D1571408

to Faith
w/ appreciation &
best wishes,
Cathey

ANOTHER SIDE OF THE LINE

CATHERINE COMETTI SAMARGO

CCSamargo   7/12/12

BrownWren Press

2012

BrownWren Press
P. O. Box 86
Dellslow, WV 26531

ISBN: 978-0-9852326-0-3

To the memory of my paternal aunts,
the Cometti sisters:
Josephine, Elizabeth, and Anita

Sit down and read. Educate yourself for the coming conflicts.

—Mary Harris "Mother" Jones

Logan

LOGAN

MINGO

Williamson

Matewan

Bear Hollow
Richfield

Tomahawk

Laura
Dawson

Mc   D.

Tug Fork River

0   10   20   30   40   50

Miles

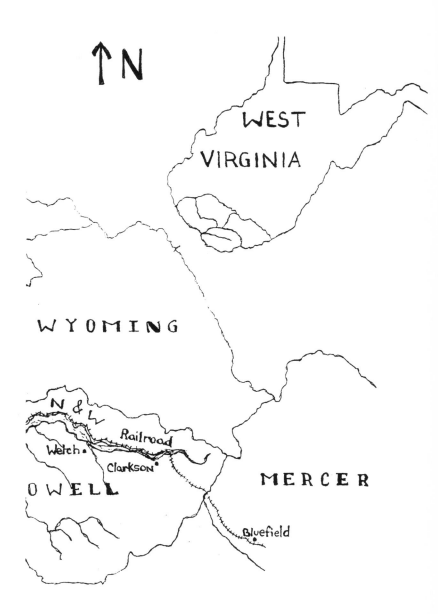

PART ONE

1

AT FIRST LIGHT Sarah Jennings left the boarding house and set out into a chilly drizzle, sidestepping puddles and peeking from beneath her umbrella at the small town that was still foreign to her. Beyond the company store and Clarkson's train station, squat rows of houses huddled under a blanket of mist and the smoke that rose from their chimneys. No one was about, but engines and machinery thrummed and clanked nearby, and she heard an occasional shout in the distance.

It took her less than twenty minutes to reach the one-room schoolhouse. She had been hired to complete the term of the teacher who had quit to get married. It was the first day of Sarah's first job, and despite her youth and lack of training, she was eager to begin.

She unlocked the door and stepped inside. Even on a chilly October morning the empty schoolhouse held the faint odors of close-pressed young bodies, stale food, and dusty textbooks. Iron-framed desks were bolted down in rows, and a potbellied stove stood in the center aisle. Sarah started a fire with kindling she had brought in the afternoon before, but she had neglected to gather any coal. From the heaping pile out back she fetched wet chunks, but the fire only spat and sizzled without producing much heat.

The students arrived in small groups and headed for the vestibule at the rear where they hung up dripping coats and deposited lunch pails on the shelves. Younger children began chasing and shrieking and running about the room, while boys around age ten stood together provoking the younger ones with loud taunts.

Sarah rapped her ruler on the edge of the podium and announced with a smile, "All right, children, it's time to get settled down." They stopped momentarily and regarded her, then resumed their roughhousing.

Sarah folded her arms, puzzled by their disobedience. A few older girls were sitting in their seats talking quietly and eyeing the raucous children with annoyance. One young man, more mature than the others, was slouched forward in the back row, head down and eyes closed. Another boy who appeared to be around twelve or thirteen sat at his desk, his nose in a book in serious concentration. Oblivious to the commotion around him, he seemed to be the only student in the room with the slightest interest in learning.

Suddenly the older boy raised his head and bellowed, "Y'all sit down and shut up!"

Sarah nodded to him. "Thank you," she murmured as the children scrambled into desks and sat at attention, watching her with eager, mocking faces. "Good morning." She smiled and tried to project enthusiasm. "For any of you who weren't here the day I visited a couple of weeks ago, I'm Miss Jennings. I'd like to learn your names and find out where you are in your texts. I'm somewhat new at this, and I won't have a completed schedule until I see where each of you is working. I promise you that we are all going to learn a lot and enjoy the time we spend here together."

Sarah called the first name on the roster. "Gerald Boone." There was no response and Sarah repeated the name.

"He ain't here," came a small voice from a stringy-haired girl in the front row.

"And where is Mr. Boone?"

"He's a-working," the girl answered in a soft drawl. "Went in the mine same as my brother Willard," the girl said proudly. "Daddy said he could go in, so he done went."

"What's your name?"

"Stella Lively."

Sarah approached her. "I'll start with you, Stella. Can you show me where you are in your reader?" As she went around the room, some of the students opened books and began working. The older girls continued to talk and giggle, sometimes much too loudly Sarah thought.

Leaning over a desk with her back toward most of the class, she felt something hit her lightly on the shoulder and heard a twitter of laughter. She raised up to face two guilty-looking boys around ten or eleven years old.

"What?" one of them exclaimed self-righteously.

"You've thrown something at me and you're laughing about it."

Both boys shook their heads vigorously. The second boy replied, "Weren't us, Teacher. We seen it come a-flying." He glanced slyly toward the back of the room where no one sat but the boy who slept.

"Young man!" Sarah called, pointing to the boy who had been reading and ignoring the others since the start of the day.

"Yes, ma'am?"

"Did you see who threw this wad of paper?"

"No, ma'am. I's reading." He threw a contemptuous scowl toward the bright-eyed rebels to whom Sarah had already spoken. She trusted none of them now but sensed that this boy was different. "What's your name?" she asked.

"Hank Ferrell." He glanced at her sharply, as if to say *I ain't your ally so leave me alone*, and settled back into his reading.

She resumed her task. The next time she was pelted, she tried ignoring it. Soon something gooey hit her cheek, and she whirled around to face the two suspicious boys again.

With big eyes and shrugged shoulders, they both held out empty, dirt-stained palms. Out of the corner of her eye, Sarah detected a movement along the same row. She turned toward a new suspect who sat quietly at a desk cleared of materials.

"Open the desk," Sarah commanded in what she hoped was an authoritarian voice. When the boy did so, she saw a piece of paper with the corners torn away. "What's your name, young man?"

"Willard," he said softly and added, "Lively."

"Stella!" Sarah called out. The girl turned around in her seat. "Is this your brother?"

"No ma'am. That there's Clyde Poling."

"Thank you. Now, see here, Clyde. I had better not catch you at this again, do you understand me?"

"Yeah." But the boy's tone indicated a deliberate absence of such an understanding.

Midafternoon after the last child had bolted out the door to freedom, Sarah drew her first easy breath since morning. She had blundered through the day meeting one small incident after another, her initial enthusiasm and confidence draining rapidly away. She was unable to always have her back away from Clyde, and twice more she had to threaten him. When pleasantries got her nowhere, she switched to a stern demeanor. As the day progressed, the entire schoolroom seemed to regard her with hostility, and Sarah was exhausted from her efforts.

Where had she gone wrong? She had directed group games and scholarly activities she hoped would reveal the children's abilities and personalities, and they had cooperated in varying degrees. The young children followed seatwork directions automatically. Most of the older students halfheartedly completed assigned tasks, but some of them refused to participate altogether.

Clyde Poling made consistent attempts to sabotage the games and often rankled her, while Hank Ferrell, despite his willful academic separation from the others, was a natural leader and possessed his peers' unquestioning respect. Sarah could see Clyde's quiet deference to Hank, who in turn ignored him, allowing him free reign, even if he could have straightened out Clyde's shenanigans with a look.

Her predecessor, Miss Huffman, had told her, *the students want you to win.* How easy that had sounded! Standing alone now in the schoolroom-turned-battlefield, upon which she had lost the first skirmish, Sarah was too shaken to sort things out. How was she to win with these strange children, so different from the Sunday school classes she'd had charge of in the past? They didn't seem like the same students she had observed on her initial visit to this schoolhouse two weeks earlier.

That day had been an Indian-summer swelter of goldenrod and falling leaves overlaying the percolating stench of coke ovens and sewage. A dusting of cinders covered the scant vegetation near the train tracks where steam hissed, engines rumbled, and coal cars coupled. The wrench and crash of metal against metal reverberated through the narrow valley where trains came and went.

After interviewing her in his office, Mr. Satterfield, the school administrator, had brought Sarah to the schoolhouse. Despite what she had seen along the road they walked—rows of frame houses cramped close together with outhouses perched at the far end of each narrow fenced-in yard, faded clothing flapping on clotheslines, peeling paint and dirt yards sparkling with black grit—Sarah had seen the schoolhouse as a refuge, its occupants innocent souls with minds yearning for knowledge.

Inside, Miss Huffman was staring out the window in what looked like utter boredom while a young girl stood in the aisle next to her desk reciting in hesitant starts and stops. Even with the open windows the room was stuffy, reeking of stale food and sweat, humming with lazy flies. The three oldest boys, in the back row, had stared at Sarah.

One of them, a big blonde boy dressed in stained overalls, rose. "Look here, it's the trustee and a pretty gal. This here a new student, sir?"

Miss Huffman rapped a ruler on the desktop. She regarded the boy with withering disgust, and he sat down immediately. The boy beside him elbowed him and smirked.

"Boys and girls, say good afternoon to Mr. Satterfield," the teacher said.

"Good afternoon, Mr. Satterfield," the group, including the boys in the back, replied in unison.

Satterfield nodded. "And this is Miss Jennings. She's thinking about becoming your teacher." A few students mumbled greetings.

While Satterfield spoke privately with Miss Huffman, Sarah had gazed around the room. There were around twenty students; some were writing, while others read. A roll of maps hung at the front, arithmetic problems had been worked out on the blackboard, and a neat bulletin board expressed October's themes of pumpkins and Columbus's ships. The pupils wore threadbare clothing and unremarkable features as they went about their tasks, whispered together, wrote, or pored over a book.

Then one of them caught Sarah's eye. He sat on the back row, and his black eyes pierced hers with an insistence that obliterated all else. In a long, electric moment the boy transfixed her with his gaze. He languidly rolled a shoulder back, one eye melting into a calculated wink, his lip curling in a skewed grin full of purpose, of warmth and suggestion. In her peripheral vision she was aware of his sinewy build; his complexion was smooth and swarthy, his features square and handsome.

She wrenched free of his look and turned away, trying to hide her blush and control the pounding of her heart. The boys she had known at home would never have taken such liberties. He's probably fifteen and in the second grade, she thought in a panic—and he could certainly use a wash. She assumed he was Italian and wondered if he could even speak English.

That boy had not been in school today, but Sarah had encountered him the previous day. It had been a mild Sunday afternoon, and she had walked up to look at the schoolhouse. Three men approached with rifles slung over their shoulders. Observing their overalls and faded shirts, Sarah surmised that they were miners on their way to the woods to hunt on their day off. Drawing near to her, the men tipped their caps and nodded.

The closest one stopped to stare at her, and she recognized him—the boy, actually he was a young man, who had winked at her in the classroom. He was tall, muscular, and handsome with a burnished olive skin tone. His dark, compelling eyes, gleaming at once with intelligence and scorn, smoldered as his lips curled and slowly pursed into the wet smack of an irreverent kiss.

One of his companions yanked his sleeve. "Leave her be, Dom. Them squirrels is waiting on us." To Sarah he said, "Pardon him, miss. He ain't learned how to behave hisself around ladies."

They turned toward the woods, leaving Sarah standing outside the schoolhouse without a shred of dignity. She heard a laughing comment from one of the men, "…you ain't never gonna learn…"

She had worried about meeting him in the schoolhouse today and his absence, a reprieve, was the only thing for which she was thankful. But what about tomorrow?

2

SARAH CLOSED UP the schoolhouse, locking the troubling day inside. Things might look brighter in the light of tomorrow's dawn. But the steady rain was disheartening and after a walk down the hill that soaked her shoes despite her attempts to dodge the puddles in the slag-filled road, she started to wonder what she was doing in such a place.

In the quiet of her upstairs room at the boarding house, where the heavy oak furniture smelled of fresh polish, Sarah took her time changing out of her wet clothes. While unpacking some of her things, she began to relax into the serenity of this private place.

She glanced into the mirror. Although others often remarked upon her beauty, her looks were sometimes a source of embarrassment for her. Her complexion was clear, her lips were full, her forehead high and framed in a striking widow's peak. She wore her silky brown hair in a pompadour that stayed mostly in place even after the day she'd had. She was uncomfortable, rather than flattered, when people commented on her hourglass figure. Her father had often suggested that she herself was responsible for a look of "sinful allure." Sarah stared into her almond-shaped hazel eyes, thinking about her father for the first time all day, and was suddenly pleased with herself.

By now her parents would have read her brief note: *I took the teaching job after all, will contact you when I'm settled*. But they had no idea where she had gone.

When she had told them two weeks earlier that a coal company had hired her to teach school, they had reminded her that she was not to make such decisions on her own. Their crashing arguments had taken several directions, none of them winnable for Sarah.

"I won't have you working for one of those outfits," Ray Jennings bellowed.

"Daddy, I signed a contract today and I'm going. You can't tell me what to—"

"You're a seventeen-year-old girl living under my roof—"

"I have a high school diploma and a teaching certificate. I'm qualified and you can't stop me." Having never before talked back to her father, her defiance left her lightheaded.

"You'll get a teaching position here in Bluefield and live with us until you're married."

But Sarah dreamed of college and that required money. She had gone to the interview—fibbed to her parents and ridden the train—imagining that something glamorous or noble awaited her in Clarkson because of what she saw daily in her hometown. Coal was transforming Bluefield into a center of business and finance, drawing prominent people from New York and Pennsylvania. Strings of cars heaped with coal jammed the vast rail yard that rumbled day and night with trains hauling coal from all over southern West Virginia.

Ray Jennings complained about coal companies and inhumane practices in the mines, but what did he know? He owned a store. "They're robbing the state of its minerals and breaking the poor miners' backs and spirits in the process," he was fond of saying.

Sarah didn't see it like that. In Bluefield people associated with the coal industry commanded respect and lived in style. As a teacher for a coal company, her salary would be comparable to that offered by the public schools. She could start saving for college right away. And best of all she'd be gone, free of her parents' unending criticism and scrutiny.

After her mutinous action, her parents had badgered and harangued her, holding her virtual prisoner, until she had agreed to write the letter they dictated turning down the offered employment. But she addressed the letter and handed it to her father to mail—to a company with a fictitious name at a nonexistent address. There were scads of coal companies along the Tug Fork River, and Ray Jennings didn't know the difference.

Sarah believed that Clarkson was her only way out. Getting out—it had been her dream for years. Getting through high school as quickly as she could, getting double promotions, testing out of classes, anything to earn her diploma and become independent. She'd graduated last spring at seventeen—in 1914, a full year before her classmates. Now here it was fall and she was still at home, working part-time at the Methodist Church because she had not found a teaching job—at least not one that suited her father.

With the bogus letter sent, routine returned, and Sarah packed on the sly, imagining she would never again return home. In secret she mailed packages of her belongings to Clarkson. And on the final night she filled two suitcases and slipped out of the house before dawn, lugging the bags on foot to the train station.

Now in her very own room, Sarah smiled at herself, invigorated suddenly with renewed energy. "If you can do that," she told her reflection, "surely you can take on those children."

In the kitchen Mrs. Means, who ran the boarding house, was preparing supper. "God-awful weather," the woman commented to Sarah as she floured pieces of chicken and put them in hot, melted lard. Her wrinkled body seemed to sag inward, caving in on flat feet, and her deft movements belied her worn look. "Glad I ain't had to go out. They say it might get colder."

She wasn't as cordial as she'd been the day before, appearing instead preoccupied and edgy, while turning chicken in the frying pan. Sarah tried to make conversation. "Have you been here long?"

"Four year." The woman lowered the heat, shut back dampers, and searched for a lid for the skillet.

"I was so busy in my room last night I didn't meet the others. Who else lives here?"

"Ida Swindell, postmistress; Ruth Crantz, nurse; Ethel Bosely, bookkeeper." Silence reigned while Mrs. Means peeled and chopped potatoes with lightning speed and tossed them into a pot of boiling water.

Sarah tried again. "Who lives in that big house at the top of the hill?" The large three-storied brick house had seemed out of place amidst the dusty rail yard and little houses crowded together in the creek bottom.

"Company supervisor, Mr. Savage." Mrs. Means answered with a scowl.

"And what about those boarding houses and houses just below it?"

She spat out her reply. "Company's hired guns."

Mrs. Means mixed biscuit dough in wordless concentration, and Sarah remembered Satterfield's comment about ignorance. *You're just a girl yourself, and I imagine you're in for a shock. You've probably not seen this kind of ignorance before. You've got foreigners here too. Some of them can't speak English...* Did the term apply to this woman? Already she had given the impression of disliking Mr. Savage, who, Sarah guessed, was judicious and kind. Sarah had read about violence during strikes and had seen men with guns in Bluefield. But hired gunmen?

"What do you mean, 'hired guns'?"

"They's hired to protect Mr. Savage and National Coal's property, and some of 'em would just as soon shoot you as look at you."

"Why, Mrs. Means! This isn't the Wild West, after all. Perhaps you've read—"

The look on the older woman's face cut her short. "My daughter was kilt at Cabin Crick during the big strike in Kanawha County. Murdered by them guards, and her only seventeen. Her husband was shot up bad hisself. She left him two young 'uns to raise. He's got him another woman now and another baby, but he has a hard time working. Something in him never healed right after them bullets."

"Oh! I'm, well, I'm sorry." But the woman's story sounded preposterous to Sarah—a girl her own age shot to death.

"Gun thugs, we call 'em, but the polite thing to call 'em's mine guards. Or Baldwin–Felts men." Sarah knew of the Baldwin–Felts Detective Agency located in Bluefield.

"Do you have family somewhere?"

"Nope. They's all gone."

"I'm terribly sorry."

"'Cept Dottie's man and my grandchildren." She cut biscuits from the rolled dough. "I lost two of my children to the flux before they's growed up. My boy, he took off out west and I ain't heard from him. My girl was kilt at Cabin Crick like I told you. During the strike."

"What about your husband?"

Mrs. Means looked out the window. "An accident. Gas blowed him to bits along with eight others." She contemplated the rain. "Hit were a day just like this. Rainy, cold, and we heard that there whistle a-blowing. We's all standing out there hoping and a-praying it weren't our man but we knowed it had to be somebody's."

"Oh, Mrs. Means, I'm so sorry."

"Seems something about this kind of weather. Sometimes when the weather gets colder... They brung some out today, did you know that? Ain't no one kilt. Just some hurt bad."

Sarah had not heard a whistle. "What kind of accident?"

"Cave in."

Sarah learned more about it at the supper table.

"Ruth won't be in tonight," Ida, the postmistress, commented, referring to the nurse. "Went to Welch with Doc."

"Them boys hurt bad?" Mrs. Means asked.

"Couple of them. Lots of blood all over the tracks." She paused. "Till rain washed it away." Ida's harsh tone seemed incongruous with her ample curves and smooth, soft-looking skin, but there was a glint in her eyes. Her attitude seemed provocative, as if she were deliberately taunting the woman.

"It's terrible," Sarah said. "Those poor men. And their families."

"It wouldn't happen if they were more careful on the job," Ethel, the bookkeeper, observed with distaste. She was an attractive blond with an absent look about her. "They don't think about safety. Don't have sense enough to avoid accidents."

"Doesn't the company teach them safety procedures?" Sarah asked.

Ida and Ethel exchanged glances and grinned.

"Where'd you hear something like that, honey?" Ida asked.

"You been listening to union propaganda? You got some Bolshevik friends?"

"I don't know anybody. It just makes sense. If I went into a mine, I would hope somebody would explain to me what to do to keep myself from getting hurt."

Later Ida, with a devilish twinkle in her eye, asked Sarah, "You got someone special, honey? I mean, a man?"

"Well, no, I—"

"Good, 'cause there's plenty of fellows around here who'd like to show you a good time."

"Oh, I couldn't do that. I was told that it's against the rules to see men." Satterfield had been very specific. *No smoking, no drinking, no keeping company with men, no bright colored dresses. You aren't to be out past eight o'clock, your dresses aren't to be any shorter than two inches above the ankle. You're to wear at least two petticoats.*

Ida and Ethel hooted. "Company men?" Ethel mocked. "Do you think the school trustee would object to your association with company guards?"

Sometime during the night the shrill cry of a train whistle drew Sarah out of a sound sleep. She nestled down into the blankets and rolled to her side. Just before she drifted into a dream it came to her that she could not win the schoolhouse without Hank Ferrell's respect, and she would have to earn *that* by controlling Clyde all by herself.

3

SKIRMISHES IN THE classroom continued, then escalated, in an atmosphere clouded with discomfort and mistrust, all made worse by Sarah's awareness of Hank Ferrell's unobtrusive observations of what she knew was her ineptitude. Clyde Poling had ready a full arsenal of petty provocations, assailing her at unexpected moments, and when Sarah confronted and then argued with him, others often joined in, or picked up where Clyde left off. The only thing Sarah had to be thankful for was the continued absence of "Dom" from school.

Away from the schoolhouse she focused on lesson plans and tried not to think about her struggle with Clyde. One evening as she descended the stairs for supper, Sarah heard male voices and female laughter coming from the dining room. Entering, she observed Ida, Ethel, and four men in the process of seating themselves around the table. Mrs. Means pattered back and forth between kitchen and dining room placing steaming serving dishes on the table. One of the men, already seated, was scooping up large portions of ham, boiled potatoes, and cooked greens. The room seemed foreign and full of maleness—tobacco, sour sweat, and guns. Rifles lined the far wall and pistols were evident in hip and shoulder holsters.

Sarah was introduced to Carl Eschman, Porter Thomas, Paul Lessing, and the man with the big appetite, Doug Burnside. All thickset and husky, they wore starched collars, coats, and ties.

"So you're mine guards?" Sarah asked.

"Yes, ma'am," Doug answered with his mouth full. "Work for Tom Felts's agency out of Bluefield." He patted the empty chair beside him. "Come over here and sit down, Ida."

Somebody steered Sarah to a seat next to Paul Lessing. Serving dishes were passed around, and for a few moments serving spoons scraped and clanked as all concentrated on filling their plates.

"Mrs. Means, your garden is amazing," Porter said. He was leaner than the others and wore the somber look of a preacher. "Still producing good, fresh greens at the end of October."

"What's so amazing about that?" Ida remarked. "All the gardens still have spinach."

"Well, maybe it's your cooking. This tastes as tender as the first spring crop."

"Thank you," Mrs. Means mumbled, keeping her eyes on her plate.

"Got to put in a good word for a lot of the womenfolk here in Clarkson," Paul said. "Their gardens are showcases."

The subject of gardening gave Sarah an unexpected pang of homesickness. The day before she had left, she had gone out back to get a last look at the garden, the only thing in Bluefield she thought she would miss. The weather had turned colder, she remembered, but there was still a patch of dark green kale and a late crop of peas that she would never harvest.

When Sarah began helping her mother with gardening as a young teen, she found comfort in every aspect of the operation. The damp, soft earth seemed to hold a mysterious key to life; seedlings sprouting in shallow pans on the back porch responded to her tenderness and solicitous care. Plants grew quietly, trusting that their caretaker would protect them from insects, provide them with water and nutrients. They stood majestically—luxuriously in the sun, slick and shiny-green in the rain—and in the end bore fruit, giving their all for someone who cared for them.

Comments from neighbors to her father had filled Sarah with pride. "Your daughter can make anything grow. Just look at your tomatoes! I wish I had half the crop."

"It's God's work," Ray Jennings had corrected.

Sarah's patience, her willingness to work, and her curiosity to experiment surpassed any effort her mother was willing to give it. Her father sold the extra produce at his store, his standard reply to customers' praise being, "Our garden is a family effort, but it grows by the grace of God."

"It made a difference, the company sponsoring that contest," one of the mine guards was saying. "Everyone wanted to win the money prize."

"I like to see them out there, toiling away in their little patches. All those neat rows. Gives the town an orderly feel."

"Keeps 'em out of trouble. That's the main thing."

After dinner Ida propelled Mrs. Means into the kitchen with an armful of dirty dishes. "We won't need anything else, sweet thing. You just wash up those dishes and get off your feet. Get to bed." Then she brought in a bottle and said, "Let's have some fun."

Porter lit a cigarette and offered his pack to the women. Ethel shook her head, but Ida partook, and Sarah accepted one also, reminding herself, "I'm an adult. I need no one's permission and I have nothing to hide." Nicotine and alcohol raced through her blood, and Paul Lessing's smile and manly good looks began to affect her. He was gentlemanly and she enjoyed his attentions, unable to think of him as a hired gunman.

Doug Burnside was different. Sarah felt an air of menace around the man. He was much larger than the others, possibly three hundred pounds. Not all of it was muscle, and he was as eager for the bottle as he had been for the food. Sitting beside him, Ida slid her arm under the table in the vicinity of his lap.

The rest of them told jokes, and their voices grew louder, the talk more irreverent. Sarah and Paul talked, sipping their drinks slowly, and Sarah asked him many questions.

"Sure they're backward," Paul said of the miners. "They haven't had much schooling, but National Coal looks out for them. Union agitators try to stir things up and make people think otherwise, but the company has the interests of its employees at heart. We've got a good bunch here in Clarkson. Never have much trouble."

Paul smiled and leaned closer to Sarah while Ida added more whiskey to Sarah's glass. "Do you know National Coal just went to the expense of opening up a movie house?"

"Some of the children mentioned it."

"That's one of my jobs. I help manage it. How would you like to come along some Saturday afternoon soon? We could watch the picture together. I've seen a lot of them, but it would be swell to have a pretty girl sitting beside me."

"I'd like that." But Sarah didn't think she could venture forth yet, risk seeing her students in public, unless things changed in the classroom.

When talk turned to the subject of education, Doug Burnside offered his view on maintaining classroom authority. "There's only one thing these people understand. The figurative whip. On their own they don't know what to do."

He swigged whiskey from the bottle, let out a noisy sigh, and looked away in disgust, and Sarah suddenly understood Mrs. Means's evaluation of the Baldwin–Felts men. "Why do you say 'these people'?" she couldn't help asking. "They're no different from the rest of the school population in this country."

He replied with certainty. "You're dead wrong there. They're sure as hell different from, say, a class of school kids in Bluefield. Look at where they come from. The foreigners, they don't understand America or the English language. They need guidance. And the niggers, they've been sharecroppers, and before that, slaves. Of course they have their own school across the creek. They've always had smarter people, whites, looking out for them. And these locals, these folks from back in the hills and farms and lumber mills. They're the same as foreigners. Don't know the first thing about civilized living in a modern industrialized setting. That's why the companies hire social workers to give the women a hand with things they don't know much about, like how to make good meals for their families and how to take care of their kids.

"As a teacher, you gotta look at things pretty much the same as we do. Sometimes the only way to make these folks listen to you is with force. That's why we have to get out our guns occasionally. I reckon you'll find same is true in the schoolroom."

Porter Thomas laughed then. "I was whipped plenty when I was in school."

The men finally left and Sarah was glad to be rid of Doug Burnside. Paul Lessing was another matter. He told her as he left that he would like to see her again, suggesting the movie theater once more. She didn't care what Mrs. Means or her father had to say about Baldwin–Felts men. Paul was a different kind of man than the others.

Stuffing kindling into the stove the next morning, determined to have a decent fire going for a change, Sarah mulled over the problem of Clyde Poling, whose antics were commanding much more of the class's attention than she seemed able to do.

She remembered her predecessor's words. *They want you to win so they can get on with their studies.* Sarah wasn't sure she believed that. So far very few students had displayed much interest in their books. Hank Ferrell was the only one who needed no prodding in that area.

"All right, so be it," Sarah thought. "Clyde Poling is twelve years old and ignorant to boot. Why should I let him run this school? If it's me or him, I intend to win." She looked with disgust at her poor attempt at fire-building. The kindling hissed and coal chunks sat on top of it, black and dead-looking with only a hint of smoke curling around them.

But the clock was ticking and soon the children, including Clyde, would arrive. Grabbing the hatchet, she hurried out the back door and across the schoolyard to the brush that lined the clearing. She cut the branch of a sturdy maple sapling and ripped off its few remaining leaves. Back inside she leaned it against her podium and tended the fire.

She heard children's voices in the distance. Glancing toward the switch to calm herself, she saw how prominent it appeared and decided that surprise might be the best method of handling Mr. Clyde Poling. She pulled down the rolled maps at the front of the room and slipped the switch inside the roll.

4

THE CHILDREN BEGAN to arrive. Several went to their desks without removing their coats.

"Hang up your coat, Hank," Sarah said and nearly gasped. The sharp words had come out of her mouth before she had thought. This boy was self-disciplined and had no interest in confronting her for the sake of mere provocation, but he would challenge her now.

"I'm sorry, I cain't, Miss Jennings. I'm near half-froze."

"Well…" Stunned, Sarah noticed his blue lips and thin jacket.

"Want me to show you how to build up that there fire?" He was already grasping the poker and opening the stove door.

"I know all about building fires!" Sarah snapped. He shot her a quick glance. *Sure you do*, his look seemed to say. "But I can't always seem to get them started right."

He knelt before the pitiful smoking pile of fuel. After an expert shake of the grate and a few well-placed prods with the poker, the coal and remaining pieces of wood burst into pure yellow flames. "She ain't gonna burn without no air." Hank placed a couple more chunks of coal carefully onto the fire. He closed the door and pulled out the ash pan, shoveling ashes into a bucket. "Miss Jennings, you ain't never gonna get a good fire going with an ash pan this full. It's gotta be emptied every day." He carried the bucket toward the back door, his palms gray with coal dust, fingers blue with cold.

When he returned she asked, "How would you like to do that every day?"

"Hain't my job, but I could show you how."

"But it could be. Your job. I'll pay you ten cents a day."

His eyes popped wide open. "Just to build a fire? Sure thing!"

"And keep it going."

"Hey, that ain't fair," Tom Murray complained. "I wanna do it."

"Sure, you ain't here half the time," Hank said to him, "and I never miss for nothing."

"Well, I'd be here for pay. Got any other jobs I can do, Teach?"

"Anything you got to be done, I can do it better than Tom Murray," another boy said.

Soon half a dozen others were clamoring for a job, and Sarah held up her hand for silence. "All right, boys and girls. Get to your seats and we'll discuss this in an orderly manner." She had never seen the children take their seats and get quiet so quickly, and Sarah suddenly realized Clyde was not there. "I have one other job, but I'm not sure what's the best way to go about choosing someone to do it. Any suggestions?"

"Let one person do it for a month, then pick someone else."

"We can apply for the job. You pick the best qualified."

"Split it up between two of us."

"Draw names out of a hat."

"That ain't fair. Hank didn't have to do nothing and he's hired."

"He got her fire going, didn't he?" Warmth was radiating from the potbelly stove, infusing the room with pleasant, cozy comfort, and just then Clyde walked in. His entrance went unnoticed by the students who were all focused on the possibility of a job.

"All right. Drawing names seems to be the fairest way, but there are certain things that you must do to keep your job, and that goes for Hank too. You must be here every day, and if you can't be, then you must arrange to have someone else do the job. How you pay him will be up to you. You must also do a good job or you'll be fired. It looks as though I won't have any trouble finding someone to replace a shirker. Is that agreeable to everyone?"

"Yeah, but what's the other job?"

"I need someone to clean up. You'll have to stay a little extra every day after school, do the dusting and sweeping, keep the outhouses presentable, that sort of thing."

The students agreed to the fairness of the plan; Harvey Casteel was chosen, and the class settled into the daily routine.

Each morning Sarah put a verse on the board for a student to read and for the class to discuss. She read a short story, usually with a moral lesson at its end and then talked briefly, often with an aid such as a picture or a map, about a famous person—connected to history, the arts, or science—whose name she wrote on the board, often in honor of a birthday.

Things seemed more peaceful than usual. The room was comfortably heated for a change and the students were working. Sarah hoped she had gained some sort of victory by assigning the jobs and allowing the children to have a say in how she went about it. An hour passed quietly enough; then Clyde was up out of his seat walking around, talking to some of the others.

"Sit down, Clyde."

"Nope. I cain't, Teacher."

So much for the quiet day, Sarah thought. "And why not?"

"I have to use the privy."

"You could have asked."

"I'm asking now. And you gotta let me go."

"Don't you know that you are to raise your hand and ask, and when I give you permission, then you may go?" Sarah heard herself whining. Of course Clyde knew that.

"But this is an emergency!" He was out the door in a flash. The others snickered and glanced at Sarah, doubtless taking note of her reddening face.

"Can I go too?" George, a friend of Clyde's, asked.

"Absolutely not."

George shoved his hands into his crotch and writhed in discomfort. "But it's an emergency!" he howled. "Please!" The rest of the class laughed and Sarah's ire increased.

She slammed her fist onto the podium. "Get quiet!" Some of the students flinched at her outburst, and Sarah's fury began to rise. How dare these boys and girls, whom she had wanted to love and to teach, whom she had met fairly, how dare they treat her like this! How dare they revel in such nonsense when there was pleasurable studying to be done!

More than anything she was furious with Hank Ferrell. Every time an incident of this nature occurred, she knew he inconspicuously watched her, sometimes seeming to roll his eyes. *He* wanted to learn, so why didn't he help her? The others revered him. He could shut Clyde or George up with a word, so why was he allowing this?

George was not backing down. Rocking back and forth, he moaned, "Please, Teacher."

Sarah glanced hesitantly toward Hank. He pressed his lips together, shook his head slightly, and looked away. Embarrassment and rage consumed her. She pounded the podium again and shouted, "George Mundy, sit up straight this instant and act your age! You may go outside when Clyde returns." She turned back to her math pupils.

"But, Teacher—"

She whirled around and pointed a finger at him. "Not another word out of you, young man, or I'll take you outside and whip you till you beg for mercy!"

He was cowed and she could see it. The others seemed to be as well, and she didn't dare look at Hank. *The figurative whip.* Perhaps a little playacting at the right moments was all that was needed. Perhaps.

Clyde was gone much too long. Sarah began to wonder if she should go after him but chose to enjoy his absence instead.

"Miss Jennings," an older girl named Stephanie said with her hand in the air. "I'm worried about Clyde. Suppose he's sick? I expect someone oughta go after him."

With the girl's comment blood began pounding in Sarah's temples. Stephanie Polaski was fourteen, three years younger than she. How did she presume to tell Sarah what to do! She opened her mouth, ready to screech out her anger; instead she glared at Stephanie, who shrank back into her seat.

I am the boss in this schoolroom, Sarah told herself, but her heart was racing. Suddenly Clyde burst into the room, smirking and cocksure. He surveyed the room and took the long way back to his desk, deliberately stopping to whisper something to one of the boys. The strong, fresh odor of cigarette smoke reached Sarah's nostrils.

"Clyde! You've been smoking, haven't you?"

He grinned before assuming a pained, self-righteous look. "Smoking? Me? I admit it smelled a little smoky out there, but I don't know where it come from."

"What have you been doing out there?"

He put his hands on his hips and rocked back and forth. "You want me to tell you what I done in the privy, Teacher?"

His question brought hoots of laughter from the rest of the students, and Sarah turned away. An image of the switch, rolled inside the maps entered her mind briefly, but she could only say, "George, you may go now. The rest of you return to your books."

The remainder of the day was a continuation of small confrontations with Clyde. He was often out of his seat, but he always had an excuse. He interrupted the class continuously, communicating his irreverence to others who were halfheartedly involved in projects that Sarah considered exciting and necessary—for example, an in-depth study of 'Hiawatha' for the younger grades that would culminate in the making of booklets to hold their material on Indian culture, animals, and geography. Simultaneously, the older grades were studying Indian history and Longfellow's life. Clyde could make her efforts seem irrelevant by asking questions like, "What's this for? Why do we have to do this? What's this got to do with us?" If Sarah tried to defend herself, Clyde made it appear as if she were unfairly attacking him. "I just wanna know!" he would say, throwing up his hands. Once she found "Teacher is stupid" written on the blackboard. Another time, horror-stricken, she hurriedly erased "fuck," and heard the soft laughter of the class behind her back. She fought tears and wondered how she would even go about using the switch.

By the end of the day she was angry with herself and vowed that tomorrow she would try to rediscover the control she had almost won.

On her way home from the schoolhouse she passed a cluster of mine guards standing on the steps of the company store.

"Afternoon, Miss Jennings." Paul Lessing stepped away from the group and tipped his hat. His smile radiated kindness that she had not felt all day long in the hostile schoolhouse.

"Hello." She paused in front of the store.

"On your way home?" She nodded in answer. "May I walk with you?"

"I'd like that, Mr. Lessing."

Along the road, he took her arm and said in an abashed manner, "I'd like to get to know you better. I confess I'm very attracted to you." She glanced at him. "Don't get me wrong. I'm not trying to… Well, I… I thought we might be friends, thought we might call each other by first names is all."

He seemed old to her, twenty-five or thirty, and yet he was shy and hesitant, sincerity itself. He was the strength she craved at that moment, someone to lean against at the end of such a trying day. "All right. Paul."

They continued up the hill, making small talk about the weather. Then he asked, "How was your day?"

"Oh, fine. A little exhausting, I guess."

He touched her elbow in a kind of caress. "Trying you out, are they?"

Sarah sighed. "Yes. Yes, they are, but I won't let them get the best of me."

Paul chuckled. "Let me see if I can guess who's giving you trouble. Hank Ferrell, Roberto Fucelli, Tony Amato."

"Oh, no!" And Sarah found herself defending him who was testing her the most harshly. "Hank is an angel, so careful of his little sisters, and Tony is so quiet I hardly know he's there. I don't know Roberto. Where did you get such ideas?"

He shrugged. "From knowing the parents, I suppose."

"They're trouble?"

"As much trouble as there is around here. They talk and grumble. And what about the Morton kid? Ferrell and Morton. We can count on those two to stir up the weighman issue from time to time."

"What's that?"

"The miners sometimes think the company weighs their cars short so as not to give them all the pay they've got coming. That was one of the grievances in the Kanawha strike. They want their own weighman along with the company's."

"And do they weigh the miners short?"

Paul snorted. "The miners get paid fair and square for everything they bring out. They're all the time coming up with a new complaint. If the union were allowed in here, they'd have the miners demanding so much it would bankrupt the company. Then where would the miners be? High and dry without a job."

"I'm sure you're right, Paul. All this is so new to me. I don't know the first thing about coal mining. Well, here we are. Thanks for walking with me."

"It was my pleasure." Sarah turned up the stairs of the boarding house. "Sarah!" Paul called to her and she turned. "You didn't tell me who those troublemakers are."

She regarded his eager face, his thick hair blowing in the chilly air. She was aware of his power, his knowledge, his age and worldliness, all of it blending to create a smugness that existed separately from his boyish ardor. Clyde Poling couldn't hold a candle to the likes of Paul Lessing, and Sarah suddenly felt wildly protective of a boy who would never be anybody.

"Oh, it's nothing, Paul. A few of them are just ornery. I expect we'll work it out."

5

THE NEXT MORNING a shivering Hank Ferrell was waiting at the schoolhouse door when Sarah arrived. He emptied ashes and built a fire in no time, then settled into his desk with a book. He nursed the fire as he had done throughout the previous day, and soon the building was snug with welcoming warmth. Sarah had so many preparations to make that it was easy to ignore his presence.

He spoke quietly to her after a while. "Miss Jennings, if you wouldn't mind to give me a key, I could come early every day, get a fire going, and then run back home."

"Would that help you out?"

"Yes, ma'am. I could help Mommy with the chores, help get my sisters up here to school. Corey, she gets sidetracked sometimes and don't keep her eye on Annie the way she oughta."

"My, you're a hard worker, aren't you, Hank?"

"Won't get nowhere without a lot of hard work."

"You need an education too." Sarah considered whether to talk to him about the conflict she was having with Clyde, possibly ask him to intervene.

"I'm figuring on a high school diploma."

"But there aren't any high schools around here."

"We got kin in Welch that offered to board me. My uncle, he ain't got much, so I'll have to pay him. I'll have to find work, but this here'll help out too."

Sarah wondered at Paul's assessment of him. Hank was scrawny, in the throes of rapid physical growth, but tough-looking like the others. His thin mouth was set in a hard line Sarah was beginning to recognize as poverty's sculpture. All these children had some measure of it, no matter what their age. Yet this boy was remarkably different. His hunger for knowledge and his determination to make academic achievements set him far apart. He was breezing through eighth-grade texts, tackling ninth-grade material on his own, outgrowing the one-room, eight-grade school. And there was simply no way she could bother him with her troubles.

The others soon arrived and another day got under way. The first time Clyde Poling rose to start roaming around the room she didn't look up from her place in the fourth-grade reader. Instead she said quietly, "Clyde, would you please sit down."

"Not now. I gotta borry something from George."

"No, you don't. Have a seat."

He muttered, "I'm helping him, Teacher," then leaned over to whisper to George.

Sarah stood. "No, you're simply being a nuisance. Get back to your desk now, young man, or you'll get a whipping you won't soon forget." Clyde scurried back to his seat, and she hoped this would end it.

Throughout the rest of the morning he remained in his seat, but he variously slouched, put his feet up, hummed, drummed on the desk with his fingers, and whacked his feet across the floor. He sighed and squirmed; he mumbled to himself, drew pictures, and wadded up pieces of paper. He blew his nose and had a coughing fit. Everything was somehow excusable; he apologized and then went on to some other irritating behavior. Many of the students kept looking at Sarah expectantly, and by noon recess she knew they were as tired of his tricks as she was.

She stepped outside. Midmorning, Hank had wisely let the fire go out. Bright sunshine was warming up the day to Indian-summer temperatures, and the children were making the most of it. Younger girls jumped rope and chanted while the older girls at the far end of the yard giggled and talked and screamed heartfelt cheers for the baseball game in which all the boys were involved.

Sarah settled on the steps to watch, wondering about Clyde's ability in this game. Hubert Shalp and Milty Furgeson, the two oldest boys, were coaching their respective teams, and the students took the game with seriousness that surprised Sarah.

The teams seemed unevenly divided, Milty's team consisting of fewer and smaller boys. His five players were in the field, spread thinly to cover bases and outfield. However, they managed to keep their opponents from scoring even though some base hits were accomplished. Clyde did not get to bat, but he would be up first in the next inning, and Sarah watched him take his position at third base, where he immediately began yelling taunts at the other team.

The first of Milty's batters was More Morton, and to Sarah's surprise, George Mundy showed no mercy toward the eight-year-old, pitching what looked like to her a dangerous fast ball. Amidst cheers of encouragement from his teammates and jeers from the others, a brave little More held onto his concentration and on the third swing hit a ground ball past Clyde. Hank, who appeared to be helping Milty coach, urged More to second base, where he dove in, just barely safe. The girls on the sidelines shrieked wildly.

The next batter was Harvey Casteel, who had an awkward gait and seemed the type who might grow to become pudgy. He suffered similar jeers from Hubert's players, and even though Hank stood close by encouraging him quietly, he struck out.

Hank stepped up to the plate next, amazing Sarah with his cocky stance and his hard, gleaming eyes. She had thought of him as a bookworm with no interests beyond his studies. George Mundy of the fearsome fast ball looked toward his coach in apprehension. Hubert shrugged as if to say, *You're on your own.*

George threw what appeared to be two deliberate balls. Taunts from his team were scattered, as most of the players watched Hank cautiously. After the third ball Hank stood the bat on end and cried, "You're a damn coward, George, and I ain't walking!" The apprehension in George's eyes affirmed Hank's accusation. His fourth pitch was again way outside, but Hank went after it and slugged it halfway down the road.

"It's outta the field!" someone yelled as a little girl scampered after it. Everyone else either booed or cheered while Hank and More took their time rounding the bases.

Sarah secretly rooted for Milty's team against Clyde, who proved to be a fairly efficient hitter. Hank Ferrell was unquestionably the best player on the field, consistently slamming out powerful hits that bounced out of ratty gloves or traveled into the trees. He fielded well too, and Sarah asked him about his game as they returned to class.

"Practice," he explained.

"You have a lot of talent."

"Seems like it 'cause these boys cain't pitch good. I go to ball practice with Daddy and try hitting against somebody who knows what he's doing. Then I cain't hit nothing."

"Nothing?"

"Well, seems like I miss an awful lot."

The afternoon session remained orderly for about thirty minutes. Sarah was in the back of the room discussing a history lesson with the older children when Clyde made his first move. He sauntered over to George's desk and said, "Got any more tobaccy?"

"Back to your desk, Clyde."

"Why should I, Miss Teacher Lady?" he replied with haughty irritation.

"Because!" Sarah threw her book down and rose. "This is a schoolroom!" She marched around to the front of the room. "I'm the teacher!" She yanked down the maps, grabbed the switch, and whirled around. "And I said so!" She dealt him a vigorous blow across his chest, and he took a couple of steps backward, eyes wide with surprise and fright. "Do you understand me?" she cried, delivering another whack. "Or is this"—she let fall another lash— "the only thing you understand?"

He cringed away from her as she switched him around the arms and shoulders, missing more times than she hit, following his backward footsteps to the rear of the room and up the aisle, past the stove, and around her desk. She seemed to be getting nowhere. "Turn around and bend over!" she commanded, and he obeyed instantly, not even noticing that his position was center stage for all to observe. Wishing more to scare him into submission than to actually hurt him, Sarah aimed for what appeared to be a full hip pocket.

One blow and then another, and Clyde Poling was whimpering, "Please, Miss Jennings, I'm sorry, I won't—"

With a furtive, unexpected little puff, the back of his trousers burst into flame. The class gasped in unison as Clyde howled and leaped about, actions that only encouraged the blaze.

My God, have I struck him that hard? Sarah thought as she cried out, "Fetch the water bucket!" Milty was on his feet at once. She snatched the pail from him and quickly doused the fire, drenching Clyde, the floor, and a nearby student at the same time. Clyde turned around to face her, his mouth hanging open, tears filling his eyes.

She realized then the origin of the fire, and despite Clyde's utter defeat, she chastised him further. For all these pupils knew, she whipped boys until their pants caught fire as a matter of course. Reaching into his back pocket, she seized a handful of soggy matches and held them up to his face. "And this! You know better than to bring matches into a schoolhouse. Lord knows the danger you put yourself in and every other child in this room! And I'll not tolerate cigarettes or any other kind of tobacco. It's a filthy habit. You had better pick your teeth clean before you come in here and leave your cigarettes at home in case I take a notion to search your pockets."

He hung his head, squeezing back tears. A few of them trickled down his cheeks and he sobbed, "Yes, Miss Jennings."

Sarah's heart wrenched with pity. This was no time to let go of her victory, but she softened her tone. "I suspect you're a bright boy, Clyde, and I think you know the rest of the rules." He nodded. "Then see that you follow them, because I'd like to throw out this switch."

"Yes, ma'am," he murmured and turned toward his seat.

The room was deathly still. Most of the children had their faces poked fearfully into a book, but a few of them eyed her in terror, all except Hank, who sat with arms folded, the bare suggestion of applause twinkling in his eyes.

6

THE CLASS DISPLAYED a new eagerness. Several students Sarah had not seen previously, whose names were nevertheless in her register, appeared, including Stella Lively's brother, Willard. All were accounted for now except the one Sarah dreaded—Dominico "Dom" Cinelli. Despite her newfound control, she worried about his sudden appearance. His irreverence would be an entirely different matter, something that could not be contained or repressed by a whipping. He was working, of course, and as far as Sarah was concerned, he could stay in the mine.

Several students complimented her bulletin board, and the whole class took a keen interest in the science project Sarah introduced relating to seeds and harvesting. Before she knew it, they had brought in an array of fruits and vegetables and couldn't wait to cut them open, make drawings and models, report on harvesting methods, and compete with one another in spelling words related to the project.

When the weather became miserably cold, Sarah suggested that if any of them wanted to sit and talk informally at lunch time rather than go out in the cold, it might be a good time to share problems and ideas and an opportunity for her to get to know them better. It was an instant success. The lunch-time break quickly became a gripe-session time in which students complained about each other, their siblings, and the small miseries of their lives at home.

One day Sarah announced, "I thought we might do a program in the spring for your parents. I was wondering if we might come up with some ideas together."

"I don't wanna sing!" Tom Murray protested.

"I do," Stephanie exclaimed.

"It doesn't have to be all one way or the other," Sarah said. "If you all decide, we might have one or two songs. Let's plan it now so that we can have the winter to work on it."

"All winter?"

"Well, I'd like for it to be something big. I'm not even sure what it is I want. Just something that might demonstrate a variety of things we've learned."

"You mean we'd be learning it while we was doing it?" Hank asked.

"Something like that."

"Our folks ain't gonna be interested in a program that shows about all the math problems we've learned," Harvey said.

"Or spelling neither."

"Let's have a spelling bee!" Stephanie, an excellent speller, exclaimed.

"A wonderful idea," Sarah said. "When would you like to have it?"

"How about Thanksgiving time."

Enthusiasm radiated from the students' faces and Sarah asked, "Does everyone want to do that? Maybe the Wednesday evening before Thanksgiving? Or the Friday evening afterward? Will your fathers have to work on Saturday?" She didn't have all her questions out before many hands went up.

But Hank said, "What about you, Miss Jennings? Ain't you going home to Bluefield? We don't want no spelling bee less you're here."

"Well, I…" Sarah had sent further communication to her parents, saying, *I have begun teaching. The children are wonderful. I'm sorry for leaving as I did, but there was no other way.*

Their brief reply had not encouraged her: *You have done a great wrong disobeying your parents, broken a Commandment. We are praying for you. You might at least come home on weekends.*

She was not ready to go back at all and dreaded the Thanksgiving holiday. Now the children had given her the perfect excuse for staying in Clarkson. She smiled. "No, I'm not going home. Stephanie, would you and Donna Mae like to make the plans?"

"You'd let us?"

"Of course. But you'll have to consult with me on everything. I have some ideas. I think we should have refreshments, and I might be able to get food for nothing. But you girls are going to have to do most of the work."

After Stephanie and Donna Mae whispered and giggled together for a few moments, Donna Mae said, "We need to decide when to have it. Y'all go home tonight and ask your folks which would be the best day."

"All right, that's settled. You girls have about two weeks," Sarah said. "Now back to my spring program. It's not going to emphasize spelling or mathematics."

"Let's have a play," Clyde shouted. "I wanna be George Washington!" After the whipping, Clyde had rapidly endeared himself to Sarah, surprising her in many ways. Not only did he become an avid student, he was genial and polite as well. His father had even visited Sarah at the boarding house to extend his humble thanks for the thrashing she had delivered. The man confided that Clyde's goal had been to run her out. He also confessed his hope that Clyde would stay in school rather than follow his older brothers into the coal mine.

"Or a presentation," Hank said. "Have a narrator and different speakers to represent different historical characters."

After much discussion, with consideration of Clyde's interest in Washington, the class decided upon a pageant outlining colonial life and bringing the founding fathers into perspective. Sarah was secretly overjoyed, this being her favorite part of history and the students proving in their discussion that they knew very little about it, yet wanted to learn.

She envisioned incorporating portions of literary contributions from the period, imagining someone like Hank proclaiming in a good Patrick Henry voice, "Give me liberty or give me death!" She envisioned Clyde holding the Continental Army together, Hubert as John Paul Jones, exclaiming, "I have not yet begun to fight!" And Donna Mae daintily stitching the country's first Stars and Stripes. And she knew that bubbly little Corey Ferrell, Hank's younger sister, with singsong voice and fiery chestnut hair would narrate, captivating the audience with her natural ebullience.

That evening Sarah pulled out her history books and borrowed the only other one in the house. She began scanning material, making notes, and thinking about a trip to the library in Bluefield. She had a copy of Thomas Paine's *Common Sense* and perused it with interest. It was certainly the literary work for Hank to interpret, the Revolution's political heart and soul: independence was the destiny of Americans, he could point out, independence from an absentee oppressor. He could end with a rousing, "Ye that dare oppose not only the tyranny, but the tyrant, stand forth!" There was also Jefferson's *Declaration* to consider and Franklin's *Almanack*. Sarah's ideas tumbled out faster than she could make notes.

She was absorbed in the task when Paul Lessing appeared, looking forward to spending the rest of the evening with her.

7

PAUL LESSING HAD enlisted in the navy for a short stint after graduating high school. Then he took a job as a prison guard in the penitentiary in Moundsville. When Tom Felts contacted him saying he was looking for some good, tough men, Paul accepted the job as mine guard, having worked with strikebreakers as a teen in Pittsburgh. He had worked in several coal towns in southern West Virginia before coming to Clarkson. He liked his work, he liked Tom Felts, and Sarah liked Paul's philosophy: *The miners might be backward, but they're men just the same. They'll work for you if you treat them with respect.*

It had become routine for Paul Lessing to call on Sarah for a little while several evenings a week. They might sit together in the parlor or go walking if the weather was nice. She thought they had reached an understanding in the manner of their relationship. "Stop saying those things," she had finally told him on the porch one night when he continued professing his improbable emotions of love. "I'm only seventeen…"

"Seventeen!" He let out a soft, whistled breath and studied her for a long half minute, surprise written across his features. "I don't know what I thought, but I guess I thought you were older, maybe eighteen, nineteen."

"It makes a difference, doesn't it?"

He appeared thoughtful for a moment. "No," he decided. "You're old enough."

"For what?"

"For me to fall in love with. You might be the age of a girl, but you're a woman." He was still watching her closely, his mind working so hard Sarah could almost hear the cogs whirring. "Well, look at you. Out on your own, away from home. What'd you do, finish up high school early? All right with your parents, is it?"

"No!" she answered with all the defiance she could put into one syllable, proud, when she thought of her parents, to be in Paul's company.

He smiled slowly. "Don't need mommy and daddy to tell you

what to do. See? You're old enough to do your own thinking, plenty able to take care of yourself."

But tonight she was studying history, impatient with him when he showed up.

"What do you want to get rid of me for, honey?"

"I'm working on a project. Do you or any of your friends have any history books?"

"What for? Sure, we might. Ruel Savage has got a regular library up on the hill."

Eyes shining with the possibility of her first tangible educational success, she was outlining her plan to him. "And we'll have a narrator who'll serve as a transition type of person. Then somebody will speak as Benjamin Franklin, and Jefferson, and maybe even a King George character—"

Paul put up his hands. "Whoa, whoa, honey! Slow down. In fact, stop!"

"Don't you like it?" She did not recognize the look on his face. She was hurt and felt a need to explain. "Don't you see, Paul, it's the perfect opportunity for them to learn and then apply what they've learned. They'll learn history better this way, and remember it. They'll work together in groups, they'll put their writing and grammar skills into prac—"

"That's enough, honey," he said firmly.

"But even the older boys and girls are excited. Clyde Poling was thinking of quitting school and now—"

"Sarah," Paul said sharply. "Sarah," he repeated more gently. He rose and took her by the hand, leading her to the deserted dining room, where he shut the door and took her in his arms. He held her like a child. "Sarah, little naive teacher, you can't do this. Do you understand?"

"What do you mean, can't do it? Of course I can. The students want to, we all want to."

"You'd better start thinking more like a company employee

and less like a teacher. That kind of thing would have gone over big in my school or yours, but you do that here, and you'll get yourself fired, no matter what I could do to protect you—"

"Fired! But why!" She suddenly remembered something Satterfield had told her. *The coal company doesn't allow certain topics. You aren't to mention labor unions or socialism, that type of thing. Any subversive talk and you're fired on the spot. No warnings, no second chances.* "This isn't about unions or socialism," she went on. "It's colonial history, way before our modern labor problems. It's about democracy. It's about the beginnings of our country, about great thinkers and dreamers—leaders who had enough vision to organize and lead scattered groups of people to a common goal, freedom. It's about brave people who had enough courage to rise against an oppressive, unfair system, and demand their rights, and risk their lives. It's about high moral ideals, fighting to the death…"

He was staring at her so hard, so accusingly, that she floundered. She didn't understand him. He didn't understand her. This was her own passion, her own inspiration, the private battle she had fought for years in her own home. *Give me liberty… Of the people, by the people, for the people*—no monarchy, no select few to decide things benevolently or despotically, paternalistically. She concluded, "It's about revolution!"

He said quietly, "I know what it's about, Sarah. And National Coal doesn't need a revolution on its hands. Teachers aren't hired here to provide instruction in the fine points of what exactly constitutes oppression and unfairness. We throw the UMWA out of here for all their talk about workers' rights, and we don't need no school teacher indoctrinating young minds about constitutional rights."

Sarah's jaw dropped. "But the constitution—"

"Is something for politicians and judges and lawyers to worry about. You don't need to know no constitution to dig coal, and that's all these people can ever expect to do."

"Not Hank Ferrell! He's going to high school. He's getting out of here, and so will some of the others if I have any influence at all."

"That may be. We have no control over that, but you're teaching on company property and these people are living in houses provided by the company, and as long as that's the case, we teach what we see fit, and organizing and rebellion aren't fit topics." He was stern, doing his job, and blind to all else. However, he was neither hostile nor threatening. Sarah realized that if she were brought before Ruel Savage or Mr. Satterfield, there would indeed be no sympathy and no second chances.

His features softened and she was his girl again. "Do you understand, honey?"

She nodded.

"A fine mess you'd be in if Ruel ever got wind of this. Have you told anyone else?"

"I mentioned it at the supper table tonight, but I'm not sure they were paying much attention to me. They all had their own troubles to complain about."

"Is that so? Like what? Let me see if I can guess. Ethel can't stand working the accounts for Ruel because he's old and he's always got his hands on her."

Sarah made a face and nodded in agreement. "He's married too. Imagine that!"

"Doesn't make any difference. He gets what he wants. Ethel likes to complain about it, but she gives him what he wants."

"What!" Sarah was dumbfounded by the insinuation. She clasped her hands together, taking refuge in primness and prudery, not wanting to hear any more horrible things. She wished fervently for an impossible haven in study—Jefferson, Paine, the men who had followed. Why was there no vision in the present time?

They were still standing in the dining room. Paul reached for her hand, pulling her gently toward him. He put an arm around her and played with her hand, kissing her fingers, nuzzling her neck from time to time. "And what about the nurse? Ruth was probably complaining to high heaven about that foreign amputee patient of hers and how bad their house stinks—"

"Paul!" She was amazed that he knew. Except Ruth referred to the man as a "greasy dago" and described the house as a cesspool.

"And Ida made fun of what she read in people's letters today. And their socialist magazines that she'll throw out."

"No, she didn't," Sarah exclaimed, glad he wasn't right about everything. "I don't think she reads their mail much. She didn't talk much."

"Come here," he said gruffly, and he kissed her hard, the way he had more often taken to doing lately. He crushed her against him with such force that his pistol and shoulder holster were jammed painfully into her collarbone and his erection pushed against her pelvic bone. She was mildly frightened by his unashamed demonstration of desire, but the assurances he gave her were more than enough to calm her, his welcome words making the rest of it worthwhile. "Oh, I love you, little girl—love you! Say you're my girl. Tell me."

"You know I am."

"Don't you love me too, honey?" he asked, hurt written across his features.

"I don't know, Paul. I'm sorry. I just don't know."

The next day Sarah told the students they could still do the pageant but that the subject matter would have to be changed. She explained that she had received a summary of the material that must be covered during the term and gave them a choice— westward expansion, diplomacy overseas, or the lives of the presidents.

With fondness she watched them argue over westward expansion and the presidents. The boys wanted to be soldiers and Indians; the girls wanted to include first ladies, costumes, and changes in the White House. Finally when it seemed that no compromise could be achieved, Clyde Poling, who had appeared lost in thought, spoke up.

"Let's do presidents."

"Siding with the girls," someone teased.

"If we do presidents we can have both," Clyde announced proudly.

"How do you figure? Indians fighting at the Capitol?"

"I don't know much history, but seems like some of them presidents got famous as Injun fighters before they's presidents. Ain't I right, Miss Jennings?"

"That's exactly right, Clyde."

Donna Mae Brown came to Clyde's defense. "Some of 'em fought other things besides Injuns. You stupid boys could do all that there fighting, then let us girls do the interesting stuff."

"What other things them presidents fight, Donna Mae?" Hubert Shalp asked. He was one of the few boys who Sarah believed had no desire to work in the mines. However, as far as she could tell, he didn't take much of an interest in anything and remained in school to avoid the world of real work. He was cooperative in the schoolhouse, though, always polite to her, and the others respected him.

"Mainly wars, I reckon. Ain't that right, Miss Jennings?" Donna Mae answered.

"Yes. Some of them, before they were presidents, fought in wars. They also fought Indians, as Clyde said. Then after they became president, some of them fought the country's wars from the White House."

"Let's do presidents then," Hank said. "Who votes for presidents?" All the students raised their hands.

Sarah was elated by the students' ability to cooperate but somewhat overwhelmed by the prospect of covering so much material.

Most of the students settled into groups in quiet conversation. It was a day full of wind and drizzle, the kind of weather that kept demeanors calm. Hank opened the stove door, stirred the fire with the poker, and added coal. Then he turned to Sarah who sat nearby and asked softly, "You have to consult with them company men on everything?"

"Of course I don't! What do you mean?"

"You know what I mean," he answered quietly so the others couldn't hear. "You got them gun thugs all over you, telling you what's what. They told you you couldn't tell us nothing about no American Revolution. Might give us ideas we ain't supposed to have."

Sarah saw a sly, steady fire in his eyes and knew he hadn't learned that kind of talk on his own, in school. Hadn't Paul pinpointed him as a troublemaker? "How old are you, Hank?"

"Old enough to know that folks without schooling don't win revolutions no matter how angry they get. They just get kilt or stay down on their knees to the boss man."

"Hank!" Sarah breathed, catching the defiance flaring in his eyes. "You—are *you* angry?"

"Alla time, 'cept when I'm here. Today's the first time I got mad here." He set his jaw. "I said too much, but you cain't do nothing to me."

Sarah lowered her voice to a whisper. "Hank, I promise you, I'll never repeat what you've just said."

His relief was evident. "And I can keep my job too?"

"Yes, you can, but I'd like a turnabout here. I'm a teacher minding my own business. Don't you repeat what I've said."

"Yes, ma'am."

"How old are you really?"

"Going on fifteen."

"I don't believe you. Fifteen goes to high school."

"Nearly fourteen. And I *am* going to high school next year."

"That's better. Have you ever been in the mine?"

"Yes, ma'am. When school's out. I work alla time."

"Maybe you know what you're talking about then."

"Maybe I do." He stuck his chin in the air.

"I've thought it might be interesting to have a tour sometime."

He shook his head. "Ain't nobody'd let a woman in them tunnels. It's bad luck. But if you could, then maybe you'd know what some folks is talking about. Specially when them thugs talk about putting down insurrections of dumb rednecks that oughta know they got it made working for a company that gives 'em such nice houses to live in, making 'em buy outta that high-priced store, giving 'em nice churches where a company preacher tells 'em what to believe, and ball fields for recreation so all they'll think about is winning games against each other."

Hank's words, quietly spoken, stirred discord in Sarah, for the first time demonstrating a reason for the guns Paul and his friends carried. For a terrifying instant, she glimpsed two sides of a well-defined line and didn't want to think about where she belonged.

She changed the subject, fearful of this liberty Hank was taking, revealing too much of his mind to her. "What do you do, Hank? When you work?"

"Last couple years I worked with Daddy. He's a coal loader. You know what that is, Miss Jennings?"

She suddenly felt afraid of him, afraid that he could read her thoughts. She imagined his mockery of her and her position. "I don't know much about mining. What's a coal loader? Somebody that loads coal?"

He smiled at her, friendly with no condescension, but she felt like the one laboring under so much ignorance. Even in the schoolhouse she was an outsider—the company teacher. "I reckon it is. But before he can load, he has to undercut the bottom of the face, then he has to bore holes above his cut and fill 'em with black powder for blasting. After the coal's shot, that's when he loads. You think that don't take skill, Miss Jennings? You gotta know where to put them holes and how much powder to use, and they's plenty of considerations that goes into making them decisions. In the near dark. Cain't learn a job like that in a week. Takes working with a craftsman like my daddy for a long time."

"You've worked with him for two summers. Could you do it by yourself?"

"Not yet. Most boys don't make it to loader till maybe twenty, twenty-one years old. Daddy says I'm good, but I gotta get bigger, stronger. It's hard lying on your back and digging with a pick for an hour or more at a time, sometimes lying in water. Then you gotta use your weight to crank the auger into the face. Faster you work, the more you get paid, because you get paid by the car. A real loader's in charge of the work place, takes charge of the safety, has his own check number on his car. I'm gonna be a loader by the time I'm eighteen."

Sarah had no doubt that he could do it by age seventeen, but she didn't say so. She didn't want him to be a coal miner. "I thought you wanted to go to high school."

"I do. I am."

"You can't do everything, Hank. If you have a diploma, you won't have to be a coal miner."

He looked out the window and grinned. Then he said, "What do you suppose a coal miner with a high school diploma could do, Miss Jennings?"

8

"HONEY, YOU EVER been riding in a car?" Paul asked Sarah one Friday evening.

"Yes."

He looked at her skeptically. "When?"

"My uncle has a friend with a car. He's taken my family for a drive several times," she said, not wanting Paul to know the truth. Several times over the past year she had slipped out of her house late at night, or invented pretexts to leave the house, to meet Mike

Brooks, an older boy who drove his father's automobile. He had taken her to some adult parties where she had tasted a few drinks of alcohol and tried cigarettes.

By that time she had given up on boys her own age, as they wanted nothing to do with her. Several boys had tried to become friendly with her, only to suffer severe rebuffs from Ray Jennings. Sarah had lost her close girl friends as well, so harsh was the atmosphere in her home, and she wasn't allowed to go to nonchurch-related social events. She took up with Mike simply because he was there.

But he hadn't lasted long. For one thing he had frightened her, once shoving her into an alcove, kissing her and pawing at her, and then unaccountably crying when she pushed him away. Another time, riding in Mike's car, she thought she had been spotted by one of her parents' acquaintances. Unable to muster any real affection for Mike, she had given it up.

"I've got to run an errand for Ruel tomorrow," Paul was saying. "I'm taking his car. Want to come along?"

"Sure!"

So on Saturday she had a tour of National Coal's other McDow-ell County holdings at Apple Bottom and West Camp, both east of Clarkson. Paul also drove into a couple of other towns. At each stop Sarah waited in the car while he talked to armed mine guards at mine entrances, which he referred to as the drift mouth. Then he visited supervisors' or operators' homes.

"What are you talking to them about?"

"Just business, honey."

The towns looked much the same, whether they were owned by National Coal or another company. A large company store stood close to the train station. Houses and other buildings were located around the nearby hillsides. In each of these towns Sarah had a closer look at the actual mine entrance than she had in Clarkson, owing to its location on the other side of the railroad yard, which was often clogged with cars. When she asked Paul what the various buildings were, he pointed out stables, blacksmith shops, and engine and supply houses. Coal tipples seemed to grow out of hillsides while squat coke ovens rimmed the train tracks.

It was easy to distinguish the residents—company officials looked one way, like Paul, dressed in coats and ties, cocksure, arrogant. Coal miners worked on Saturdays, but Sarah picked out their wives and children, not only because of their shabby dress and sometimes grimy skin, but because she saw what she had missed in the familiar setting of Clarkson—a suggestion in their stature that showed they were aware of their own position, as Hank had said, down on their knees to the boss man.

After the messages had all been delivered, Paul said, "Let's just drive for a spell." He drove the car along a narrow road in concentrated silence for a while, carefully avoiding holes in the road that was becoming little more than a path. Eventually he turned off onto a much narrower lane running up a little hollow and pulled into a wide spot where other tire tracks were visible in the drying mud. When he stopped the car, he reached into the back seat for a brown paper sack. "Thought we'd relax in a little privacy for a change before heading back. All right with you, honey?" His warm smile sent a pleasant shiver through her.

"Yes."

"This is the best 'shine you can find in these parts," he commented, producing a jar and two glasses. "Smooth as silk and expensive as hell."

She was conscious then of perhaps too much privacy. "Is it really?" she said nervously. Ida would have had a better reply. Paul was looking at her as though he thought so too.

"Yeah." He handed her a glass and watched her take a drink. She was unable to meet his eyes, aware that he continued to observe her. He cleared his throat and spoke softly, faltering. "An old hillbilly lives so far out, I don't know how he brings this stuff in. Well,

I guess he's got a mule. Sarah, I—holy smoke, but you are beautiful! I—did anybody ever tell you that before?"

Sarah shrugged and blushed, then looked out the window, where brambles, bare trees, and a lonely road going nowhere were the only things visible. And here she was drinking moonshine with a mine guard—a gun thug in the estimation of some—in an automobile in this deserted place. "We ought to go back," she said. If she screamed, no one would hear her.

"I suppose you're right. Your parents wouldn't like it if they knew you were out here with me and a jar of good whiskey." Their eyes met and he seemed hurt and lost, sincere, all pretenses of tough manliness gone. He seemed remorseful. "I just love you is all. There's so much filth and meanness everywhere you go around here, I just wanted to look at you—how pretty and pure you are in the middle of all this."

No, her parents wouldn't like it, but he was a good man. When the guards were relaxing on the steps of the company store, Paul's was the only weapon which leaned untended against the building. Her parents would never understand how gentle he really was despite his occupation. She touched his hand. "Sure. It's all right if we stay for a while."

Their eyes held and he closed his hand around hers. She tried to control her rising breath. She heard him swallow. "If we were to get married, I could make you so happy." The word struck her a dizzying blow, and she closed her eyes, felt the warm, gentle pressure of his hand around hers. "I'd get you anything in the world you wanted." His voice was tender, going toward a whisper. "I've tried to think about the things you want. Thought maybe diamonds, but I think maybe you'd rather go to college." She opened her eyes. For the first time she understood that there was depth to his feelings for her. "Marshall? You want to go to Marshall? I could get good work close to Huntington. Ahh!" He kissed her hand, and leaned back in the seat with his eyes closed. "Can't think of anything that would make me happier than coming home from work every day to see you sitting there, pretty as a picture, studying at your books." He took her hand to his lips again. "After a while, though, you probably wouldn't want anything to do with a dumb guy like me."

"You're not dumb, Paul!" She slapped his chest playfully and he caught her in a partial embrace, his eyes gleaming with the light of his reverie.

"Could you ever consider that, Sarah? Could you ever love me?" With ever so much tenderness, he pulled her closer, and she yearned to press close to his body. *Yes!* she wanted to shout, but she only wanted to love his body. She thought of the little she knew of a man's anatomy and nearly groaned with wanting to touch him. "I've killed five guys. No, ten," he said, nuzzling her neck. "Do you love me now?"

She pulled away from him and burst out laughing. "You haven't!" He remained motionless, smiling like a drunk, drunk on love.

"Honey, please…" She fell into his arms then and accepted his tender yet impassioned kisses, snuggled close in powerful arms that were all sweet gentleness. Her mind floated away to images of his mercy, of his dissatisfaction with the company, and a picture of her enraged father if he could see her in the arms of this kind man. Her father would never even try to understand. Paul began to stroke her breasts so softly she could feel the love in his touch. She had but to ask him and he would stop, but she didn't ask because she was in love with the rightness and harmony of the moment, her need meshing so neatly with his understanding of her. He moved to caress her thigh, then left his hand in a light grasp just above her knee. The gentle pressure began to play on the nerves of her desire.

"Oh!" came his whispered sigh, as he straightened up and eased away from her. "I'm afraid your old man is very displeased with me at this moment." He held her chin with his fingertips and kissed her quickly. "We'd better get you back to where you belong."

Back in Clarkson he turned up the hill instead of going to the boarding house. "It's high time you met the boss." He kissed her before opening the car door and said with a wink, "Don't tell him we're getting married, honey."

Paul opened the front door and ambled in as though he owned the place. He led Sarah through a front room decorated with plush furniture and oil paintings in fancy gilded frames. Everywhere polished woodwork gleamed, but the air was stuffy with stale tobacco smoke. Down a hallway they passed a large dining room, and Sarah stopped momentarily to observe the luster of the mahogany furniture, the heavy, elaborately carved, untarnished silver service, the chandelier with facets glittering in the fading late-autumn sunlight.

Farther along Paul opened a door and shoved her inside. "This is what you want to see, honey." In the gloom she saw books lining three walls from floor to ceiling and easy chairs facing a fireplace of marble and brick. Sarah took quiet steps around the empty room, stopping at an opened writing table adorned with feminine articles—rose-embossed stationery positioned neatly in the left corner, and a heavy glass inkstand in the right. Unopened letters were stacked in the center beside a silver-handled letter opener carved in a pattern of roses; a matching set of small oval picture frames decorated the table's raised shelf. Sarah stooped to observe two smooth young faces peering from the frames— teenage boys, stiff and unattractive, plump and formally dressed. Next she moved to a roll-top desk where cigar butts were half-buried in the ashes of a large, translucent yellow glass ashtray. She ran her hand lightly across piles of papers—invoices and letters—and traced a finger across two leather-bound volumes— *Stockholders Annual Report...* and *Bituminous Coal, Industrial Conditions in...*

Sarah turned her attention to the books and gazed with longing at the floor-to-ceiling shelves. She turned to Paul who stood in the doorway with his arms crossed. "What does he do with all these books?" she whispered.

"I suppose he reads them. Come on."

The staircase was wide and curved and carpeted. The banister was smooth and embellished underneath with floral carving. The second-floor hallway stretched out past six closed doors. Paul pushed one of them open.

Inside, several men in shirt sleeves were sitting around a table playing cards and drinking whiskey. Thick cigar smoke stung Sarah's eyes, and she recognized several of Clarkson's mine guards.

"Hey, Less," a middle-aged man with thinning hair and a ravenous look said, "get my dirty work done for me? Well, look at this, will you!" He rose, smiling a gulping, leering grin with a wet mouth that was clamped around a cigar. "You the new teacher, are you?" He came toward Sarah with an outstretched hand, tall, so commanding that nobody had to tell her he was Ruel Savage. His hand was slick and dry, and she had to force herself not to shrink from him. He held onto her hand too long, appraising her, and Sarah was aware of Paul, restless at her side.

"Sarah Jennings, Ruel Savage," Paul said.

"Well, I'll be. I should have come by the schoolhouse to see you before." He looked from her to Paul and then back again. Then he turned again to Paul. "She, uh—?"

Paul stood up straight, not as tall as Ruel, and grasped Sarah's arm possessively at the elbow. "Yeah."

Ruel continued to regard her. "You're... uh... right young."

Sarah nodded.

He was thoughtful for a moment. "From Bluefield, are you?"

"Yes."

"Ever been in a coal camp before this?"

"No."

"Suppose you know what you're doing in that schoolhouse?"

"Leave her alone, Ruel. The trustee said she was well-qualified. And I'm helping her along when she needs help."

Ruel Savage lost interest in Sarah. "Well, wait outside the door while I talk to Less."

9

SARAH RETURNED TO school on Monday, hoping to forget all that she had been exposed to over the weekend. Although Paul had been a part of it, she was able to keep him in a separate compartment in her mind. He was, after all, different from the other guards.

The schoolhouse had become a pleasant haven for Sarah, an adventure in imagination, creativity, and learning with a crew of eager, trusting children. Work had begun on the Pageant of the Presidents, as the students had named it, and every day a study group gave a report on some fact related to a president or some aspect of the plans for the pageant.

But at noon Sarah glanced around with new eyes at the lunch fare of her students—cold fried cornmeal mush or biscuits, beans or a strip of fried salt pork, occasionally a wrinkled baked potato—and her thoughts went immediately to the grandeur in Ruel Savage's house.

The children ate with fingers, dark with ground-in dirt and black under the nails, that no amount of washing could cleanse. Here in the schoolhouse they acted like children, but the boys, Sarah realized, were familiar with a man's kind of work, and the girls knew about making a meal out of nothing and keeping a house clean with no running water in an environment that was constantly sifting out thick black dust.

She asked, "What is it you boys do in the mine?"

They looked at each other, wondering which one she addressed.

"She asked me that last week," Hank said.

"You told me about loaders," she said. "What else is there?"

"She sure asks a lota questions, don't she?" Stella Lively said with a giggle.

"How else can she learn anything?" Tina Furgeson, Milty's twin sister, said.

"You ever ask your gun-toting friends any questions, Miss Jennings?" Hank asked, startling Sarah with the pointed ferocity in both his tone and the question itself. His arms were crossed and his eyes compelled her.

"Hank!" she exclaimed. She tried to deflect his question, brush it off. "Well, yes, of course I do. I always ask questions, like Stella said. So, boys, what about—"

He persisted. "Ever get answers?"

"Yes." She turned away. "Some." The look in his eye, his tone of voice, made her feel she had done something wrong. Over the weekend Paul had answered none of her questions, had only said *just business, honey.*

"Their answers okay with you?"

Sarah could not look at Hank, nor could she reply. The students remained quiet, waiting. Nearly half a minute passed, during which the muted hiss from the fire in the potbelly and the chug-chug of a passing train in the valley were the only sounds.

Hank's quiet voice finally broke the silence. "We, uh, usually start out as trappers, Miss Jennings." The rest of the students began to breathe again. "Or carrying our daddies' tools."

"What's a trapper?" She looked at him, hoping he understood her gratitude before turning her attention to the younger boys. "Is that what you do, More?"

"I ain't never been in. My daddy says I gotta wait till I'm twelve."

"I been a trapper boy," Tom said. "You take care of the trap-doors."

"Trapdoors?"

"Doors that closes off sections of the tunnels."

"It's to keep fresh air circulating so gas don't build up at the work face."

"Gets pumped in from a ventilating furnace."

"You open the doors every time you hear a motor coming or the trip for the mules or when men walk through," Tom continued.

"What do you mean, a motor?" Sarah asked.

Tom shrugged. "You know, a motor."

"It's a locomotive," Hank said. "A little thing, run by electricity. Pulls cars through the mine. Cars usually carry coal or supplies, sometimes men."

"Being a trapper's the most boring job there is, ain't it?" Tom observed and several others nodded.

"Lonesome too."

"Not scary?" Sarah asked.

"No!" they answered emphatically together.

"What else is there?"

"Stable boy."

"And that ain't no fun. Them mules is mean. Ain't never knowed a friendly mule."

"Really? Why is that?" Sarah asked.

"They go blind," Clyde remarked. "But they ain't nothing for 'em to see anyhow."

"They're always getting shocked in the head," Hank said. "Hit their heads on the trolley wires running along the top of the tunnel."

"My, my. So many things you children know that I've never even thought of. What other jobs do you have?"

"I been in charge of the ventilating furnace before."

"And I been a breaker boy."

"What's that?"

"Picking pieces of slate outta the coal after it come out. You ain't inside with that job."

"Is there a one of you, besides More, who hasn't worked inside the mine?"

"The girls."

"They don't allow us," Stephanie said. "It's bad luck if a girl goes in."

"I don't think Hubert has," George said.

"Yeah, he has," Milty said. "We was trappers at the same time about five years ago."

"He didn't do it long, I don't think," Stephanie said.

"He don't like it inside," Clyde said. "He gets labor work on the railroad sometimes."

Sarah noted Hubert Shalp's absence. He was usually there, even if he did sleep half the time. "Is that where he is today? Working on the railroad?"

George answered. "They say Dom's took a turn for the worst and Hubie won't leave him."

"Who's Dom?" Sarah asked. The one who had never shown up?

"His buddy."

"Is something wrong with him?"

"He got bad hurt in a cave-in. Don't you remember that, Miss Jennings?"

"Are you talking about Dominico Cinelli, a student who's enrolled here?"

They all nodded gravely. "Dominick, we call him," someone said. "Or Dom."

"But I just saw him a while back," Sarah protested. "When I first came here. He was going hunting."

"Hit musta been about that time," More said. "When you first come."

"What happened to him?"

"A piece of the roof give way and smashed him up bad," George explained. "Him and a couple others."

"Cap and Rob, them's the other two," Clyde said. "They wasn't so bad."

Sarah felt Hank's rage burning, and she glanced at him, almost timidly, feeling guilty, as though she were to blame. "Bones in his legs was crushed into a thousand pieces," he growled. "Doctors had to cut 'em clean off."

"What!" Sarah whispered. "Oh, no, Hank. He lost his legs? Oh, no!"

"Ain't no reason why he shouldn't go on living, right?" Hank continued. "Only his spirit's crushed worse'n his legs."

Sarah's thoughts whirled together, part of her mind refusing to accept such horror. "But we can't think that! There are things he can do. Perhaps we could do something for him, something to cheer him, give him a reason to go on..." She stopped. They were all staring at her as though she had lost her reason.

"He ain't got legs," Hank said. "He ain't nothing without legs."

"Shame on you, Hank Ferrell, for giving up on him. You've got a lot of fight in you. You should try to infect him with some of that spirit."

"He ain't nothing without legs," he insisted. "He's seventeen, he cain't speak much English, much less read it nor write it. All he ever done was work in the mine. He don't know nothing else. He had him a gal. They was gonna get married, and here she already took up with another feller. What's he got to live for? His mama cries alla time, and that there nurse that comes in to check on him practically sneers her disgust right in his face. Dom's the kind of guy some folks takes a look at and all they can think of is 'dago bastard, filthy foreigner.' "

Hank spit his accusation at Sarah as though he knew her initial thoughts about Dominick had been similar. Tears blinded her. One of the students embraced her. She sensed that it was Donna Mae, and before she realized how unseemly her behavior was, she was sobbing her grief, devastated because she should have known. She had wondered about him and had asked no one. She swallowed hard, reserving the rest of her tears for later.

"Well, I'm going," she said to Hank, wiping her eyes.

"Going where?"

"I'm going to see him. I'll try to cheer him, give him reasons to have hope. I could teach him—"

Hank rose and stormed out the back door, slamming it behind him. All eyes turned to Sarah. "Well, I will," she sniffed.

The afternoon went by in silence, as though everyone were taking refuge in learning. Hank let himself back in once class was under way, taking his seat quietly and doing his math lesson with a vengeance. With half her mind, Sarah listened to the intermediate students read, quizzed the primary children on sums, then challenged the older students with spelling demons, but her thoughts were on all she now realized she knew about Dominick.

Ruth's abrasive complaining echoed in her mind: "Dago scum! I swear they must bathe in garlic and shit, if they ever wash. That old lady of his doesn't help out none. I wish she'd learn how to take care of him. I tell her over and over how to turn him, what to feed him, how to change bandages, how to give him medicine, and she stares at me like I'm crazy, like *I'm* crazy! Then she grins like a fool. And cries. I sometimes wonder if she hears a word I'm saying. I wish he'd drop dead. He's no good to anybody and he looks at me like he wants to kill me. He could probably reach out and grab for my neck. I don't like it when the old woman leaves me alone with him. Truth is, I'm afraid of him…"

Once Sarah had been with Paul and another mine guard, who had commented about Ruth, "I don't know why Ruel has her wasting her time on that tally. He's half dead. Somebody ought to put him out of his misery."

"You know damn well why he does it," Paul had answered. Sarah had asked Paul about it and he had answered, "Just one of the miners got hurt when a roof fell in. Wasn't watching what he was doing…"

Everyone in town had known but her! Poor Hubert Shalp! Now she could see it. He came to school every day half-asleep from sitting up nights with his friend. Well, now Sarah knew it too, and she would visit Dominick. She would teach him and help him and inspire him. Dismissing the students for the day, she said, "Hank, please stay for a moment." He sighed and sneered and remained in his seat.

When the last child was gone, Harvey Casteel stood indecisively with a dust rag in his hand. He gestured toward the back door. "I'll... uh... go see about the privies." He had just done that job the previous Friday, and Sarah nodded her appreciation.

She turned to Hank who stared straight ahead. "Will you take me?" He was silent and Sarah took a step toward him. "Hank?"

He began to speak barely above a whisper. "There was a buildup of coal dust in the room that day when they was setting charges. Dust caught fire, just a little fire, but they hit a roof support while they was trying to get free of it, and a piece of the roof come down. You ask company folks about it, they'd say 'stupid foreigner weren't paying no mind to his work.'" Hank went to the cloakroom and picked up his coat and his lunch pail, stopped at his desk for his books, and said, "Yeah, I'll take you, but it won't do you no good."

They walked down to the rows of houses which Sarah had never seen close up. Square bungalows of board-and-batten siding and black paper roofing, each house had a chimney in the center, a covered porch, and a small yard, many of which had been used as gardens. Most of the once-white houses had weathered to gray. Chickens and dogs scavenged around some yards or wandered beneath the houses that were set on posts without underpinning.

"Which one's your house?"

He pointed to the top row. "That white one."

"Why is yours white?" She counted five white houses in the whole vicinity.

"Mommy tries to keep the place up. She whitewashes and puts up wallpaper and fixes the leaks in the roof herself. Don't do much good. Soon as one thing's fixed, another gets broke."

At approximately every fifth house, Sarah observed a hand pump at the side of the road but was afraid to ask Hank about them. Two women were pumping water into gallon buckets at one, and they stopped to stare as she and Hank walked by. Every so often they came upon a pile of garbage that smelled even in the cold weather, and Sarah knew there was more in the creek. She had listened to Ruth complain about it; she had heard Doug Burnside making excuses for National Coal's lack of garbage service for miners, but the problem had never seemed real until now, and it became appalling to her when she realized that there was no garbage accumulation either at the boarding house, the schoolhouse or, she was sure, at Ruel Savage's fine house.

It was mid-November, few people were outside, but Sarah could hear voices coming from inside the thin walls of several houses. As they walked by one house, the door squeaked open and Stella Lively scampered out, wildly waving her hand and grinning with enthusiasm. "Hello, Miss Jennings! Hi, Miss Jennings!"

"Hello, Stella." Sarah smiled, trying not to stare at Stella standing on a crooked porch with a mud-caked dog at her heels, and she saw that this was the real Stella, grinning in ignorance and clutching the splintered porch railing, the bars of a prison from which she would never escape. Framed in this impoverished landscape, Stella's grimy little hands now made sense to Sarah. The pump down the road and the hollow space beneath the house sucking up a cold wind explained the oil in the little girl's hair, the yellow mucous always clogging her nose.

Sarah glanced at Hank. Could *he* live here too? He and his sisters were cleaner than most and their house was white, but their clothes were still faded, their hands still gray. He plodded along by her side, more bitter and angry than a thirteen-year-old should have to be, but he would break out of his prison by means of that very fire and anger. Nevertheless, he was a child. "Hank, you shouldn't—" she blurted, not knowing how to finish. His stormy eyes snapped at her, but she tried again. "Maybe you should try to—"

"Forget it?" he asked through clenched teeth. "Is that what you think I oughta do, forget it? Go somewhere and play with pretty toys? Dream pretty dreams? And forget it? You go in there and take a look and see if you can forget it. Come on." He bounded toward one of the houses and knocked at the door. Sarah followed and arrived just as a big-boned woman opened the door. "Hello, Mrs. Cinelli." Hank spoke slowly, enunciating each syllable carefully. "This here's the schoolteacher, Miss Jennings." To Sarah he mumbled, "She don't know much English."

The woman smiled, exposing crooked teeth. Sarah smiled back.

"She come to talk to Dominick."

Mrs. Cinelli's smile vanished and tears welled in her eyes. "Oh," she moaned, her head shaking. "He no good."

"What's the trouble?" Hank asked. She began to weep into her apron. "She does this every time," he muttered to Sarah. Then he raised his voice as though the woman were hard of hearing. "Can we see him?" She moved aside to let them in and Hank asked, "Hubert here?" She nodded, and Hank said to Sarah, "C'mon."

They left the mother crying on the doorstep. Hank led Sarah through a front room littered with a hodgepodge of the family's belongings—piles of clothing, tools, plates, a few books—all scattered around on the table, the sofa, and the floor. There was a table reserved for a crucifix, a rosary, and a Bible. They passed a closed door on the right. In a corner located in the middle of the house an open grate burned coal, and live ashes spilled out onto chipped firebrick. A film of grit covered everything. They walked through the kitchen, which was in the same untidy condition—dirty dishes stacked on a lopsided wooden table, sacks of flour and meal in a corner on sooty floorboards. Onions, garlic, and red peppers hung from nails, and a single light bulb dangled from the ceiling.

In the bedroom, where junk was scattered about and a combination of odors—tobacco and feces the only ones Sarah recognized—nearly overpowered them, they interrupted Hubert and Dom who were sharing a cigarette. Hubert quickly handed it to Dom and scrambled to his feet when he saw Sarah.

"Miss Jennings!" he croaked, as though he had been caught in a criminal act. "Why, what—hey, Dom, this here's the teacher. Remember her?"

Sarah met the same doe eyes that had arrogantly violated her before, now flat, staring at her from a sunken, yellowish face etched around the edges with uneven stubble. His dark hair was wild and long and matted, and his lip curled and trembled. She held his eye, determined to reach for his soul and never see the stumps of his legs she was fleetingly aware of outlined under the bed clothes. "Hello, Dominick," she said, trying to sound bright, instead of as nervous as she felt. "I don't know if you remember me, but I remember you. I've just now heard about your accident. I had no idea—"

He had dropped the cigarette into an ashtray full of butts, and his eyes seemed to wake up as she spoke. She took a step toward the bed and reached for his hand. In that instant she read the resentment in his eyes, and with the furious power of a wild thing cornered, he rose, half-sitting for a moment, and rolled as far from her as possible, hugging himself, his face half-buried in a near-featherless pillow. His body trembled; his breath was loud and shallow. His violent shift of positions had partially pulled the cover away from what remained of his legs, and Sarah looked away from dirty bandages.

Hubert knelt next to him. "C'mon, Dom. Say how-do to the teacher." Dom said nothing, only shook the harder. "She wouldna come if'n she didn't give a shit. C'mon, buddy." Hubert stroked his friend's face and oily hair, grasping strands of it in a gesture of affection. He looked up at Sarah. "What'd you come here for, Miss Jennings?"

Sarah tried to pack everything into a few words, taking care, as Hank had, to speak clearly, slowly. "To tell him I want to give him something, anything, whatever I can. I can teach him in the evenings, write letters, help him find a job somewhere." She shook her head sadly. "Hubert, why didn't you tell me?"

He shrugged and grimaced, swallowing hard to fight his tears.

Dominick's muffled voice came through the pillow. "Tell her go way."

She stared, first into Hubert's eyes glistening with sadness, then at Dominick's trembling shoulders.

"Let's go," Hank whispered.

"I'll come back to see you again, Dominick," she said before turning to follow Hank.

Dominick cried out, "Tell her don't come no more!"

Outside in the narrow street of packed slag Sarah stopped with Hank. "See?" he said in bitter triumph and Sarah nodded. He looked up the street to where a mine guard was now purposefully loitering and turned to her, spitting out words in a loud whisper. "You think I'm going to high school so I can get a job somewhere else? After I graduate I'm gonna join the United Mine Workers union and learn about organizing. Then I'm gonna come back here and help tear this place down." He turned on his heel and dashed down the street.

10

"WHAT'D YOU VISIT that boy for?" Paul asked Sarah that evening. She did not respond, didn't ask him how he knew. His tone seemed mildly threatening. "Come on now."

Something was wrong, but she didn't think visiting Dominick
Cinelli was the problem. How could they know everything? She
had walked with Hank, had stood in the road with him, but they
could not have heard the words that passed between them.

They. Paul Lessing was one of *them*. And they could not have
known what occurred inside. They could not have known what her
mind had seen in the vision of little Stella Lively.

His voice, a question, was intruding on her thoughts.
"What'd you say to him?" Which must be why Paul was questioning her now.

"Not much. It was a disaster. He didn't want me there."

"Of course he didn't. What'd you go for? What are you, some
kind of self-appointed Florence Nightingale going around visiting
the sick?"

"He was one of my students. That is, he was on my register,
the only one who's never shown up. The kids told me today about
the accident. It was the first I'd known about it. I felt I should go
by, see if he needed something, maybe some kind of evening
tutoring or something."

Paul nodded. "Okay. Yeah, I get it now. Why didn't you say so
in the first place?"

"Why do I owe you an explanation? When I ask you questions, all you say is 'I don't know' and 'Just business.'" He didn't
answer. She saw the wreck of the Cinelli home again in her
mind. Paul still hadn't answered and in a clouded way she saw
red. "Why? It's another question you're not answering for me.
You're combining business with pleasure. One of you must have
been assigned to keep a watch on me." She recalled the splen-
dor of Ruel Savage's house, built on the backs and broken legs
and beaten spirits of men and boys like Dominick Cinelli. "You
don't love me." She saw it was true—a man like Paul Lessing
could never love her. "You just want to make sure I'm not up to
anything."

Paul's face was the vision of sheer panic. "Oh, God, honey! That isn't true at all!"

Sarah no longer cared what he said. She was remembering the stench in that little bungalow where there was no running water. "How can your big, powerful, rich coal company be so suspicious and deluded as to think that a seventeen-year-old girl who's just left home for the first time has come to town to hatch plots with... with children!"

"So help me, it's not like that at all, Sarah." His eyes were full of pain.

She crossed her arms. "What's it like then?"

"You're right about the suspicions. That strike a couple years back has the coal companies so scared they worry when a stray cat wanders into town. But it's not my job to watch you. There are others who do it instead of me. It's all our jobs to keep tabs on everything. I can't see past the end of my nose when it comes to you, honey, and it worries me when the men talk. I don't want anyone to decide to give you a hard time. Now there. I've said enough. Come, let me hold you, honey. Ease my mind. I didn't like that look in your eye just now. Like *you* were suspicious of *me*. That's no way for us to be."

Sarah wiggled away from him. "You haven't said enough. Who's going to give me a hard time? And why?" She glared at him. He looked away.

"Look, around here, names aren't important. Your little friend Hank can tell you that. Ruel's is the only name you need to know."

"But the *why* is important," she pressed and he conceded with a look. "Now why, Paul?"

"Just... Honey, you've got to keep away from that boy is all."

"But I didn't even know about his accident until today! I thought he was working and that's why he wasn't in school. This is crazy!"

"I'm not talking about the Cinelli boy," he said softly.

Sarah's heart was suddenly thudding in her throat. How could anybody know so much? What had she done besides listen? Her eyes met Paul's, and she saw that he was only pleading, not accusing. "If you want me to throw him out of my school, I won't," she said quietly. He shook his head sadly. Hank Ferrell had evidently established a reputation for himself before she had ever come to Clarkson. "Don't walk down the street with him, is that it?"

Paul nodded. "Keep away from him, Sarah. He's trouble." He kissed her forehead and his lips were soft and loving. "Look, honey, confidentiality is the nature of my work. I'm a detective, deputized by the McDowell County Sheriff, and whether you like it or not, I've got a boss to answer to. It's nothing personal against you, and it's got nothing to do with us."

"Have you ever been in any of those houses?" she asked him later in the week because she had been unable to forget Dominick's house or Stella's porch.

"Yes, I have."

"The Cinellis'?"

"Nope. I hear it's a pigsty though."

"Are they all like that?"

"Some are worse than others. Some stink, some of them are dusty. Some have decent belongings. Some are clean as a whistle. That house you went into used to be spotless and tidy."

"What's going to happen to them?"

"I don't know. It's awful to say, but they'd be better off if the kid would die. The old man doesn't go home much anymore. Stays drunk when he's not working."

"Oh, Paul."

"Look, I didn't invent the system. Somebody brought these foreigners over here to work cheap, didn't tell them anything about how it is. There's poor people everywhere. They were poor before they came, some a lot worse off before they got here."

"But they're worse off now because of the language barrier."

"That's right. Look here," he said, kissing her hands, "it's okay to sympathize with them a little, I suppose, but you ought to be glad you won't ever have to live like that. How would you like to raise kids in a little village like this?" Sarah tried to imagine her future children growing up with schoolmates like Donna Mae or George or Clyde or any of them, whom she nevertheless dearly loved. "I make good money, and I've got plenty saved," Paul continued. "If you don't like the idea of Marshall and Huntington, there's opportunity in Pittsburgh. Once the school term's over, I'll take some time off and we'll do some traveling to those places. You can make up your mind then."

Sarah found that in a way she loved Paul after all. True, he was a mine guard, but he was protective of her and caring, and he simply had nothing to do with conditions in the coal mine that had caused a roof to fall on Dominick Cinelli.

11

THE DAY BEFORE Thanksgiving Sarah met Stephanie and Donna Mae at the company store. The girls had so desperately wanted to bake treats for the social hour following the spelling bee which was to be held at the schoolhouse on Friday evening that Sarah invited them to use the kitchen at the boarding house, equipped as it was with running water and an icebox. The light in their eyes told her that this was one of the most exciting experiences of their lives. And thanks to Paul, National Coal would pay for the groceries.

A train had just pulled in and several mine guards and other company officials were unloading items and tossing them into a horse-drawn wagon: turkeys, oranges, nuts, sugar, and butter, all were being provided to the miners' families. In addition, Ruel Savage was closing down the mine on Thanksgiving Day and on the

Saturday afterward. The miners were to have a bonus of anywhere between twenty-five cents and a dollar.

In the store Sarah stood by while the girls put their heads together with their list of groceries. Several other women were lined up to make purchases. There was usually a mine guard on duty, and this afternoon Doug Burnside strolled around the store. He had an ear tuned to a conversation at the far end of the counter, and Sarah couldn't help listening as well. An accountant was discussing figures in a ledger with a thin Negro woman who was shaking her head vigorously from side to side.

"No. No, sir," she said, pointing to the book. "He had fifty up here, see? Then you took off all these deductions, which is right, but then you added fifty again, and that ain't right. He didn't get no credit for Thursday. He worked that day, but he gone in late 'cause he weren't feeling good. He brung out four cars that day, and you ain't put it on his pay. Now he got a paper at home and y'all oughta have it on your weigh sheet."

Doug Burnside stepped up and leaned on the counter, staring at the woman. "Miz Webster, what are you telling Walt here?"

The woman turned Walt's ledger toward him. "Now look here," she began. "Up here, where they put on fifty—"

Doug held up his hand. "Miz Webster, I don't give a shit about that. I want to know what it is you're saying to Walt."

"I's saying—" She threw up her hands and sighed.

He leaned an elbow on the counter and leered. "You saying he's wrong?"

"Yes, sir. You see—" She put her finger on the ledger.

"Let me get this straight. You're accusing one of our accountants of making a mistake?" Mrs. Webster folded her hands. "Is that what you're doing?" She nodded with eyes lowered.

Doug reached into his jacket and pulled out his pistol. With exaggerated slowness and seeming indecision, he took it first to the woman's head, touching her frizzy gray hair, then changed his mind and jammed it between her breasts with enough force to push her.

"Let's get something straight, nigger lady. National Coal don't make mistakes." He shoved her with the pistol and she stepped backward to keep her balance. Doug frowned. "Don't be moving away from me when I'm talking, do you hear me?"

"Yes, sir."

"Now listen to me one more time, nigger bitch. National Coal don't make mistakes. Can you say that? Let's hear you say that."

"National Coal don't make mistakes, sir."

"That's a good girl." He shoved her again and she lurched backward, falling on her behind. The hem of her faded print dress rose over bony knees. Doug stood over her and grinned as she scrambled about, reaching for her bag and yanking at her skirt. She staggered to her feet, and he made a face of disgust. "Get out of here, nigger. And don't come back here accusing the company of making mistakes, or your husband will have to look for work elsewhere." He followed her to the door. "I don't want you walking on the road, nigger. Walk in the ditch, you hear? I'll be watching."

He closed the door, pocketed his pistol, and shook with laughter. Walt laughed with him. The customers and the store clerk were all going about their business as though they had not noticed anything out of the ordinary. Sarah, feeling as though she herself had been shamed into submission, concentrated intently on Stephanie and Donna Mae's progress.

Mrs. Means and the other three boarders were away. In the boarding house kitchen that day Sarah supervised as the girls baked fancy cookies, laughing and talking with them about their troubles and concerns over boys. Sarah was surprised at the girls' confessions about their exploits with boys, young men she did not know. They were seventeen- and eighteen-year-olds employed full-time and doing their best to lure these girls into marriage; moreover, their parents encouraged it. These girls were barely fourteen years old.

Sarah did not mention the incident they had all witnessed at the store, irrationally fearing that the walls had ears. She thought about asking Paul about it later but knew she wouldn't. Hank Ferrell was the only person in Clarkson she could imagine discussing it with, but even that seemed risky. The best policy, she realized, was to do what everyone else did—ignore it.

The previous week Hank and Sarah had been victims of Ruel Savage's own idea of mistreatment. He had walked into the schoolhouse with two guards, who positioned themselves at either end of the room while Savage strolled around the room, stopping at Hank's desk. There he hauled the boy out of his seat and sent him staggering with a hard slap across the face, demanding the return of "company property," which turned out to be the schoolhouse key.

By that time the guards were standing with rifles pointed at Hank, and Sarah did the only thing she knew to do. She stepped into the line of the nearest guard's aim, exclaiming, "Mr. Savage, he's only a boy!"

Rather than have Hank whipped as punishment for his alleged theft, Savage threatened to deduct five days of Drew Ferrell's wages, all the while shrieking, "This is company property, kid," while waving the key in the boy's face.

"But I gave it to him," Sarah said. "If you want to cut somebody's pay, take mine."

"*You* gave *him* the key?" This was information that none of his detectives had discovered. She had never even told Paul. "Don't you know who this kid is?" Savage asked.

"He's my student, one of my best, and he works for me. That's why I gave him the key. He comes here in the morning and gets the fire started. Then he goes back home and helps out there. It's an arrangement we've worked out. The building is warm by the time I and the other students arrive."

Savage ordered the students and the guards out of the building, leaving Sarah to contend with the leering bully on her own. She was able to convince him of Hank's innocence, but not without much trouble and deliberate misunderstanding on his part, as he seemed unwilling to believe that the boy didn't have devious purposes of his own while alone in the schoolhouse. Once Savage's mission was deflated, Sarah became his target, and the man's lewd suggestions, his proximity to her, and his attempts to touch her made her skin crawl. When she understood his intention, she sprang for the bell rope and began to ring it madly. While the students poured into the building and took their seats, Savage whispered his threat. It was simple, he said—tell Paul about Savage's remarks to her and Drew Ferrell would suffer the results.

"Boy, tell your dad I haven't made up my mind yet whether to dock his pay," Savage said to Hank. "It'll depend on some things that unfortunately are out of his control." He winked at Sarah and chuckled, then turned and sauntered toward the door.

As though nothing had occurred, Sarah said, "Mr. Savage, I'm keeping Hank on as my fire man." He dug in his pocket and flipped her the key, smiling in a congenial manner. Once the men had gone, the class returned quietly to work. Sarah and Hank exchanged a look but had acknowledged it no further.

Thanksgiving Day was a dreary occasion for Sarah, and if it hadn't been for the school program planned for the following evening, she might have wished she were with her family. The company officials remaining in town without families enjoyed a huge feast at Ruel's house, and Ruel's absence was the only thing for which Sarah was thankful.

Doug Burnside crammed in plate after plate of food and later emptied one whiskey glass after another with seemingly no effect on his sensibilities. His remarks and stories left Sarah with no appetite, especially when he discussed what he apparently considered a sport.

"...and he did it without legal hassles. Absolutely none. Here's what you do." Doug talked with a mouthful of food. "See! You shoot a guy, and it don't make any difference if there's witnesses or not. You just bend over him and slip a gun in his hand. Gotta make sure you have that extra gun. Then you stand back and say, 'look there, that fellow went for his gun and I had no choice but to defend myself.' Ha, ha, ha. I'm gonna try that sometime on one of these damn rednecks. Ha, ha, ha."

To Stephanie and Donna Mae's credit, the spelling bee at the school on Friday was a success, with various recitations and contests that gave most of the students an opportunity to shine in some way. Sarah met many of the students' friends and families, with one disappointing exception. She had been eager to meet Hank's parents, but neither was present. Belinda Ferrell had gone to Welch to be with her ailing brother; Drew was helping a neighbor whose floor was falling in. Hank and Corey attended alone.

After Thanksgiving Sarah focused the class's attention on making Christmas presents for Dominick Cinelli. They spent the last hour of each day working on their gifts, which included a bird feeder, a stuffed animal, a lap quilt, a simple gun rack, a small Christmas tree with crocheted ornaments, and an illustrated book of Italian poems several children collected from neighbors.

But the coming of Christmas made Sarah feel sad in a way she couldn't explain, and taking refuge in the good relationship she had with her students only heightened the feeling. Regardless of their meager expectations for the holiday, there was a cohesion among them that seemed to Sarah more important than all the food and gifts in the world. She was keenly aware of her separateness from them.

Considering her only alternative, the family she had run away from, Sarah sometimes felt a deep and overwhelming isolation. She sought comfort with Paul, but he was agitated and preoccupied, hinting that the mine guards were on the lookout for an incident "because of the Cinelli boy's accident."

"That's the kind of thing gets these guys stirred up," Paul told her. "Every last man is thinking the same thing—that could be me instead of him. Then they have the same second thought—thank God it's him and not me. That's where a guy like Drew Ferrell makes his move. This is the ideal time for the union to try to grab these men, because their next thought is, it could happen to me tomorrow."

"Is Ferrell a union man?" Sarah asked. "I thought you didn't let union people in." Paul said they weren't sure about him—a man who appeared to have the trust and respect of all the miners, no matter their race or nationality. He said they'd surprised Ferrell with searches of his person and his household trying to find union cards and other subversive evidence, but they had found nothing.

"How very clever you are," she murmured, hoping he couldn't read her inward shock at the idea of surprise household searches.

"Not clever enough. One of these days he'll make a mistake. And we'll be watching. And there are ways to watch a person without them suspecting."

"Such as?"

"The easiest way is to let some of the seditious mail go through. Then it keeps right on coming, and you can weed out the guy right quick."

Sarah couldn't help herself. "Reading people's mail is against the law, Paul."

"Honey, about half the things the coal company does are against the law, you know that."

"Why do you work for them then?"

He put his arms around her. "Why do *you*? We're no better than anybody else. It's a job and that's all. Good pay, and besides, I hate the United Mine Workers. They threaten our rights, bring in communist ideas, and cost coal companies extra money. The union's the real threat to free enterprise, and that's what our country runs on."

"How is it a threat?"

"Why, the union's controlled by Bolsheviks trying to destroy industry. They want to run it themselves. Think about it. This country runs on coal. Do you want outsider radical groups to get control of the country's fuel supply? It's a dangerous proposition."

Sarah didn't quite believe him. She didn't know much about labor issues, but she knew that coal miners in every other state belonged to the union, and that southern West Virginia did not produce all of the nation's coal, even if it did produce the best.

"The part I hate worse than anything," Paul told her, "is working with informers. We couldn't do our job without them of course, but they're scum, snakes slithering in Ruel's back door, drinking his best whiskey, telling who did this and who said that, pocketing that extra wad of cash he shells out. It's sickening."

"Which is worse, them or the UMWA?"

"There's nothing worse than a spying, double-crossing rat. You see them around town or going in the mine, buddying up to the other men, especially a guy like Drew Ferrell. We're on opposite sides of the fence, but he's a good man and I respect him. Then I see one of the snitches hanging around him, lying through his teeth just to get a little extra cash, and it makes me sick. Could be Ferrell and his friends have them pinpointed and I'm glad. I'd never admit that, but I'm glad. Snitches are just about the only ones I ever fool with."

"Fool with? How so?"

"Sometimes we have to get a little rough with the miners."

And their wives and kids, Sarah thought. "So if I ever see you roughing some man around, I'll know right off he's an informer?"

"Usually. Yeah. If I have to put on a show of force, I'll pick on the snitch if he's around. I can't stand them. Unless some other man's legitimately out of line, I'll bash the informer if I get the chance. But most of the time I leave everyone alone."

One evening at a holiday party at the Savage mansion Paul persuaded Sarah to go up the back staircase and into a third-floor bedroom where he turned the key in the lock. They kissed for a few minutes in the dark.

He stumbled around until he found a lamp and switched it on. Leading her to the bed, he murmured in reassuring tones, "I don't want to hurt you. I just thought it might be more comfortable here. You trust me, don't you?" He held her eyes and she nodded. She felt safe in his arms, pleased to be in his company. There was indeed no place else she would rather be. Was this love? "Say you love me," he commanded softly.

"No. You tell me."

"You know I love you. And you know I'm hoping to marry you next summer."

He kissed her all over her face and neck, and they sank onto the bed together. When his hands began to move, hers did too, and she found that she was more impatient than he was.

He soon put a stop to it, pulling her to her feet and straightening her hair. "Don't make this easy for me, honey. This kind of thing can get out of hand."

12

A COUPLE OF days after Christmas Sarah was in Bluefield, at home with her parents, and feeling as miserable as she had expected she would.

Only this was even worse. She stared into the dark recesses of her own bedroom, reliving events of the previous evening, trying to push away both horror and disappointment. In his unthinking passion Paul's gentleness had vanished, and he had hurt her with his penis and his fingers; she felt sliced to bits by his nails, and she didn't know if she was imagining it or not. Judging from the comments he had made, the experience to him had been close to heaven; to her it had been messy, awkward, and painful. While he grunted and shoved against her, she ran her hands over the knotty muscles of his back and shoulders and thought about Doug Burnside and Tom Felts with full realization that the whole bunch of them were indeed thugs and that there was nothing nice about any of them. *Except Paul!* her heart kept crying out.

And her father wasn't any better. He had caused her unimaginable embarrassment when Paul had come to see her at her parents' home the previous evening.

Ray Jennings thought the mine guard system in coal towns was criminal and that workers' bondage to the company was the next thing to feudalism or slavery. Sarah had heard his ranting all her life, never paying much attention to what he said because she loathed him and knew he must be wrong. He had grumbled endlessly about Baldwin–Felts men living it up in elegance in Bluefield, and then she had done the unthinkable. Arriving home at break, she announced that she was in love with one of them and planned to marry him come summer.

"He's nice," she tried to say in Paul's defense.

Her father had cut her off. "Tom Felts doesn't hire nice men."

And then last night Paul had surprised her with a visit. After the initial blowup, Paul had miraculously managed to win over Ray Jennings, and Sarah's father had allowed him to escort her to a party. All the boys Sarah had ever known had backed down and run from her father. Next to that, Paul's persistence appeared heroic. When he stopped the Dodge sedan in front of a large brick house, she asked, "Do we have to go in yet?" and threw herself into his arms.

"I could kiss you out here all night, honey, but we ought to go in. Let's take care of business first, then maybe we can find a cozy corner to snuggle up in." Then he told her the bad news, his arm going around her. "You have to try to come back to Clarkson tomorrow. You're going to have to help the kids with this, but you've got to get through it yourself first. The Cinelli boy has killed himself."

His words were cold, heavy blows, and this time, more than just words about violence. Dominick—she had known him, her students had made gifts for him; he was real and now he was gone. "Oh, Paul! Oh, no! How?" Her eyes brimmed with tears and he pushed his handkerchief into her hand.

"Shot himself."

"What!" And then it hit her. "But he couldn't have done that by himself."

"That's right. Somebody's bound to have helped him." She sobbed against his chest, and he held her until her tears subsided.

"Who did it? Who would give him a gun?"

"You tell me."

She suggested the nurse, but Paul shook his head. "Ruth's in Charleston."

"Well, then, one of your associates."

"The company didn't want him dead."

"But some of them have said—"

"It was just talk. That boy's a martyr now. He was hurt in the worst way, he suffered in the worst way, so bad that somebody had to help him die, and now that somebody is going to have to live with what he did."

Harshness Sarah had never seen before was evident in Paul's features, visible in the pale light of the street lamp. She knew a part of him must hate the coal company now as much as Drew Ferrell did and wondered how he justified working for a man like Ruel Savage. "There might be some kind of trouble now, is that it?"

"Might be. Ruel wants everything back to normal fast. To hell with the holidays."

"What do you mean?"

"People find comfort in day-to-day routine when they don't have as much time on their hands to think or talk. The funeral's tomorrow," Paul continued, "and it would be a good idea for you to go. Everybody ought to be there. Even the niggers are going to this one."

They went inside where a party was in full swing. Paul took Sarah to a room at the back of the house, a library of sorts. Six or seven men were there whom Sarah recognized as mine guards from Clarkson. Ida, the postmistress, was there too, swirling ice around in a nearly empty glass, smoking a cigarette, and caressing Doug Burnside's leg with her stockinged foot.

Gesturing toward a man with light hair, a square jaw, and eyes that gleamed hard behind spectacles, Paul said, "Sarah, this is Tom Felts; Tom, my girl, Sarah Jennings. She grew up here. You two probably know each other already."

Felts nodded. "Your family own the grocery?"

"It's my father's."

He laughed gruffly. "Does he know you're here? Hell, does he know you work for National Coal? That man's a union sympathizer."

Paul put an arm around her. "He doesn't know anything. I think I won him over tonight, didn't I, honey?"

"Yes, you did." Sarah was still furious and embarrassed by her father, and she smiled warmly toward Tom Felts who winked his reply.

"All right," Felts said. "It's time to quit drinking and start talking." Sarah took a seat next to Paul and sat transfixed for the next hour listening in silent horror to the kind of insider talk she had not been privy to before.

She tried to recall it now in the stillness of her bedroom to keep her mind away from the discomfort in her body and poor Dominick. His funeral was to be held the next day, the mine would be closed, and Felts had warned the men to keep their eyes open for trouble. He insisted upon the mine guards' attendance at the service, cautioning them to remain visible.

Ida contributed her cynical two-cents' worth. "They're having a party afterward. Lots of food and tears. None of us got an invitation."

Paul had just come from Clarkson and said of Ruel Savage, "He's scared to piss. He wants you to send in more men. I advised him against it. I told him, let's see what develops. So he says you're the expert, Tom, he'll take your advice."

Felts chewed his knuckles. "Strange thing about Ruel's town, the way everyone gets along. Niggers, tallies, hillbillies, polacks. I wonder if there's a way we could drive a wedge in somehow."

And Doug Burnside suggested, "Suppose we arrested someone for aiding and abetting a murder. Suicide's murder, ain't it? Taking a life and all that? The dago would be alive if somebody hadn't put a loaded gun in his hand. My guess is it was the Shalp kid. He's white, he's American. If we do it right, say the right things from the beginning, we might be able to divide them. Miss Jennings, you could be real helpful on something like this."

All eyes turned to Sarah and she felt like a hostage in a den of thieves, a spy herself. "How?" she whispered.

But they forgot about her and went on with their ideas. "It'd be easy with them tallies. We could say, look what them interfering hillbillies done to your boy. Helped him take his own life. Now he's gonna spend the next two thousand years in purgatory, ha, ha. Or look at what those dagos did to this kid. He's going to have to live with a murder charge."

And Felts agreed, saying, "If they got involved in backbiting, they might forget organizing for a while. It might divide the leaders, half of them locals, half of them foreign. Yes, it just might work."

But Paul pointed out something else. "Or it could easily blow up in our faces. It'll only work if Shalp's the one gave him the gun. Suppose it was his own mother?"

Then it was back to Sarah. Felts asked, "Suppose you could find out, Miss Jennings? If one of the kids is upset, they might spill the beans to you."

"I could try," was all she said. She would never tell these people anything.

They talked on, arguing about Felts's idea that the men should attend the funeral without their guns, as mourners themselves rather than law enforcers, while Sarah's thoughts returned to her father. He treated her the way these men treated coal miners. She was tired of it all and longed to be alone with Paul. After the endless meeting she had gotten her wish in an upstairs bedroom, there surrendering her virginity to Paul.

He's nice. He's different. He loves me. In the dark in her room back at her parents' she repeated these things, trying to wish away the vaginal burning and dreading the coming day—getting out of her house, attending a funeral escorted by mine guards.

On the train back to Clarkson with the whole lot of them who had been at the previous evening's meeting, except for Tom Felts, Sarah asked Paul, "If I found out who gave Dominick the gun and then told you, wouldn't that make me an informer?"

Paul laughed at her. "You've got it backwards, honey. A snitch is someone who sells out his own kind. It's unheard of, but suppose as a company employee, you were to sell information to the other side, sit in on a meeting like the one we had last night, then tell Ferrell or some UMWA rep what you heard, in exchange for, say, five dollars—you see? *Then* you'd be selling out your people."

"I think I get it," she answered. Watching Doug and Ida giggling and poking at each other a couple of seats in front of her, she was getting it more and more clearly.

She counted the months until April. It seemed a long time off. She would honor her commitment to teach at the Clarkson school until the term was over. Then what?

She and Paul would move to Huntington. She would go to college and forget the horror of coal mining towns. He would get a different job. He had said so. And as for the physical part of it—she didn't know when they would have the opportunity again, but the next time, she would ask him to be gentler with her.

13

THE CHURCH, A simple wooden structure, was packed, and the place was too warm, perfumed with a strangling mix of body odor. The Catholics knelt in the front pews; the Negroes sat in the back. Everyone else was in between, and the closed pine casket at the front, decorated with a spray of holly and pine boughs tied up in red ribbon, seemed almost insignificant in such a crowd.

"Make sure that priest doesn't have a problem with burial rites or putting him in the cemetery. Sure it's a suicide, but the fellow was sick," were the last words Tom Felts had spoken to his minions at the Bluefield meeting. Now Sarah, with Paul, was standing among them—the rest of the Baldwin–Felts operatives, and various other company employees—along the back wall, facing a sea of bowed heads. Ruel Savage was not there. The service, conducted by the company priest in low tones of mumbled Latin, was interspersed with much weeping, nose-blowing, and rattling coughs.

At the conclusion of the formal service, the priest took a seat, and a man of medium build stepped forward, doubtless dressed in his humble best—jacket, faded shirt of an indistinct color, string tie, and overalls. He contemplated the congregation for a few moments, and the coughing and weeping ceased. The absolute quiet of so many people was disconcerting to Sarah, demonstrating better than anything else the cohesion of the group. She had never seen this man before, and yet he was familiar because of his very ordinariness. *Every miner*, she thought of him as he surveyed his audience. "Every miner" except that he stood proudly; ordinary except for the subtle command and fire snapping from his eyes; he was an example for all of them as he cast defiant eyes slowly across the back wall, a look that caused a few of the guards to stiffen. Sarah saw in him Hank's square jaw and thin lips, the same intelligence on his brow. He took a deep breath and then spoke, his voice measured and eloquent.

"Friends," he began, "I wanna take a few minutes to remember Dominick Cinelli with y'all. I tried to think of one or two words to describe him, and I come up with one. He was a lover. Our Dom loved to hunt, he loved to swim, he loved to work. He never liked schooling much, but he didn't mind setting there in the school-house looking at the gals. He loved to drink and eat; he even liked to play poker once he figured out the game. He loved his mama too. Remember how he used to slap her on the behind and kid her and then kiss her on the cheek? He loved teasing folks and singing and dancing whenever somebody brung out a fiddle or a banjo. And he loved his friends. He and Hubert been showing folks for a long time that it don't make no difference where we come from or what language we speak, we can love each other anyways. And Dom loved loving. Some of you gals can attest to that, and some of you fellas that wanted to give him a good sock in the teeth sometimes."

Drew Ferrell paused to let his words sink in.

"Dominick Cinelli was a lover, all right. He simply loved... living." Ferrell's voice rose, carrying with it the weight of everyone's sorrow and frustration. "He's seventeen years old, shoulda had thirty more years coming to him. He woulda loved living them years. But he's gone now, dead by his own hand 'cause he couldn't face being half a man for the rest of them thirty." His tone dropped, his quiet voice compelling his audience. "But that ain't really why. You wanna know why there's just pieces of our boy a-laying in that pine box? I'd like y'all to turn around and take a good long look at what's lining them walls and think about what it represents."

With a swish and rustle the congregation turned, and Sarah closed her eyes, streaming with tears, unable to bear the accusation in so many aggrieved stares. The speaker was silent until everyone had settled down again.

"And take a look sometime at that fancy house up the hill. That's why Dom ain't with us no more. 'Cause there's a system here that don't wanna treat men like men, that thinks human life is cheap. But there don't have to be no more after Dom." Ferrell raised a clenched fist, then bowed his head for a moment and said softly, "There don't have to be.

"Jesus loved Dom as much as we done, and He sent him to us for a reason. Jesus sent Dom to show us all about living life to the fullest, to show us about love. And He sent him... He used Dom to show us that things has got to change. If things is changed 'cause of what happened to Dom, then he won't've died for nothing."

Ferrell wiped at the corner of his eye. "Dominick—" His voice cracked and he stopped to breathe deeply before he began again. "That young man suffered more'n any of us should have to, and we give him as much comfort as we could. It hurts us a lot to see him gone, but we gotta take our own comfort now, knowing Jesus loved Dom enough to help get him outta here, outta his earthly hell, and on home to where he can laugh again and find some peace at last. Amen."

The man took his seat amidst a scattered response of "amens." Then there was perfect silence. The priest rose to perform a final blessing but stood for a moment, fidgeting with a sleeve of his vestment and glancing around in a defensive manner.

Sarah remained in her shameful place against the wall as the people filed out. Behind the pallbearers Hubert walked with Mrs. Cinelli, an arm around her shoulder and their hands clasped, and a tall tired-looking man who Sarah guessed was Mr. Cinelli, with deep circles under doe eyes that could have been Dominick's, followed them. He was accompanied by two weeping young women and three solemn young men, possibly other siblings. Several Italian families came next. Then came the rest, Drew Ferrell among them with no particular place of honor. Holding his arm was a small, thin woman whose attractiveness had been overtaken by lines made by hard work and poor diet; nevertheless, Sarah thought she could sense the woman's strength of character and nurturing kindness. Hank and Corey came behind, each holding the hand of a younger sister. Last of all came the Negroes huddled together with eyes cast down.

Sarah walked with Paul and Carl Eschman along the frozen path to the cemetery. "Guess we're stupid, ain't we?" Carl muttered. An impotent sun tried to peak from behind clouds.

"I'll say. We played right into his hands."

"I was ready to go for my gun."

"You and probably half the others."

"Think it's a good idea for us to walk up here?"

"Sure. We don't want him to think he's scared us." Paul spoke to Sarah for the first time since the service. "You all right, honey?" She nodded and kept walking, looking straight ahead.

"For all his inspirational talk, he's not so smart," Carl said.

"He's got four kids and a wife. They're going to be out on the street someday soon."

"Bastard probably knows it too."

"What do you mean?" Sarah asked in alarm.

"Guys like him don't last long," Paul explained. "His wife and kids can't live in their house unless he's gainfully employed as a miner."

"But he is employed. What'll happen to him?"

"Jesus, I don't know." Paul seemed annoyed with her. "He'll probably get fired and blacklisted. And don't ask why like you always do. You've seen him now. You know Ruel can't keep a guy like that around here whether he's associated with the union or not."

At the graveside Sarah separated herself from Paul. She bowed her head and watched Drew Ferrell. For a while he kept his own head bowed, then he looked around until he found the smallest of his redheaded daughters and picked her up. He rocked her and bounced her slowly as though comforting her, but then

Sarah realized that with all of his slow twisting and turning and snuggling his face into his daughter's hair, he was keeping his eyes on the mine guards.

Paul moved toward Sarah and reached for her hand. He squeezed it to reassure her and searched her eyes, and the contact sent a thrill of physical desire lilting through her.

Furious with herself, with her body's betrayal at such an inopportune moment, she concentrated on the pine box as it was lowered into the ground and recalled Hank's words. *I'm going to join the union, then I'll come back here and tear this place down.* The Catholics were crossing themselves and muttering prayers, the Baptists were crooning, and the Negroes were humming along, swaying rhythmically from side to side. Felts's men stood motionless, some, like Doug Burnside, with looks of contempt on their faces.

Sarah remained focused on her surroundings: the gray afternoon, the smell of coal fires burning, the hum of machinery in the distance, clods of earth thumping softly upon the casket, and Hubert's hand clutching Mrs. Cinelli's shoulder which shook with silent weeping that reminded Sarah of Dominick's own impotent sobs when she had visited him. Her hand gone numb in Paul's, Sarah closed her eyes and made a silent vow to help Hank, his father, and the UMWA tear the town apart.

14

SCHOOL WAS BACK in session the next day, two days before New Year's Day. Walking toward the schoolhouse in the gray, windy early morning, Sarah was afraid to face her students and anticipated melting in shame when the first pair of eyes regarded her in cold appraisal.

Hank Ferrell was the first to arrive, without his sisters, so she supposed he meant to chastise her. He had been there previously to light the fire, and he slipped in again, going to the stove to add more coal. She was working at her desk, scarcely able to concentrate. When he finished, he turned toward her with the poker still in his hand.

They watched each other for a long moment before she broke the ice. "Your father gave a beautiful talk. It broke my heart, Hank."

He nodded. "You didn't wanna be standing where you was, did you?"

She shook her head. "I was so ashamed."

"We knowed you didn't."

"How's Hubert?"

Hank shrugged. "He's leaving town for a while. With some other fellas."

"I just wanted to know how he's doing, how he's holding up."

"He ain't. He's mad, and he and Matt and Randall—"

Sarah slammed her hand on the desk. "Hank!" she cried. He was so startled he could only stare at her with an open mouth. "I don't want to know anything, do you hear me? Don't tell me anything. Do you understand that?"

"But I thought—"

"For all your father's brilliance, hasn't he trained you to keep your mouth shut?"

"I know who I can talk to."

"Well, you can't talk to me." She came around her desk and stood before him. "Look at this." She pointed to the floorboards beneath their feet. "There's a line right there. See it?" She traced it with her toe, sliding it along the crack between the boards, a line dark with sifted coal dust that separated the two of them. "I'm on this side, you're on that side. You stay over there and keep all your secrets over there with you."

"But why? You said it yourself. Your own heart's broke."

"That may be." They were alone but she dropped her voice to a whisper. "But I've been instructed to find out things from you kids. I'm engaged to marry one of Tom Felts's men, and he was standing outside the Cinellis' house last night. You and I are on different sides of this line, and everyone will be better off if I know nothing. Just ask your father about that."

Hank hung his head and went to his desk. Sarah returned to her work. The boy was restless and couldn't concentrate on the book opened before him. He went to the window. In a little while he said, "They's some of them coming. I reckon I'll go fill the bucket." He passed her desk and loitered there. Sarah's head was lowered as she tried to skim a textbook, but she watched his hands run lightly over her glass paper weight and the primitive coal sculpture of a bird a student had given her. As his thin, nail-bitten fingers traced the rim of a wire basket, he commented, "At least you picked the fair-minded one, the one that ain't so rough." She couldn't think of an answer but was relieved that Hank approved of Paul. "But none of them's really civil nor trustworthy, and I bet you ain't gonna marry him."

Her heart constricted and she pounded her fist on the desk. "Mind your own business and don't get personal!" she exclaimed.

She caught the hurt in his eyes before he turned and snatched up the coal bucket.

Most of the others filed in just after that, and class resumed as it had before Christmas, Sarah's position with her students unchanged.

15

ON NEW YEAR'S Eve Paul took Sarah to Ruel Savage's house. They walked in, and a cluster of men, including the superintendent, turned expectantly toward her as if they had been awaiting her arrival.

"What've you heard at the schoolhouse?" Ruel asked her.

"I—"

"Just a minute," Paul said. "You start hitting her with questions and don't even offer her a drink first. Honey, don't tell him a thing till I get you a drink."

"I've heard nothing," she told Savage without waiting for Paul.

"Well, have you asked them?"

"Asked them what?"

"It would be nice to know where those guys took off to," Doug said.

"And how they did it."

"What guys?" Sarah asked Paul as he handed her a drink.

"The Shalp kid and two or three others," Doug answered. "Surprised the hell out of us. Disappeared. Musta cut through the woods and hopped the train outta here."

"You know anything about that, Miss Jennings?" Porter asked her.

"All I know is Hubert's not in school."

"It don't take a genius to figure they went to Charleston," Carl commented.

"I told you she didn't know anything," Paul said, "so we're leaving."

"Come on, Less, you two stick around."

"Sorry. I've got to work midnight. I'd like to spend some time alone with my girl."

They stepped outside into the frigid air. Paul said, "I've got a surprise for you, honey."

They walked down the hill toward town, and Sarah snuggled against him to keep warm. The blue-black sky was sprinkled with icy stars.

"What's happening, Paul? Why'd those people go to Charleston? What's there?"

"A UMWA district office. They've probably gone to ask for help with organizing."

"Then what?"

88 | *Catherine Cometti Samargo*

"Sometime soon some new guy will show up to work here, an undercover man. He'll contact Ferrell and Amato, and they'll all start sneaking around trying to organize. Chances of success are so slim that the union might not even send anybody."

Sarah's mind came alive with hope and excitement. "Why wouldn't it work?"

"Why, honey, you almost sound disappointed. But let's not talk about it now."

He stopped at the post office and fumbled in his coat for a key. "What are you doing?" she asked while he tried to get the lock to turn.

"Damn thing's frozen," he muttered, banging it with the heel of his hand. "Ah. There we are. Come on inside, honey. It's plenty warm in here." He closed the door and moved a chair up against it.

"Come here," he whispered. He led her through the darkened building toward the rear, slowly feeling his way.

"Why don't you turn on the light?"

He turned a corner and started up some stairs. "No one's supposed to be here." At the top of the stairs he pulled her into a room, stuffy with closed up heat, and went to the one window to check the blind. Then he turned around and struck a match. He held it up and she glanced around the crowded little office. There was a desk, a file cabinet, a small table, and a narrow bed with an iron frame. Before the match went out, she caught his eager expression.

He kissed her. "This time it'll be better," he murmured, "I promise you."

It was better, Sarah mused the next morning as she walked toward the schoolhouse. It was New Year's Day, but she intended to get some work done. Paul was standing in the lane with another guard, both of them red-faced from the cold, rifles slung over their shoulders, and bundled up to their ears. The warmth in his smile seemed incongruous on lips blue with cold.

"You two look like you could use some hot coffee," she said.
"Have you been standing out here all night?" Sarah asked.

"More or less," the other guard, John Harless, replied. "We busted up a few celebrations. Only time we were warm all night. Ain't that right, Paul?"

Paul grinned like a fool. "Nah. My thoughts kept me warm."

"What did you have to do?" she asked him.

"Just keeping the noise down is all. Don't you worry about it, honey. Folks get too much 'shine in them, they're liable to fall off their porches and kill themselves."

"Well, I better get to the schoolhouse. I've got a lot of work to catch up on."

Paul walked with her a little way. Neither of them could find anything to say. He stopped and said, "Guess I better get on back. We still have some things to check on. You look so pretty today, honey. I wish I could kiss you right out here in the daylight."

"Me too." But with the gun on his shoulder, he looked like someone she didn't know.

Yes, it had been better, she assured herself as she continued walking—but not much. He had gone about the process with trembling and intensity, apparently under the illusion that the very *force* of his touch would transmit his passion to her. She couldn't decide whether it was her own misguided assumption that intercourse should be a kinder experience, or perhaps Paul had only figured out one way of doing it, when there might be alternatives. At any rate, she was unable to say what she had wanted to communicate: *You're hurting me.*

Instead she cringed away from him. "What's the matter, honey? Am I too rough?"

"Uh-huh," was her timid reply.

"Sorry." After that he stroked her softly—for a little while.

A few feet from the schoolhouse door Sarah stopped. She smelled it first and then saw smoke rising from the chimney. She had imagined that today, a holiday, she would have to build the fire herself. It was evident that to Hank Ferrell, every dime he could earn was significant.

She worked for several hours, once getting up to throw a few lumps of coal into the stove, aware of her amateurism when the coals stopped burning and started smoking. She applied the poker but her efforts seemed only to smother every remaining ember.

Eventually Hank opened the door. He went directly to the stove, poked and shook the grate until a blaze roared and the acrid smell of burning coal reached Sarah's nostrils. Then he went out back to refill the bucket. She could tell by the way he walked and went about his work that he was in a temper. He had not looked at her, and when he returned, he avoided her eyes. He let the bucket drop with a clatter and headed toward the door.

"Hank?" He froze. "What's wrong, Hank?"

"Nothing." He sighed and studied his feet.

"Did something happen last night?"

"We got too much law enforcement in this here town."

"What happened?"

"Just thugs busting up folks' fun. For no particular reason."

"How so?"

He shrugged and seemed tired. "I don't feel like talking about it, Miss Jennings. You said we ain't supposed to tell each other nothing 'cause we're on different sides."

He ambled slowly toward the door and she rose. "Hank. Did somebody get hurt?"

"Ain't nothing that cain't be fixed. It ain't nothing." His drawl was soft and sweet, and for all his anger and hostility, he seemed to Sarah like a boy who knew only innocence.

"Who was hurt?"

"It don't matter." He peered out the window, his nose nearly touching the pane. "John Doe, Jim Doe, Jeff Doe. Nobodies—to you."

He would make her ask what she really wanted to know. "Who did it? Which guards?"

"Already told you. Thugs." He seemed a restless animal in a cage. "Bastards," he whispered.

"Hank?" She was ashamed to press, but she wanted a name, any name but *his*.

"I don't know!" He bolted toward the door and shot out like a cannonball.

16

TENSION CREPT IN, slowly permeating the town, until it was entrenched within all aspects of life. Tempers everywhere were short. At the company store people made their purchases and left quickly. In the schoolhouse Sarah noticed more inattentiveness and daydreaming, even if the students continued to treat her with the respect she had earned. At the boarding house Mrs. Means was hostile to the boarders, and she stayed in her own room more often.

One evening Sarah came to dinner and found Ethel slumped at the table in tears. "What's wrong?" she asked. The bookkeeper only cried the harder, and Ruth, ever the nurse, shoved a whiskey bottle into her hand. Ethel took a couple of swallows and left the room. "What's wrong with her?" Sarah asked again.

Ida gave her a look and snorted.

"She's fired," Ruth explained.

"She'll be out of here on the morning train."

"Boss's getting some brains," the nurse observed. "I hear Walt's going to replace her."

Ida hooted. "What! Has he turned queer, or what!"

Some evenings Paul pulled Sarah out into the cold for a brisk walk to the post office. They seemed to have less to say to one another than they once had, but he often vowed that he would love her until he died, and that one day soon they would get out of Clarkson and marry. He held firmly to the notion that there were certain areas of the female anatomy that were only to be pushed upon and prodded at in a rough manner, while other places, such as fingers, cheeks, shoulders, and lips, on occasion, could be handled with gentleness. She was unable to stop what had begun between them and told herself that things would be fine after they were married. It really didn't hurt with the same severity as it once had, and there was a certain something about him she had learned to love and now needed—a kind of protectiveness, a hard masculinity that nevertheless seemed patient and understanding.

Every once in a while he asked, "Kids telling you anything?" She answered truthfully negatively. During the schoolhouse conversations at noon, the talk seemed to stay, by unspoken consent all around, away from certain topics.

Sarah was vaguely aware of some incidents—men arrested for disorderly conduct, among them Angelo Amato and a Negro, Gabe Lawson. Mine guards had become much more visible—even Paul made no bones about carrying and holding onto a rifle—and much more strict in their refusal to allow men to gather in the street or even on porches.

And then on a heavily overcast night Sarah and Paul stood together in the little upstairs room at the post office, ready to leave and sharing desultory kisses before they faced the cold outside. A noise, a muted thud outside, as though someone had stumbled over something, sent Paul to the window.

"Holy smoke!" he muttered, holding back the blind.

Sarah peered over his shoulder and caught a glimpse of silhouetted figures scrambling alongside the railroad tracks, slipping behind coal cars. "What is it?"

"Let's go," he said and steered her quickly from the building. Outside he escorted her up the hill at such a rapid pace she could barely keep up.

"What was it? What's happening?"

"Don't know."

"Who were those people?"

"I don't know."

"What are you going to do?"

He stopped and sighed. He was swallowed in shadow and seemed to study her. "Honey, I think you know the answers to those questions—"

"But I don't, Paul."

"Well, I don't know either."

They walked the rest of the way in silence. At the boarding house he didn't go inside with her as he usually did. They stood together on the porch where light spilled out from a window. Out of habit he bent to kiss her but stopped short, and for as long as a kiss might have lasted, each gazed, through undisguised eyes, at the other's heart.

"Sarah, I love you," he whispered, but his words, they both knew, clearly came from the other side of the line. "Tell me too."

"I love you, Paul." Stunned by the hollow strength of their words, Sarah saw that regardless of the word *love*, it was a game, one they would play for a little while longer.

That night she lay awake contemplating from every angle she could think of the lowness of the informer—the rat who sells out his own kind. As the night wore on, she made futile attempts to reconcile her feelings for Paul Lessing with the kind of "people" she knew she was. And before she had figured anything out, it was morning and she was facing a roomful of children for whom she felt genuine, unequivocal love.

She detected nothing out of the ordinary, but she was aware of the inexorable element with which she was dealing—time. She had little time to measure love or sort out right from wrong. Her father's Bible had never taught her how to handle such a dilemma. Several times she tried to catch Hank's eye and read all the secrets there, but he was learning geometry, and his eyes sparkled with the thrill of discovery.

At lunch time she separated herself from the children, eating at her desk and ignoring them for the most part, trying to work. When Hank was finished with his lunch, she called him to her desk and spoke quietly in the safety of the hum of the other children's banter.

"Remember that line we drew on the floor?" she asked.

"What about it?"

"What'd I tell you then?"

He seemed suddenly alert, his eyes wary. "That I'm to stay over here and keep my secrets from you. That's what I been doing."

"But if it was the other way around, if I had a secret, I might wish I could toss it over the line. To you." His brow clouded. "But I'd have to be careful because somebody might figure out where the information came from."

His eyes narrowed then in perfect understanding. "You know something?" She nodded, unsure of what to say. "What?"

"I don't want to... I can't say it straight out." He nodded encouragement. "Maybe I could just put it this way and it would be enough. Whatever secrets or plans your people have need to be changed quickly because people on this side have discovered something about them."

17

"You're an informer now," Sarah accused her reflection each morning while wondering what effect her words had wrought upon some hard-to-imagine underground organization of labor. Had something changed?

One evening Paul sat with her on the sofa holding her hand and kissing her cheek from time to time while he imagined how things were going to be for them someday and dreamed up their own children. "Let's name the girl Daisy," he said. "I've always loved that name for a girl."

Sarah burst into tears. Days were lengthening into weeks of suspense while she waited for something to happen.

"Aw, honey, what's wrong? What have I said to upset you?" He held her against him and rocked her and ran his hands over her back, petting her gently as if she were a sad puppy.

She lost herself in his embrace, the comfort of his strength and manliness, and vowed never to know anything else that she could pass on to schoolchildren. She was beginning to dismiss the roundabout warning she had given Hank as juvenile, a child's game. And that wasn't the worst of it.

Shortly after warning Hank, somehow trying to place herself within his family, a family she knew next to nothing about, she had foolishly asked him, "Have you ever said anything to your father about me?"

"Yeah," he answered and looked away.

"Well? What does he say?" Hank's cheeks turned red and Sarah pressed him for an answer. "Well?"

He spoke hesitantly. "That maybe you're too young to know your mind."

"I know my mind, young man!" she snapped with indignation. Since then she had carried the secret hurt with her, and every day her perception of it changed. Not only had she played a child's game, trading secrets with Hank, but Drew Ferrell had commented upon her own immaturity without even knowing her. The rock bottom end of it all was the part of her that feared it was true, that she indeed knew very little.

Paul, at least, thought of her as a woman.

Now he seemed to be working all the time and rarely had time to do much more than stop for brief evening visits. He didn't even find the time to walk to the post office with her, and she missed those times when they had been closest, even if he had been rough and clumsy.

Sarah resolved to ignore the events in Clarkson and tried to concentrate on teaching. Clarkson did not concern her. Her stay in the town was so temporary that it simply did not matter. She didn't care for any of Paul's friends, and the others, the miners and their families, certainly cared nothing for her beyond the fact that she performed a service for their children.

Sarah was delighted when Paul invited her to have dinner with him one Friday evening in early February. Holding his arm as they walked, she reveled in his dreams. "Come spring, I'll take you to Charleston. We'll go to a real restaurant. Pittsburgh will be even better. I'll take you to some swell places," he told her as they entered the little diner.

Rancid cooking odors hung in the air, and grease spots dotted the bowed flooring. The food was unpalatable, but she scarcely tasted it. She was in a whirlwind of anticipation, ignoring the cigarette burns on the stained oilcloth table covering. His leg touched hers under the table and he patted his jacket, saying, "I got us a good little bottle here, honey. I expect the post office has been empty too long. What do you say we go over there tonight?"

"I'd love to, Paul."

"I, uh… Honey, I, uh, well, I'm not very good at any of that. I'm just like any other guy, never got much of an opportunity. Some of them make regular trips over to Keystone to the cathouses and bars, but I don't. I figure sometimes I don't know what I'm doing much, and if you could maybe just tell me. We could maybe just do a little more talking is all."

She blushed and nodded and they smiled shyly at one another.

"I need to check on a couple of things at the movie house first, get that out of the way. If you don't mind coming along." Sarah didn't mind. When she was with Paul, the dreariness of Clarkson, that not even the cover of night could hide, faded away. Love was shining in his eyes, and it seemed to be a special time.

The moment was ruined when Doug Burnside, fat and officious-looking, strolled into the diner, rifle in hand, and approached them. "Somebody told me I'd find you here, Lessing."

"I'm off tonight, Doug. I'm not thinking about work."

"There's a thing going on. I don't know where you and Miss Jennings are off to, but you better stop by the jail." Doug pulled him aside and they talked in low tones for a few moments before Paul returned to her ashen-faced.

He spoke to her bluntly, while pulling her to her feet. "I have to work."

"But why! I thought—" It was useless to press.

On the porch at the boarding house he kissed her, long and tenderly, and it seemed that some kind of passion she could not understand was breaking over him and into their lives. He turned away into the night, and Sarah went in, staggering under the impact of the emptiness.

With nothing else to do, she tried to concentrate on some paperwork. Then she took a book to bed with her. She ached to be with Paul and wondered what kind of trouble the mine guards were going to try to stir up during the night. She imagined the jail would be full in the morning and tried not to care. What could she do after all? It was Friday night, but even if she had school the next day, she had no real information to pass along. She had sworn to herself not to become involved in something like that again, but seeing Hank Ferrell in her mind's eye, she knew she would say something anyway. Come Monday she would go in early and meet him when he first came to light the fire. But Monday was long hours and days away. In the meantime she had an entire weekend to get through. Without Paul, she assumed.

Saturday was a blustery mix of rain and snow that settled on the tips of brown grass and melted before it touched the ground. The drippy, gusty weather combined with bare trees and undergrowth, shiny slag heaps, and crooked tipples to reaffirm Sarah's belief that Clarkson was the ugliest, most miserable place on earth. By now Paul would be sleeping, and there was no hope of seeing him until evening if she was lucky. She settled into an easy chair with a book.

After lunch, which Mrs. Means laid out before disappearing into her room, Ida came in and sighed and paced fitfully. "I hate this weather. I hate all this carrying on in town. There's nothing to do with the men working all the time. Let's play some cards."

Out of boredom Sarah agreed. Ida's abrasiveness got on her nerves and she wished Ruth was there. "I saw Ruth go out this morning. Somebody sick?"

"She went to check on that baby that was born last week. It might not live. Jesus! Can you imagine living the way these people do? That baby might just as well die as to grow up in this mess."

"Do you ever think of going someplace else to work?"

"Oh, no. Pay's damn good, as you know."

"It's so depressing here, I'm not sure I could stay indefinitely even for that."

"Well, you got your man. I just love 'em all. That's another reason I stay. There's so many sweet men here to play around with. Um-um."

"Like Doug."

"Doug's a sweetie. Knows how to show a girl a good time, and he doesn't mind spending his money. Did I show you the red silk under things he bought me?"

"Yes," Sarah answered, trying to keep the disgust out of her smile. "And the perfume."

They started a game, and Sarah managed to keep the conversation away from Doug Burnside's virtues, although Ida seemed ready at any time to elaborate on the subject.

Ruth came in soon, dripping wet. It took her a minute to get out of her overcoat and boots. Then she sat down at the table, her shoulders slumped forward.

"You're wet!" Ida exclaimed. "Go dry your hair and change your clothes." She took a closer look at her. "Why, you're a mess. Did you deliver another baby, or what?"

Sarah glanced up and saw blood splattered all over Ruth's blouse.

"Girls, we're in trouble. If I were you, I wouldn't go anywhere without an escort. And you," she turned to Sarah, "oh, well, there won't be school anyway."

"What's happened?"

Ruth leaned forward and whispered, "They've killed Drew Ferrell."

18

"OH, GOD! NO!" Sarah shrieked in disbelief. It had been, then, worse evil than she could ever have imagined.

Ida's eyes glittered. "What happened?"

"It was an accident. Officially. He provoked them, back-talked them—"

"Then he went for his gun, I bet." Ida giggled with glee.

"That's right."

"But that man wouldn't have been carrying a gun," Sarah protested.

Ida waved an arm. "Don't you get it? That's what they'll *say*. Who got him?"

"Doug Burnside, of course. John Harless and Jim Collins were with him." Ruth turned to Sarah. "I don't know where Paul was except that he wasn't anywhere near."

"Doug got him! Where'd it happen?" Ida asked.

"When?" Sarah wondered. "Aren't the men in the mine today?"

Ruth whispered, "This morning. A couple of hours ago. As I understand it, they ordered Ferrell out on some pretext. They shot him just outside the mine. Half the town was there in a minute. So was the sheriff. They'd already sent for him, called him last night."

"Has he arrested those men then?" Sarah asked.

Ida slapped her on the shoulder. "Of course not! Ferrell went for his gun, silly."

"Doug's given his statement," Ruth said. "Shot him in self-defense."

"Otherwise all three of them would be dead," Ida added. "They knew there would be trouble. That's why they called the sheriff." Ida turned back to Ruth. "What about the rest of the town? What about the crowd? I bet all hell's gonna break loose now."

Ruth shook her head. "You'd be surprised. They're kinda quiet. Belinda Ferrell showed up right quick and lit into every one of them—the sheriff, the guards. You should have seen her shaking her little fist in Doug's face. Then her boy showed up and she forgot everything to see to him." She paused. "I didn't much care to see that. Anyway, they brought Ferrell over to the infirmary, but he was dead all right. Must have had six or eight bullet holes in him. I couldn't do much except clean him up a little."

"My lord!" Ida said. "I've heard that Ferrell woman can rant and squawk like a redskin on the warpath. She can get a mob fired up even without her husband's help."

"They're quiet. When I left, a bunch of them were outside the infirmary, but they were tame."

"They're scared now," Ida observed. "See? Ruel knows how to handle these people."

"They weren't expecting this," Ruth said. "Poor Belinda's in a state of shock."

Paul came on Sunday evening, shy, reserved, in his best clothes, a three-piece suit and starched collar. He dragged nervously on a cigarette, put it out, and lit another. Sarah had never seen him smoke before and commented on it.

"It's a bad habit. I keep going back to it." He ushered her into the dining room and shut the door.

"Look, honey." He was so agitated his hands seemed to shake. "I, uh, I'll get directly to the point." But he stood still, smoking, staring at the floor, and Sarah touched his arm. She was relieved to see him, to finally have someone to talk to. He flung the cigarette into an ashtray and pulled her to him. "Aw, honey!" he exclaimed softly and held onto her for some time. Then pushing her away, he said, "This isn't gonna work, honey, we're gonna have to call it quits."

"Call what quits?"

"Us. This thing we got. It's just no good." He tried to be tender. "We're fooling ourselves and each other if we try to go on."

"Why that's not true!" Was he abandoning her because somebody he worked with had killed a man? Or was it because he was tired of her, had done what her father suspected every man of doing—taking her for what he could get? Tears burned her eyes. "We do have something. We're leaving here. Together. You've been saying we'd get married—"

"It'd never work."

"But it could! It has! I love you, Paul."

"No, you don't, honey. Take a good look at me." She regarded him, handsome, sincere, certainly embittered by Drew Ferrell's death, and she loved what she saw. "Look at what I am. You couldn't love me after what's happened here."

"But you didn't do it!"

"No, I didn't, but it wouldn't take you very long to figure out how much of a hand I had in it. I knew it was going to happen. I was sick about it but didn't do anything to prevent it."

"But what could you have done?"

"Maybe nothing."

"You can get out of this, Paul."

He shook his head. "I'll never get out, honey. I'm in this thing till the end."

"The end?"

"For as long as we're needed to keep the union out. No union will come in here without a tough fight and I'm in it."

"But why? It's so ugly."

"You know why. Unions are ruining the country. It's what I believe." He stood up straight. "Take a good look at me, Sarah. What am I? I've never killed anybody, but I might someday. Then what? Would you be able to love me? Would you want these hands on you?" He held them out, and to Sarah he looked charming and innocent, a man who could never hurt anyone. She believed nothing he was saying. She only wanted it to be as it once had been, to be back in his arms.

"Yes. I would! I want you to touch me!"

He shook his head. "You don't know what you're saying, little girl. I tell you, I've learned more... I started out with you, just out to get you is all. I swear it, I saw you were a pretty young thing. We all did, and the guys said, go on, Paul, make a try for her. We all figured I'd be more likely to get you than any of us. But something happened." He put a gentle hand on her shoulder. "I messed it all up, and while I was lying to you, saying I loved you, I really fell for you. First time I ever said let's get married, I never meant it. Now there's nothing I want more. You taught me a lesson I'll never forget, sweet little teacher."

She laughed nervously. "You scared me for a minute, Paul. But see, you do love me. You do want us to marry, so I don't know what else you're talking about."

"It's not going to work out, Sarah, and I'm telling you I'm calling it quits."

"No! There's no reason—"

"Let me tell you something else, and then you see if I don't know what I'm talking about. They're going to bury Drew Ferrell tomorrow, and day after that, Tuesday, we've got to run the family out. Ruel wants them out fast. Do you know who's doing it? Me and Mel. We're going to knock on the door, ask them real nice to pack up and get out, but I doubt they will. Belinda Ferrell is a fire-breathing radical, probably learned from Mother Jones herself, and she'll do just like her husband did at the Italian boy's funeral. She'll try to make an issue of his death, use it to stir up trouble. She'll refuse to leave. She'll make us pick up her belongings and throw them in the street. She'll scream at us and tell us National Coal owes her something. She'll make us push her kids out the door at gunpoint, and she'll holler about it, make sure everyone in town sees with their very own eyes what monsters we are."

"Well, then, don't do it."

"The company's not a charity organization. That house is needed for another man and his family who will work."

It had been a long time since Sarah had noticed any real toughness in Paul Lessing. There had been a time when he had frightened her. She had a glimpse of him now as that kind of man but said, "You couldn't do that to them."

"I can and I will. I don't want to, but if you want to come and watch, come on. Then you'll see whether you can love me. If I have to pick those little girls up and set them in the street, I will. If I have to slap the boy to make him get out of my way, I will."

"Oh, my God!"

"Sarah, the truth is, you're more your daddy's girl than you know. You think I can't see where your sympathies lie?"

"Oh, no. Oh, Paul!"

"Don't worry, I won't tell a soul." He emitted a short, bitter laugh. "See, you've got me protecting a union sympathizer. This is crazy."

"But together we can—"

"We aren't together on anything. I started out to try to use you, but you're the one that's been using me. Do you think I can't see that?"

"Me? Using you? Why, I would never—"

"Yes, you would, honey. Something inside you loves how much your daddy hates the likes of me, something that makes you get back at the hurt he's caused you by loving me. You're not crazy about what we do over at the post office, but if it hurts him, you'll settle for it. If we kept on, one day you'd wake up and look at what's lying beside you and be sick with yourself."

"You're wrong, Paul," Sarah protested, but the truth of his words flickered momentarily deep inside her.

He drew himself up. "I can't live in the same town with you, so close to your sweetness. It'd kill me knowing you're here, knowing you're so pure and innocent, and feeling that unsure little spark in you that wants to blow into a real fire."

"What are you talking about?"

"I aim to do that messy job I just told you about. Then I'm leaving myself."

"Where are you going? Take me with you!"

He shook his head sadly. "I'm not going far. There's plenty of other towns around here like Clarkson. Felts has got another place for me. I can't prolong this, Sarah. So long."

He turned on his heel and reached for the door. "How can you leave me like this?" she cried.

He sighed, approached her again, pulled her close, and kissed both cheeks. "It's better this way," he said. He ducked away from her then, was out the door quickly and gone.

19

TUESDAY'S TREK TO the schoolhouse was the first time Sarah had been out of the boarding house for three long, harrowing days. She had considered attending Drew Ferrell's funeral, but was told by Carl Eschman, who stopped by the boarding house, "Those people don't want to see any of us right now. No telling what they're likely to do. We've all got to tread lightly till that family's gone."

Since Paul's visit Sarah had cried so much she could not get the swelling out of her puffy eyelids, and her nose seemed permanently red and swollen. She was glad to be going back to school, happy to have something to get her mind off her misery—glad until she unlocked the schoolhouse door and walked into a building so cold that the outside was warm by comparison.

It was then that the loss of Hank, Hank's own loss, and the terrible upheaval of his family—far worse than her own petty trouble—hit her squarely. She realized she'd never see the boy again and she was devastated, wondering if she could even teach without him there. Even worse was the realization that never seeing *her* again was the smallest of his concerns. Once Paul and Mel got through with him and his family today, Hank would grow up remembering her as the teacher who had been engaged to marry the thug who threw his family into the street.

She struggled to build a fire, but when the children arrived, the building was still chilly, reminding them all of their loss. No one volunteered to take over Hank's job as Sarah had expected them to, but the sullen students took turns throughout the day bringing in coal and stoking the stove.

Sarah taught her lessons self-consciously, feeling like an outsider, wanting to make some sort of terse speech that would help them all feel better, but nothing came to mind. She was unable to compete with the empty seats that had belonged to Hank, Corey, and Annie Ferrell. Sometime during the day Paul and Mel would perform their job, and while all these students would know about it, perhaps witness it, Sarah would never know when or how it happened.

At the boarding house that evening Ida and Ruth were as kind as they knew how to be, keeping their distance and not mentioning

Paul's name. The only thing said on the subject was Ruth's comment at dinner, "Belinda and her boy managed to get most of their belongings packed up. I saw them get on the train. Nice of the men to let them store things next door."

"Too nice, if you ask me," Ida muttered.

The following morning Sarah arrived at the schoolhouse an hour early to make a determined effort at getting a real fire going. She tried to do everything she had seen Hank do, stirring the powdery ashes in a futile search for live coals. She carefully stacked kindling in the stove, blew on the flame she finally started, and was rewarded by a little blaze that didn't seem to need much coaxing.

She whirled around at the sound of three sharp raps on the door and voiced a small cry. With an instinct she was hardly aware of, she picked up the poker and called, "Yes? Come in."

Her heart raced when she saw that it was Paul who pushed open the door, pausing first to toss his cigarette out. She ran to him, but he put miles of distance in his hard glance. He set down a bulging traveling bag next to the door, and she backed away from him, still holding the poker.

"I guess you're leaving." Sarah couldn't control the trembling of her lower lip. "Oh, Paul, please don't. I already miss you so much. I can't stand it, I really can't." Tears skidded down her cheeks, and the poker clattered across the floor.

He ignored her and strode toward the stove. "I kicked that widow out yesterday, Sarah. She wouldn't go on her own, so I went around the house and picked up armloads of their stuff and dumped it in the street."

"Stop it, Paul. I heard you let them store their belongings next door."

"Hell, I… I grabbed up one of those little girls by her hair. I loved hearing her scream."

"I don't believe it! They said you let them store—"

"That was afterward," he said, and his look was so bitter she didn't know what was the truth. "A neighbor came by while they were picking things up and offered. I said why not. Half of it was ruined anyway."

They stood for a while in silence. She glanced around the room, sniffing back tears, afraid to look at him.

He muttered in a half-choked voice, "Don't make things so hard on me. Hell, you're like a kid sometimes." She still couldn't face him. "I'm on my way to the station. I came by to give you something." She gasped as he removed a pistol from his coat pocket. He let the corner of his mouth turn up in a quick half-smile as he sauntered slowly to her desk and laid it down. "It's loaded," he said. "All you have to do is point it with a steady hand and pull the trigger. You might get lucky and hit your mark."

"You're giving me your gun? Don't you need it?"

He patted his chest, indicating his shoulder holster. "It's another one I had."

"But I don't have a permit. Don't you have to be licensed or something to carry one?"

"Honey—Sarah, if something is staring you in the face threatening you, you're going to use that thing and not worry about whether you have a permit." His voice was hard.

"But who—? Paul, I've never needed a gun before."

"Maybe you did," he said with so much tenderness she wanted to run to his arms. "Maybe somebody else was carrying it for you." He busied himself consulting his pocket watch and pulling out a pack of cigarettes. "Sarah, there's something else I want you to have." He came a step closer. "I know you'll try to refuse, but do me a favor, honey, and please take it." He stuffed his hand in his pants pocket and pulled out a folded stack of ten-dollar bills. "It's a hundred dollars, and it would sure ease my mind if you'd take it."

"You know I can't accept money from you."

"Well, look here. You're not going to be staying here much longer yourself. I expect you'll be going back to Bluefield when school's finished. Why don't you just keep it till then. If you need it, fine, if not, just send it back to me. It's a loan is all. Just in case."

"Just in case what?"

He shrugged. "I don't know. It'd just make me feel better is all. You can send it back, honey—Sarah. If you need it, don't worry about it. Just pay me back sometime. A year or two, or ten. It doesn't make any difference. I don't care if you never give it back."

She didn't like the desperate feel of this "loan." "But I don't know where you'll be. And after I leave, you won't know where I am." Finality echoed in every word they spoke. She wanted to take his money just so she could have something of his to hang onto.

He smiled weakly. "We can always find each other. You can write to me in care of Tom Felts. And I know where your folks live."

He stretched out his hand; she opened her palm and he placed the bills in it. When he did so, she clasped her fingers around his hand, and he closed it over hers. Their eyes met, and with the strength of her gaze she tried to hold him and keep him from leaving her.

"Sarah, I… Look, some men are bound to mess with you, and what you do is your own business, but I want you to know that no matter what any of them insinuate, I never told them a thing. Take care of yourself," he mumbled, brusquely hurrying past her, grabbing his bag, and opening and closing the door quickly as he left.

Clutching the money in her hand, Sarah went to the window and watched him. He stopped to light a cigarette and then took heavy strides down the lane. Tears were starting in her eyes again when she spotted some children coming the other way. They left the path to make a wide arc around him. Sarah remembered the pistol on her desk. Before the students reached the building, it was safely hidden in back of the bottom drawer.

20

IN A DREAM Sarah met Paul Lessing on an unfamiliar street. Then they were on a train and he held her hand in the warmth of his. At the station in Clarkson, they peered out at Savage, Burnside, and the others who were unable to board the train. In the basement of her parents' house Paul held her, filling her with sharp passion. Somebody was watching outside a window. Then one person became many, and they were inside, milling around, clumping their big boots all over the place, asking for her...

She awoke in the living room to find Porter Thomas, Mel Greathouse, and Doug Burnside standing over her, Mel stooping to touch her shoulder. Doug's hand was on his hip, holding back his jacket so that his shoulder holster was visible, his expression hard with accusation. They were going to get her right here. She had been expecting something like this all evening and had fallen asleep with her coat on, her hand in the pocket where it rested on Paul's pistol.

"You awake, Miss Jennings?" Mel asked—gently, she imagined. She nodded, paralyzed with fear. "Well, we got some talking to do."

"What is it?" Maybe if she played dumb, they—Doug—wouldn't shoot her.

Doug answered. "Boss says you gotta clear out."

"Clear out?"

"Out of town. Train leaves at seven-thirty tomorrow morning. We'll be here at seven to see that you get down there and get on it. Understand?"

Sarah nodded without understanding. Doug stuck an unlit cigar in his mouth and wandered over to the stairway. "Hey, Ida!" he barked. "You up there, good-lookin'?" When he got no answer, he started up the stairs.

"You got anything at the schoolhouse you want to take with you?" Mel asked Sarah.

"Yes, I suppose I do." It was slowly dawning on her that she was to leave with an escort in the morning.

Leave Clarkson!

"If you want to tell us what all, we'll go up and get it for you."

Sarah stood up. "What's going on?" she asked. "Am I fired?"

"I expect you are," Porter answered.

Was it really going to be this easy? "Do you know why?"

He shrugged. "We're just following orders. But I expect you know why."

Yes, she knew why. She hastily wrote a list of everything she could think of that belonged to her at the school and went to her room to pack up. But to go where? Could she go home now? She knew if she tried to tell her parents what had happened, they would put the blame on her. And it was indeed somehow her fault. In a daze she threw her things into suitcases, trying to relive the nightmare, this month-long ordeal that seemed to be ending, in case she had misunderstood some detail.

Shortly after Paul's departure, Ruel Savage had begun showing up at the schoolhouse asking Sarah questions—what do you teach? may I see the books? how are the children doing? He stood around the classroom and watched her teach, sticking his nose and his ideas into Sarah's lessons. He peered over children's shoulders, corrected their written work, seeming to enjoy their nervousness and timidity. At times he took over, asking the students questions, drilling them, grilling them, belittling them with a look or an insult. Some of them stopped coming to school.

On one occasion when the students went outside during recess, Sarah asked him if there was something wrong with her teaching. "You're an excellent teacher, Sarah. You don't mind if I call you Sarah, do you?"

"Yes, sir, I do," she replied, no doubt her first mistake. Then she asked him why, if there was nothing wrong with her teaching, he kept coming around.

"Schoolhouse is on company property, Sarah. I have a right to be just about anywhere I feel like being in Clarkson."

"I'm sure you have that right, but the fact is, you're interfering with my teaching and the children's learning." Looking back now, Sarah saw that she had indeed provoked him.

"*I'm* interfering, Sarah?"

"Yes, sir. You see, the children aren't at ease when you're here, so they don't perform as well, and I don't either. In fact, there have been times when I've found myself asking them easy questions I know they can answer correctly because they get upset about making a mistake in your presence. So if there isn't a problem, it would help if you didn't visit us so often. My job is to challenge these boys and girls, encourage them to learn..." It had clearly been her fault.

He took hold of her arm, and when she struggled, he gripped her tighter. His upper lip curled into a sneer. "You've turned into a bitch, Sarah." When she continued to squirm, he pushed her ahead of him until they reached the stove. He shoved her so close to it that a move on her part would cause her to burn herself. "Now we can talk, Sarah."

"I've said all I have to say." No doubt, another mistake.

He leaned closer and she felt each of his fingers digging into her arm. "You're a cold bitch and I'm trying to thaw you out, Sarah." He paused, then asked, "Do you miss your boyfriend, Sarah?" He was looking at her greedily, his eyes traveling slowly over her face and down to where they settled for a moment on her chest. "Do you miss all those things he used to do to you?" She whipped herself around angrily, only succeeding in burning her hand on the stove. When she drew it back and cried out, he laughed softly.

He grabbed her breast, at the same time increasing the pressure on her arm. "Like this? Do you miss this, Sarah?" He squeezed and kneaded her so roughly that she cried out again. She struggled, certain that being burned was preferable to this, but he pulled her close to him, shoving her even closer to the stove, and she was powerless.

A guttural laugh came from his throat. He moved his hand from her breast, placing it on her shoulder, and squeezed. Then he bent as if to kiss her. His sour breath of stale cigars nauseated her, and she clamp her teeth and lips together firmly. He pulled away and laughed again. "Don't you want to kiss me, Sarah?"

She was so close to the stove she feared her clothing would catch fire. He placed thumb and fingers on either side of her face and applied pressure, all the while grinning with a sly leer, until she was forced to loosen her jaw. "Now, let's see what we've got here." He jammed two fingers into her mouth, poking around, sliding them over her gums and teeth and tongue. "I bet you know what to do with this pretty mouth, don't you, Sarah? Mouths are for more than kissing, you know. Did Paul Lessing put his prick in your mouth, Sarah?" He continued to probe, while his tongue hung from his mouth.

Drenched in humiliation and anger that flamed hotter than the stove, Sarah bit down on his fingers, felt her teeth sink into his flesh. He roared with rage, staggering away from her and holding onto his fingers that were oozing blood.

She bolted toward him, pointing at him as she spoke—her worst mistake of all. "Leave me alone, you filthy worm! Get out of my schoolhouse and let me teach!" He backed toward the door as she marched in his direction. "And don't compare yourself to Paul Lessing. You're a filthy low-down scum of a pig, and I can't stand the sight of you!" Then she whirled around and rang the bell.

The children filed in past him, and he stood with a handkerchief wrapped around his fingers. Sarah smiled at the children, while Ruel Savage threatened her in a whisper. "I'll be back. You're going to do it to me too, and you'll like it better with me. If I'm a pig, you're nothing but a whore. You were fucking him, and now you're going to fuck me too."

Thus began Sarah's vigil against his promised rape, something her father would say she had brought upon herself. When would he be back? It seemed unlikely that he would attack her at the school-house. The boarding house? Would he send his men to escort her to his home? With the snap of his fingers Savage had ordered his men to kill Drew Ferrell. Being with other people at all times was no protection against such a powerful man. With a wave of his hand, he could send them all away. Was there even one of the mine guards who would come to her defense?

Paul, of course! Paul would have killed him. That's when she remembered the gun. She opened her desk drawer and took it out. The cold, heavy hunk of iron in her hand reassured her. With a timid finger on the trigger, she practiced pointing and aiming it a few times. Then she slipped it into her pocket. From now on she would not be without it.

She felt isolated and vulnerable at school. Her students, cowed along with the rest of the town after Ferrell's murder, could do nothing to bolster her confidence, and Sarah had fleeting thoughts of Hank. The Hank she had known would not have tolerated Ruel Savage's behavior, might somehow have even protected her; but that Hank was gone now, broken down in grief somewhere with his shattered family. Sarah tried to be ready to leave the schoolhouse every day with Harvey Casteel after he completed his cleaning duties, his company, as they walked down the hill together, distracting her and providing her with the illusion of safety.

Now in her room she kept unpacking and repacking a suitcase, trying to cram in more of her belongings. She wondered what else she might have done than carry on as usual. Of course, she should have left Clarkson that very first day after his ugly threat instead of waiting around for him to carry it out. The fact that she had stayed had been an invitation in itself.

It finally happened that very afternoon after the children left for the day. Despite the gun in her pocket she began trembling in a sweaty panic the instant Savage walked in and ordered Harvey to leave. She tried to breathe deeply, remembering his fingers inside her mouth, forcing herself to imagine what else he intended to prod her with. The resulting anger steadied her.

Savage said to her, "You've had time to think about your actions the other day, Sarah." He took a step toward her and she stepped backward, her hand thrust into her pocket in what she hoped was a nonchalant manner. "You called me some names that people don't call a supervisor for National Coal. You owe me something—whore."

He took a few more steps and she slipped between a couple of desks. "Wait a minute!" she shrieked, her mind about to splinter into a thousand pieces. "What do you want? What do you think you're doing?" She was shaking so badly that the idea of hoisting the gun seemed a physical impossibility, but she kept her fingers around it.

He gritted his teeth and curled back his lip. "I've come for you, bitch. You're going to spread your legs for me right there on your desk, and make no mistake about it, because I've got ways to make you." He went to the stove and picked up the poker. He tested its weight in his hand and moved slowly as though he planned to enjoy every minute of the chase.

She put another desk between them, her heart beating so violently in her throat it felt like she was choking. Pretending coolness, she pulled the pistol from her pocket and leveled it at him. The action calmed her somewhat as fear leapt into his eyes.

"Let go of the poker!" she cried, and to her astonishment it clanged to the floor. "I don't care who you are. You'll not touch me. Try it and you'll be a dead National Coal supervisor." Surprise and terror were written upon his features. That and her own words gave her strength. "I've been target-shooting since I was six years old," she said with such conviction that she almost believed it herself, "and I can hit anything, even a worm." She jerked the gun to emphasize her words, and he tensed.

He held up quivering hands and shook his head. She took a rapid step forward.

"Get out of here!" she exclaimed.

He scuttled toward the door but turned to face her with his own threat. "You think this is the end of it, do you? You think it's this easy? You'll see. I promise you, you'll see."

He stepped out onto the front stoop and she followed. She was elated, drunk on her power, outside herself now, saying things that people only imagined saying. "Go ahead and sneak up on me, you bully. Have your big strong men come for me. And *I* promise *you* that I'll shoot anybody that comes for me." He was walking away, but she continued to shout. "If your goons shoot me down the way they shot Drew Ferrell, then fine. I'd rather be dead than be touched by you!"

She had gone about in fear the rest of the afternoon and evening, waiting. But he had only dismissed her. She remembered Ethel, the bookkeeper who had been terminated, but this didn't seem like the same thing.

The next morning Doug and Porter carried her bags down the hill, and Mel walked beside her. The men put her things on the train and before she boarded, Burnside said, "Boss said to tell you you're blacklisted."

Sarah frowned. "What does that mean?"

"It means there ain't a coal company anywhere that'll hire you." He added with a short nasal laugh, "And whatever pay you think you got coming, you can forget it."

She stepped into the car. What did she care about a few more dollars? She found a seat and looked at them standing out on the platform, their attention already gone to other things.

The train hissed and groaned as it rolled forward, and Sarah gazed out the window watching Clarkson disappear. Never again would she enter such a place. Ruel Savage had taken care of that for her. Each time the train rounded a bend and called over the hills with its shrill whistle, a thrill plunged through Sarah's body. For an instant she imagined that she was riding a triumphant train out of a bad dream toward freedom. But the truth was that she had no idea where she was going.

PART TWO

1

Welch, West Virginia, Spring 1915

AFTER TWO WEEKS of floundering in Bluefield, dodging her parents' questions and halfheartedly looking for employment, Sarah boarded a westbound train. With no real idea of what she was doing and fearful of spending any more of Paul's loan, she got off in the town of Welch, forty miles northwest of Bluefield and county seat of McDowell County. Despite her lack of a plan, things fell quickly into place.

She found a room with a sweet elderly woman and a job doing clerical and reception work for a printing company. The pay was meager but adequate for the time being. Since she was unable to return Paul's money in its entirety as she had originally intended, she deposited the large remaining chunk of it into a savings account, planning to send it to him when the balance returned to one hundred. Meanwhile she would collect the interest. As for the pistol, she had never felt quite safe since her ordeal in Clarkson and did not intend to get rid of it. She kept it loaded and hidden in a bottom drawer in her room. Whatever she now felt about Paul Lessing, it was his pistol that had saved her from unimaginable horror.

Worry and vague uneasiness nagged at her. Like Bluefield, Welch was crawling with men associated with the coal industry. Those men looked at her often, usually when she was alone, and around every corner she imagined meeting Ruel Savage. One day from a distance she saw Doug Burnside ambling toward the train station with men who could have been lawmen or coal company officials, and she wondered why she had not stayed on the train and gone farther west. She should have taken the N&W all the way to Huntington where she hoped one day to enroll at Marshall College, but she wasn't quite ready for that yet. Perhaps she could take the summer months to regain the self-confidence that had been peeled away from her in Clarkson.

She tried to play down her attractive features, but her landlady said to her constantly, "What a beauty! You'll have no trouble finding a husband. There are plenty of men around here with money." But Sarah wanted nothing to do with moneyed men, men related to coal.

Spring came on early, warm and certain, carrying fragrance in on its breezes, freshness and hope in the evening air, and brought handsome, fun-loving Denny Sable into the print shop ordering handbills advertising a festival in the park in May, where he and several others would be playing music. His affable manner charmed her. He wore dark trousers and a shirt of no particular hue buttoned to the throat, and Sarah could tell he had nothing to do with mines.

Throughout a glorious, carefree summer, Denny courted Sarah. He played guitar and sang with a band and lived with his aunt Sadie. His voice was as voluptuous as his kisses, as sleek as his lean body. Sarah felt safe with Denny Sable, safe with his poetry, his untroubled spirit that knew nothing about games or deceit, cowardice or violence.

Sarah buried the loneliness and fear she had taken with her from Clarkson. She had grown up in an atmosphere of severity and threats. Now, with Denny, life could be carefree and fun. The ordinary things they did seemed significant and special. They walked over Welch's steep streets and strolled the banks of the Tug Fork River, discussing the books he read and the movies they saw. They watched a July Fourth parade and a traveling show, and enjoyed other musicians when Denny wasn't playing with his group. Most important of all was the laughing, snuggling, and kissing. Sarah had sworn to herself after Paul Lessing that she would never again be so free with herself. But she longed to have Denny's body next to hers, washing away forever the memory of Paul's touch. She didn't encourage him though, still ashamed of her forward behavior with Paul. Denny didn't press her, other than to kiss her and kiss her until she felt wild and drenched in a clean desire that every day seemed to free her from the filthy claim she had mistakenly allowed Paul to lay on her.

Denny Sable was as lavish with words and dreams as a philanthropist could be with money. "I love you, Sarah Jennings." He repeated the phrase often, and similar ones, and then wrote them down in songs that his band arranged and performed. Those songs included an oft-repeated declaration: "I'll marry you someday." Soon he was speaking the words to her in heated moments of kissing. "Let's get married someday, woman. I ain't never had such a sweet thing."

He was tall, good-looking, and cocksure. On his arm Sarah was undeniably taken and safe, off limits to other men, the same as invisible, and she again became careful with her looks, happy now to appear stunning. Denny also had the kind of friends—musicians and laborers—who had nothing to do with coal operators, and Sarah retreated into friendly camaraderie with those people. In late July she took Denny to Bluefield to meet her family, expecting her father to despise him for his imperfect grammar. Instead her father took to him at once. They sat on the porch together passing the time, and Ray pried into his background.

Denny was twenty-one years old. His father was deceased and his mother had moved to California. He wasn't close to his far-flung siblings and an uncle had died in a mining accident. Aunt Sadie was his only nearby kin. Denny had been raised in Kentucky in the Old Regular Baptist Church, also known as the Hardshells.

"My folks went to church every chance they got," he told Sarah's father. "Me, I lost interest in it once I found out about real music.

The folks at church didn't believe in no instruments besides the human voice. Well, I heard a fiddle and a banjo and never wanted to sing no more hymns, which is what folks was always trying to get me to do."

"You do have a nice singing voice," Ray Jennings said. He did not object to music and listened appreciatively as Denny strummed guitar and sang softly on the front porch.

"I never cared a whole lot for the dancing part," Denny continued. "I just wanted to play. Banjo and a fiddle was too hard though. You gotta start picking and sawing when you're a young 'un to get really good. There weren't no other instruments besides a harmonica. Then I seen I could order a guitar out of a Sears and Roebuck catalog for around seven dollars. I got some guitar music too, but I couldn't figure it out, so I picked it up by listening." Denny's favorite subject was music. Given the chance, he enlightened everyone on the subject. "Ain't too many can play a guitar or even seen one where I come from. Back home they just got fiddles and banjos. But we got us a modern band. Ain't many around that's got a guitar and a mandolin."

Denny had left school after eighth grade and had done a little bit of everything in the way of work. "I'm a good carpenter," he said. "Used to get work around home when I wasn't in the coal mine or building coke ovens. I was gonna go back there if the band splits, but I aim to stick around Welch. Lots of building going on. I've already got two men says they'll hire me. All I gotta do is pick which one. I'm gonna be my own boss, fix my own hours, work more when I need more money. I really wanna make furniture. Set up a little shop and take orders. Maybe have a catalog made up of all the different things I can make and mail it out to rich folks in big towns. Then when I wanna take off some time to play music, I can do it."

Denny was a voracious reader. "Getting into a book is like being somewhere else, being other people and doing exciting things," he said. "I read the Wild West stories and don't have to worry about getting shot at." He loved Owen Wister, Jack London, and Zane Grey. He also read Mark Twain, James Fenimore Cooper, and everything in between.

Sarah tried to find a teaching job, but there were no immediate openings in Welch, and when she was referred to a district just outside of town which provided teachers to a coal camp, she retreated. She assumed she was on a blacklist somewhere but didn't want to get close enough to find out. She asked the Welch district to keep her name for consideration if anything should become available and continued at the printing company.

The marriage proposal that eventually came wasn't entirely Denny's idea. "When were you thinking of getting married?" Sarah asked him.

"Married?" He seemed astonished at the idea.

"You say you love me."

"That ain't the same as saying let's get married."

"But you've talked about us getting married and written all those songs about it."

"Ain't we having fun just the way it is? It is fun, ain't it?"

"Yes, but can we keep going like this?"

"It just ain't never crossed my mind before."

"But you talk about it, you sing about it, all the time."

"I suppose I's mainly thinking about what we could do if we was married. You know—in bed. I ain't even got a job. And I don't figure you'd have me anyhow."

"Well, I'm working, and you've got two offers. Just pick one."

"Two offers? What're you talking about?"

"You said two different men want you to do carpentry work for them."

"Well, that was a while back. I could maybe go back and ask them."

"You really don't want to, do you?"

"Now don't be putting words in my mouth. I been thinking maybe one of these days I might see if you maybe wanna get married."

Denny and Sarah parted in a storm of misunderstanding and didn't see each other for almost a week. During one of her crying spells, Sarah saw how irreconcilable Denny's free-spirited ways were with the actual idea of entrapment, and while a part of her knew that marrying Denny would mean giving up her dream of college, she didn't know anymore how to get along without him. She was perhaps even afraid without him. She berated herself for the fool she had been, counting on him while he was merely having fun. He had deceived her with his laughter and lightly spoken words, betrayed her with technicalities—where she came from, words and acts of love led to marriage; to him those things were only a part of the fun.

She dared to think of Paul Lessing in a kinder light. Mine guard or not, he would never have done this to her. In his own clumsy way, he had been more considerate than Denny, who made the world believe he was sensitive and gentle on the strength of his charisma, his good looks, his sensuous voice, and the little bit of poetry in his songs.

But Denny came back for her. "Sarah, I never asked because I figured you didn't really want somebody like me. Look, I'm asking now. I reckon I won't never find nothing as sweet as you if I looked for the rest of my life." They were married at a small service in the Methodist church in Bluefield under Ray Jennings's watchful, questioning eye. Then they returned to Welch, there to discover the rest of it, the reason for their attraction, and it wasn't long before Sarah was pregnant.

It was fall; the rest of the musicians had drifted away to take jobs that paid decent wages, and Sarah and Denny awoke to reality at the same moment. "I reckon I better get me a job," Denny said, and his search took him out of town.

Several days later he returned beaming with good news. "We'll have to move, but it's a good job, good pay. Aunt Sadie says we can have that old furniture in her basement."

Sarah was full of questions. How much did the job pay? Where were they going?

"Pay's good and there ain't much in the way of living expenses. It's all provided. A house with running water, a store with everything, a nurse, a doctor. It's a little town west of here, owned by Dry Creek Coal."

2

Dawson, West Virginia

THE ONLY COMPANY-OWNED house Sarah Sable had ever been in was the Cinellis' in Clarkson. The house she and Denny shared in Dawson was a dream by comparison—a sturdy two-story house, underpinned and painted yellow, with a large front porch with all its boards in place and a dirt yard of more than adequate size whose fence was also in good repair.

It was a half house, shared with another family, with separate entrances on each side. The running water Denny had bragged about was a hand pump on the back porch just outside the kitchen door, both porch and pump for the mutual use of both families. The outhouse, a two-seater, also accommodated both families.

The kitchen, at the back of the house, opened into a middle room that might be used as a dining room, which in turn led to the front room. Stairs hugging the inside wall of the front room led to two bedrooms upstairs.

In the kitchen was a coal cookstove with a large tank for hot water attached. The house had the capacity to breathe dust and grit all over the floor and their sparse furniture. Sarah quickly developed an efficient system of wiping up dust and pumping, carrying, and then storing water in the house. And she learned to build fires. There was a stove for heating located in the middle downstairs room. She banked fires in the evening and stirred the hot coals in the morning, shoveling ashes and scattering them neatly outside on the patch of ground where she intended to plant a garden in the spring.

The house was equipped with electricity, which the neighbors seemed to think was a great luxury, and Sarah agreed, remembering the one bulb dangling from the ceiling at the Cinelli shanty. But there was no icebox, and she had no idea how she would get used to that. The weather was cool now in fall, but summer would be impossible, and she foresaw two or three daily trips to the store.

Sarah and Denny adjusted to the Morris family who lived in the other half of the house. They were loud and smoked so incessantly that the odor permeated the thin walls. The couple was much older with several grown children and three still living with them. Harriet Morris was sloppy and unfriendly. George Morris had black dirt under his nails and ground into the creases in his neck. But he was friendly enough and helpful too, not averse to giving Denny a hand at tasting the home brew he occasionally mixed up in the galvanized bathtub.

Dawson was owned by Dry Creek Coal Company. Its owner and operator was Orville Sanders Jones, who lived in the big house on the hill. He was often away, in one of his other towns—Tomahawk or Laura, named for his wife—or in New York City, and Sarah wondered if the owner's residence in town owed to the better conditions of the houses.

Denny surprised Sarah with his ability to adapt to work in the mine. She had never considered his roots so carefully. His father had stayed on the land, but his uncles had worked in the Kentucky coal fields, taking young Denny on as an apprentice. In Dawson he fell in easily with the other men's talk of mining; there was no doubt that he was intimately familiar with what to do at the working place and that he knew his tamping bars from his pry bars. He became a part of a group of men solidly bonded together even if he chose to remain at its outskirts. He worked with a buddy, Arthur Caldwell, a man in his mid-thirties with years of experience and much respect among his fellow workers, which put Sarah's mind at ease. With a man like Arthur in charge, Denny was most likely as safe as he could possibly be in this most dangerous of occupations.

Ray Jennings came once to visit her. He had little to say, standing at the window in her neat living room and pointing in the direction of a church.

"You should go, Sarah. If not for yourself, for your baby."

"I don't have much free time. Sunday is Denny's only day off and we need the time together."

He sighed. "You'll do what you want, I suppose, but you should take him with you. With his job, he needs all the praying he can get. Go to the Baptist church with him."

"Denny's more interested in playing music than going to church, and I'd rather be with him. Anyway we won't be here long, Daddy," Sarah assured him. "We'll stay till after the baby's born. Then he'll look for something else."

Ray Jennings looked at her, resigned and distant. "Denny's a good man, Sarah, a delightful person, happy, always has a smile for everybody, but I'm not so sure about anything else. You've got a good house here, probably better than what he was used to in Kentucky. It'd be mighty easy for him to stick around here."

Sarah met many of the families in the community while Denny managed to find the musicians and the men who lost the most sleep and took the most time off work going on drinking binges. Arthur Caldwell stopped by the house from time to time and talked to Denny about the time he was taking off the job.

"You ain't gonna make nothing if'n you don't work," was Arthur's admonition.

"We're doing fine," Denny told him hotly. "I'll dig as many ton as I need."

Arthur, a compactly built man with a confident swagger, had a deep rattle in his chest. "Suit yourself, Denny. You're a good worker, but I need you there. If this is how you wanna do it, I'm gonna talk to the foreman about making a change. You don't wanna lose your house. You got lucky with this."

"Oh, I'll be there." After Arthur left, Denny complained, "He's an asshole. All he thinks about is work, work, work."

"He's got a family, Denny, five children."

"Well, a man's gotta have him a little bit of fun. Guys like him die young, always pushing theirselves to be at the top of the weigh sheet."

3

ALTHOUGH LIVING IN an environment she had once assumed would be intolerable, Sarah enjoyed her position as Denny Sable's wife. Clarkson was her example, and even in that camp of stricter limits, she had recognized the range of human differences. From the lost hopes of the Cinellis to the ignorance of the Livelys; from Clyde Poling's narrow personal aspirations to the boundless vision of Drew and Hank Ferrell, Sarah saw that she didn't have to settle for what little the company provided.

When she bought a piglet from Boris Tonkovich with money from her secret stash of cash, scrounged some fencing from the dump on the other side of the slag heap, and built a pen in the woods just beyond the clearing, she raised her fist in a private celebration of victory. Whatever else happened, she would enhance her income. She moved the pen every time the pig rooted out what was edible. With her meager table scraps and the ones the Morrises threw out she supplemented the animal's diet and collected the pig's dung for her future garden.

If there weren't any organizers with whom to involve herself, she would at least take on the challenge of earning a better-than-average living. Looking around the town she found nothing to do at first that would earn her more money and for the moment was satisfied with her efforts with the pig and planning her garden.

But Denny provided the incentive she needed one day when he brought home a pay envelope with a note for scrip only. "That's all?" Sarah exclaimed.

He glared at her. "You spend too goddamn much at the store."

"Me? What about the days you don't go to work?"

"There's a lot of guys that don't get nothing on payday. Only way they get anything is to take an advance against their next pay. We ain't done that yet."

"And we won't either."

"At this rate we will. Ain't there something you can do? I mean, hell, you got time on your hands. You're twice as smart as the rest of the women in this here town. I bet there's ways a woman could make money that none of them's ever thought of."

Denny shocked Sarah with the amount he spent on liquor, and it didn't make any difference if he had no cash. Scrip would buy moonshine from a couple of brothers who lived around the mountain and traded when they had to at the company store for their still's ingredients. Sarah began to evaluate everything within her control and possession in terms of its earning potential. One morning standing in the empty upstairs bedroom, she saw a gold mine with potential even greater than that of the pig. Not wanting to give Denny the chance to react negatively, she went straight to the coal company office next door to the store and said she wanted to take in a boarder.

"What!" Denny exploded when she told him. "Jesus Christ almighty, woman!"

"It's extra income every month, in cash. I'm doing it. And please don't complain until you can bring in that amount."

She bought a used mattress and bedstead from a family that was moving, and Denny quit complaining when a man showed up on their doorstep with a suitcase in each hand and a beat-up banjo slung across his back. Stocky, a jovial smirk on his bearded face, he stuck out his hand and said, "Catfish Johnson. Foreman said you have a room for me."

Denny could hardly wait to talk music with him, but Sarah silenced him with a look until she had made the necessary arrangements with her boarder. "I'm doing this because I need the money, Mr. Johnson. Having you here means extra laundry, extra cleaning, extra groceries, and extra cooking for me. There aren't going to be any excuses on the rent. I need the money in cash and on time."

"Yes, ma'am!" he exclaimed with a grin, pulling out his wallet.

When Denny reached for the cash, Sarah snatched it from him and said to both of them, "This is my job and my pay. Mr. Johnson, you will pay *me* no matter what my husband says." She turned and smiled sweetly at Denny, who laughed in appreciation.

The new boarder picked up his suitcases. "Well, I'll try to stay outta your way as much as I can, but see here. Long as I'm eating out'n your kitchen and sleeping next door to you, just call me Catfish. Most folks does."

Catfish played music with Denny every night after they ate, and drank as much, and to Sarah's relief, he realized his obligation to provide his own liquor. After work on Saturdays, he bathed and left, usually not returning until Sunday evening.

His presence in the house was an inconvenience that Denny sometimes grumbled about, even though it was harder on Sarah, but she learned to tolerate it, seeing the gross overcrowding and lack of privacy in most of the other homes where several children lived. She got used to his evening bathing alongside Denny in the kitchen, and if she was cooking, she turned her back, ignoring them both.

She was self-conscious at first when she and Denny made love with Catfish in the next room, until she remembered that the Morrises were just as close and that Harriet Morris had made a sour comment to her more than once. "You and your man having too much fun at night, ain't you? And in your condition?" If Sarah hadn't felt so sorry for the woman—tired, wrinkled, disgusted with everything around her that suggested life or happiness—she might have told her to mind her own business.

In early spring Catfish cancelled his weekend plans to help butcher the pig. Sarah had to run to the store to buy eggs for their breakfast, and on her way back it occurred to her, "If I had chickens I wouldn't have to buy eggs, and we could kill one occasionally for fresh meat." That day she traded a piece of fresh pork for a dozen chicks.

Arthur Caldwell eventually made good on his threat to have positions changed, and to Sarah's surprise, Denny was given charge of his own working place, taking on a seventeen-year-old as a helper.

But one day after work, he stormed in, sprinkling grit everywhere. He walked from one end of the house to the other, kicking furniture, picking up unbreakable objects—books, pillows—and hurling them across the room, while Catfish quietly sponged off in the kitchen and slipped off to his room. Denny grabbed the whiskey bottle and stomped out the front door. He stood outside in the cold, gulping whiskey until Sarah heard glass tinkling in the street.

She went to the door. "What is it?"

He was stepping out of his clothes, flinging them everywhere. "Goddamn weighman bastard," he muttered. He walked through the house naked, and Sarah followed him, taking note of his taut leg muscles working beneath skin that was translucent and flecked with patches of coarse, dark hair. Nude, with legs gleaming like the pallid mushrooms which occasionally popped up as mere accidents in the mine, he was vulnerable, one man, whose impotent anger changed nothing. He washed off with the rest of the hot water, silent while she handed him clean clothes and put dinner before him. Sarah went upstairs and knocked on the closed bedroom door.

"Supper's on," she called to Catfish.

On the stairs he said to her, "Bad day. Don't like to get in the way after a bad day."

Both men ate without speaking. Catfish finished quickly and returned to his room.

After Denny ate two helpings of stew and half a loaf of bread, Sarah asked, "What did the bastard weighman do?"

He leaned back in his chair when she brought him coffee. "I didn't do nothing different today than I do every day, but that there weighman at the tipple tells me there's too much slate in one of my cars. Tells me he's docking my pay on five hundred pounds." He slammed his fist on the table. "Five hundred pounds! The sonofabitch! I seen there weren't more'n about twenty pounds of waste in my car. That ain't fair, is it? I done all that work for nothing."

"Did you say anything to him?"

"Sure I did. I let him have it." Denny crossed his arms over his chest and stared at the table. "He sent me to talk to a couple of the guards, told them I was getting out of line and rowdy. But, dammit! I wasn't! I's just telling him what I thought."

"Of course you weren't, Denny." She took his hand. "What'd they say to you?"

"Said the company would lose money if everyone sent up cars with a lot of waste, and they was docking me to teach me a lesson. And they said not to back-talk the weighman."

"Did they touch you?"

"No. That there weighman's the one got to me. Hell, I'm gonna have to be extra careful now, make sure I don't ever got no slate in my cars. That right there's gonna slow me down. I'm gonna be lucky to get five cars loaded in a day."

4

SARAH'S SON WAS born in late June of 1916, and in a moment of sentimental weakness she named him after her father, Ray

Alan, who visited to honor the occasion. To avoid confusion they called him Alan. She had such an easy time of it that by the time the midwife arrived, Sarah and her friend, Millie Owens, had delivered the baby themselves. Denny celebrated with moonshine and music.

He and his friends played late into the night on the front porch—Denny singing in rich, full tones which were somehow enhanced by alcohol, Mark Hilling and Catfish picking banjos, Millie's husband, Harry, fiddling and exchanging it occasionally for a harmonica, and Denny strumming guitar. Others came and went, passing the jug and joining in on choruses.

Sarah lay in bed with Alan and smiled at all the noise that she could sleep through at will. Next door Mrs. Morris was less accepting. "Shut up, you goddamn hell raisers!" she yelled.

"Shut up yourself, old woman!" Mr. Morris, who kept the young hell raisers company, replied to his wife.

Over the summer Denny worked long hours with seemingly boundless extra energy to stay up late with his music and a little home brew. He was proud of Alan and indulgent toward Sarah, lavishing her with praise for her own hard work in what was becoming the most prosperous garden in Dawson. His broad smile and sensual laughter infected everyone. Sarah fell in love with him again, hungering for him when he sat shirtless on the porch in the evenings, his skin glistening with a damp sheen, his hard muscles rippling with each movement.

Up nights with the baby, working in the garden during the day, and putting up canned goods when the harvest came in, Sarah ran on energy she didn't really possess, but she hummed throughout the days, anticipating the good times when Denny came home.

In early fall Sarah noted that she and Denny had been in Dawson for a year. For several months no mention had been made about leaving. So far Denny had earned little in cash. Sarah had managed to take a small portion of the money Catfish gave her every month and return it to her savings account, and she was now up to ninety-nine dollars. Nearly enough to return to Paul.

She and Denny were about where they had been the previous year, except for the addition of some extra food and another mouth to feed, and Denny had not gone elsewhere to look for a job. "Once a miner, always a miner," it was often said, and Denny had been in the mines off and on since his early teens.

The idea of staying in Dawson might have been tolerable if it had just been herself, but Sarah looked down at dark-haired Alan falling asleep at her breast. How would this boy resist following his daddy into the pit as those Clarkson boys had? It was no different in Dawson. A slew of boys always tagged along with the men walking to or from work. It was one thing to have a husband for a coal miner, but she vowed that no son of hers would ever dig coal.

She set her mind to figuring out how to get them out of Dawson. Maybe Denny wasn't bound to earn anything besides scrip, but she, Sarah, might be able to. What else could she do besides keep a boarder and raise chickens, pigs, and a garden? She heard that the Valentinos were moving to another town, and Rose Valentino had a job doing laundry for mine guards.

She would try to get the job.

As for Paul Lessing's money, Sarah stroked Alan's silky hair and decided to keep it for her child and his future. She was certain Paul had known when he left town that Savage would come after her and had left her with the only protection he had to offer. He had wanted to give her the money. Well, she deserved it for all her trouble with Savage.

She accompanied Rose on her last laundry day, learning the particulars of the job. Handling the mine guards' laundry, with its odor of stale tobacco smoke, cologne, and sweat, was like mucking around in a bad memory or a nightmarish dream. Her own laundry was no picnic with Denny's and Catfish's coal-soiled work clothes and Alan's diapers. She scraped dirty laundry across the washboard until her fingers ached and fed a fire all day to keep hot water for the many necessary washes and rinses.

One evening when Denny and Catfish came home, and Sarah was trying to get their supper in the midst of an irritable baby and crisply starched and ironed shirts hanging everywhere, Denny lost his temper. "Good god, woman! I cain't even get around in my own house no more without having some other man's shirt slapping me in the face. And why's he so goddamn cranky?" He pointed to Alan.

"He's teething. His gums hurt."

"Seems like every time I come home, he starts to hollering. Hell, I cain't get my supper without putting up with all this fussing and mess. A man cain't have no peace in his own house!"

"This ain't your own house, Denny!" Sarah exploded. "It belongs to Dry Creek Coal. We're never going to get any place where we can have our own home unless we earn some money. Real cash, not scrip. And that's what I'm doing. Earning extra. As for the baby, he's your son as well as mine. I listen to him all day. Why can't you take it for five minutes?"

"I been working all day, ten goddamn hours. I'm tired."

"Me too," Catfish said, pushing back his chair. He stole quietly to his room.

"And I haven't been?" Sarah exclaimed. "This is just an ironing day. I've made three trips to those boarding houses today. I've ironed twenty shirts and twenty pairs of pants, I've carried wood and coal, I finished building a new pigsty, I made your breakfast, dinner, and supper, I carried groceries from the store, and I cleaned the house. Most of it carrying Alan in the sling. I've also fed the chickens. And I was up an hour before you and once during the night. That ain't work, Daddy? If that ain't work, I'd like to know what is!"

"All right, all right. It does sound a little like work now that you put it that way."

"And what will you do after supper? Play music? Read another book? Go drink with the boys? What do you think I'm going to do?

Carry coal and water to begin with. I've got diapers to rinse, dishes to wash, and bread to make, so don't you tell me about working, Denny Sable!"

All the while her voice had been rising and he was trying to calm her and quiet her. He managed to capture her in his arms, and she burst into tears. "There now, woman, don't you cry. I love you. I *love* you, dammit. I'll help get in some coal later."

Sarah was so agitated she couldn't tell Denny what was really bothering her, that she was pregnant again.

5

ON APRIL 6, 1917, Sarah's twentieth birthday, the United States entered the war in Europe, and two weeks later on a Sunday Orville Jones, Dry Creek Coal's owner, held a meeting for coal miners and their families at the recreation hall where he gave a rousing speech.

"We're in this war to keep liberty alive!" he barked. "Democracy and freedom are sacred, rights that we should all be proud to fight for and protect." So now it's all right, Sarah thought, recalling her efforts to discuss such topics in her classroom. "Some of you men have already announced your intentions to quit your jobs here and enlist in the service. That's a noble act to be sure, and of course you can go. I commend you for your sacrifice." Sarah noticed his tone—like a father advising his sons.

"The noblest effort might be to remain here digging coal. Our country needs coal. Seventy percent of the energy in America is provided by coal, and twenty-five percent of that comes from the mines here in southern West Virginia. Now there's a war on, and the need for coal is going to go sky high. Orders from the navy are already coming in. Boys, they want our coal first because it's the best in the nation, the best in the world! So don't think you have to enlist to do your part in our fight for freedom. Just remember, every ton you dig is a ton dug for America! For freedom!"

Such speeches continued, along with pamphlets and leaflets full of inspirational propaganda, urging greater coal production, the purchase of Liberty Bonds, and contributions to the Red Cross. Nevertheless, Catfish Johnson enlisted in July, so Sarah notified the company office that she could take another boarder.

In August her second son was born, and Sarah was exhausted. Her delivery was not as easy as the first, and she seemed to have a less than adequate supply of milk.

"You work too hard and you don't get enough to eat." Millie chastised her while Denny stood in the background nodding his head in agreement. "I'm gonna go tell them mine guards to find somebody else to do their washing."

"No!" Sarah cried in alarm. "I can't quit. We need the money."

Millie leaned close to her. "You need your health and your little one's health more. Last thing you need is a baby to get off to a poor start. You don't wanna lose him, do you?"

Millie's speech frightened her. There had been sickness the previous winter in other homes where it had sometimes seemed to Sarah that ignorance was in greater abundance than food, and she had taken good health for granted.

"Stay in bed," Denny ordered indulgently. "Millie'll help with Alan, won't you?"

Millie nodded.

"I don't mind getting my own supper."

"Nonsense," Harriet Morris, who had just walked in, spoke up. "You c'mon over and eat with us. I'll make sure Sarah gets enough to eat too." The newborn, it seemed, had softened her.

Sarah ate and rested, and after two weeks she felt strong, her health restored. The newborn, named Colin Robert after his paternal grandfather, began to gain weight, and she concentrated on harvesting what little there was left of her garden after so much neglect.

"Your garden is beautiful," a woman said to Sarah one day while she picked green beans.

"Thank you, but it's a mess right now. I've just had a baby, and I haven't kept up with it. Look at the weeds!" She thought the woman was married to one of the mine guards.

"Would you sell me anything you've got extra?"

"I don't know that I'll have extra." She held out a large bean, fat and yellowing. "Look at all this overripe stuff. But if I have anything…" She took to selling produce on "Silk Stocking Row," where the better houses reserved for company officials were. They were so enthusiastic about the fresh produce that Sarah planned to increase the size of her garden the following year.

It was pitiful recompense compared to her former earnings from laundry and boarding, and she felt down and worried. She stopped into the company office several times and bothered Mr. Chandler. Once he said, "Only new man we got is a nigger."

"I don't care. I'll take him."

Chandler shook his head. "Sorry, Mrs. Sable, we don't put niggers in with whites. We don't need trouble, and that would cause trouble with your neighbors, even if you don't care."

A boarder showed up on her front porch shortly after Thanksgiving, and after what seemed a meager holiday, Sarah was elated and dared to charge him a bit more than she had Catfish. She told him, "I take cash, not scrip, paid to me, not my husband. And I've got to be paid on time. You'll get your meals, your dinner bucket, your laundry, a room, and I'll have hot water for you to clean up with when you come home in the evenings. You've also got to put up with my sons."

The new man, Floyd Hopewell, laughed and said, "I don't mind young 'uns. And as for your pay, well, my mama used to run a boarding establishment, and I know what that money means to you."

Floyd Hopewell did not play music, but he spent more time with the family. Without being asked he carried coal and water for

Sarah, and he sometimes put Alan on his knee and distracted him while Sarah was getting supper or nursing Colin. He also fixed a broken door and put up some trim, and Denny grumbled about it in private.

"What the hell does he think he's doing coming in here and taking over like that?"

Sarah defended him because Denny never helped her with those things.

"Like hell. The son of a bitch is after you."

"He certainly isn't. I'm married after all."

"That don't mean nothing. If he tries anything, I'll bust him up good."

"He's not going to try anything."

"And if you let him, I'll let you know who's boss here." He brandished an open palm.

Sarah stared at him. "Are you threatening me, Denny?" He didn't answer, and she shook a finger in his face. "You ever even think of touching me and you'll be sorry. And how dare you to think I'd encourage that man!" Tears sprang to her eyes. "I'm your wife! That means something to *me*!"

"Aw, hell, I'm sorry. I's only kidding about that, about you anyway. Not about him though. I don't want him doing nothing else round here."

"Surely you don't mind him carrying water and coal. I need the help and as long as he volunteers, I won't discourage it and you'd better not either."

One Saturday evening when Denny had already wandered up the road with his guitar, Floyd came to Sarah with an apologetic look. "I got plenty of scrip here, but I ain't got no cash, and I sure would like to go out and have me a good time tonight. Suppose I could trade you some of my scrip for some of your cash?"

Sarah could find no words for his audacity. Didn't he know that cash was more valuable than scrip? But he held up a coupon book. "I'd sell it to you at a discount. You give me four of your dollars for this here five dollar book."

"Three fifty," she said.

"You drive a hard bargain, but I'll take it."

"Oh, all right. Three seventy-five, but that's the best I'll ever do."

"I ain't arguing," he said with a smile. "I reckon I cain't do no better."

The next evening he said to her, "They's a couple others might be interested in trading their scrip to you, if you was willing."

Sarah was thoughtful for a moment. "All right," she answered. "As long as they agree to the rate of seventy-five percent. I'm not bargaining. And I don't want my husband involved. Tell them to stop by in the morning after you two have left for work."

Denny had relegated the family's financial affairs to Sarah. He didn't want to fool with it, he said. He didn't want to know how much scrip they had or how much cash, and she had never told him about her savings account in Welch. The arrangement suited Sarah because he was dangerous with his earnings. No matter what he carried in his pocket, cash or scrip, it didn't remain there for long, and afterward, he was either unable or unwilling to account for it. He also had a habit of picking up things at the store which, in Sarah's opinion, they didn't need: new tools, simply because he liked their shine; an extra pair of overalls, so Sarah wouldn't have to wash his others as often; a new lamp, a decorative item to hang on the wall. Such things he bought on credit, infuriating Sarah, because even as she accumulated more scrip, she had to hand it over to the store to keep them free of debt.

Sarah got tired of Floyd bringing papers, pamphlets, and letters to her and Denny and asking, "Can you read this for me?"

One evening instead of answering him she asked, "How would you like to learn to read?"

"I sure wish I knew how."

Denny burst out laughing. "Sarah here used to be a teacher, but lately she's turned businessman. If you wanna read, I bet she'll teach you for a price. Ain't that right, woman?"

Sarah grinned. "That's what I was thinking."

"Well, how much you want?"

"That depends on how often we work at it." Soon they had agreed upon a schedule and a rate of pay—in cash, Sarah insisted, before Floyd could offer to pay with scrip.

Floyd spread the word, and after Christmas Sarah increased her earnings by spending her free moments teaching miners to read. She had turned the front room into a bedroom for Colin and Alan. The middle room served as a living room, where Denny often sat strumming the guitar and drinking moonshine. Sarah tutored at the kitchen table. She discovered that teaching two men at a time worked well because they could not refrain from competing against each other. She instructed three groups of two, and after saturating them with the religious stories, myths, and morality tales that she found in her old readers, and after listening to their wry comments, she looked for more interesting material.

On her trips to other towns along the railroad line in search of bargains, she picked up newspapers and magazines from the train "butcher," a man who peddled candy, toys, food, and reading material up and down the aisles, striking a bargain with him for his old papers. She also collected the informational pamphlets that the company distributed about the war's progress and the miners' obligations to help win the war by digging more coal.

The miners grasped the patriotic spirit of the war. Sarah taught them with her own secret zeal, sure that for all the miners' extra digging, the operators were pocketing profits too large to contemplate in the wake of a growing coal shortage. When full coal cars sat for days in the rail yards, it was evident that they were delaying shipments, holding out for higher prices.

With a heart full of vengeance dedicated to the memory of the people she had known in Clarkson, Sarah taught her willing pupils to read about making the world safe for democracy, and she discussed every aspect of the meaning of democracy with these men. Without mentioning their own situation, she encouraged them to think about what it meant to be an American, to live in a country that guaranteed to every citizen equality, liberty, freedom, and constitutional rights—as opposed to the autocratic rule imposed by their enemy, the Kaiser of Germany. She helped them read the Bill of Rights and saw to their understanding of each section.

For her own part, Sarah read with a silent cheer of the stepped-up efforts of the UMWA to increase its membership in southern West Virginia. The coal companies and the governor attempted to thwart such efforts with the establishment of anti-vagrancy laws which allowed the arrest of strikers, and "Work or Fight" programs that allowed companies to have draft deferments withdrawn for men who were not working, a policy meant to render strikes ineffective.

But she was unable to discuss such matters with Denny, who was content to leave things as they were, who would probably never fight for anything besides his right to have a good time, and gradually she began to feel empty and deserted.

As winter gave way to spring and Sarah began to plan an expanded garden, she looked around more often to find Denny gone. When he seemed to take more care with his appearance and seemed to be more aware of his good looks, she suspected him of cheating. He no longer showed much interest in sex, yet he seemed wilder, more distant, more given to moodiness. At home when he wasn't playing the guitar, he sat for long periods engrossed in the popular books he bought by the armload at the company store or ordered through the mail. He even brought them to the supper table sometimes. His attention absorbed by improbable adventure and romance, he was able to ignore his family at will.

Like a schoolboy he belched and passed gas loudly, teaching Alan to think it was as funny as he did. Instead of taking the time to walk to the outhouse when he had to relieve himself, he stood on the back porch and watered the yard. Sarah protested and he eyed her with contempt, as if he thought his beauty gave him the right to be vulgar.

"Hell, woman, I'm fertilizing that patch of dirt for you. And I'm getting Al out of diapers sooner'n you could." It was true, the boy copied his father. Then Denny might narrow his eyes at her and gradually brighten with a broad grin. At such times she knew they had lost their connection, that she had charge of three boys rather than two.

Denny was uninterested in Sarah's gardening plans. "Don't bother me with woman's work," he complained, picking chords with greater concentration. When she pointed out the presence of an ice wagon in town and suggested they buy an icebox, he said, "Whatever you wanna do is fine with me," and pulled his book closer to his face.

During the summer Denny practiced often with his musical friends with the idea of playing for money in a saloon down the road, and in his absence Floyd Hopewell helped Sarah in the garden. She knew Denny would be furious, but she also knew he would never be home long enough to find out.

"Look here," Denny said, waking her when he came home in the early hours one Sunday morning. He waved a dollar in her face. "You think you're the only one that's making any extra around here."

She smiled at him. "You made that playing tonight?" He beamed and broke out into an old familiar smile. "That's wonderful, Denny! I wish I could come see you."

"Get that old woman next door to watch Al and Colley and come with us next weekend."

But when she said, "I think I'll do that," his face fell noticeably.

He recovered himself quickly and snatched the covers away from her. He raised an eyebrow and made growling noises in his throat. "You look awful good tonight, woman."

He slid in beside her and made love to her for the only time she would remember that summer, and he smelled foreign, with other people's cigar smoke in his silky hair and other people's beer spilled on the clothing he quickly removed.

Harvest was exhausting, but Sarah threw herself into the work. She enumerated her material riches—plenty of food, a new icebox, and a relative fortune in money and scrip, some stashed in the bank and more hidden under a floorboard in the kitchen out of Denny's dangerous reach, not to mention a pig in the woods and chickens in the yard. There were at least two jobs that she did not mind leaving to a couple of older women— midwifery and the peddling of mail-order merchandise through the town and up the hollows. She did find other ways to make additional money—selling her extra eggs and produce at lower prices than the company store, packing lunches for single miners, and tending children from time to time. They were far better off than most other families, but to remain so, Sarah could never let up in her own work.

6

ONE EVENING AS Sarah was clearing dishes from the supper table, Denny reached out and wrapped his large hand around her pelvic bone. "Christ, but you're a scrawny woman!" Sarah heard the disgust in his voice. "Look here, boys. Can you believe I married something this bony? What happened to all them nice curves I married, woman?"

Sarah set the dishes down and ran from the room to hide her tears.

She felt numb a few minutes later when Denny wandered in to find her. "I was only teasing you, Sarah. Christ, not only are you scrawny as hell, you cain't even laugh at a joke."

Seeking relief from sadness, Sarah finally went to church and found much more than she had expected. She settled into her seat with a sleeping Colin on her lap and Alan quiet beside her, ignoring the men who were passing a liquor bottle two rows in front of her, to listen to the preacher's words of solace.

"The war's over, praise God!" he began, "and it's time to take a look around and assess what we got here in Dawson. We got a lot. Today, folks, let's give thanks to the lord that we have among us here in Dawson one who is most favored by Jesus, Mr. Orville Jones. I don't need to tell y'all that along with Mr. Woodrow Wilson, Mr. Jones is the foremost protector of your rights and your freedoms. He's doing everything in his power to keep wicked, ungodly secret organizations outta our beautiful town—"

Secret organizations? In Dawson? Sarah glanced slyly around her to observe the reactions of others who were either sleeping, talking quietly, drinking, or listening. The company preacher droned on, and Sarah could scarcely believe the disingenuous sermon laced with ambiguous warnings.

"Here we want for nothing… We're cared for by Mr. Jones, who has seen Jesus Christ himself… And I was with him the day Jesus come to him… All of us, in God's hands, with Mr. Jones's help… He's personally sworn to Jesus to fight the evil, to run off the devil who tries to sneak in here in the form of illegal organizations…"

By the sermon's end Sarah had forgotten her own sadness and emptiness. Raising up her voice to heaven, she sang the doxology as strength and purpose renewed her and filled her with a religious fervor she had never felt in her life. The congregation bowed its collective head to the preacher's benediction, and she made her own promise—to God and Jesus, she supposed, but mainly to her children.

She raised her head and scanned the sparse congregation. They must believe this pack of lies, otherwise why would they come? They were ordinary people, scorned, she remembered so well, by mine guards. But she wondered—*why such a sermon?* The miners and their families were indeed scorned by the mine guards, but perhaps they were feared as well, otherwise—*why such a sermon?* Walking home, Sarah studied the two Baldwin–Felts detectives on duty and thought of Clarkson again. In that town who had feared the miners the most? Who had ordered Drew Ferrell's murder? Ruel Savage. In Dawson, who might it be? No doubt it was Orville Jones—Jesus's buddy.

She looked again at the mine guards and wondered why they were patrolling Dawson even on Sunday. There must be a union movement in this town, she thought, and then it struck her. With Denny's leave-me-alone attitude, it was no wonder she was in the dark. She suddenly longed to talk to Hank Ferrell and wondered if she could find him. She had run into him the summer she and Denny had courted in Welch, the summer after she had been thrown out of Clarkson.

She and Denny had been strolling together in a grassy public area toward a copse of trees where a creek ran. Denny's guitar was slung backwards over his shoulder, and he carried a bottle of whiskey in a brown bag. A ballgame was in progress nearby, and people were out in force, picnicking and visiting.

She had heard running footsteps behind her, catching up to her, and then the person turned to block her path. Noticeably taller, wiry and almost gaunt, dressed in an oversized shirt and threadbare trousers that were too short and had seen too much patching, Hank smiled uncertainly and said, "Howdy, uh"—then glancing at Denny, added—"Miss Jennings?"

"Hank Ferrell!" she cried softly, and tears brimmed in her eyes. "I thought I'd never see you again." Sarah had introduced Denny, who nodded a greeting to the boy and then continued on to wait for her by the stream. Sarah turned to Hank and said, "I never had the chance to tell you how sorry I was about your father. That was an unspeakable thing they did."

He nodded. "He knowed it could happen. He and Mommy used to talk about how it could happen, but they mostly figured he'd just get fired."

Hank told Sarah his family was making out all right in Welch. He had two part-time jobs, and his mother was doing housecleaning, even, he told her with some pride, working one day a week for a wealthy local railroad man called Fleming. They were all cramped together living at Uncle Slim's. Hank was still planning to finish high school by the time he was sixteen, then he was going to join the miners union.

"Does your mother know this?" Sarah asked. "I'd think she would've had enough of it."

"Course she does. She's the one's got all the contacts."

"She's not *making* you go back in, is she?"

"We're of the same mind, Miss Jennings. My daddy didn't die for nothing. I expect there'll be plenty more like him to get beat up and killed before we get the union. I'm bound to be part of it and I aim to make every minute count."

Sarah voiced her concern. "You're fourteen years old, you've got two jobs and you're studying nights. That's too much for a boy." When he protested, she added, "Well, I wish you'd do something lighthearted or fun occasionally. You're a boy after all."

"You sound like Mommy. Anyhow I do. I play baseball." Then he told her he was glad she hadn't married Paul Lessing, that he had known she wouldn't.

"I'm ashamed now that I considered it," she confessed. "Those people are horrible, aren't they? Every last one of them."

"Well, as a class, they're terrible folks, but that one wasn't really so bad."

"How can you say that, Hank? He tossed you and your family out in the street."

"Couldn't've had a nicer toss though. Mommy tried to make him get mean with her, but he wouldn't. He said he's sorry, he didn't make company rules. Said if it was up to him, we could stay. He went round to the neighbors and asked if he could put our stuff in with them. Then he and the other man helped us pack up our things real careful and moved it for us. One of Mommy's friends here in town says he was deliberately taking the wind outta her sails, that the whole thing was a company trick, but I don't think so."

Sarah tried to use what influence she had to encourage Hank to do something else. "Organizing is dangerous work," she told him needlessly.

"You'd do it, Miss Jennings. I seen how mad you was and how tight your hands was tied. If you was to live in one of them towns, you'd do it yourself."

"I'll never get near a place like that again. I was lucky to get out of Clarkson alive."

Hank studied her. "Is that right? Alive? Something happen?"

She nodded.

"Mommy writes to folks there. They said you quit, just up and run out. They had to close down the school before the term was over 'cause it was too late to get another teacher."

Sarah's meeting with Hank had been more than three years ago. Maybe he was working in a mine somewhere close by now. *He* wouldn't be afraid to talk to her about the organizing efforts in Dawson. Could she find him?

7

ON THE EASTBOUND train to Welch Sarah saw Porter Thomas. It had been almost four years since she had known him as a mine guard in Clarkson, but she recognized him. He was part of a contingent of guards intent upon something, but she could see nothing for them to be occupied with. They simply rode the car, their guns visible, along with several ordinary-looking people also seated in the car. The mine guards were alert, and some of them rose whenever the train stopped in a town.

Sarah didn't like having her children in the same car with a gang of gunmen who appeared ready to use their pieces. Other people boarded and found seats, and their presence made her feel somewhat safer, a feeling she knew was ridiculous.

Then suddenly four or five mine guards rose up together, drawing pistols and aiming rifles, and Sarah shoved her sons to the floor and covered them with her body. When a few seconds had passed with no gunfire, she rose up slowly and peered over the seat.

An unarmed man stood motionless in the aisle watching his would-be assailants. "I gotta use the john. Is that a crime?"

One by one weapons were put aside. "No, it ain't," one of the guards answered. "But we'll escort you." Porter Thomas and two of the others left the car with the man.

Sarah leaped up, jerking Alan by the hand and carrying the baby. As she approached the front of the car, one of the guards blocked her path.

"Where do you think you're going, ma'am?"

"I'm moving to another car. This is no place for children."

The man glanced at her sons and smirked. "I reckon it ain't, at that." He stepped aside.

In Welch Sarah relaxed for a little while with Aunt Sadie. They ate and exchanged bits of news. Sarah feigned interest in large homes owned by prosperous men of industry and asked, "What about a man named Fleming who has something to do with railroads? Where does he live?" Sadie wrinkled her brow. She wasn't sure, but she knew of the general neighborhood.

It was Sarah's only lead. She left her sons with Aunt Sadie and said she was going to visit a friend. As the weather was mild for mid-December, she didn't mind the walk to a street where the houses were of an imposing new style. After asking for directions, she stood on a rambling porch where the wicker furniture had been covered with canvas and shoved against the back walls. A maid answered her knock and peered at her suspiciously.

"Hello. I'm looking for, well, is this where Mr. Fleming, the railroad man, lives?"

"Who wants to know? Who are you?"

"I'm looking for someone who works for him, or used to about three and a half years ago. Is this his house? Who lives here?"

"This is Flemings."

"I'm trying to locate Belinda Ferrell. Does she work here?"

"No."

"Do you know her?"

"Not directly, I don't. Ain't she Slim Osborne's sister?"

"Yes! That's it! Do you know where I could find him?"

"He lives in a little blue shack a good mile and a half outside of town," the maid said and gave Sarah directions.

"Thank you!" Sarah turned down the walk.

"I doubt you'll find the sister," the maid called out. "She and her kids moved away. I think she got married."

"Thank you anyway."

Sarah had difficulty finding the Osborne place on an unmarked road outside of town, and walking over the many ruts and holes was a strenuous task. Once there, however, it was easy to spot the faded blue house with peeling paint. A couple of scrawny dogs guarded the front porch and they rose together and howled at her when she tried to approach the steps.

From inside Sarah heard a man's voice complaining to his dogs and uneven footsteps coming toward the door. "Where's yer manners? Get back under the porch and shut the hell up!" The dogs crept back toward the hole under the porch, reluctant to make a full retreat. "Well, c'mon up." The man leaned on a crutch, the right leg of his pants rolled up and pinned just above where his knee should have been. His face was gray-stubbled and he squinted as though he could barely see. "C'mon up." He beckoned with a wave of his arm.

"Are you Slim Osborne?"

"That's me. Come in, ma'am. I cain't stand out here in the cold."

Sarah hurried up the steps and crossed the porch, taking in a general impression of piles of junk, broken and rusty things—jars, tool handles, old furniture pieces and machinery parts, and the strong odor of dogs.

Slim held the door for her and she entered the dimly lit front room, where furniture and boxes were pushed close together in the cramped space that was stuffy with heat from a small potbellied stove. A tiny brown dog danced around Sarah's legs, trying to sniff at her and leap at the same time.

"Go on, Buffy. Get away now. Have a seat, ma'am. Lemme get rid of the dog." He led Buffy into another room and shut the door. Then he returned, moving almost as rapidly as a man with both legs might.

When he returned, he waved Sarah to a chair. He sank into a rocker next to the stove and leaned forward studying her through his cloudy eyes. "What can I do fer you?"

"Mr. Osborne, I was wondering if, well," she hesitated, almost afraid of the cranky old man, who probably wasn't nearly as old as he looked. She took a deep breath. "Your sister, Belinda Ferrell—"

"She's Harmon now. Been Harmon going on three year."

"Could you tell me where she moved? I want to talk to her."

"You a friend of hers?"

"Well, I… In a way, yes. I know Hank, and it's really him I was trying to find."

"Bel moved to Montgomery. Up to Fayette County."

"Is Hank with her?"

Slim seemed suddenly on his guard. "Who'd you say you was? What's your name?"

"Sarah Sable."

"Ain't never heard of you. What do you want with Hank?"

"I want to talk to him."

Slim was quiet for a moment. "I don't know where he is."

"All right. Well…" Sarah had not expected such a response. "Does he visit you?" Slim didn't answer. "Could I maybe, uh, write down a message for him, and you could give it to him next time you see him. Or send it to him."

The old man shook his head. "Ain't putting nothing on paper. I cain't see it anyhow."

"Could you please tell him something for me? If you were to see him?"

"Sure. I got a good memory. Your name's Sarah Sable. What else?"

"He won't know me by that name. Tell him Sarah Jennings."

"Jennings."

"Tell him… Tell him I've got two children, sons, and I want to do something. Tell him I've been looking for a way to get on his side of the line, but I don't know how. I live in Dawson." She stood up. She wasn't going to spill out her heart to this skeptical man. "Do you know where that is? Dawson? It's owned by Dry Creek Coal."

He shook his head. "He might." Sarah had imagined his suspicions would vanish upon hearing her message.

"Will you remember all that?"

He rose and shoved the crutch into his armpit. "You got kids in Dawson, and you want on the other side. Name's Sarah Jennings, married name's Sable. I'll tell him if'n I see him."

"His side of the line, Mr. Osborne." Tears started behind her eyes but she forced them back. She met his milky eyes and he stared, not really seeing. "We drew a line on the floor once, Hank and I. We were on different sides then, but we aren't anymore."

8

ON THE RETURN trip to Dawson Sarah wrapped herself in the familiar cloak of solitude. She would never hear from Hank. Everything for her was, as usual, wrong. She had no outward scars like people in Hank's family, but she had been violated, and now she felt defeated.

She dozed, a part of her mind still functioning, keeping her aware of Colin's every wiggle in her arms, and Alan's squirming by her side. She took vague mental note of the train's movements—stops, starts, jolts, screeching metal wheels on metal track—and the mumbled conversations of other passengers, aware of Alan's movements as he bounced around in the seat. She heard his gentle voice and felt his soft little hands pat her wrist.

"Mommy? Wake up, Mommy. Open your eyes." His laughter, already a little like Denny's, rang through a dream, and as she slowly came fully awake, his sweet, cajoling voice echoed pleasantly in her head. "Come on, Mommy. Open your eyes..."

She smiled at him. He was patting her bag. "Are you hungry?" she asked, pulling out a sandwich.

She watched him eat for a while, then glanced out the window. Around every bend, it seemed, a coal tipple stood out against a hillside shorn of its trees. Every few miles railroad yards fanned out alongside the track indicating the presence of another center of industry stacked up on itself in a mountain hollow.

Come on, Mommy, open your eyes...

Colin awoke. She nursed him, using her coat as a screen. Out there, mines were booming, towns were thriving. Thousands of men toiled underground to fill cars with coal—coal which miraculously turned into gold and eventually went up in smoke.

Open your eyes, Sarah...

She saw gold riding the railroad lines out of West Virginia, never to return.

Alan put his sticky hand around her face and hugged her. All I've seen are these little babies, she thought. I've only thought to keep my house clean and make extra cash. Maybe things are going on around me. Denny doesn't want to see anything. But if I opened my eyes...

At home that evening she and Denny shared news, and as they talked he drifted to the corner and picked up a mandolin that leaned against the wall beside his guitar.

"Whose is that?" she asked when he sat down to play.

He beamed. "It's mine."

"Yours! Who gave you a mandolin?"

"I bought it."

"Bought it? With what?" She didn't think he had suddenly made so much extra playing music. "Payday's three days away, and even then there isn't extra."

"Well, it ain't paid for yet. We got us an account at the store, remember?"

"Oh, Denny!" Her tone suggested anger or frustration, but she regarded her husband with tenderness. His back, along with thousands of others, brought out the coal that was taken away and turned into gold elsewhere. Somewhere else there were men who could afford to buy a whole orchestra because of Denny's labor.

"Now look here, woman. I'm tired of you telling me how to spend my money. It's my pay. I'm the one goes to work every day. I'm the one that earns it, and I reckon I got a right to spend it."

"You're just earning the right, if you can call it that, to pay triple-high prices at the company store," she said gently. "If you'd waited till Christmas, you could have bought a mandolin in Welch or Bluefield for cash."

"Shut up and leave me alone! The way you talk reminds me of Med Givens and his buddy Pierce, and I don't want to hear no more of it. I'll spend my credit the way I see fit. I wanted the god-damn mandolin now, not next week."

He turned his attention to his instrument, and Sarah stood gaping at him. *Med Givens and his buddy Pierce.* Who were they? People she didn't know, living in Dawson, talking that way. Where did Denny hear them talk?

Sarah changed her way of life. She began to let some things slide around the house, partly because she no longer had the time, but also because it didn't matter to Denny. How many times had she spent hours scrubbing the house only to have him come home and grumble, "Jesus, when are you ever gonna clean up around here?" How often had she taken extra time to make something special for supper, only to have it go unnoticed? The times she had taken such care to pack extra treats in his dinner pail, even to slip in a sentimental love message, were innumerable, and he rarely showed appreciation.

It wasn't because he didn't notice things. On the contrary he was very observant, taking care on a regular basis to point out the stretch marks on her breasts and belly, the calluses on her hands, the plainness of her lackluster straight hair, and her broken nails.

She had always had a bent towards solitude, but now she made herself become more sociable. She stopped longer to talk to other women at the store. She accepted Millie's invitations to go to the movies on Sunday afternoon. Christmas came and went, the weather grew bitter and wet, and Sarah didn't like taking the boys out in it, but she continued to do so, to go with Millie to the movies. There was no real opportunity to socialize, but many people were there. She tried to keep her eyes open and notice everything about everyone.

She imagined more than she saw, and eventually she gave up and faced reality. Every coal miner in Dawson was aware of Denny's let-me-do-my-job-and-play-music attitude. As Denny's wife she would never be invited into the fellowship of a hidden radical movement. Besides, she herself was scorned by some because of her own competitive, get-ahead inclination. Winter settled in and began to numb her spirit.

One Sunday afternoon as she and Millie and the children left the movie house, Sarah glanced up at a miner standing outside. He tipped his cap and smiled—at her, not Millie. Later during the week she saw the same man again standing outside the company store, which also housed the post office, rifling through magazines and letters. As she passed, he looked up casually, nodded, and went back to the perusal of his mail.

Two days later less than five minutes after Denny and Floyd had left for work, there was a knock at the back door. She opened it to find the same man standing there.

"Sarah Sable? They say you buy scrip." He was holding out a booklet and began pushing his way past her into the house when she nodded. Once inside he put a finger to his lips. "You alone?"

She nodded. "My sons—"

"My name's Pierce. I got a message for you," he muttered. His complexion was swarthy and his glasses were bent, giving his face a distorted look. "Friend of mine says he talked to his uncle. Says you're to meet him at Slim's a week from next Saturday, in the afternoon. Says he'll talk to you about his side of the line. That okay?"

Sarah's eyes lit up. She nodded and started to smile. "Oh—"

The man narrowed his eyes. "Hey!" he warned. "If anybody asks, I stopped to sell you some scrip." He pulled two one-dollar bills from his pocket. "See. I got the cash right here." He was out the door and gone as fast as he had come.

PART THREE

1

SNOW WAS FALLING in the gathering gloom as Sarah approached Slim Osborne's little blue shack. Her train had been late, and Aunt Sadie, although willing to watch Sarah's sons, was skeptical about her going out at all, but Sarah lied: she was meeting an old friend who was in town, and it was only three blocks away. The actual trek over nearly two miles was difficult and disheartening, even though she had worn boots in anticipation of the weather. Large flakes, thick in the air, mounted up in inches on the ground, deadening sounds, so that the rattle of chains and low growls from under the porch weren't as loud or menacing as they had been on her first visit.

A man stepped out on the porch, flipped a cigarette over the rail, and spoke sharply to the dogs. "Hey! Enough of that!" The animals scuttled back under the porch, and Sarah stiffened, wondering how many strange, unfriendly people she was going to have to prove herself to this time. The man turned toward her and said, "That you, Miss Jennings?"

She looked closely at the figure silhouetted in the dim light of the porch. "Hank?"

"C'mon in. You must be froze."

She mounted the stairs. Inside she forgot manners and stood staring at him. He grinned and looked away. "What're you looking at?" he muttered.

He was wiry, not much more than average in height, with reddish highlights in his fine sandy hair. He was freshly shaved and wore a shirt with no collar under suspenders. "I think I imagined I was coming to see a fourteen-year-old boy," she said, smiling. It was true; she had not expected this young man.

His sinewy, agile look was almost deceptive; there was the hint of a solid musculature beneath his loose clothing. "Well, quit your looking. Still makes me nervous having a teacher stare at me like that."

"I'm not a teacher anymore."

"I know," he said. He took her coat and waved her to a chair. Slim Osborne dozed in the rocking chair next to the stove. Hank smiled and said, "You've changed too, Miss Jennings."

She lowered her eyes, unaccountably shamed by his words. "Don't call me that." The part of her past that she tried never to think of was all Hank knew about her. Memories of Clarkson flooded her awareness. Must she face it all again, with him standing in judgment?

"All right." He sat across from her. "Mrs. Sable."

"Sarah."

"Sarah." He touched her arm lightly. "You wasn't never on their side. I know that." She glanced at him, at his sincere face. "We ain't never gonna forget that it's on account of you we had a little more time with Daddy before them bastards got him."

"If you only knew how I..." ...*where I was and what I was doing that night.* She could scarcely stand to recall those nights in the Clarkson post office.

He rose and reached for a pack of Camel cigarettes on a table and shook one out. "I don't wanna know. It don't matter anyhow." He lit a cigarette and sat back down. "You didn't always know what you was doing back then." He was silent and she was unable to speak. With her eyes fixed on dusty floorboards, she listened to him smoke.

"I was just your age," she whispered. "You seem so much older than I was then."

"I reckon you've made up for it. You figured out how to build a fire yet?" They both laughed. "You was a good teacher, Miss Jennings—"

"Sarah."

"Sarah. I'll have to get used to that. I had lots of 'em since, but you's good."

"Oh, I—well, you just said I didn't know what I was doing."

"Maybe not in everything, but in the schoolhouse you knowed what you's doing. You's what they call a natural."

"I was good with books. I wanted to go to college, but, well, things have changed."

"You still might get there yet."

"I have something more important on my mind, Hank. I need you to teach me now."

"I can try. Lonnie says you been in Dawson about three, three and a half years."

"Who's Lonnie?"

"Lonnie Pierce. Ain't he the one give you my message? Dark-haired fella in his thirties? Nose bent like it's been busted a few times? Eyeglasses setting on him crooked?" Sarah nodded. "He says you're the type minds your own business, tries to make a little extra money. Says—" He stopped.

"Well? What else does he say?"

Hank dragged on his cigarette and shrugged. "Says your husband's a wild ass. Likes to do lots of celebrating on payday and a few of the days in between."

"Denny does like his good times."

"Denny. That the feller you's with when I seen you that summer in Welch?" She nodded. Hank grinned through a curtain of smoke. "You know how to pick 'em, don't you, Sarah?" He was a man now and yet not much different than he had been four years ago in Clarkson. Of course he was aware of the poor choices she had made.

But she didn't want to talk about Denny. She said, "When we first moved there, I thought it was temporary, but he liked it. Now I can see I'm stuck. I've got two boys, and I've vowed to myself that if they're bound to follow their father, it's going to be better and easier for them. I've been around for several years and I don't understand anything."

"For instance?"

"When I was in Clarkson, things were happening, things the company and the guards didn't like. I was never sure of what, but in Dawson there's nothing like that going on, no one I can connect with. I've made a point of being observant, but I can't see a thing."

Hank smiled slowly. "Looks like that, does it?"

"To me it does, but Denny has mentioned that name, Pierce, and he named another. Med Givens. He doesn't want anything to do with them, and he doesn't want me talking like them." Hank was thoughtful, fingering a cigarette, tamping on the ends, and Sarah noticed his hands, scabbed and rough, fingers slender with nails bitten to the quick. "Hank, I want to be involved whether Denny's interested or not, but I need to better understand. Why isn't West Virginia unionized? My father says every other state has the union."

"Lots of reasons. And it's the southern part of West Virginia that ain't unionized. When the mines was first opening up here about thirty-five years ago, the union's interests wasn't exactly in line with what the people here thought was important." He scratched his head. "Hey, you want coffee or something? I ain't real good at entertaining."

"No, thanks. I'm fine."

"The hell you are. You just come in outta the snow."

"No, really—"

He rose and looked down at her, the hint of a grin at the corner of his mouth. "Well, I'm getting me some. It's already made. I'll bring you some." He turned toward the door.

She jumped up. "Let me help."

He motioned her back to her chair. "You stay there, Miss Jennings. You don't need to see how we men keep a kitchen."

He returned with two steaming mugs of coffee, smelling as though it had been warming in a pot of thick grounds for some time. He handed her a cup, and a look of confusion came over him again. "You want cream or something?" He shook his head, smiling sheepishly. "I mean, well, we ain't got cream. I shouldn't have asked. There's probably some sugar."

"How about water?"

"Water? You want a glass of water?" And off he went to fetch it.

When he returned, she added some to her coffee, aware of his frown. "It's just a bit strong," she explained. Something about him made it easy for her to relax and forget pretenses.

"Oh, sorry. I guess I kinda like it that way."

He sat down, lit another cigarette, and began a lengthy explanation of the UMWA's history in the southern West Virginia coal fields. At the turn of the century, he told her, the labor union had fought for shorter hours and higher wages, but most of the local miners had been satisfied with piece rate, which allowed them more freedom than working a factory job would have. They could come and go as they pleased; if they wanted to call it quits and go hunting after half a day, nobody stopped them. Nobody bothered them if they decided to go on a three-day spree at payday. But such a system enabled them to get in the hole charging things at the overpriced company store, where they were often required to make purchases.

Why were so many satisfied with such an existence? Hank explained it in terms of demographics. Coal companies recruited Negro sharecroppers from down south and poor Europeans and also hired the locals, once farmers or lumbermen. None of these groups had union, or even—in most cases—mining backgrounds. The sharecroppers and Europeans had come from even more deprived circumstances, so at first they thought living in company towns was a fine way to live. The local mountain folk, always independent, had felt fairly free and in control at the outset.

"We were all different folks looking at each other suspicious-like," Hank said, "just earning our own pay, and not feeling like we belonged together or nothing."

But as time passed, the workers began to see that they were in it together. It was no longer an issue of a black man against a white man. Foreigners weren't any better or worse than Americans. They all lived in the same houses, worked side by side taking the same risks and the same abuse from the company. A company deputy might hit a black man a little harder than he hit a white man, but he hit them all—black, white, Polish, Italian, all were cowed by the same guns. Southern West Virginia mines had the highest death and accident rate of all the coal-producing areas. The Workman's Compensation law was a joke—"a joke on the worker," Hank noted. The law exempted companies from lawsuits filed by injured workers who were blamed for accidents. When a group of miners went on strike, the company threw them out of their houses and brought in scabs. The miners had to fight the scabs and the Baldwin–Felts men who broke up strikes and protected scab labor.

"It's hard to organize independent men," Hank said. "You gotta have a group of committed, organized men who'll stick together, who ain't gonna get scairt and back down. It's hard to get them all thinking that they're better together when they got families to feed and with the coal companies doing a smooth job placating them, telling them the union's bad business. We don't come from union heritage, and we ain't got feelings of solidarity." He clenched his fist. "But every day we work together we feel it stronger, that we're a class of working people, that we got rights and that together we can be a powerful force. Take a look at the Kanawha County strike six years ago."

That strike, Hank said, had been a start. They had obtained union recognition. It had given them an identity and shown them how powerful they could be using collective bargaining. A U.S. Senate investigation revealed that the coal companies, the governor, and the military had violated the Constitution on several counts. Since the miners had not been well-represented by the national union, local men had agreed to head up the district office.

The demands themselves indicated that the miners had come to understand modern issues. They had asked for union recognition. They wanted to get rid of the mine guard system and demanded their own checkweighmen. They also asked for cash wages instead of scrip, and to be allowed to trade at stores other than the company store.

"The entire *system* has gotta change," Hank told Sarah, "before higher wages mean a damn. We got a long haul just to educate coal miners. It's gonna be a long fight. The union cain't get in here mainly 'cause of Baldwin–Felts guards which are technically illegal.

"This fight's about more'n what's going on today. It's for the next generation. It's gonna take a lot of daring 'cause the companies'll do everything they can to keep the union out." He looked through her with cold fire burning in his eyes. "And it's gonna take hurting people."

"Hank, you're advocating the kind of violence most people don't want. No matter what kind of hold the company has on them, they'll leave before they'll get involved."

"That ain't true, Miss Jennings—"

"Stop calling me that. I'm not your teacher."

"Sorry. It's hard to break the habit. I always thought of you like that. Anyhow, what you said ain't so. We've just spent a year and a half listening to everyone—the government, the coal companies, and the union—telling folks it's good and right to fight for freedom, to kill for democracy, to die trying to bring the Kaiser to his knees. People who didn't know nothing before know it now. In the coal camps folks know who the oppressor is. A man can only take so much, and having them men strolling round town intimidating folks with their hardware is gonna exact a cost someday. If they got guns, then we're getting them. They got machine guns hid, so we're stockpiling our own arsenal. They kill people for no reason, then you just wait and see if it don't get turned around on them."

"But, Hank, in Clarkson, after your father—" His father! She was suddenly keenly aware of Hank's position.

"Go on," he said, but she remained silent. "You see where I'm coming from now, don't you?" She nodded and he made a fist again. "I know what you's gonna say. You think after Daddy was murdered and we was throwed out, everybody just went back to the way things was before. That they quit trying to organize 'cause nobody wanted to end up like Drew Ferrell. Well, it ain't so. They was quiet for a spell, and scairt, but it didn't take 'em long to get mad again. Plenty of folks there remember Dom Cinelli and my daddy and what they stood for and how they's kilt. And it'll keep happening in other places too. Until *we* throw *them* out."

"I only saw your father one time, but I saw that he was gifted with words," she murmured. "You've got the same gift."

Hank looked down, embarrassed by the compliment. "It ain't no gift, Miss Jennings. I mean Sarah. I just copied him. He was a preacher. Did you know that?"

"Instead of a miner? I thought he was always a miner."

"He preached too. Sometimes a man gets the call, or has the gift, even if he's got another trade. Daddy preached radical, talked about the real Jesus, and the company didn't like it. So he mostly prayed with the others when they went in and after they come out. Then he quit preaching about Jesus and took up talking about the union. That was the next logical step. Jesus woulda been a union man hisself. Everyone liked listening to Daddy. Words just rolled off his tongue. I listened to him for fourteen years. I reckon I'm just a cheap imitation."

"Don't sell yourself short, Hank. You're what, eighteen?"

"Next month."

"Then you're seventeen and quite articulate. He'd be proud of you and you know that."

"That's what Mommy says. Anyways, I try." The fire still burned in his sepia-toned eyes, and Sarah had the feeling that no matter how hard he tried or how successful he was, he would never be satisfied with himself.

"I imagine you're proud to be his son. I would be. Are you a coal miner?" He nodded. "You've done what you said you would then. You work and organize?"

He nodded. "It's slow. But I'm making it slow. I ain't making no mistakes. I ain't getting caught and I ain't getting kilt. We got us a network connecting several towns. That's tough. Communicating between towns. Thugs wanna know a stranger's business in town. They pay attention to who you visit. If they figure you out, they dog you till your hands is tied."

His words called to her mind the scene she had witnessed on the train, Baldwin–Felts guards harassing an innocent-looking man. She described the occurrence to him. "They don't have the right to bother ordinary people on a train, do they?"

"They take plenty of liberties. That man musta been an organizer. If they get wind of one, they'll dog him. One comes from out of state, they'll ride with him clear from Cincinnati—"

"Cincinnati?"

"Cincinnati, Pittsburgh, Washington. Them guys operate in the big cities too. And you question their jurisdiction on a train in McDowell County. Anyhow, they come into the state with the union man. Once they're in West Virginia they won't let him off the train. Or else they'll let him get off, then force him onto one that's leaving the state. I've heard about guys, organizers, that get off a train, and then them thugs beat 'em senseless and throw 'em back onto the train. Who knows where the man is when he wakes up. *If* he wakes up. Something like that was probably happening on your car."

"But that's absurd! Would they shoot at him if he tried to get off the train? In full view of witnesses who could verify that he was shot down in cold blood?" But she remembered Doug Burnside's ugly words. *You bend over him and slip a gun in his hand. Then you stand back and say, that fellow went for his gun and I had no choice but to defend myself.* And she remembered Ruth's words in Clarkson—Drew Ferrell lying in a pool of blood with bullet wounds in his chest and a pistol in his lifeless hand.

2

"WHAT CAN I do, Hank?" Sarah asked. "There must be something I can do."

"All the time we been talking I been thinking about that. Lonnie says you teach folks to read, and you use some interesting materials to get them thinking. That's helpful, but I don't suppose that's what you want. You buy scrip. That's all I know. That's how Lonnie figured to explain why he stopped by to see you. You do anything else?"

"I'm having trouble with scrip."

"Yeah. New court ruling says it's same as cash. That's bull. A lot of store keepers'll only take it for half or less of its face value."

"Some still trade with me. I also have a boarder."

"Lonnie says that boarder ain't one of ours. So if you're with us, that's two you gotta hide it from. Him and your husband. Well, let's keep talking and I'll keep thinking. More coffee?"

"No, thank you." Hank went to the kitchen to refill his cup. When he returned, Sarah indicated Slim who continued to snore softly in the rocking chair. "He's sound asleep with us talking."

"Yeah, poor fella. Stays awake half the night, then sleeps half the day. Claims he cain't sleep. It was awful when we was all living here a few years back. He's got a big heart. He woulda never said no to us, but you could tell we drove him crazy. He don't mind me by myself. When Mommy and the girls moved, I stayed here till I finished school."

"That must have been hard on you."

"It was easy. I made better grades'n most anyone. And I was working too."

"I've no doubt about that, but I meant wasn't it hard on you for your mother to marry somebody else?"

"What makes you say that? We was glad."

"Because, well, what about your father?"

"What about him? Daddy's dead. Cain't buy food with memories of a dead man." He waved his thumb in the direction of his sleeping uncle. "Uncle here, he don't make enough to keep hisself going, much less his sister and four kids."

"He has a job?"

"Ain't much. He goes out in the woods and collects herbs and roots. Sells 'em. You think that ain't hard work with only one leg? He runs a still sometimes, but he never gets much good liquor. One of these days Mommy'll have to take him in. I try to do my share when I got time—keep things fixed round here, buy him a few groceries, give him a little cash. Make sure the family down the road looks in on him."

"How long did your mother wait?"

Hank glared at her. "Now look. Sometimes a woman ain't got a choice."

Sarah shrank from both his look and his words. "I didn't mean anything—"

"Miss Jennings, I gotta figure you're still playing at being poor. Maybe your folks got some money. Maybe you got your own stashed away somewheres. But if you lost all that and your man got hisself kilt, how would you raise your sons? You'd find yourself another man, that's how."

"I could still teach."

"That's so, but Mommy cain't. A lot of women cain't, and maybe a lot of women don't wanna leave their young 'uns with someone else while they work."

"Why can't she teach? All you have to do is pass a test. She must be as smart as you."

"Maybe she is, but not so's she could change her ways of speaking to sound as smart as she is. Anyhow, she ain't graduated high school. Ain't very many's graduated."

"Are you smart enough to change your ways of speaking?"

He whistled softly and smiled. "I'm smart enough not to. Suppose anybody'd take me seriously if I's to talk like some damn coal operator? And don't ask me questions like that, Miss Jennings. Puts me in a mind like I'm a student again."

"I just asked because you mentioned it."

His eyes lit up with pride. "Anyhow, I can if need be. I got me a job, a writing job, and I don't make mistakes. Not on paper."

"A writing job! How so? I thought you were a coal miner."

He laughed. "I am. But I write for the union, you know, stuff for pamphlets and magazines. Not all the time. Just sometimes. It ain't a steady job."

"Do you belong to the union?"

"You still ask a lot of questions, don't you, Miss Jennings?"

"Yes." Sarah was delighted to be in his company again. It seemed that no time at all had elapsed since they had been separated, and yet they both had years of experiences now that had changed them. "Are you a member?"

"Course I am, and I ain't the only one. Now it's my turn to ask you questions. What do you do with all that scrip you buy?"

"I save some of it for slack times, and I buy things with it."

"At the store?"

"Where else?"

He shrugged. "How come you don't tell your husband about your trade in scrip?"

"Because he spends everything we have."

He emitted a brief snort of derision and watched her through a cloud of smoke. Sarah felt fury toward Denny for embarrassing her. "You smoke a lot," she commented to distract Hank.

He chuckled. "And you sound like Mommy. That's one thing Daddy never done, she says, but I cain't help it. Seems like I'm tied up in knots all the time. It helps."

"Cigarettes and strong coffee. Do you drink?"

"Occasionally. Not much."

"It seems you've been running at full speed ever since I've known you. You ought to slow down. Take things easy sometimes."

"You ain't my teacher. Don't give me advice. You wanna know how many ton of coal I can dig on a good day? You wanna know how many companies want me working for them and offered me bonuses 'cause I can play good baseball?"

"No. I want to know if you have a girl."

He glanced around and was silent for several moments, as though unsure of himself. "What do you wanna know that for?"

"You need a girl. A girl might help you take it easy." She was advising him again and about something so personal. Angry with herself, she tried to change the subject. "By the way, not just at the Dawson company store. I go to different towns, different stores. To find the best prices."

He drew on a cigarette and looked around the room lost in thought, his leg bouncing on the ball of his foot. "I had me a girl." He spoke in a near whisper. "Daphne. Still love her yet. That is, seems like I might. We was gonna get married but then decided not to." He grimaced and picked pieces of tobacco off his tongue. "Thugs ever ask you where you're going when you go to them other towns?"

"Maybe once or twice, but they're used to my traveling. Why? Why not get married?"

"'Cause she said I loved this fight more'n I loved her, even though I said it's two different kinds of passion. But then she asked did I wanna bring babies into the world the way it is. And I told her I wanna wait and win the fight first." Hank threw Sarah a sad smile. "A woman's different'n a man. I love her, but I can wait easy. Ten years, if that's how long it takes. A girl cain't wait that long."

"Oh, Hank. She's found somebody else." He nodded. "I'm so sorry."

He waved his hand. "It don't matter. It's her happiness that counts. She wouldn'ta been happy with me anyhow."

"Why not?"

"Some people's got choices, Miss Jennings. I just got big shoes to fill, a legacy I'm bound to." He held up his hands knowing she was about to protest. "And there ain't nothing you or anybody can say about that. Maybe I got choices too, and this here's what I choose to do. Probably ain't a girl anywhere would wanna live with that. Besides, no matter how careful I am, I could wind up like Daddy. If I had young 'uns, they might feel some need to carry on whatever I don't get done. I wouldn't wish that on no son of mine. Nor a daughter neither." Hank stopped and sighed. "Ever go as far as Bear Holler?"

"Where's that?"

"It's Richfield station just into Mingo County. Ever go that far?"

"That's too far. Well, maybe not far, but I just don't go out of McDowell County. I don't know why."

"Suppose you had kin there. You'd go then, wouldn't you?"

"I don't seek out relatives."

"You would if you's close to them, wouldn't you? Maybe combine your outta-town shopping days with visiting."

"That's too much for one day."

"But if you stayed overnight with your kinfolk, you could get up early next morning and go on back, make your stops along the way. Would you ever do that?"

His voice was hypnotic, relaxing and soft-spoken, and Sarah wondered that it came from someone tied in so many knots. "I don't have relatives in Mingo County, so what difference does it make?"

"The hell you don't."

"What do you mean?"

"Hmm. Cain't be a brother. How about a cousin? Somebody you growed up with, somebody you's close to. Just moved to Richfield, name of Ben Stevens." He was speaking with a playful smirk on his face. "Just married a redheaded gal named Corey—"

"Your sister!"

"Yeah."

"Are you serious? She's only, what, fifteen?"

"Fifteen and pregnant."

"Oh, Hank."

"I know. Mommy give her hell. So did I. I give Ben worse hell though."

"How old is he?"

"Twenty-three, twenty-five, something like that."

"No wonder you gave him hell. She's just a little girl."

"Well, I seen 'em married at thirteen. I reckon if she's old enough to lay down with a fella and get with his child, she's old enough to get married."

"But you just said you gave him hell."

"I did, but the damage was already done. Me and Mommy wanted her to graduate. Daddy wanted us all to graduate. I had to let Ben know she's got someone looking out for her."

"You don't think he will?"

"Sure he will. Ben's a good man. Been a friend of the family for a long while. Corey's been running after him long as I can remember. Something happened to her after Daddy was murdered. She's jumpy and scairt even of little things and needs folks around. Anyhow, Ben, he takes good care of her. He's crazy about her."

"Why are you inventing this cousin for me?"

" 'Cause I figure that's what you're gonna do to help out. You buy scrip behind your husband's back, so just about any man can come to you after he goes to work, and them guards don't get suspicious if the man only stays a few minutes. Don't ever keep them longer'n that or they might think you're laying with them—"

"Hank! How dare you—"

"Don't go getting all ruffled up now. I'm telling you the way things is. You got a reputation for hustling extra cash. If them guards think that's what you do, maybe they'll figure you're game for their money too. You're awful pretty. Lot better'n what they're likely to find where they gotta go. If you's to refuse them, they might get to wondering, start watching you. Lonnie knowed you's having some rocky times with your man. I expect the guards know it too."

"I don't like this. Everyone knowing my business. Lonnie probably just knows it because Denny runs his mouth at work. He wouldn't tell the guards."

"He wouldn't? He drinks with them sometimes, don't he?"

"I suppose he does," Sarah said. "Tell me the rest."

"Just act like you done all along. They ain't really selling you scrip, but be prepared to say they was. They give you information that needs passed along. Then you go on one of your shopping trips, go to spend the night at your cousin's at Richfield. You'll probably wanna get to know them here real soon. Bring your kids. Become part of the family."

"Then what do I do with the information? Give it to my cousin Ben?"

"Depends. If I ain't there, you will. Or I might have a message for Lonnie or somebody close to Dawson. An arrangement like this would help. I had to be careful setting up a meeting with Lonnie. Took me a long time."

"Do you work in Richfield?"

"I work at Bear Holler. It's a couple miles round the mountain from Richfield." Hank blew smoke from his nose, snuffed out the butt between his fingers, and rose to stir up the embers in the stove. "You decide, Sarah. You think it's more risk'n you're willing to take, say so. You got young 'uns, after all, and your husband don't want nothing to do with unions. It might complicate things too much for you." He shoveled coal, clanging the shovel against the edge of the bucket with no regard for Slim's nap. The older man stirred slightly.

"Do you worry about informers?"

He closed the stove door and picked up the empty bucket. "Sure do," he answered, heading toward the door. "I'll be right back."

In Hank's absence Sarah became aware of the cramped room for the first time. The walls had no decoration besides faded paint, and two overstuffed chairs of brownish plush seemed ready to belch clouds of dust if touched. Several boxes were crammed into a corner. A crooked bureau that seemed to lurch forward on the uneven floor was littered with two cheaply framed photographs and a jumble of personal items—a clock, a train schedule, a pipe, and a leather pouch. A film of soot covered everything, and the room, much too warm, was strong with the acrid odor of coal and perspiration. It was poorly lit by a smoking kerosene lantern on the bureau and an electric pole lamp standing behind Sarah's chair.

The table next to her was stacked with reading material, which surely did not belong to Slim Osborne, and Sarah was curious enough to investigate. A book was open on top of a handful of newspapers, copies of the *Charleston Gazette*, and she tilted it up to peek at the title—*Sons and Lovers*.

A small volume with a page marked lay closed on the larger one. She opened it at the marker, surprised to find poetry—"The Eve of St. Agnes." She read a few lines, and her breath caught. Here was part of Hank's world, perhaps where he had been before the dogs had alerted him to her approach. Observing the room again, its shabbiness rendered incongruous by Hank's intellect, she couldn't understand his single-mindedness, his drive, in light of the poem's sensuous images.

His footsteps sounded on the porch, and she guiltily slapped the book shut and glanced at Slim who continued to doze. Fleetingly she thought of Hank's fearlessness. Everything about him frightened and excited her. A world like his, so full of meaningful things, was what she had sought in Dawson.

He returned, stomping his feet and slamming the door. Letting go of the bucket an inch above the floor, he commented, "I seen you sticking your nose in my books. You always done that in school."

"You were always reading." She returned his smile. "I guess you still are."

He shrugged. "Bad habit I got."

She observed him standing before her. A more hard-hitting realist she had never known, but she couldn't get the haunting glimpse of St. Agnes's Eve out of her mind. She couldn't remember exactly what the long poem was about, but it didn't matter; it was pure passion. "Keats, Hank? It doesn't fit."

He looked slightly confused. "Sure it does. You don't know me that well." He turned away. "Besides, I'll read anything, you oughta know that. Just so's I can say I read it. Look, Sarah, hit's really coming down out there. How long a walk you got?"

"Almost two miles."

"C'mon and get your coat. It's gonna be dark soon. You best get started."

"What?" She rose but had no wish to leave. Besides, they weren't finished with business. He held her coat out for her and she reluctantly slipped into it. While she fastened buttons and wrapped up in her scarf, he pulled his coat off a hook by the door. He turned and waved a mock salute in Slim's direction, then opened the door for her.

"You ready?" he asked. She pulled on gloves and nodded. "Let's go," he said and followed her out the door. Going down the stairs he took her arm and said, "Careful. It's slick."

"You're coming?"

Her threw her a look full of scorn. "You think I'm some kind of bastard, or what?"

They walked through fresh snow into the hushed, whitish glow of nightfall, making new tracks, grabbing each other's arms when they slipped, and Sarah asked questions.

"How did you get so far in so little time?"

"What d'you mean?"

"You're just eighteen, you're organizing and you've probably got your own working place in the mine, don't you?"

"Yeah."

"You're probably one of those men Denny gets upset about. What is it he says about them? They do more work than anyone else, and he says they lead the shit. I don't know why he says that."

"Lead the sheet, the weigh sheet. Your husband's a smartass."

"Well, do you?"

"Try to."

"How'd you do it so fast?"

"Ain't fast. I been working summers since I's eleven. Only summer I wasn't in the mine was that summer I seen you. That was right after Daddy died and Mommy wanted me home."

"Lots of people do that, but they don't get as far as you."

"Miss Jennings, I am just a coal miner."

"And modest too. When you were a student in my school you always had to do everything right. Remember?"

"After Daddy died, there just wasn't nothing else to do but try harder to do everything right. I just done it for him, 'cause he shouldn't have got hisself kilt."

"I hope you don't blame *him*."

"No. He just underestimated the enemy. He trusted in God too much, or so Mommy always said. What she meant was he overestimated them, didn't give them credit for being the cowards they was. Anyhow, I seen what they can do, and I ain't afraid to fight back using the same weapons they use. Daddy was more kind, ready to give folks the benefit of the doubt. You see where it got him."

When they came to within half a block of Aunt Sadie's house, Sarah stopped.

"This where you're staying?" he asked.

"It's down the street. Listen, Hank, I want to help out, even if there's a risk."

He was lighting a cigarette around cupped hands. Snow was falling so thick she could barely distinguish the swirling flakes from the cigarette smoke. He peered at her in the faded light. "You sure?"

"Yes. But I could be an informer, and you've told me so much. Why do you trust me?"

"Trust, Sarah?" He blew out smoke and sighed. "You and me ain't got nothing else."

"But why would you? I was a company teacher. My husband's against the union."

He looked down at her, considering his answer for a long moment. Then he said, "If I was to tell my associates that you once thought you's engaged to marry a Baldwin–Felts operative, they might say I's crazy to trust you." She winced and he took her arm tenderly, pulling her up close and speaking quietly, passionately. "But you know what I'd tell them?" She shook her head, shame consuming her. His warm breath, perfumed with tobacco, touched her face. "I'd tell them that it's 'cause you walked on the other side that you're so firmly on our side. You seen and heard things we can only guess at. I'd tell them that the day you was told you couldn't teach us about the War for Independence was the day you come over to our side. And I'd say you're as courageous as a man. Ain't many women nor men coulda done what you done—alone and isolated, surrounded by people you knowed wasn't really your friends, and risking yourself by warning me that they's onto Daddy's activities. And taking up for me when that bastard come for his precious company key.

"Something else happened to you in Clarkson, Sarah, something you still ain't told me about yet. Something you got hid in your heart." He held her arm firmly and looked into her eyes through a whirl of smoke and snowflakes. "You wasn't no model company teacher, we all knowed that. You was with *them*, but you loved *us*. That's why I trust you, and my word's good enough for anybody. All I'll ever tell is that a long time ago, before I grew up and you got married, you and me, we made a connection strong enough that it ain't broke after all this time."

3

SARAH BUSIED HERSELF gathering up valise and children to mask the anxiety she felt about establishing contact with her long-lost "kin." The train was pulling into Richfield Station. She spotted Corey Ferrell at once. Standing on the platform in the hopeful sunshine of early spring, she was a young woman now, small and lovely, with thick, shining dark copper hair, cut short, just below her ears. To Sarah, Corey seemed much too young to have such a protruding belly. They exchanged greetings, embraced, and pretended with ease to be family.

When the letter had come from "Cousin Ben," inviting her to visit, Sarah had to explain him to Denny, who was surprised about a previously unmentioned relative. "We were neighbors when I was growing up," Sarah had practiced telling him. "We went to school together and played together. He moved to Tennessee when I was fourteen. I haven't seen him much since, but he's awful close by now." At first Denny had seemed interested in accompanying her on the trip but had begged off at the last minute.

As Corey and Sarah went about household tasks together, they became acquainted with one another as women. Sarah found that Corey, like her brother, was mature and self-possessed beyond her years, but unlike Hank she had a flair for fun and warmed to Alan and Colin.

The house, another design of double house, was of a poorer quality of construction than the ones in Dawson, but Corey had made it homey, even with sparse possessions. The long living room was twice the size of the two rooms opposite it. The one at the back was a kitchen; the other might have been a dining room, but Corey and Ben had put a bed in it. Their main bedroom was the only upstairs room.

Sarah studied a little collection of Corey's family photographs. In one a young Drew and Belinda Ferrell posed with their children in front of a dilapidated board shanty in a bare dirt yard. He held an infant in his arms; she had two little girls by the hand. Sarah concentrated on the oldest, the boy Hank, squinting and frowning intensely under a thick mop of blond hair, in overalls and bare feet. He stood next to his father, his small fist entwined in Drew's trouser leg, and a scrawny black dog sat in the dirt next to him. Sarah studied the parents' faces. Behind their bland half-smiles she thought she detected pride but knew it was something she only imagined, for how could pride exist in these impoverished surroundings? And yet, for all their threadbare looks, something in the picture left her with a feeling of belonging nowhere.

"That one there's me." Corey pointed to the tallest of the girls.

Sarah continued her scrutiny of the picture. Perhaps not pride, she decided, but determination—probably made all the stronger by the surroundings.

Ben came home from work early, Corey said, in honor of Sarah's visit. He washed up in the kitchen, then came to the living room to greet her. "Well, hello, cousin!" he said, embracing her with a chuckle. "Been so long I hardly recognized you." He was a bear of a man, over six feet tall, and Sarah couldn't imagine Hank or anybody giving him hell.

"It's good to see you again, Ben." While she exchanged pleasantries with her "cousin" and watched his friendly overtures toward Alan, Sarah thought these people must know every horrible detail of her life.

At the supper table Ben ate like Sarah imagined a bear might eat, with mute concentration, while Sarah and Corey talked about children and helped Colin with his food and drink. Then Ben poured himself a cup of coffee and sat back down with them.

"Hank tells me you're one tough old lady," he said, stuffing a pipe with tobacco. "First thing he told me about you was how you whupped a boy so hard his pants caught fire."

Corey howled at the remembrance. "I's scairt half to death! I thought you's the meanest, awfullest thing in the world."

Sarah had nearly forgotten her long-ago confrontation with Clyde Poling. "I was probably more scared than any of you."

"Didn't seem like it. I thought you just naturally knowed you's gonna hit him that hard."

"It was all pretense." Sarah shuddered, remembering the only other time in her life she had used a weapon. "And the element of surprise helped."

"Oh, is that it?" Ben's eyes became slits in his jovial, grinning face.

"Well, of course a big man like you probably doesn't see things quite the same way."

"It ain't size makes you mean." He glanced at Corey. "Her brother's the brawler."

"Hank? A fighter?" He had neglected to tell Sarah about this aspect of his life.

"Pisses Mommy off like nothing else," Corey remarked.

"He's beat the tar outta men bigger'n me."

"You got your own licks from him," Corey said slyly.

Ben pointed a finger at his wife. "That there's something you don't need to be talking about outside of the family."

"But Sarah here's your cousin!"

Ben and Corey laughed together, and Sarah forced a smile. They were united in their love of fun, and their closeness made her feel diminished. To end the uncomfortable moment she asked, "Doesn't Hank live around here somewhere?"

"Up Bear Holler. He'll be down later."

"Wanna take the boys to the playground?" Corey asked, rising to carry plates to the sink.

"Sure." Sarah, too, busied herself with dishes.

Ben reached out a brawny arm and caught Corey around her thick waist. "Y'all go on over there now while you still got daylight. I'll wash dishes for you, darling."

"Oh, Ben! We'll do 'em."

"No, you won't. Now get. I want you people outta the house so I can just listen to the peace and quiet for a spell."

"He treats me like a baby sometimes," Corey said as they strolled down the lane to the playground. Alan took off running when he spotted the swings, and Colin trotted behind him.

"He treats you awful nice."

"'Cause he got me knocked up and he feels bad."

"Didn't he treat you good before?" Sarah asked.

"Oh, sure. I wouldn'ta let him get me knocked up if he hadn'ta."

"Has he been your man long?"

"All my life, seems like. Mostly it was just me wanting him to be. 'Specially after Daddy got kilt. I growed up fast as I could just to get Ben to look at me like a woman." She smiled a secret smile. "Didn't take him long."

"Did you mean to get pregnant?"

"Lord, no! But I ain't as worried about it as Mommy and Hank is. And I expect Ben is too. They say hit's gonna ruin my figure and make me grow old too fast and put on me too much responsibility, but I can take any of that stuff long as I got Ben. I know I could lose him anytime, but I got him now, and I'll enjoy every minute I got with him. If he's taken from me, well, then I got his kids, and I'll love them as hard as I love him."

At the playground they made small talk with other women, and the refrains were similar to ones Sarah heard at company stores, on trains, and in her own community.

"My well water's turned rusty. Ain't no good for washing, but I cain't hardly collect enough rain water for that."

"Could be worse. My sister over at Vivian says they got worms in their water. Even in the company officials' places."

"Cain't get no worse than it is up the holler yonder. Their well water's contaminated."

"They say some kids up there got sick after drinking from a pump."

Sarah and Corey found a bench where they watched as Alan amused himself making tentative friends with other children and Colin played in the dirt at their feet.

Sarah asked about the Bear Hollow water and Corey said, "They got wells dug too close to the outhouses. It ain't no good for drinking. Makes you sick. They gotta carry water from springs. I'm glad I don't live up there. All we got to worry about is a little rust."

"Those poor women!" Sarah said softly, thankful for what she had in Dawson.

"Hey, look there." Corey nodded in the direction of the road bordering the playground. She waved, and Sarah saw Hank coming along the path. He returned his sister's greeting and then stopped to talk to two men. "You shoulda seen him when he found out me and Ben was getting married. He busted Ben up bad. I thought my baby was gonna be an orphan and I was gonna be a widow before we's even married. I thought Hank was gonna kill him. And Mommy, she just stood by and allowed it. First time she didn't mind him carrying on. He told Ben if he ever got hisself hurt or kilt, he'd kill him all over again."

4

SARAH WATCHED HANK approach. If she didn't know him, she would never guess he was just eighteen years old. He seemed older than Denny, and in some ways he was. And so different. If Hank were married, he would work all day, organize all evening, bank fires and carry water, take time with his kids, and make love to his woman all night. And he would admire her clean house and all her efforts. Because of his fierce class pride, he would find beauty in the things Denny scorned—her rough, calloused hands, her thin body, and drawn face. Her faded dresses, and her drab, tied-back hair.

He was suddenly standing in front of her and she was embarrassed, wondering if he could read her thoughts. He nodded and sat down beside her. "I's trying to pick out your boy. I know this little one here's yours, but the other one…" His eyes were scanning the group of young children congregated around the swings.

Sarah pointed. "The dark-haired boy in the blue shirt."

"What you been up to, Hank?" Corey asked. He shrugged and shook his head, pulling a pack of cigarettes from his pocket. He was hunched forward, staring straight ahead. He lit his cigarette, took a couple of drags and started picking tobacco from his tongue. "Well, I hear you got a girl," Corey teased.

"I ain't got no girl."

"Priscilla says you do."

He snorted in disgust and glanced at Sarah. "How's Dawson?"

"Okay."

He looked at her more closely. "You don't really know, do you?" She shook her head. He smoked and watched the children. "Good looking boy you got."

"Thank you." Hank's intensity was making Sarah feel tense. She was still unsure of her position in her newfound "family." "I know another name." He turned toward her expectantly and she said, "Mace Elder."

A few days before, the evening air had remained warm with a real hint of spring on the faint breeze, and Sarah had stood on the porch watching Denny stroll down the street. He stopped at Mace and Darlene Elder's house, where a group of men was gathered. About an hour later he returned with Mark Hilling and Jim McCartney. They rounded up instruments, glasses, and the bottle and settled in on the front porch. Sarah went about her evening chores expecting them to strike up Denny's hackneyed rendition of "Alice of Aire" at any moment, but they continued to tune strings and talk.

She caught a remark: "…Med and them guys. They're crazy."

Then another: "Hit ain't smart associating with 'em. I ain't going down there no more."

She continued to listen. "I don't want no trouble neither," Denny said.

"They might have a point though."

"About that new supervisor?"

"It's gonna be tough taking his shit."

"He's just one man."

"Him and the boys with the guns."

Denny reiterated, "I don't give a shit what anyone does. Me, I'm doing my job, keeping outta everyone's way, minding my own business."

"Yeah. The supervisor ain't nothing to lose your job over."

"Or your life."

"Givens and Elder don't know what they're talking about anyhow. The union's same as the company when it gets right down to it. You work for the company, the company tells you what to do. Belong to the union, union tells you what to do. They tell you when to strike and what to strike for. Them union leaders is futher away from us than the company is."

"Yeah, how does some guy from Charleston or Pittsburgh know how things is here?"

"It don't matter," Denny said. "I ain't listening to none of that shit. You guys can take your political talk somewhere else. I wanna play—with or without y'all."

"Speaking of names," Corey was saying, "Priscilla says her name's Natalie Phillips." She crooned in an exaggerated drawl. "Says she's *cr-aazy* for you. Natalie's a widow, Sarah. Priscilla says all she talks about is getting Hank here in bed—"

"Shut up, Sis! That ain't no way to talk round Miss Jennings."

Sarah sighed. "You think I don't know about that kind of thing, Hank? If that's what she wants, maybe you should take her up on it."

Corey hooted with laughter and hugged Sarah in appreciation. Hank went back to staring ahead of him. "I ain't fooling with no widow, and I don't wanna hear no more about it."

"What's wrong with a widow?" Sarah asked.

"I fool with her, next thing you know, she'll be trying to get me to marry her."

Corey sighed. "You're hopeless. You won't court no girls since Daphne took off, you won't let no widow get you in bed, and you're probably too busy to go to one of them places." She rose. "We better get started back to the house."

Sarah dusted Colin off and called for Alan. They left the playground, and Corey returned to her harangue. "Hit's no wonder you're so serious all the time. You're worse off'n a hermit."

"Hell if I am." Hearing the smile in his words, Sarah glanced over and caught his grin. "I got me a married woman." He leered at Corey. "Them's the best kind," he continued with a wink. "Their man's tired of 'em, but they still need loving. Best part is they cain't trap you."

Gripping his arm, Corey walked beside him in sheer admiration. "But if her husband—"

The hint of a twinkle lit up his eye. "I think I could handle him."

They walked on in silence and Corey was thoughtful. "What about that old lady over by Ironweed? Ain't you seeing her no more?"

"She ain't old and it ain't your business."

"She's thirty, almost as old as Mommy." Corey explained to Sarah, "This old lady, she's a union sympathizer. She's got her a run-down farm and lets the boys meet over there sometimes." She turned to her brother. "She sure likes Hank, don't she?"

"Shut up, Sis," he said under his breath.

"Probably taught him everything he knows. And I hear he knows a lot." Hank stopped in the street and glared at Corey. His patience and lightheartedness had vanished, and Corey seemed to shrivel. "Sorry," she said meekly.

Later that night after Sarah put the boys to bed in the spare bedroom and Corey and Ben had gone to bed, Hank sat with Sarah at the kitchen table. She related to him the talk she'd heard about the men's concern over a new supervisor causing problems, about Givens and Elder trying to stir up the men. "Denny won't talk to me about the mine. If I ask, it starts a fight." Sarah also told him of Denny's lack of interest in her "cousin," which led to Hank's observations about husbands in general.

"A thing makes 'em mad and they cain't do nothing about it, so they take it home with 'em. Then things ain't so good." He tapped his finger on the edge of his coffee cup, and his eyes traveled slowly to hers. Meeting him eye to eye was unnerving, like having a bright light shining uninvited into the private hollows of her heart. He didn't say so, but she felt that he read her too well, and his intensity unsettled her. She tried to deflect his mood. Perhaps she could treat him as kin, like Corey did. "Is that how it is with your married woman?"

He laughed softly. "You believe that? I's only kidding her to shut her up." Then he feigned alarm. "But don't you tell her now."

"I won't. But I'm disappointed—"

"And don't you start in on me like she does. I'm content to be as solitary as a hermit. I ain't got much time for romancing anyhow."

"But the widow, Natalie—"

"Why, Miss Jennings, don't you bust up my idealized image of you." He frowned as he spoke, and she couldn't tell whether he meant what he said. "Surely you ain't like my sister and a lot of women who's only interested in one thing and thinks that's all men think about too."

Sarah didn't understand him.

He raised his arm on his elbow and kept his eyes on her. "I tell you, that there's all Corey thinks about." He was pointing casually to the ceiling, and Sarah was suddenly conscious of the whispered squeak of bedsprings overhead.

She lowered her eyes, blushing profusely, and he persisted. "That's why I ain't fooling around." He nodded toward the ceiling. "All that loving's just making more misery. I'm gonna be an uncle ten times over in the next few years, and my sisters are gonna look round 'em and try to remember why they done it."

"Where do you get that idea, Hank? It's not that way with your mother, is it?"

"Not with her, not exactly, although she's got herself a couple more babies by her new husband. But I seen it and seen it..." He talked on about the pitfalls of love and desire. And the consequences. "One day we wake up and find we got us a lot of young 'uns stuck in this same hellhole that we're in."

In just the past couple of weeks Sarah and Denny had somehow revived the passion in their marriage, and she didn't want Hank to make that seem wrong. While reason had caused her to at least verbalize caution, Denny had been heedless in his lovemaking, possessing her repeatedly, holding onto her tightly, and she felt the warm puddles he made inside her with misgiving. Their revived ardor was probably temporary, and more than anything in the world she wanted no more children. "But it's not wrong, Hank," she insisted.

"I know it ain't. You think I ain't wanted? And loved? You think I ain't seen men wanting it every day, and women too? It's just that there's something else, something more. Lot of people ain't got much sense, and sometimes when things ain't going right, first thing they do is use them feelings to try to make everything seem right."

Sarah suddenly felt the isolation and loneliness in Hank's conscious decision not to risk fathering children. She thought of the family picture she had studied earlier that day. Hank was too complicated for her. Everything about him seemed tentative, like a risk taken, like she could easily turn around and find him gone forever.

5

SARAH'S SECOND TRIP to Richfield did not begin auspiciously. The cars swayed and bounced, and waves of fear and nausea roiled over her. She was forced to leave Colin with Alan and go to the tiny lavatory, where the smell of warm urine overpowered her, and she vomited until she thought her guts were turning inside out.

At Corey's house she shivered violently, wrapping arms around herself to calm her shaking. She kept running to the privy until Corey ordered her to bed, helping her to undress and slip into a nightgown. She put Sarah in the spare bed where she and the boys had slept on their first visit and set a pan on the nightstand. "You get some rest, sweetheart. I'll see to your boys." On her way out she added, "I won't shut this all the way. You holler if you need anything."

Sarah fell asleep. Later she awoke and heard Corey and Ben putting her sons to bed on the living room couch. "Your mommy ain't feeling good," Corey crooned. "But we're giving her a good, long rest. She'll be better in the morning. You fellers can help her out by being real quiet and sleeping in here."

Some time after that she heard footsteps in the living room and Corey's whispered admonition. "...ain't feeling good, and you drug her all this a-way just so's you can hear more of the same shit."

"I didn't do no dragging. She come on her own," Hank replied in a low murmur.

"Well, you keep her for about fifteen minutes and then let her go back to sleep." Corey pushed open the door and spoke softly as she approached the bed. "Sarah, you awake, sweetheart?"

"Yes." Sarah sat up and pulled the covers around her.

Corey switched on the lamp and said in a flat drawl, "Surprise! Look who's here to make you feel worse sick." Hank picked up a straight chair and brought it to the bed. "You shouldn'ta come, Sarah," Corey continued. "Not that I don't like having you of course, but traveling just give you a worse flu."

"I've had a lot more rest here than I would have had at home."

"I reckon maybe you have. Can I get you something?"

"Yeah," Hank answered for her. "She wants a glass of water and some crackers."

"You got fifteen minutes, brother!" Corey said sternly as she left the room.

Hank regarded Sarah for a long moment. "I'll wager you ain't got no flu."

She turned her face to the wall. His words felt like a reprimand, even though there had been no hint of reproach in his voice.

"It was never like this before," she whispered. Tears started. She squeezed them back and breathed deeply for a few moments. She had been jittery and sick at her stomach off and on for days, feeling as though she was crumbling and falling apart, and now it came out in tears.

Hank met Corey at the door, took a plate and a glass from her, then shut the door with his foot. Putting down the plate, he tugged at Sarah's arm and said, "C'mon. Drink some water." She took the glass. "Sip it real slow," he said, finding the chair again.

She sipped water and thought her stomach might cooperate. Then she told him what she had come to say. "They've opened a new room in the mine. Lonnie says it's low and narrow and has rich coal but a lot of gas, that is, sometimes there's a gas buildup, then other times it's okay. The company has a new supervisor baiting the men. If they talk back, he calls in guards to rough them up and threaten to fire them. As further punishment they're sent to that section to work the next few days. Three or four men have to go in there every day."

"Strange way to get men to work. What's wrong with the room?"

"They're upset about the gas. Lonnie says they can't control it."

"They're running fans, ain't they?"

"Yes, but it builds up too fast. They have the fans going at one speed, then gas comes in before they realize it, before they can make changes. I don't understand it. They say it's dangerous because they can't regulate the fans or the accumulation of gas."

Hank gnawed voraciously at his nails. "One day they'll be an explosion."

"How can they do this? Even if there was an explosion, couldn't the miners say how this supervisor—"

"Who they gonna tell that to? The operator? The deputized men in the operator's town?"

"What can they do then?"

"Better question would be what should the company do about it. They oughta close it till the engineers can work it out."

"That hasn't happened."

"What do they think they oughta do?"

"Lonnie says he and Med were thinking about a strike, but they're afraid they don't have enough support."

"They had a strike backfire on 'em once before, two, three years ago." Hank was grinding his teeth together. "Couldn't get enough of the men organized. Ended up with guards all over 'em. Looks to me like they got three choices—"

"Hank—"

"They can refuse to go down and maybe get hell knocked out of 'em—"

"Hank, I feel okay now."

"Huh?"

"Smoke. I don't care."

"You sure?"

"I'm sure."

He already had his pack of Camels tipped upside down. "Lemme know if it bothers you," he said. "Now, trouble with letting the guards beat you up is you cain't fight back, and if you do, they might kill you or maybe they'll whup you, then fire you."

"What're the other choices?"

"Go down in the gas and hope you don't get blowed up, or take the supervisor's mouth."

"What would you do?" Their eyes met, and Sarah knew the fourth choice was the only right answer. He didn't speak and Sarah said, "I don't think they'll go for it."

"They've got to. Things ain't the same as they once was. I don't know exact numbers, but I believe they got three-quarters of the miners organized. Tell Lonnie I'm passing it on. He already knows the men could wildcat on this. He and Med oughta be working for that right now."

"Somebody like my husband would never do it."

"If the majority was to strike, they wouldn't let your husband go in. And with the gas and them guards, they don't need no prior go-ahead. The union'll back 'em on this. I wonder... D'you know if they been stockpiling any more guns?"

"Hank! Guns?"

"Yeah, guns. High-power rifles, shotguns. We got 'em here. Used to have some there. We got 'em other places too. Getting more all the time."

"Hank!"

"Don't act surprised, Sarah. This here's a war. We just got outta one war for freedom. Now we're in another. Don't you think that there supervisor bastard deserves a bullet or two? And them guards? They're deliberately sending men to possible death. Just to bring out a few more ton of coal to line the operator's pockets." His eyes blazed. "Your own husband! He could be the next one to lose his temper. And what the hell would you do if they sent him down the day that room decided to blow? That there young 'un you're carrying would be born without ever knowing his daddy, and if that don't make you mad as hell I don't know what would."

Sarah hung her head. "I can't make a strike happen all by myself, Hank. And I'm scared." She couldn't stop her tears this time.

"I know, I know." He picked up her hand and cradled it next to his rough cheek. "I try hard never to lose my sense of unreality."

"What do you mean?" she sniffed.

"That this here, the way we're all living is like a bad dream that shouldn't be happening, I don't care how low-down ignorant a body is. Most folks in America go through life never thinking much one way or the other about guns. They go to work every day, and ain't nobody's threatening 'em with fists and guns."

"Why don't you get out of it, Hank? You don't have to be here like most of the rest of them. You're young, you could do anything."

"And you know I ain't here just to dig coal."

"Well, I've been around it a long time now, and this doesn't make sense. What's Dry Creek Coal up to anyway? That supervisor's not even real. He's a Baldwin–Felts detective, so he's not just a supervisor with a bad temper. He was put there deliberately."

"What do you mean, a Baldwin–Felts detective? Lonnie tell you that?"

"No. Millie told me. Her husband talks to her. She said the man's name is Doug Burnside. I knew him in Clarkson. He was an awful man, hard and vicious, thought violence and bullying were fun. He was one of the men who shot your father—" She stopped, realizing the enormity of her words, clapped her hand over her mouth, and murmured, "Oh, my God."

His eyes watched hers for so long she thought she would wither before he spoke, almost inaudibly. "You mean all this time, all these years, you knowed who shot him?" Sarah nodded. "And you never told me?" She nodded again. "Why didn't you tell me?"

She whispered her answer. "I don't know. I only heard about it. I didn't see it. It was a terrible time for me, Hank. I know that sounds trivial compared to what happened to you." She started to cry again. "It seemed like everyone in Clarkson knew."

He lit a cigarette with the remains of the previous one. "Doug Burnside," he mused. "If he was in Clarkson, I oughta know him too. Describe him." She tried to control her tears. "C'mon, Sarah. This ain't no time for crying. Tell me what he looked like."

"In Clarkson," she sniffed, "he was the biggest one. Fat too. Mean. Receding hairline, if you ever saw him without a hat. He liked working around the portals or anywhere he might get an opportunity to hit someone. He bullied women at the company store. He had a thing with the postmistress, Ida Swindell."

"I know who you mean. At Dom Cinelli's funeral, he was the only one carried a rifle."

"Yes."

"I wonder if I'd still recognize him. He wouldn't know me of course. You seen him?"

"I took the trouble to get a look at him, to be sure it was him. He looks the same."

"Sarah." Hank's teeth were clenched and his jaws were working. "Who're the others?"

She didn't answer. "Now look." He rose and began pacing the room. "Somebody kilt someone you loved, you wouldn't wanna go round for the rest of your life thinking it was just some faceless, nameless mine guards. This way I hate 'em all the same. If I knew who to hate, then maybe the rest of 'em would turn into people again. I used to see 'em as people. Sorta."

Corey stuck her head in the door. "Hank, I'm telling you—"

"Get outta here, Corey!" he exploded. "I'll talk to Sarah all night if I've a mind to."

"But she ain't feeling—"

"She ain't sick. She's expecting. Now get outta here!" Corey closed the door quickly.

"How do you know I'm expecting?"

"Well, you are, ain't you?"

"But how do you know?"

"Just a guess. Now tell me them names."

"I thought your mother knew. Didn't she know?"

"She said they wouldn't tell her. There weren't no friendly witnesses. She didn't have much time before they pitched us out. Now c'mon!" Sarah kept quiet, trying to decide if it might not be better to shield him from such useless knowledge. "Please, Sarah."

"John Harless and Jim Collins. But I didn't see it. I just heard it. Maybe I heard wrong."

"I wonder if I oughta tell Mommy."

"Now you know how I felt before you bullied me into a confession."

"Look, I woulda bullied you to hell and back if you hadn't told me."

"I thought your mother knew. The nurse said Doug Burnside did the shooting and that your mother was shaking her fist at him. What a horrible thing for you, Hank."

"Yeah, Mommy, she got there first." He gazed at the floor. "Somebody come to fetch her. She made me stay home with the girls, but I knowed something weren't right so I made Corey watch 'em. Time I got there, they's a lot of people round. Miners, women, guards, deputies. Seemed like the whole town. Even the sheriff from Welch. He was brung in *before*. Like them guards was after some outlaw. Well, there Daddy lay, in the rain bleeding outta them bullet holes and a gun in his hand, and some men a-telling Mommy about how he tried to shoot 'em."

"What an awful thing for a boy. I'm so sorry..."

"Mommy, bless her, she seen me there and quit hollering at them lying sons a bitches, trying to get me away. But I seen him, Sarah. I seen my daddy laying in black mud with blood running everywhere, rain splashing his face, a kinda surprised look froze on it. Eyes open, mouth open. But there weren't no fear on his face." Hank stood in the middle of the floor holding a cigarette so short it might be burning his fingers. "Mommy tried to keep me from seeing it, but I did, and I ain't never gonna forget it."

6

"Okay, Miss Jennings, you give me them names, now I'll let you have you a good cry." Hank sat down beside Sarah on the bed and pulled her to him. She wept hard for several minutes, thinking of Denny's vulnerability at the whim of Doug Burnside and the frightening possibility of a strike with guns on both sides.

"There now," Hank said. She felt comfort in his strange embrace. His chest was as rock-hard as granite, his wiry arms as solid and unsupple as a branch of oak, and his scent was sweet–sour strong with soap and tobacco. "You're too brave to be scairt," he murmured. "But you are. What're you afraid of?"

"Everything. A strike. Without Denny involved with the men, I feel isolated. If there's going to be trouble, I want to know what's going on. I want to be close to a leader."

"Don't you worry about nothing, Miss Jennings. There won't be no trouble."

"And I'm afraid of having another baby. It was a surprise, and now with this trouble..."

"Maybe they ain't gonna be no trouble." He eased away from her and found her eyes. "Least ways, maybe no strike. Not for a while." He took her handkerchief and wiped her face. "You feel better now?" She nodded and settled back into the pillows. "I wish you's closer to your husband."

"How do you know I'm not?" Her eyes met his but he didn't answer.

He went on. "You'll be all right. Women and children's usually left out of things."

"Usually."

"And if they ain't, then you'll pick up a gun like everyone else and do what you gotta do for your boys. You ever use a gun before?" Sarah kept still for a long while, then closed her eyes. He looked at her more closely. "You ever?"

Was this the time to tell him? She wished he already knew. Ever since she had discovered the presence of Doug Burnside in Dawson, she had been afraid with the same fear she had taken with her from Clarkson, and she was terrified that the man would recognize her. He might then seek her out to purposely bait her or try to hurt Denny.

"Sarah? What is it? You shot someone?" She shook her head. He scooted the chair up close to the bed and tentatively stroked her hand with his finger. "This here's that thing, ain't it? Something that happened in Clarkson?" She nodded vigorously. "Something has to do with that bastard Burnside?" She shook her head. "Who?" It was buried so deeply, she was unable to speak the name. "Not that there fella you was seeing?"

"No. He gave me the gun. Then he left me. Alone. He left town."

"*He* left *you*? I figured it to be the other way round."

"He knew where my sympathies were. He knew I'd learn to hate him. He was right."

"You don't hate him, Sarah. Just what he does."

"No. I hate him."

"Maybe it ain't him you hate. You was awful young." Her tears started again. Hank knew almost every horrible thing about her and could probably guess the rest. "What about the gun?" He stroked her hand again. "You want to tell me?"

"I want to, but—I'm not sure I can say it."

"All right then, lemme guess. Your fella, he left town, but he give you a gun 'cause he thought you needed protection. From his buddies?"

"No."

"Well, don't say it was none of the miners. I'm too class loyal to believe that." She shook her head. "They's plenty of people round. Doctors, accountants, foremen, company store clerks, railroad men. You gonna make me guess through all of 'em?"

"The same one that hit you."

"Savage." Sarah winced at the name. "Damn head man! I feel like killing him already. Maybe I'll have a better idea of how to kill him after you tell me what he done."

"He done lots of things, Hank. To you and to me."

He smiled and lit a cigarette. "Well, I got a coupla guns and some knives. Where do you think I oughta start? Cain't get him less I know what he done."

His banter gave her courage. "That day he came after you for the key, he talked filthy to me, but he was afraid of Paul. He said if I told anyone what he'd said, he'd dock your father's wages."

"And you kept quiet."

"Yes, and later after I had the gun and Paul was gone, he came after me. He—" She stopped, scarcely able to think of what had happened, much less translate thoughts into words.

"He?" Sarah could not find her voice. "He talked dirty to you again?"

"Yes, and—"

"He hurt you. He hit you." Hank was growling.

"He shoved me up against the stove, but he didn't hit me."

"They's ways of hitting that don't use a hand."

"And I bit him."

"You bit him?"

"Yes. Hard. I drew a lot of blood. He—" Sarah covered her face with her hands.

Hank touched her arm. "What part of him you bite?"

"His fingers. The children were outside. He forced his fingers into my mouth and talked awful to me, said he'd rape me when he came back. A few days later he came back after school when I was alone. He picked up the poker and threatened to, well, force me. And I pulled the gun out of my pocket. Shocked him!" Sarah wasn't expecting Hank's reaction either. He was grinning. "I told him he was a pig and a worm and said I'd kill him if he touched me. I told him he could send his goons after me, but they'd have to kill me because I'd die before I'd let him touch me. He left the schoolhouse in a hurry."

Hank laughed, a quiet, heartfelt laugh. "And all he done was run you outta town and blacklist you."

"Hank, it's not funny. I was afraid! I've been afraid ever since. And I've felt awful and filthy and here you are laughing." She thought she should be crying by now but couldn't find her tears. "Why are you laughing?"

" 'Cause you same as castrated the bastard. And here you been keeping it a secret all these years. Why, you oughta be telling that story all over McDowell. Make that son of a bitch a laughing stock. He slapped me, and what'd I do? Nothing. He threatened you and attempted rape, and you bit him and pulled a gun on him."

"But you were just a kid."

"And you wasn't?" Hank chuckled again. "I'd love to tell that story around, 'specially to some of them guards that try to buddy up to us." He added quickly, "Course I wouldn't. But I gotta tell Mommy. And Ben and Corey."

"Oh, all right. Them, but nobody else. Now tell me about the guns."

"What about 'em?"

"How do you get them? How do coal miners stockpile guns?"

"Takes work and planning. Money too. Anyhow they's lots of ways. I've stolen 'em."

"From who?"

"From the thugs who already got the guns. And we order 'em and have 'em sent to commercial towns. I get 'em in Williamson or have 'em sent to Uncle Slim. Lots of guys gets 'em."

"Where do you keep them?"

"Around. Different places. People living back in the hills hides 'em for us. And people in commercial towns. Old mine shafts. Stills. They's plenty of places to hide 'em."

"And you think you'll have to use them?"

"They's already been used some places. In Clarkson. Remember?"

7

BACK AT HOME Sarah looked for a way to talk to Lonnie Pierce, but she was unable even to catch his eye. In any case she didn't know what she would have said to him since Hank seemed unaccountably to have dismissed the possibility of a strike by the Dawson miners, as if the problem with Burnside was of no consequence. Burnside's presence in town still caused her discomfort, along with her nausea, but she felt like a different person since her confession to Hank. The woman she saw in the mirror was thin with dark shadows under her eyes, but now a little spark of pride shone, and she saw that she wasn't actually unattractive after all.

Denny was tense. He drank more in the evenings and played music less often. He opened a book and five minutes later threw it down in frustration. As disturbed by Sarah's pregnancy as she was, he lost his appetite for sex. But Sarah wondered if his mood of despondency didn't come from daily occurrences in the mine that she knew little about.

"How were things at work today?" she asked him sometimes in the evening after supper, after Floyd went to his room.

"Dark."

"Is that all?"

"I spend ten hours in that hole. I ain't spending my free time talking about it."

"We used to talk about leaving this place."

"I don't wanna talk about nothing right now. I just wanna play my guitar and relax."

There had been a time when such a remark might have angered her. Now her heart went out to him, and she tried to let him know. "I love you, Denny. We all love you. We think about you every day when you're working."

"Love you too," he muttered, lowering his head and concentrating on the strings.

A few days later shortly after Denny and Floyd left for work, Sarah was straightening up the kitchen when she heard frantic knocking on the front door. Before she could answer, Millie burst in shoving her children ahead of her, a look of alarm on her face.

"What's wrong?"

"I ain't sure, but something sure is. Come and look." Sarah stepped out on the porch with Millie, who pointed down the road toward the mine entrance. A large crowd of miners was standing outside.

"Why aren't they going in?"

They stood in the garden patch, Sarah stirring up clods of dirt, feeling her stomach turn into a hard knot as they kept an eye on the men near the mine entrance. Mine guards walked around officiously conferring with one another. Eventually most of the men sat down on the ground, while guards fanned out in various directions, rifles menacing. Some stayed to watch the miners, and there seemed to be more guards on hand than usual.

A woman came running up the lane. "They say a supervisor's been kilt," she said. "Name of Burnside. Murdered, they say." Some of the other women gathered around to listen. "They got his body down there showing our men, but I didn't see it. Wouldn't wanna look. They say they're gonna keep them all out there till every man's been accounted for. Some of the guards've gone to check the boarding houses. We might as well expect a search of our houses."

"This ain't right," a woman complained. "Our men's losing pay setting out there."

"Is somebody missing?" Sarah asked.

"They think they can catch the guys that done it easy 'cause the dead man's got chunks of skin and blood under his nails and broken bones in both hands like he musta lit into somebody defending hisself. He's beat up bad too, but he done his own damage before he died, and them guards expect to find men with black eyes and skin all tore up."

"How'd he die?" one of the women asked.

"Knife in the gut. I never seen Burnside, but my man says he's bigger than most."

"Whoever did it ain't gonna stick around here, do you suppose?"

"The guards is taking care of that. They're calling up and down the railroad lines to the other towns. Oh, now what?"

Sarah turned around to see the group of miners rising. Mine guards had guns pointed into their midst.

Another woman came running up the road. "They're gonna let 'em work."

"Smart," Millie said. "It's obvious none of them's been in a fight."

"They're gonna check 'em over good first," the woman continued.

"Men are going in by twos and they gotta strip down in case they're hiding gouges or bruises under their clothes."

The group of women began to break up, some of them still speculating, heading back to their houses.

"Suppose they'll find the guys that done it?"

"Bunch of men get drunk and decide to take on a company man, kill him, then light out. They'll leave a trail."

"Had to've been drunk to pull a thing like that."

"Drunk or crazy."

"Or full of courage and drunk on vengeance," Sarah murmured to herself. "And tougher in a fight than Doug Burnside." She turned away and concentrated on her garden, taking idle note of the kale and spinach sprouts. She was sure that none of the miners was missing and that nobody in Dawson had any telltale gouges.

During the morning she carried out her household chores guardedly. Mrs. Morris eventually yelled, "Here they come! They's checking houses." Mine guards entered the Morris residence first, and Sarah stood in the living room with her children listening to the thump of boots and the crash of objects next door.

"What are they doing, Mommy?" Alan asked.

"Looking for some people they think are hiding. They'll be here in a few minutes."

"But there's nobody here but us."

"They don't know that."

The guards finished at the Morrises' house and started across the porch. Sarah already had the door open. Mrs. Morris stood in her doorway and looked at Sarah. When Alan popped his head around Sarah's skirt, the older woman said, "Let them boys come over here with me."

Sarah scooted her sons out the door and said to Alan, "You and your brother go sit with Mrs. Morris." Taking Colin's hand, Alan scurried past the guards, who walked right in.

"What are you doing?" She felt a lump in her throat and tears stinging her eyes.

"Taking a look around."

One of them went upstairs; the other went directly to the closet in the front room which was the boys' room, and Sarah didn't know which man to watch. She was halfway up the stairs when she heard a loud crash. She looked over the banister to see the items she had stored neatly in the closet tumble out onto the floor and the guard poking around the relatively empty closet with the butt of his rifle. As if a man could hide in there! She stared, speechless for a moment before she found her voice. "You *are* planning to put those things back!"

He turned and looked at her with contempt. She heard thuds and thumps overhead and took the stairs two at a time. In Floyd's room the man had tossed her boarder's belongings—magazines, photographs, cigarettes, tools—all over the floor. Clothing was thrown in a pile in a corner. The man was kneeling, shoving his rifle under the bed.

"Oh!" Sarah stood in the doorway trying to calm her racing heart. "This is unnecessary! Whatever you're looking for—"

"If you don't like it, complain to Mr. Jones," the man said as he rose. When he walked past her, he nearly stepped on her foot and she had to move to avoid him. She watched him methodically tearing apart her own bedroom, trying to ignore the noises she heard in the kitchen downstairs. The man held up a pair of her faded underwear on his fingertip and sneered.

Her thoughts flew to her gun—Paul Lessing's pistol, stashed with cash and scrip under the floorboards in the kitchen, and she raced down the stairs. The other man had made a mess of the kitchen, taking a few swigs from Denny's whiskey bottle, but the important thing, the hiding place under the boards, had gone unnoticed. When the other man came downstairs, they both went out the back door and down the path to the outhouse where they looked around carefully inside and out. Then they moved on to the next house.

Sarah watched them crossing the yard. "You bastards won't find a thing in this town," she whispered with a silent cheer for the man she was certain had bested Doug Burnside. Then she turned to the task of putting her house back in order.

Later she went to the store to pick up the mail and get milk. When Colin stumbled on the sidewalk, she stopped to help him up and retie his shoelaces and heard some men talking.

"What'd you find out, Meeks?" one mine guard shouted to another as they approached each other in the street close to Sarah.

"We might have something. They pulled a guy off a train down past Keystone. Had blood caked all over him…"

The men wandered off together, and she continued to kneel on the sidewalk, a new fear taking hold of her. He'd have to be courageous and able to take Doug Burnside, but for it to work, he would also have to escape. Was he more impulsive than he was smart?

Maybe they ain't gonna be no trouble, he had told her. *Least ways, maybe no strike…*

When Denny and Floyd came home, Sarah said of the search, "They didn't put anything back. Floyd, I didn't want to mess with your things, so I left it for you. I'm sorry."

"That's okay," he answered despondently and went to his room.

"You have got to talk to me," Sarah said to Denny.

"All right." He put his head in his hands and said, "How about getting me some whiskey first." She poured it for him gladly. After he bolted it, he told her, "You know about that supervisor getting kilt, I reckon." She nodded. "They told us they's gonna find the ones that done it. They made us strip, looked us over good. Too good. Kept a close eye out all day. The foreman didn't make a move less he had a coupla guards with him. They've brung in extras."

"Did they put anyone in that room with all the gas?"

"How'd you know about that?"

"I ask, Denny. You don't tell me, so I ask. Did they?"

"No."

"Why not?" He shrugged. "Are they going to send them down tomorrow?"

"I don't know."

"Do you know who killed the supervisor, Denny?"

"Hell, no! Near as I can tell, ain't nobody knows. Them union agitators, they're as surprised about it as me."

8

THREE DAYS LATER nothing had changed. No men were sent into the dangerous tunnel, and no word had come of any arrests. A letter arrived from Corey, and out of habit Sarah examined it closely before opening it. It *had* been opened, and no precautions had been taken to conceal the fact. Sarah was dizzy, nearly reeling with anger at this violation. They had entered her house and poked their rifle barrels into her closets, but this seemed like an attempt to invade her mind. Her hand shook as she unfolded the letter.

Dear Sarah,

Well, I aint feeling too great, being so big. Im tired and the midwife tells me, any day honey, she says! I don't feel like company. So dont come. Ben says after the babys born. He says for me to write you the family news instead. Aint heard much from Mommy except she says sister Annie done real good in school. And so did Libby. Course your more interested in Bens family. Only news we got from them is his pa sold two cows and he just got enough together to fence in his south field. And your cuzin Linda had a accident with one a her kids—little Henry. You remember him—that cute boy in the pictures we looked at thats

*standing with the black doggie and hanging onto his daddys
pants. He fell down the stairs and busted up his face. But hes
doing good cause his moms taking care of him. And Bill finally
got that job hes been hoping for in the mill. Its so much more
money for them that they are planning to buy up a few acres
close to Bens pa. And Ben hes working hard here. Now that
springs come hes starting baseball practice. So is my brother
only he took a week off to visit Mommy. The foreman let him
cause hes about the best miner they got up the holler. Ben says
maybe later bring everyone over to watch a ballgame. After the
baby comes. Well, I'm running out a room so I'll close just don't
want you to come till I feel better, but we love you, Sarah, and if
you ever felt like you just <u>had</u> to, you know you are welcome.*

Love,
Corey and Ben

Sarah read the letter over three times, afraid she had missed
something. She laughed, remembering Ida Swindell's complaints
about people's boring mail. Whoever had read this probably didn't
even get to the end. They certainly couldn't see that Hank had
indeed planned every detail. He might even have composed the
letter himself for Corey to copy and mail.

She threw the letter into the stove and started supper, wondering how he had escaped. That evening just before supper, Denny
came into the kitchen and told Sarah, "I'm taking my guitar down
to Mace Elder's tonight. Wanna come along?"

"Why?"

He shrugged, embarrassed. "I just want you along."

"Are you going to Mace Elder's to play music?"

"No." Denny's black eyes slid sideways, avoiding hers. "To
talk."

Was this, then, the upshot of Burnside's death? "Are you joining up with those men?"

"I'm thinking it over. You know about them guys?"

She rushed to him, ecstatic, and opened her arms to hug him.

"Hey now." He pushed her away. "It ain't nothing to get all worked up about."

"But you're fed up, aren't you?" She relished this precious moment, when they might form their pact together to fight for the union for their sons.

"I might be." He helped himself to a spoonful of beans out of the pot, and Sarah wondered at his capacity to be so noncommittal. "It ain't a good situation."

"What is the situation, Denny?"

"Ain't nothing's changed. Everyone's just looking over their shoulder, including the company men, the guards, and us."

"Oh, Denny, you've got to get involved with those men! Every new person counts. I've always wanted you and me to be in this together."

"You!" he exclaimed. He stared at her. "You ain't got nothing to do with this, you hear!"

"Yes, I do."

"You ain't no coal miner."

"I'm the wife of a coal miner, and I've got two boys, maybe three, that might see those pits someday. I'm also a human being who can't stand to see the way any of us gets treated, you miners on the job, us wives, and the kids in these slave towns."

His eyes popped open and she caught their gleam of hostility. "Woman, you're talking radical, and I don't wanna hear no more of it."

"What do you think you're going to hear tonight at the Elders' house?"

"I don't know, but I don't wanna hear it from you."

9

A PACK OF youngsters congregated outside Mace and Darlene Elder's house, and Alan and Colin joined them to play around the garden and the road. Denny had already gone inside with a man carrying a banjo. Sarah entered the house, eager for the politics but uneasy about the group, people, mostly women, who had often shunned or ignored her. Some women sat in the living room with their men; others sat around the kitchen table with their mending baskets swapping gossip. They eyed Sarah and returned to their business.

Denny sat close to the front door with the banjo player. He kept glancing around as if worried that someone might point an accusing finger at him, even though he worked with these men every day. He and the banjo player were joined by a harmonica, and soon they had worked up an improvisation that set people's toes to tapping while they continued to converse in circles that seemed closed to Sarah.

Darlene Elder, heavyset with rough features, freckles, and a dark shadow on her upper lip, smiled warmly at Sarah. "Nice to have you, Sarah. Make yourself to home." Sarah hesitated halfway between the kitchen and the living room, casting about for likely women to join. When Darlene started making coffee, Sarah volunteered to help, but Darlene waved a hand. "It don't take two to make coffee. Just relax."

There was a cake on the table. The gathering was ostensibly a wedding anniversary celebration in case mine guards showed up. Standing in the doorway between the kitchen and living room, Sarah recognized most everyone but didn't know them all by name. Altogether around twenty-five men were present. Was this the entire group? Harry Owens was there, and Sarah wished for her one real friend, Millie, who had stayed home with a sick child. Lonnie Pierce caught Sarah's eye momentarily, but that was the extent of his acknowledgment of her.

Med Givens rose and said to the musicians, "All right, boys. Pick it up again if we get company." The room grew silent, the only sounds the carefree shouts of children outside. Med sauntered slowly toward Denny, then grasped his hand and clapped him on the shoulder. "Glad to have you with us, Denny Sable!" The others shouted their approval.

Then Med asked, "Anybody heard anything?" Everyone shook his head. "Nobody?"

"I heard they arrested a coupla men at Tomahawk, found their union cards," a man said.

"Aw, that's bull and you know it," another man said. "Ain't no one been arrested or Linhart woulda told us."

"You're right, Al."

"Rumors is flying."

"Some thug told me today they's bringing in a squad of 'em to interrogate us all separately."

"Hard to tell what to believe," Lonnie said. "Fella at the store said the company's holding Tom Felts responsible for the whole mess."

Med rubbed a hand over his short, gray hair. "Cain't figure whether this is good or bad."

"Long as they closed up Room 13, I say it's a good thing," Mace Elder remarked.

"Didn't pain me none to see that fat son of a bitch all stiff and tore-up dead," another man said, and they all mumbled agreement.

The house was suddenly stifling with bodies pressed close and the strong aroma of brewing coffee and acrid whiffs of smoke from the cookstove. Sarah felt momentarily giddy with the idea that she knew more about Burnside and his death than the forefront of union men in Dawson. The man was probably dead because of her. The snubbing from the other women suddenly hurt a little less.

"I'd be willing to bet it were some of their own that done it," Lonnie said. "They didn't like him much neither. Somebody that had a private score to settle with him."

"He's right," one of the men said. "Look at where they found him."

"Where?" Sarah asked without thinking, blushing when they all turned toward her.

"Found him in front of his boarding house, but he'd been drug round from behind. The fight evidently took place there."

"Oh, my God!" Sarah whispered. Her pulse began pounding behind her eyes.

"See," Lonnie said. "Hit don't make no sense. None of us would get him up there so close to all them company employees. But if one of them done it…" He paused for a moment, confused. "Maybe they brung him round front to make it look like we'd done it. Or something. I ain't never come across nothing like this before."

Med hooked his thumbs around his belt. "We can speculate all we want and we won't get no answers. The company's gonna speculate too, but they's gonna do something about it."

"Spies," somebody said.

"You can plan on it. New guys'll show up to work, probably single miners. They'll try to be your buddy right off, trying to find out who kilt the supervisor. The company probably thinks we got a plot and that Burnside was the first. Now we ain't gonna let any new guys in on these here meetings no matter how right they seem. Tell 'em all your troubles, tell 'em about how your kids is sick and your credit's outta sight and your wife ain't giving you any, but don't—"

One of the Elder boys stuck his head in the door and barked, "They's coming!" Then he screeched, "Mama, make Buddy give me my ball! He's took it and run off with it!"

Darlene went to the door to pretend to discipline misbehaving children as Med, like a conductor striking up a band, pointed to the musicians. The banjo and harmonica picked up easily, but Denny floundered with incorrect chords through several measures before he got it right. Mace Elder rose and came to Sarah. "You about ready with that there cake, Miz Sable?"

"Oh," Sarah went into the kitchen where one of the women had begun cutting the cake. The miners in the living room were getting rowdy with whoops and yells and foot stomping. A jug of moonshine had appeared, and some of the men had glasses in their hands. Three men were on their feet clapping their hands and doing an extemporaneous dance together, and a couple of the wives joined in.

The woman continued cutting the cake while Sarah found more plates in the cupboard and listened to an escalating mock argument between Darlene and her sons on the front porch. Sarah picked up two plates of cake and carried them to the men sitting nearest to her. There was a commotion at the door as she brought in two more servings. Two men armed with rifles barged through the front door, with Darlene close behind them.

"…and my husband's fifteenth anniversary and you wasn't invited," she was saying.

One of the intruders smirked as he surveyed the room. "An anniversary party, eh?" He was smoking and he dropped the cigarette, grinding it into the worn carpet with his foot. His eyes settled on Sarah. "That cake for us?"

"No!" Sarah snapped without thinking, jerking her arms back.

"We want a piece, don't we, Herb? Looks mighty good."

"There isn't enough for you." Sarah felt outside herself, out of control, isolated.

She heard Med's even voice. "Go on, Miz Sable. Let 'em have it if they want." Eyeing them with loathing, remembering the intrusion and mess in her house, she stretched out her arms but did not budge from the spot.

"Aw, that's okay," one of the men said. "Probably tastes like shit anyhow." They walked around the room, then glanced into the kitchen before leaving.

At the door the man called Herb turned toward the miners and said, "There's a law on the books. Too many of y'all congregating in one place at a time is—"

"This here's a private residence, sir," one of the miners said.

Herb's gaze swept the room. "Yeah and your little party'll get busted up if we hear the slightest disturbance."

After the guards left, the banjo and harmonica started up again more quietly, and soon Denny was strumming along, a shocked expression on his face. Sarah stood frozen to the spot. Soon she was weaving, barely able to control the nausea rising in her gut. I can't keep being like this, she told herself. If I'm in this fight, I've got to learn to be tough. Someone took the plates from her hands, and Darlene guided her to a chair in the kitchen.

"It won't do to challenge 'em, 'specially not now," Med said in a low voice. He and Lonnie were leaning over her. The room was noisy with several conversations rising above the music and Sarah's head spun.

"You shoulda seen the look on your husband's face," Lonnie said. "I hope this little incident don't scare him off."

"You're an important link for us, Miz Sable. Don't want 'em getting suspicious of you."

"I suppose they will be now," Sarah answered in dismay. "I was here tonight. And Denny's here. I hope Denny's always here from now on."

"Don't know why he brung you, but you keep away from our meetings from now on. Go on the way you been. Only don't go to Richfield for a couple weeks. Maybe write letters—"

"They must already suspect me. Some of my mail has been opened."

"They ain't singling you out," Med said. "They's checking everything right now." He seemed troubled. "It ain't for me to say what goes on between man and wife, but if you ain't told your husband about what you're making them trips for, I wouldn't tell him for a while yet, Miz Sable. He don't look any too sure of hisself tonight."

Sarah could not get her trembling under control. Soon her legs were shaking. Expecting another bout with nausea, she excused herself.

"I've got to go home," she told Darlene. "I'm pregnant and I'm sick."

"Do you need someone to go with you?"

"I think I can make it home."

But Darlene accompanied her and Alan and Colin down the lane. Sarah thanked Darlene, then told the boys it was time for bed. They grumbled but cooperated, and Sarah felt so weak she had to sit in a kitchen chair while she sponged them off. It was dark by the time the boys were under the covers, and she took a lantern with her to the outhouse.

Her head was whirling. Swaying on her feet, she suddenly realized she was bleeding. With a groan she collapsed onto the toilet seat. She was losing the baby! She should be glad, she knew, but tears sprang from her heart.

10

"I reckon I'm gonna be moving on," Floyd Hopewell said with fried eggs dripping from the end of his fork.

"You quitting?" Denny asked.

"Gonna find work somewhere else."

"Oh, Floyd!" He was Sarah's largest source of income. "We hate to see you go."

He smiled at her. "You can find somebody to take my place,

Sarah. I already paid you through next week, but I'm leaving this morning."

"What'sa matter?" Denny asked. "All this shit get to you? Least they closed up that hole fulla gas for now."

Floyd shook his head. "I got a sick ma I'm helping to care for, and I'm hoping to get me a wife someday soon, and when the men get restless like this and start thinking about maybe they don't wanna work, that's when I gotta leave. Don't wanna be involved in no bad business, no strikes fighting scabs and strikebreakers. I just wanna work."

Cleaning Floyd's empty room, Sarah was heartbroken. One of the high points of her life was her bimonthly visit to the bank in Welch where she deposited every penny she could spare. Of course Paul Lessing's original contribution had helped, but over the years Sarah had managed to more than double the amount, and she had kept it a secret from Denny.

As she swept up the last of the dust, she mulled over Floyd's words. *That's when I got to leave. Don't want to be involved in any bad business, no strikes. I just want to work.* That was the kind of talk she had heard from Denny in the past, not long ago in fact. If he hadn't seen reason and become involved with the union men, she might be packing up her family's belongings now. She couldn't be sure he would stick with it though, and now her relatively secure existence seemed threatened.

Two days later a man knocked at her door, removed his cap when she answered it, and set down his battered suitcase.

"Hello, ma'am," he said. "My name is Edward Billings. Mr. Chandler sent me here for a room."

"A room?" She had not told Chandler to send anybody else.

"Yes, ma'am. Didn't you just have a boarder to leave?" She looked at him. *How would he know that?* "And I can pay you good money," he said, putting cash in her hand. Observing the stack of bills in her hand, Sarah stepped aside and showed him in.

216 | *Catherine Cometti Samargo*

She didn't like him and neither did Denny. He seemed different from the other miners, and he intruded in their family life far too much, making them uncomfortable in their usual routines. When Denny played his instruments, Edward sat around and watched him and asked questions. He followed Sarah around in the evenings asking her questions as she carried buckets of water to her garden, but unlike Floyd, he never took a full bucket from her. He seemed to be all around the neighborhood with a smile too bright and a nose too long.

He's a spy, Sarah decided. When she told Denny her suspicions he looked at her in alarm, then told her to mind her own business.

But spies hired by the coal company are my business, Sarah reasoned, and one morning after Denny and Edward had gone to work, she did her own snooping. His room was neat with scant possessions. On the nightstand was a writing tablet, a bottle of ink, an ink pen, two pencils, and a large, new Bible, and she felt that the tablet and writing implements were reason enough to look around.

Her search was thorough. Taking care to cover her tracks, she checked every pocket of every item of his clothing; she looked under the mattress, between the sheets and pillowcases, under pictures in the picture frames she found in his otherwise empty suitcase. She ran her fingers over the top sheet of the note pad, looking for the imprint of freshly written script, and picked at each floorboard and trim board to see if he had loosened any to create a hiding place. She found nothing, and with a mixture of relief and disappointment, she left his room.

At noon she fed the boys and hustled them into their room for a nap, and Alan reached for the book Sarah was reading to them. As he stuck his index finger in and open it at the marked place, she realized what she had missed in Edward's room. She read to her sons while her apprehensive mind worried her into jitters.

As soon as the boys were asleep, she tiptoed to Edward's room. She carried his weighty Bible to the window and began paging through it. She eventually came across a handwritten page and froze as she read the few sloppily scrawled lines:

> *Tom:*
>
> *Got in, am boarding with miner—Sable, & family. Wife a good cook, boozing husband plays guitar. Have made no contacts. These people are too wary, must be union activ. here. Seen it before. Will wait for Jones's men to contact me. Will not risk approaching them. Will wait a few days before posting.*
>
> Op. 32

Tom? Felts, no doubt. Hands shaking, Sarah replaced the Bible carefully. She went to the living room and sat down on the couch, breathing deeply, slowly, fearful of making any moves now because they might be the wrong ones. Eventually she decided on two things.

First she went to the coal company office and waited a half hour until Mr. Chandler could see her. "Mr. Chandler..." She was trembling, visibly shaking and she let it be to her advantage. "I... I didn't ask for another boarder and I..."

"Well, you were so insistent the last time that I just assumed—"

"But I've been ill. I lost a baby." She mopped her face with her handkerchief, playing up how sick she felt. "Floyd was sort of part of the family. He helped..." She shook her head dramatically. "Mr. Chandler, I just can't manage another right now. I'm just, well, I can't tell you about the female trouble I'm having, but I... A boarder other than Floyd... no, I'm sorry." She made herself burst into tears. "I need the money, but..."

"All right, all right, Mrs. Sable." He ushered her from his office, making it plain that he was disgusted with her. "We'll have somebody tell him. Next time I'll know better than to assume anything." As she left, she heard him muttering, "Damn bitch!"

That evening Denny arrived before Edward did, and while he sponged off, she told him the same story she had told Chandler.

"So that's why they called him over to the office." He toweled himself dry, pulled on a clean pair of trousers, and combed his wet hair. "Well, good. I didn't like that son of a bitch anyhow. And I don't want no more boarders in here for a while."

"We need the cash, Denny, but it's too much extra work for me."

He observed her carefully. "You do look tired."

Soon Edward arrived angry and wary. "I don't know what the problem is, ma'am. You don't have that much extra to do and I'm paying you good."

Too good, Sarah thought. She sat at the table. His money was under her fingers and she slid it across the table. "You can have it back." Her eyelids drooped in feigned exhaustion.

He hesitated. "I won't cause no trouble. Just give me a chance."

Denny stepped to Sarah's side and put a hand on her shoulder. "My wife just lost a baby, Ed. Sorry, but this ain't a good time. Besides that, the company never even asked before they sent you. We didn't want nobody else in here, and I reckon when you showed up, she just didn't know how to tell you so."

11

SARAH STOOD ON Corey's doorstep in mid-May, facing a petite woman whose dark hair, knotted in a bun, was heavily streaked with gray. Her pale face was creased with what seemed like lines of worry, but her brown eyes burned with a warm fire, and her smile was welcoming as she stood aside for Sarah.

"God bless! You must be Sarah. C'mon in. Set them parcels down. Let's get them young 'uns something to eat." Sarah followed her, listening to her soothing banter, and noticed two small children asleep together on the couch. "Them two's my youngest. Finally got 'em to sleep. With Corey's baby fussing half the night, didn't none of us get to sleep much except Ben." In the kitchen she turned her attention to the boys. "Let's see. The oldest is Colin, and the other—"

"No. I'm Alan. This here's Colin."

"Oh, sorry," she laughed. "I hear things and get all mixed up. You boys hungry?"

"Yes, ma'am!"

"Are you a neighbor?" Sarah asked.

"Lordy, no. I'm Belinda, Corey's mama. Looks like I've forgot my manners. That's what happens when you become a grandmother."

"I didn't realize… I didn't know you were here or I wouldn't have come. It'll be awfully crowded—"

"For heaven's sake," Belinda waved her arm, "we're glad to have you. You wouldn't be here less Corey had asked you."

"But if I'd known—"

"Shush now and let me fix y'all something to eat. Besides, you know why you're here. If Hank don't find out how things are over your way, he's gonna worry hisself to death."

Sarah nibbled at bread and cheese and drank tea; Belinda sat at the other end of the table fanning herself and sipping cold coffee, while the boys ate leftover soup and buttered bread. The baby whimpered from the upstairs bedroom.

"I can't wait to see him," Sarah said.

"He's a little devil. Gary, they call him. Big baby, big mouth. But I wish Corey woulda waited."

"She seems so happy though."

"Oh, she's happy enough. Long as she's got her man she's happy.

I's probably like that once myself." She fanned herself harder and yawned. "Sorry to hear you lost yourn."

"Thank you."

Belinda lowered her voice and crooned, "The Lord works in strange ways, Sarah. I reckon they's reasons why He takes from us. You'll have you another one. Maybe this just weren't the time."

While her sons played outside with Belinda's and the neighborhood children, Sarah passed the afternoon with Corey and Belinda, talking and helping with the new baby. Both of the women accepted Sarah warmly, as though she were actual family, and she burrowed into their fellowship. The sun had almost disappeared when Hank arrived, and Sarah, who had been sitting on the porch among five children and three other adults, busied herself cleaning up after the children, hesitant to look at him. He leaned on a post in shadow, making small talk with Ben about baseball.

Then he spoke to her across all the people and everyone fell silent. "Sarah, it's awful crowded on this here porch. Wanna go round back?"

She rose and followed him, fearful of catching up with him, afraid of who he was now. But he stopped in the deep shadows and waited, taking her arm. "C'mon," he said. He steered her through the darkness, taking her past the back porch and beyond the outhouse, slipping into the woods and walking on for a short way. "Too many people out on a night like this. Them porches, even back porches, got ears." He wandered around in the gloom until he found a bare patch of ground. "Wanna set here?"

The air was almost chilly under the cover of trees. Sarah pulled her knees up under her skirt and Hank lit a cigarette. In the momentary flare of the match she glimpsed dark scabs over his left cheekbone.

"According to your letter, your husband's joined up?"

"Yes." Sarah, fearing the possible consequences of her confrontation with the guards at the Elder home, had written the letter deliberately, for the benefit of the prying eyes of the company, suggesting that she felt disconnected from both Denny and the people of Dawson, especially Denny's "new friends."

"Sorry about your baby." He groped for her hand and squeezed it. Slow seconds passed and she remained silent. "Talk to me, Sarah. Sometimes I ain't good with words."

Sarah described to him in detail the general state of affairs in Dawson since Burnside's death and included the specifics of the company's vain search, the new men who had come to work, and her experience with mine guards at the Elders' house. "That's when I miscarried. Oh, Hank, I think you're the bravest, most stupid man I've ever known."

"That's what Mommy says. Couldn't help myself though."

"Plenty of men are glad to see him gone," she said. Hank smoked in silence, still clasping her hand, and didn't answer. "Looks like it was a fair fight, whether you intended it to be or not."

"You think I'd knife that bastard in the back? I told him who I was and why I come for him. He bragged about what he done to Daddy."

"How did you get in and out?"

"Coal trains. Jumped 'em outside of town. Went straight away to Mommy's afterward."

"You're crazy, Hank."

"The hell I am. I planned it careful."

"Is that the first time you ever killed a man?"

He took a slow drag on his cigarette. "I didn't kill no *man*." She leaned her head against his shoulder and sighed. He was still himself after all. "It was the first time, Sarah." She heard him spitting pieces of tobacco. "But it didn't make me feel no better like I thought it would. Didn't make me feel bad neither. I just ain't felt nothing yet. And I... I settled with myself a long time ago about killing."

"How?"

"Long as it's war, long as it's a fair fight, long as people's rights is violated, well, it's gonna happen, by me as well as a lot of others. I didn't start that fight with Burnside. I made sure he come after me."

"Lonnie says things are getting tense in places like Logan County and here in Mingo County. He and Med want to concentrate on getting guns. What's going on here?"

"Same as over your way in McDowell. Coal miners are getting educated. The New River field up around Beckley was organized during the war. Why not us next?"

"It's going to be hard," Sarah observed. Then she told him about Edward Billings, "Operative 32," assuring Hank that she had warned Lonnie about the man.

He whistled softly. "Ah, Sarah! You're too damn smart and too damn brave for me to even contemplate. He put an arm around her and hugged her, laughing softly. Then he said, "So Lonnie's getting guns, is he?"

"He says they have another iron in the fire, but he wants to know what you can do."

"Nothing!" Hank sat up straight, his voice cracking with ferocity.

"Don't be angry with me, Hank. I'm just passing the word along."

"Go back and tell him I said I ain't involving you in something like that, and if he was here I'd bust his ass for suggesting it."

"Me? What do I have to do with it?"

"Anything comes from here goes through you. He knows that. He's asking if I'll give you guns to take in there."

"But I will. I'll take them."

"Now let's talk about who's crazy. You got two boys on that there train, and on the way home you gotta make stops at one store at least. How're you gonna do that if you got guns?"

"I don't always have to stop. Or I could shop on the way here. I could put a gun in my traveling bag every time. If I came to visit five times between now and summer's end that's five more guns they've got."

"Good point." He paused, then added, "but I don't like it."

"Why not?"

"Sarah, you're a woman with children. You ain't got no business taking risks like that."

"The risks I take are for my children. Your mother would do it, wouldn't she?"

"Sure, she would, but—"

"Then why can't I?"

"I'd just worry," he muttered and fell silent. After some thought he said, "Tell that bastard Lonnie I'll send what we can spare, but I gotta have cash up front."

"How much?"

"The ones we been getting through mail order runs between ten and twenty dollars. And shells. Tell him fifteen." He rose and pulled her to her feet. "C'mon. It don't look good me keeping you so long in the woods. I reckon we can measure your bag tonight to see if a gun would fit." On the way across the backyard he asked, "Your husband got hisself a union card?"

"Yes."

"Well, I don't care if he's an officer in the local. Don't you tell him about the guns."

12

THE WALK TO her house from the station seemed an interminable trek to Sarah. She had spent an exhausting weekend in Welch helping Aunt Sadie move in with a widowed friend. Denny had refused to participate, saying he had to work, so for three days Sarah had packed Sadie's belongings, cleaned the woman's house, and directed movers carrying out furniture and boxes, all while supervising her sons. The trip home had seemed never-ending;

she was now behind in gardening chores and her sons were bent on misbehavior after an unstructured weekend.

She stepped onto her porch, thankful that she'd at least been able to catch an earlier train home and too tired to care that Alan and Colin were lagging behind with some other kids they'd met in the street. She pushed open the door, took a couple of steps inside, and stood stock-still in what should have been a quiet house. Through the boys' front room, she stared into the living room. A whiskey jug and glasses were on the table, Denny's guitar rested against it, and clothing was scattered over the floor. Laughing in the voluptuous tones Sarah knew well, Denny was naked on the sofa and tangled in a woman's arms and legs, thrusting against her, while she emitted squeals of pleasure. They were unaware of Sarah's entrance.

She backed gingerly toward the door, her suitcase still in hand. She averted her eyes but the sounds followed her, laughter and moans, the rhythmic whisper of two perspiring bodies softly slapping together.

She shut the door quietly and set the suitcase on the porch, an intruder in her own home on this late Sunday morning. Clamping her jaw shut on her feelings, she marched into the street after her children. She yanked both boys by the hand, ignoring their protests. "Come with me. We're going to Millie's."

Millie was glad to keep them, but Colin protested vigorously. "I wanna go home."

Sarah shook an impatient finger in his face. "That's enough out of you, young man. Any more whining and you'll see the back of my hand! Now you mind Millie!"

Back at her house she barged straight in, slamming the door behind her. "Denny! What do you think you're doing!" She was shouting in the vain hope of drowning out sounds, but neighbors were probably listening, and she vividly pictured their smiles of amusement.

Her husband and the girl flew apart, each diving for clothing which they began struggling into. Sarah wasn't sure who she was, someone's daughter, maybe a mine guard's daughter. She was young, nearly a girl, with white skin and soft curves which undulated provocatively with each move she made.

"This ain't what you think!" Denny snarled as he jerked on his trousers. Sarah caught a glimpse of his still-moist penis and the girl's shiny blond hair falling over large breasts that were slick with sweat. But the worst was his anger at Sarah. Somehow she was to blame.

"Go on home. I'll see you later," Denny mumbled to the girl who grinned shyly at him when he touched her waist.

When she was gone out the back door, carrying her shoes and waving with separated fingers, Sarah turned to Denny, who sat down hard on the couch and poured out a shot of whiskey. "What the hell you doing here?" He threw back his head, downing the whiskey.

"No! I want to know what the hell you're doing here."

"Ain't none of your concern." He glared at her. Sarah felt shame in her homeliness in the shadow of the girl who had just left.

"Denny!" She heard the childish whine in her voice. "What do you mean it ain't my concern? I'm your wife."

He sighed. "What'd you have to come in here for?"

"I live here. I finished at Sadie's and got an earlier train."

"Where's Al and Colley?"

"At Millie's. What's going on?"

"Hain't nothing going on!" he shouted, rising to pace around the room.

"It looked like something to me." Sarah's tears spilled over as she recalled the scene, the coupling of two beautiful animals.

"Aw, Sarah," he said with false gentleness, putting his hands on her shoulders. "You know I love you. And that weren't nothing." He tried to pull her to him, but she resisted. "Jesus!" he exclaimed in a whisper. "Look... Uh..." Sarah wandered into the kitchen, but the hurt followed her and grew worse when it came to her that this wasn't the first time, it wasn't an accident, and it certainly wasn't "nothing."

Returning to the living room where she was now aware of the scent of the naked bodies that had lain together, she asked him straight away, "This isn't the first time, is it?"

He was straightening things up, the only time he ever had. "Come here," he said and pulled her by the hand to the couch. He sat down with her, smoothed back her hair, undoubtedly at its mousy-looking worst, and gazed into her eyes, attempting to communicate heartfelt, wounded sincerity. "Sarah, you know I love you. You know that, don't you?"

She didn't know anything, but she imagined she saw love in the intensity of his gaze.

"You mean so much to me, woman. Why, without you, I don't know what I'd do. You take such good care of me and the boys. You work hard. You're smart and you know how to do things other women never even thought of. When I look round this place at all the wives, I know I got the best one, and I'm sure proud of you and what I got. Now, you're all them things, and ain't nobody else could do 'em no better. But you're smart enough to know that ain't one person can be everything to another. That there's a pretty big order, don't you think? One person cain't satisfy all my needs, nor yours, nor anyone's, and sometimes a man's gotta, just, well..."

"What need of yours does she satisfy that I can't? I can do all those things..." Her tears began again. She knew the answer and despised herself for what seemed like begging.

He thought for a moment, scrutinizing her face as he did so. "Well," he grinned and said, "she don't have to help old ladies move and watch young 'uns on Sunday when I feel like getting me some."

His words drove her to fury and she forgot tears and heartache for a moment. "That was your old lady aunt I was helping. Are you telling me that if I didn't have those things to do, you'd have me here on the couch instead of that girl?"

"We used to do that a long time ago, remember?"

"Before we had kids! Are you saying that if I could get someone to watch the boys, you and I would be carrying on like that? Well, I'll ask Millie if she'll watch them next weekend."

"It ain't exactly like that, Sarah."

"Good, because I don't see why it should be up to me to find someone to watch the boys. They're yours too. Tell me, Denny. Tell me what she does to satisfy you that I can't do."

"I already told you I love you, Sarah. You know that and there ain't anyone else I'd wanna be married to. You just don't look like her, that's all."

"You mean you want to do it with someone who looks pretty."

"Yeah."

"Is that all?"

"You don't feel like her neither. Now don't you go crying about it, woman. You're the sweetest woman in the world. You had my children, so course you don't feel the same as her."

Sarah tried to control her weeping. "I just want to know three things and then we don't need to talk about it anymore."

"All right. Three things. What's that?"

She wiped her face on the hem of her dress. "Is this what you do when I go to Richfield?"

It took him a long moment to answer. "Yeah."

"Are you going to keep on doing it?"

His answer was another long time in coming. "Well, I ain't sure. I might but, Sarah, it don't have nothing to do with how I feel about you. Or our life." She couldn't look at him. She knew crying had made her face splotchy and swollen. "What's the third question?" he asked.

Sarah was twenty-two years old, her life empty and ruined, and the lump of pain over her heart was suffocating her. Reason told her that Denny was in the wrong; reason shouted to her that even the likes of Paul Lessing would never have done this to her. She wanted to provoke an argument Denny couldn't win, one that might demonstrate to him how low-down he was.

"According to you, nobody can satisfy all of anyone's needs, so suppose I decided that you couldn't satisfy all my needs. Suppose I needed a man who doesn't smell like a whiskey still or have coal dust under his nails? Maybe I'd like somebody who smiles at the supper table or who takes a little more interest in the boys." She saw his alarm and continued with an exaggerated expression of dreaminess. "Somebody who tells me I'm pretty and likes to have conversations with me." It was working and she decided to strike a full-force blow, the only kind he could understand. "Suppose I'd like a man who feels... well, nicer inside me. I guess what's good for the gander is all right for the goose. Right?"

He was on his feet with fists clenched and eyes blazing. "What the hell are you suggesting, woman?"

"I was just wondering. You didn't ask me first. I thought I'd at least ask you first."

He sat down again and leered in her face. "First? Before what? You better be joking with me, woman." He stuck a finger in her face. "I ain't married to no whore!"

Again Sarah's tears spilled over. "You know I was joking," she croaked.

"Aw, Sarah!" He embraced her, holding her hard against him. "Why, every man in town would like to get his hands on you and that's no lie. But you're my woman, now ain't you?"

He held her. Stifling sobs, she thought of the roll of bills she had already received from Lonnie Pierce, hidden under the floor-boards, and the letter she had already mailed to Corey announcing that she would be visiting in three days. Denny, too, was aware of her plans; he had probably already made arrangements of his own, and it was impossible for her to back out.

13

AT COREY'S HOUSE, away from Denny, Sarah almost forgot her despair. But as the evening wore on and Corey and Ben cooed at little Gary and at each other in happiness and harmony, Sarah thought increasingly of her own house and what might be going on there at that moment, perhaps in her own bed. Despite his feigned remorse, Sarah knew, Denny wouldn't change his plans just because he had been discovered.

When Hank showed up at about nine, a lump formed in her throat and began to choke her, and she couldn't even look at him. How was she to discuss guns? She put Alan and Colin to bed while Hank and Ben argued about baseball and Corey straightened up the kitchen and living room. The baby slept peacefully in Ben's arms.

Eventually Corey and Ben went upstairs. Hank stoked the cookstove to heat coffee, and Sarah sat on the couch staring at her hands. She touched her pocket and felt Lonnie's money. Then she became aware of Hank leaning in the doorway, arms crossed, watching her. "You wanna talk about guns, Sarah?"

She nodded, trying to appear enthusiastic. "Yes. I've got Lonnie's money—"

"Or you wanna tell me what's wrong?"

His soft-spoken voice drew her tears, and then he was beside her gathering her up in his arms. She sobbed against his chest until she was at least temporarily dried up inside, and he produced a handkerchief. "Look what you done now, you got my shirt all soaked."

"I'm sorry." She tried to laugh.

"You wanna tell me?" She told him. From beginning to end, she described the confrontation with Denny, plunging into it with no qualms about modesty or worry over the revelation of intimacies. By the time she finished, she was ready for another good cry, and he held her gently and then hard, muttering from time to time while he stroked her hair, "Ah, Sarah. God love you, Sarah."

When her tears subsided he said, "You think you can hold back them floodgates long enough for me to get some coffee?"

She nodded and covered her face, ashamed for him to see it so puffy and red. She heard him in the kitchen pouring coffee and lighting a cigarette. He returned to the couch.

"You want some?"

She shook her head, watched him sip coffee and smoke and study the opposite wall intently. Then he turned to her. "Want me to kill the son of a bitch?" His seriousness brought a momentary smile to her face. "That wouldn't work, I suppose. He is their daddy." He nodded at the bedroom door. He lit another cigarette before squashing out the first butt. "How about I just knock hell out of him, huh? Turn his nose sideways and get rid of a few of his teeth."

"It wouldn't change anything," she said. *When I look at all the other wives, I see I got the best one,* Denny had told her. What did *best* mean? Most of the other wives had less education, different goals, and perhaps less ingenuity, but most of them had good-enough marriages with husbands they could count on, and if their men were killed, they'd have good memories that would remain with them forever.

"I guess you'd still be married to him and you'd still have to look at him, at what's on the inside." He paused. "Appearance don't really mean nothing."

"It does to a good-looking man like Denny. He hates how I look."

"What? Why, you're the most beautiful woman—"

"Stop it, Hank. You don't have to say that." She felt the tears coming again. "I don't know how I'm going to live with this."

He pulled her to him and laid his cheek against her hair. "I cain't tell you what to do 'cause I don't know neither. But tonight I ain't gonna let you go, Sarah. I cain't stand to see you hurting so. I wish they's some way I could take it and bear it for you, but I cain't, so I aim to hold onto you all night. To hell with guns. We'll talk about guns some other time."

During the night Sarah was awakened by Corey stumbling half-asleep down the stairs toward the kitchen. She stopped beside the couch where the light was still on. "What in the name of God you two doing?" she asked in a thin nighttime voice.

Sarah stirred and found she was half-lying, half-sitting, all tangled up with Hank, who sat up suddenly, wide awake. He rubbed his eyes, looked up at Corey, and said, "What time is it?"

"About two-thirty."

He got up and went outside, and Corey wandered into the kitchen. She returned with a pitcher of water, a wash rag, and some towels. "Babies pick the worst time to make a mess, don't they?" She smiled like a happy girl. "He stinks so bad, hit's a wonder Ben don't wake up." She looked more closely at Sarah. "What's wrong, Sarah? Your face is all puffy like you been…"

Hank came back in and sat down, removing boots and socks. He shrugged out of his shirt, and Sarah glimpsed his own youthful beauty—lean, well-defined muscles beneath his undershirt. "Go back to bed, Corey," he muttered.

Corey turned toward the stairs. "I guess you aim to stay the night."

"I do." He switched off the lamp and pulled Sarah close. Her head against his chest, she listened to his even breathing and his rapid heartbeat as she drifted off again.

In the recesses of her mind, she had already heard Corey clattering in the kitchen, and soon she heard Alan, standing next to the couch protesting. "Mommy! Get up, Mommy. Why'd you get to sleep on the couch?"

Hank spoke quietly to the boy. "Your mommy wasn't feeling well last night so I stayed here with her."

"Me and Colin wanna sleep on the couch."

"You can next time, son."

Sarah kept her eyes closed for one long moment more, trying to soak up as much peace as she could from Hank's embrace. Then she rolled off the couch and hurried to the kitchen to splash her face with cold water.

"You all right?" Corey whispered to her.

"I suppose so."

"It's your husband, ain't it?"

"Yes," Sarah squeaked, afraid she was going to cry again.

"He's either beating you or cheating on you."

"If he hit me I'd shoot him."

"Well, if he's cheating, you can fix him. You oughta really sleep with my brother. Show that stinker of a husband two can play his game."

"Oh, Corey!" Despite her misery Sarah was enamored of Corey's ingenuousness. "Be quiet."

"Don't want me giving him no ideas, huh?" Barefoot and wearing a faded nightgown, Corey was frying eggs and sausage, while throwing sandwiches into Ben's dinner bucket. Biscuits were baking in the oven. "I'm much obliged to you for this here meat. We love your sausage."

"Let me help you." Sarah began to set the table, worrying about Colin in the back of her mind, hoping he hadn't wet the bed. She heard Hank talking to Alan in the living room.

Corey nodded toward the living room. "You think he ain't already had that idea? He's had it plenty. Everybody knows that but you."

"Corey! Stop it!" Sarah hissed. "Find him someone else. I'm married."

Corey stared at her. "So?"

"He needs a single girl."

"I know. He knows. But it don't change how he feels."

Just then Ben came in the back door, his big hands full of wild strawberries. "Anybody like strawberries with eggs, besides me?" He dunked them in a pan of water. "Jeez, Sarah. You look like hell. No offense meant. Hank beat up on you last night?"

"Shut up, honey," Corey said through gritted teeth.

"I better go see about Colin," Sarah mumbled.

In the bedroom Hank and Alan were already seeing to Colin. "We's just going outside," Hank said with a wink as he led both boys out the door.

"You stay here, Mommy," Alan said. "This is men's business."

At breakfast Corey excused herself when she heard the baby crying upstairs.

"You ain't never gonna make Bear Holler by six o'clock," Ben said to Hank.

"Yeah, I'm late already, so I ain't going in. I got things to take care of in Williamson anyway. Might as well do it today. Sarah, you feel like talking about what we was supposed to talk about last night?"

After Ben left for work, Corey distracted Alan and Colin with the lure of storybooks in her bedroom, and Hank removed the rifle from its hiding place beneath the back porch. In the downstairs bedroom Sarah dumped out her suitcase and watched him disassemble the firearm after the removal of two screws.

"This here's a high power rifle, thirty caliber," he said. "Meant for killing bear or deer. Or coal operators and deputies. Took down, the barrel's about twenty-one inches and that's perfect for your twenty-four-inch bag. But it weighs near seven pounds, and that's gonna make quite a difference in what you're used to carrying. When you pick up your suitcase, you gotta make it look as effortless as what you're used to. Think you can do that, Sarah?" He caressed her with his eyes, not allowing her to forget for a moment that he would bear her pain if he could.

"Of course. I carry water every day."

"Don't let them train porters or anyone carry it for you."

"I never do."

"Don't let your boys get into it."

"I won't."

He produced a small package, a paper sack rolled up. "Cartridges," he said. "They's about forty here. Weight's about a pound and a half."

"I'll put them in my shopping bag." She reached for them.

He jerked his arm back. "Sarah, I don't know."

"Why not? They're nothing compared to the rifle."

"You gotta be extra careful with ammunition." He went on to warn her of the dangers of black powder, with which he was intimately familiar, describing the potential for explosions, frightening himself, boring Sarah.

"Just give it to me, Hank," she complained. "The trip takes an hour at the most. Hunters carry bullets around in the woods all day."

Sarah boarded the train at Richfield with a high power rifle packed among the clothing in her traveling bag and with Hank's many admonitions echoing in her mind. He had hugged her and mumbled, "Don't let your husband get you so blue, Sarah. It's him, not you. He don't know nothing about what a good woman is, he don't know what he's talking about, and he don't know how to treat nobody right but his own self. You come back and see me anytime you need me, you hear?"

14

THAT SUMMER OF 1919 Sarah smuggled guns into Dawson. She and Lonnie established a signal—when she had something for him from Richfield, her "Welcome Friends" sign would be hanging crooked on the front porch. On the nights Denny went to meetings with the other union men, one of them would come after dark and pick up whatever she had obtained, be it a rifle, pistols, or rounds of ammunition.

Things with Denny did not improve. "D'you think that's all I do? You think I ain't got feelings for you, woman?" he might say.

Sometimes he managed to stay awake until she came to bed, and then he caught her in his arms, mumbling, "C'mon, woman. Hit's been too long for us."

"I don't want to, Denny."

But he kept after her. "You don't care for me no more? Look, if you and me was together more, maybe I wouldn't think about them other things. I wanna show you I love you…"

And she gave in.

His kisses were wet with too much whiskey; he peered at her with a too-bright smile to make sure her face expressed pleasure; his remarks—"you're beautiful, woman; forgot how nice that is"— were flat and insincere; and sweat dripped from his brow, splashing over her face while he grunted and made strained faces. Afterward he rolled away from her with a sigh that sounded like relief that he had done his duty. Sarah knew other hands touched him better and other lips kissed him better; other bodies were not stretched and misshapen from childbearing.

One morning the biscuits got too brown because Sarah was tending to Colin's fussing. Denny fumed. "Jesus Christ, woman. You cain't keep them boys outta trouble and you cain't cook worth shit. Can you do anything right? What the hell am I supposed to eat!"

She shoved another tray of biscuits into the oven, thinking, *I'm good at carrying guns and information.* She decided immediately to go to Richfield.

At Corey's, Alan begged to sleep on the couch. "People are still up, sweetheart," Sarah said. Until now she had felt like a member of Corey's family. Now she suspected her own judgment, especially when she had arrived without giving notice ahead of time. Corey assured her she didn't mind, and Ben took off on foot to Bear Hollow after supper to find Hank.

Sarah did every conceivable chore for Corey, welcoming the physical exertion. Her heart felt hard with a new kind of frost, and bleakness settled over her like a thick blanket when Ben returned at dusk to say he hadn't been able to locate Hank. There was indeed something wrong with her: what other human being would travel so far, unannounced, assuming these people had nothing better to do than cater to her pathetic whims?

She made the boys sleep in the bedroom, and Alan went to bed pouting. Colin was tired, but he copied his brother and refused to kiss her good night. *Even my own sons...*

Ben was exhausted and went to bed, which reminded Sarah again of the nearly five-mile walk he had taken for her after a hard day's work, and Corey sat up for a while with her. Sarah listened to her talk of motherhood, the physical drudgery of day-to-day tasks, and financial worries, sympathizing and offering advice from her own experience, and secretly wishing Corey's problems were the extent of her own misery.

When they heard footsteps on the back porch, Corey said, "I knowed he'd show up. He probably run all the way down here through them woods." She went to the kitchen and Sarah heard her making over her brother. "You're crazy. Lemme get you something cold to drink."

"Where's Sarah," he breathed. "Sarah!" he shouted. "C'mon in here and talk to me."

Hank sat in a straight chair, panting, gulping the water Corey handed him. His face lit up when Sarah approached, and he stretched out his hand to clasp hers. "Sorry I didn't come sooner. I just now got back to my room, and the boys told me Ben'd been by." He turned to Corey. "I's just in time to hop the freight coming down the hill, Sis, but boy I had a run to catch her."

"You're crazy. Carrying a rifle too. Guards caught you, you'd be in jail right now instead of my kitchen."

"I jumped off just before it come around the bend. I bet I run that path in less'n five minutes. Anyhow, ain't no guards gonna catch me in them woods."

"They mighta caught you hanging off them coal cars. I tell you you're crazy, and I'm going to bed."

After Corey went upstairs, Hank asked, "Why'd you come here without no warning? Something wrong?"

She didn't answer. "Aw, Sarah!" He took her hand and placed her palm against his cheek. "Come here. Sit down. Now tell me."

"There's nothing I can tell you. It's all the same. Horrible. Really, I came because I wanted—" She stopped. *To carry guns.* How silly that sounded. *Because I can't do anything else right.* Her thoughts were too ridiculous to verbalize, but he was watching her expectantly. She looked away, afraid he could read her foolish thoughts, and said the first thing that came to her mind. "I wanted to see you."

"You did?" His voice expressed delight; his ocher-brown eyes danced when she looked at him. She wished he could read her every thought so she wouldn't have to speak.

"You didn't," he realized, dropping her hand and pawing his pocket for cigarettes. He lit up and smoked half the cigarette in brooding silence. "You want me to break a few of your husband's bones." He wasn't asking. "You want me to bust open his skull, maybe. Kick him in the ribs. Castrate the bastard. I'll do it."

Sarah smiled at his earnestness. "If you did that, he'd get some of his friends together to come after you."

"Lonnie said your husband ain't got friends."

"Why, he does. He's always got people he plays music and drinks with."

"They're just people, Sarah. They ain't real friends."

"When did Lonnie tell you that?"

"Last winter. Before you come to see me in Welch."

"What else did he say?"

"He said Denny Sable's the type always has something else to do when someone needs a hand and the first to ask others to give up free time when he needs something." Hank went to the stove and picked up the coffee pot. "There's half a pot here. You want some?" She shook her head and he got a cup for himself. "That ain't what I said, now. That's what Lonnie said."

"But it's true. He's embarrassed me more than once, refusing to help someone."

Hank sat back down. "I expect he ain't the only one. Course I'd like to kill him 'cause he done you wrong. Before, I just thought of him as one of them independent types, like a lot of 'em used to be. Them's the kind that's hardest to organize. They don't trust nobody, not the union, not the company. Figures they're better off minding their own business. And that's what your husband used to say, ain't it?"

"Uh-huh."

"That's why I couldn't figure it when you said he'd decided to join our boys. Just like that, after all that time."

"He was scared. Scared of Room 13, scared of Doug Burnside, scared of the mine guards after you—after Burnside was killed."

"I reckon he had to take the pledge to get them boys to stick by him. Lonnie said he used to steal stuff from the other men at work."

"Oh, Hank! I don't know if I want to hear that."

He eyed her harshly. "Still feeling loyal to your man, are you?"

"What did he steal?"

"Stuff. Tools. Equipment. Wood, explosives. They turn their back, hit's gone." Sarah closed her eyes, hating Denny, hating herself. She felt Hank's rough hand over hers and listened to his grating voice. "See. You ain't the only one he's wronged. Well, I reckon he's quit thieving in the mine. Somebody probably called him on it. That time I talked to Lonnie, he said he hadn't done it in a good while. Now, you want me to break his legs or not?"

"Hank, you couldn't break the legs of a union man and you know it."

He squeezed her hand. "You just don't want me to."

"This is something I have to take care of on my own. You beating him up isn't going to solve anything besides your own hunger for vengeance."

"That's true enough." Something about Hank seemed different tonight. There was an edge to him, although it was muted, a loosening of his usual restraint. After a moment he said, "Say, Sarah, why don't you come over sometime for a ballgame. We got an important one coming up soon. Our toughest competition. We're the top team in our league."

"I don't know. I'll see."

"I'm a good ballplayer. I can hit better'n anyone on the team or anywhere around here."

"I know you can." Sarah thought he might want the approval he had needed as a student. "You're good at everything you do, aren't you?"

"I try to be." He rose and opened the back door, reaching outside for the rifle. "Go get your bag while I take this apart." She remained where she was, watching him separate the stock from the barrel. He glanced at her. "Part of me wants to keep you as far away from this kind of thing as I can, and another part wants you close by. If we got to shooting, it'd be kinda nice, a comfort, if you was along."

"I agree with Corey. You're crazy."

"Well, I do feel a little unhinged right now." He turned his attention back to the gun, muttering to himself. "And I gotta get outta here before I lose the rest of my mind."

Sarah found the suitcase in the bedroom, checked on the boys, and took quick inventory of her feelings. She had impulsively come to Richfield to transport a gun to keep herself from feeling worthless, but the appearance of the rifle was not what had restored her self-respect. She set her bag on the kitchen table and watched Hank arrange the pieces inside. He displayed the screws in his palm, then dropped them into the sack of cartridges. "You keep your boys away from this, you hear?"

"I will."

He took a deep breath and said, "Well, I, uh, hope you can make it for the ballgame."

"I'll try."

He touched her arm lightly, riveting her with his gaze. His fingers closed around her upper arm and he pulled her close. "Remember all them things I told you about riding the train with that rifle." His voice, muffled in her hair, mesmerized her.

"I will."

Then, index finger to her chin, he turned her head up to his and kissed her. And his kiss—gently parting her lips, searching her mouth with a mix of tenderness and aggression, burning her up in his steely embrace—was perfect. He eased away and whispered, "Yeah, I know I'm crazy. I done lost my mind. Good night, Sarah."

He left her, stunned and burning up, and disappeared out the back door.

In a few moments she opened the door and stepped outside, trying to cool down and slow her racing heartbeat. She stared into the darkness, his kiss still on her lips, wondering, *what just happened*?

15

SARAH COULDN'T HAVE said why she did many of the things she did that summer. With each firearm she handled, her resolve grew stronger; with each forced sexual encounter with Denny, the wall around her heart thickened. She tended her garden, her home, and her sons, and she didn't allow her mind to wander to the memory of Hank's kiss, which had surely occurred because he felt sorry for her.

Denny developed secretive routines, and Sarah never knew where he was or when he might return home. Sometimes he took his guitar; sometimes he went without it. Sometimes he came home elated; other times he was half-drunk or despondent. Often he brought home wisps of perfume and the odors of strange bodies that clung to the furniture and lingered in the air until next morning. He snapped at Sarah when she asked where he was going or where he had been. He wouldn't even tell her anymore when the union men met, so she found out from Millie.

When the inevitable confrontations with Denny came, he called her names to fit the subject of disagreement—stupid, nosy, nagging, bitchy. She was alternately a whore and a cold fish, a sloppy housekeeper or too compulsively neat, a neglectful mother or one so excessively concerned with her children that she didn't notice her husband. Regardless of the argument, she was always a terrible cook and a scrawny mouse with too many bones and not enough curves.

"Where the hell do you think you're going?" Denny stormed at her early one Sunday morning as Sarah was making travel preparations.

"To Richfield." This time she hadn't bothered to tell him of her plans.

"I never knew nothing about it."

"Why should I tell you? I hardly ever know where you are or where you're going."

He gazed at her with sorrow in his eyes, and she thought he might be seeing the wreck of their marriage for the first time. "But it don't matter where I go."

"It doesn't matter where I go either."

He reached out for her. "Don't go. Stay here with me."

"But I already said I'd come. Ben's got a baseball game. Everyone goes to ballgames, Denny. Why don't you come with me? You always said you'd go and you never have."

"I know." He was thoughtful.

"Well?"

"You want me to go clear to Richfield to watch baseball?"

"It's not just baseball. It's… family. The train leaves in half an hour. If you're coming, you'd better hurry."

"In a half hour?" She heard the relief in his voice at this ready excuse. "I ain't going. There ain't time." He got up and moved toward the door scowling. "I hate baseball." He walked out and did not return.

On the train the gaiety of others resonated through the hollow spaces inside her. The day was warming up with bright sunshine and the festive moods of travelers who had worked hard all week and now looked forward to the promise of Sunday with eager smiles and pleasant conversation. Sarah tried to catch their spirit, singing softly with Alan and Colin and playing games with them. As the miles between Dawson and Richfield lengthened, Denny and his ill-disguised disdain became increasingly diluted by the atmosphere of cheer and the feeling of exhilaration that was stealing over her.

Corey was flying in ten directions at once when Sarah arrived. "Am I glad to see you!" she said to Sarah. "Ben ain't here and I got so much to do, I's about to give up and stay home."

"Tell me what to do," Sarah said as Corey settled onto the sofa to nurse Gary.

"The whole town's having a picnic after the game, and I gotta pack us some food. I tell you sometimes hit's more trouble than it's worth to have a good time."

"You sound like a tired mama." Denny had nearly vanished from Sarah's thoughts. By now he was somewhere drinking. She wasn't sure anymore where his whiskey came from. Did he steal it? Did he have unlimited access to a still? There was probably no doubt where it came from: the blond girl, she had learned, was indeed the daughter of a mine guard, home for the summer. It didn't quite make sense, but somehow the two facts went together in Sarah's mind.

"It's just I ain't got time to do everything that needs done," Corey was saying. "If I had two or three young 'uns I don't know what I'd do."

"They wouldn't all be that little at the same time." Sarah poked her head into the ice chest. "You want all this in that basket?"

"I think it'll fit, don't you?"

"Corey! Fried chicken! Where'd you get it?"

"Company brought in chickens. We already got us them egg layers out back, so Ben said let's kill what the company give us. Hank says they just done it to take the wind outta talk about the union."

"But he'll eat fried chicken."

"Don't bet on it. He says most of the time they're starving us with low wages or keeping prices artificially high at the store. Now they're giving us chickens and expect us to eat 'em and thank 'em and be good dogs and lie down and shut up about the union. Well, I don't care what he says, I'm eating it. That nice social worker comes round here tells me I need to eat good 'cause I'm nursing Gary here." Sarah saw how thin Corey had become and realized she was more tired than she would admit.

Alan and Colin scampered out the door to play with the children next door, and Corey directed Sarah from the couch. Then they dressed to go. Corey took one look at Sarah's new dress and exclaimed, "God A'mighty, what I wouldn't give for something new! You look so pretty, almost like you ain't a coal miner's wife who's half-starved all the time. Tell me how you managed, Sarah."

"Oh, I... I had some extra put by, and my father sent me a little something. I haven't done anything for myself since I've been married." It wasn't quite the truth. One day, particularly down about Denny's continuing references to her thinness, she had seen the dress at the store and tried it on. Of pale green silk crepe, it was both sporty and festive with a bow beneath the collar and embroidered trim on the cuffs, collar, and bodice. Box pleats in the long-waisted skirt added fullness and gave her figure the suggestion of substance, and it cost too much. She imagined that it brought out the green in her hazel eyes in a bewitching way, so she took money from her cache of scrip under the floorboards to make what she considered a selfish, extravagant purchase. It was the same as taking food out of her children's mouths. To appease her conscience she put together bags of excess produce and peddled them on Silk Stocking Row, a gesture that hardly equaled the dress's expense.

Corey was remembering Sarah as she had been in the Clarkson schoolhouse. "I thought you was the prettiest woman I ever seen. Your clothes was so pretty and your hair was always fixed real nice. Course you still look good, but when you gotta wear the same dresses over 'n' over..."

They gathered up baby, children, blanket, and picnic basket and closed up the house. Corey remarked, "We better set in the top of them bleachers behind some fat mine guards so Hank won't see you. Even in your old clothes, he thinks of you same as when you was our teacher. He sees you in that, he's gonna forget about hitting home runs and lose the game for us."

Sarah gave Corey a wry smile, knowing the likelihood of that. Hoping to attract Denny's notice, she had worn the dress one afternoon, but he had gone about his business without a word.

16

THE AREA AROUND the ball field was crowded with spectators, and mine guards were unarmed. "They just come to watch the game," Corey explained. "See that big rat over there in the tan suit. That's Beckworth. He owns Richfield Coal and Coke, operates both Richfield and Bear Holler, so he wants to see our fellas beat Coal Ridge. Let's take this here basket over to the spring. They're supposed to have ice."

Corey led them to the spring near the meadow that was teeming with people in gay spirits. Children shrieked and scampered about, and women stood in groups chattering and complaining. Several men had already had too much to drink and amused themselves by watching or participating in fistfights that were more a show of bravado than aggression. A breeze, scented with warm earth and creosote from the nearby tracks, rippled over the sparse vegetation, and it was hot, the sun sharp and bright in a cloudless sky. The insouciance of sultry high summer wrapped around Sarah's heart. She thought of Denny, of a marriage that had become a series of broken promises, and then quickly pushed it all from her mind.

Corey jolted her out of her reverie. "C'mon. Let's get us some seats with a good view." They sat in the bleachers between home plate and third base among Corey's friends, and all the children, including Alan and Colin, slid down to the front. Little Gary slept in Corey's arms.

The opposing teams were suited and warming up, eyeing each other, and conferring among themselves. "Them Coal Ridge fellers and their families is coming to our picnic."

Sarah was eager to get into the spirit of this ballgame. "They don't look much like picnicking with each other right now."

"Oh, they're just having fun."

The spectators assumed a more orderly disorder once the game got under way. Coal Ridge batted first, and Sarah scanned the field for Ben and Hank. She found Ben easily at third base and spotted Hank just as Corey said, "There's Hank over in right field."

The first batter stepped to the plate, and Corey and several others began to shout and jeer. The pitcher threw one strike, which inflamed the crowd. The Coal Ridge hitter swung hard at the second pitch, sending the ball sailing over the shortstop's head. Center and left fielders galloped for it, and the left fielder caught it on a leap. Corey squealed so loud and bounced so hard that Gary whimpered.

"Want me to hold him for a while?" Corey hardly noticed her baby was gone as Sarah eased the infant out of her arms.

The next two batters were taken out the same way, by a catch first by Ben at third base, and then by the center fielder.

Then it was Richfield's turn at bat, and Corey and the rest of them began to yell before the first batter had finished warming up. The man promptly struck out, and Corey cheered wildly when the second batter stepped up to the plate. It was Ben. He hit two pop-up fly balls before striking out. Corey howled and clapped her hands, and Gary continued to sleep in Sarah's arms through all the fuss. The next batter swung for two strikes then managed a ground ball, base hit.

"Now we're gonna get us a couple of runs," Corey announced and motioned to the field. "You watch Hank hit it outta the field."

The outfielders spread out to cover the back field, and Sarah heard Beckworth, the coal operator, shout, "Let's go Hank. Knock one in there for us." Hank slammed the first pitch hard and fast. It barreled straight for the center fielder, bounced off his glove, and while the outfielders went scrambling for it, the first man ran home, and Hank just barely made it to third.

Corey was on her feet roaring with the rest of the Richfield spectators. Once the crowd had settled down, she cupped her hands around her mouth and shouted several times, "Hey, Hank!" waving her arm until she got his attention. She pointed to Sarah. "Look who's here!"

He grinned and saluted. Sarah waved.

The game's progress was slow, and tension mounted between the adversaries on the field as the score seemed always to be nearly even. When Gary began to fuss, Sarah accompanied Corey to a place of privacy at the end of the bleachers where the baby could be nursed and changed. At the bottom of the seventh inning Colin fell and skinned his knees. He was cranky after playing hard with the older children, and Sarah rescued him, taking him to a nearby pump where she wet her handkerchief and cleaned his scrapes. Then she returned him to the front row and sat in the midst of the other children, holding him on her lap.

Richfield was at bat, and Hank climbed out of the dugout, going to the fence to talk to her. He asked about Colin. "He fell," Sarah said. "One of the bigger boys accidentally pushed him. I think he's had enough playing for a while, and he's missed his nap."

"Poor little fella," Hank said and then smiled at her, his cheek swollen with a wad of tobacco. "This here's a good day, ain't it, Sarah?"

"Your team's behind by one. Do you think it'll be a good day if you lose?"

"Want me to hit a home run for you?"

"Hit one for the team. You need to catch up."

"I'll do it for you. Put it outta the field. For you."

"I'd like that." One of his teammates called for him. He grinned, reminding her of the boy she had once known. She carried Colin back up to her place next to Corey. He curled up in her arms, closed his eyes, and poked his thumb into his mouth. Corey was screaming and waving an arm, and Sarah saw that Ben was at bat. He hit a ground ball. The shortstop raced for it, scooped it up, and hurled it to first, but Ben was safe.

Corey was bouncing Gary on her shoulder in agitation, a pained look on her face. "Come on, fellas! You cain't let 'em take this away from you!"

"How many outs?" Sarah asked her.

"Two. This next guy, Stewart, better not strike out." But the man managed a base hit, and Ben made it to third. When Hank stepped up to the plate, the pitcher was already conferring with his manager and the catcher, and Corey moaned, "Oh, blazes, they're gonna walk him."

Sure enough, the first two pitches were deliberate balls. The pitcher fingered the ball and wiped his hands on his behind, while Hank stood at the plate, his hand resting on the bat handle, as though it were a cane, the other hand on his hip. Then he hunched his shoulders forward, spat and slung the bat over his shoulder.

The pitch came, another ball, and Corey groaned in frustration, but Hank moved toward it and swung. It went foul. The crowd shouted, and the pitcher scratched his head in confusion. Hank shook his fist at the pitcher and yelled something the spectators could not make out.

"Oh, come *on*!" Corey exclaimed as the catcher and the manager wandered to the mound again. "Just throw him the ball!" Corey wiped off her face. "Two balls and a strike. You got plenty of time, Hank!" Sarah held onto Colin and prayed for the run she knew Hank would be disappointed without.

After several moments they were ready to play ball again. This time the pitcher threw a fair ball, which connected with Hank's bat in a resounding crack. The crowd howled, and Sarah rose with them to follow the ball's progress over the fence. Her attention returned to the field where Ben had already run in and Stewart was approaching third base. Hank finally let the bat drop and began a slow trot around the bases, apparently enjoying the accolades from the stands. In two more innings of play neither team was able to score even though players got on base in each inning.

After the game the teams met and shook hands and slapped each other on the back. One of them began shouting and raising threatening fists at another player. Hank seemed to be arguing with

Coal Ridge's pitcher, and then Beckworth went to the field and had words with "his" players. Sarah watched him pull Hank away from the others and put his arm around him. They talked that way, as approving father and obedient son, for several moments. Hank had never discussed his relationship with Beckworth with Sarah and she asked Corey about it.

"Beckworth's probably giving him another bonus. Gives him cash all the time so he won't take a job nowhere else and leave the team. Hank plays along for as much extra as he can get. Then it all goes for guns and the strike fund. Beckworth had a son about Hank's age, well I guess a little older, kilt in the war, and sometimes I think he buddies up to Hank 'cause he reminds him of his own boy. He never tries to make it political or nothing, and Hank takes advantage of the fact that he ain't under suspicion 'cause the boss is so stupid. If you was to ask me, which nobody ever does, I think Hank oughta quit fooling round here and put all his efforts into baseball. They's been guys here from the Pittsburgh Pirates looking at him. Even talked to him, but he ain't interested."

17

COREY AND SARAH claimed a spot near the musicians and a tub of home-brew which Ben was eager to sample. After hours in the hot sun Corey was wilting and couldn't do much besides tend to her baby's needs, so Sarah took charge of serving and cleaning up.

"Leave that chicken off my plate," Hank told Sarah. His smiling eyes kept touching hers, and her insides boiled. She went about her chores, watching him discreetly. He tumbled with Alan and Colin and held his nephew while Ben tried to interest Corey in dancing. He clapped his hands with the music, talked in whispers to men who came and sat with him for a few minutes, and sometimes he disappeared for what seemed like long stretches of time.

"I'm so tired," Corey groaned as dusk began to fall.

"Let's pack up and get home then," Ben said and Sarah wondered at such indulgence.

"I gotta talk to one more guy," Hank said.

"We don't care what you do," Corey said. "We're leaving."

"And Sarah's staying with me." Delighted with the suggestion, Sarah glanced at Hank and caught his half smile.

By the time they were ready to go, Alan was asking to go along, and Corey said, "C'mon, boys. Looks like your mommy wants to stay out late. We'll put them in bed for you, Sarah." Corey squeezed her. "You been such a help to me all day, it's the least I can do."

Holding onto Sarah's fingers, Hank pulled her through the thinning crowd. At one of the tubs, depleted of its home-brew, he put his hand on a man's shoulder and said, "Got a minute?" and led him away from listening ears. They discussed rifles and ammunition, Hank giving the man directions for placement of various firearms.

Then Sarah and Hank began a slow walk across the meadow where fireflies winked and a tentative breeze had begun cooling the night air. Distant voices rose and fell as families made their way home. She tried to question him about weapons. "I'm in charge of distribution here," he told her, putting an arm around her shoulder. "I work with an organizer in Williamson." He sounded dismissive, as though finished with talk of union activity for the night.

"I really enjoyed the game, Hank," she said. "You played great."

"I tried to get me another homer, but I couldn't hit nothing. Nobody could. By the end of the game, the ball was beat-up and knocked outta shape. I ain't making excuses, but it's hard to work with something like that."

"Well, your home run was a grand show. It was you that won the game," she said, sliding her arm around his waist. He stopped abruptly and kissed her, long and slow, his breath coming in sighs, his hands caressing her shoulders and her hair.

"Ah, sweet Sarah," he whispered. "I told you I lost my mind. I expect it's been sneaking away from me little by little." He nipped at her ear with his lips. "Probably started a long time ago, first day you come into Clarkson school. I never seen anyone so pretty and so smart."

She fell into it with him, returning his kiss, and he tensed and sighed and drew her into a closer embrace. But almost immediately he began pulling away. "Whoa, Sarah, enough! Enough!" He stepped back, groping in his pocket for cigarettes. "Look, I'm sorry. I shouldn'ta done that, nor said them things. I wasn't thinking, and I ain't got the right—"

"Yes, you do."

"No, I don't—"

"I say you do."

"Well, I ain't so sure about this," he said, leading her toward the road, and Sarah suddenly knew that she was more sure about it than she had been about anything else in her life. "And you ain't either," he told her, as though reading her thoughts in the dark.

"I am. Yes, I am."

He stopped when they reached the road. "Look, you're all tore up about your husband. You feel bad. Maybe you need a little attention, and maybe you think I'll do all right for now till y'all get things worked out."

"It's not like that, Hank."

"Is that so?" Time stretched out as he smoked. Crickets and katydids were beginning their nighttime serenade. "Then tell me how it is."

"We aren't going to get things worked out."

"What d'you mean?"

"Oh, I don't know." Denny was far from Sarah's thoughts. "I don't know anything."

"You see what I mean?"

"Well, you could kiss me again."

He flipped the cigarette into the dirt and pulled her to him again, but soon he was trying to ease away. She clung to him, pushing herself against him, running her hands over his back and shoulders, loving the feel of him so close to her.

"Look, Sarah. This here ain't good. I mean, it is, but… My God! What am I doing? This ain't right and I gotta get you home." They walked along the road silently with arms around each other. She was almost dizzy from his kissing. On the porch she leaped into his arms again.

"Stop it now," he said firmly, moving clear away from her and lighting a cigarette defensively. "You need to go in now, Sarah. I didn't mean to start nothing. I just… My God…"

"What ain't you sure about?" she asked, strangling on his rejection. "Don't you like me?"

"Course I do." He took her hand. "I said I lost my mind, but I meant I lost my heart. I got strong feelings for you, you know that. I always have."

"Wait here while I check on the boys." She unloosed her hand from his and ducked inside. Her sons had gotten their wish and were sound asleep on the couch, and Corey and Ben were nowhere in sight. If Hank had lost his heart, Sarah knew she had lost her own mind, as well as her will. Outside again she asked, "What do you mean, Hank, strong feelings?"

He shrank into the shadows, muttering his answer with his head turned away. "You know what I mean."

"No, I don't. What about Daphne?"

"Daphne? What about her?" He spoke in a near whisper, backed up against the house, arms crossed, retreating in all ways from her. "That was a long time ago. She wasn't nothing."

"What does that mean? About me?"

"It don't mean nothing."

"Hank? Please tell me."

"I… My feelings is real tender for you, Sarah, so that I cain't care for no one else. Now I ain't saying no more."

"Will you come in the house?"

He followed her inside. She led him into the empty bedroom, shut the door, and switched on the lamp by the bed. Before he could drag on his cigarette, she threw herself into his arms, but he pulled away. "Sarah, I don't know what you think you're doing, but I ain't sure I like what it looks like." He stood alert in the middle of the room smoking and watching her.

"You once said you had a married woman. That they're the best kind because you can't get caught by them."

"And I told you I's joking." He sighed, put out the cigarette, and with hands firmly on her upper arms, he held her away from him. "Let's talk, Sarah."

"All right."

"Promise we'll talk for now, and you ain't gonna try nothing else."

"Don't you like kissing me, Hank?"

He exhaled loudly and clapped his arms around her in a bear hug that almost hurt in its ferocity, then held her away from him. "I love kissing you, Sarah, but I don't think I oughta. You're married and I—"

"Couldn't you," she said in a small voice, "I mean, will you come to bed with me?"

"Now look here! You think I cain't see you wanna get even with your husband?"

"No, that's not it."

"I reckon that *is* it, little darlin'."

"Hank, it's really not."

"Then what is it?"

"I… I well, I care for you too. I want you. You… Being close to you like this, kissing you, excites me…"

He stroked her hair, his mouth curling into a half smile. "Maybe you don't wanna get even then. Maybe you're just lonesome and want a man to love you. Is that it?" She didn't know. A lump formed in her throat. She only knew she couldn't bear it if he left her now. He kept stroking her hair. "I could love you, sweet Sarah," he said in a guttural whisper. "I could lay you down and love you like you ain't been loved in a while, I reckon. But you still gotta go home. You understand? It won't fix nothing. You still gotta go home."

She hadn't thought it out in such horribly clear language, but the prospect of Hank leaving her alone was intolerable. "Couldn't we anyway? Please?"

"My God, Sarah…"

"Stay with me, Hank. Please don't say no."

He was thoughtful for a few moments, breathing audibly. "If it's what you want. But God help me…"

"What about you? What do you want?"

"Me?" Another loud sigh escaped him. "You got me crazy outta my mind so's I ain't sure what's right. You're married. You used to be my teacher, and sometimes you make me feel like I'm a kid who don't know nothing."

"But all those things aside, when it's just you and me, then what?"

He was silent for a long moment before he whispered, "Ah, Sarah, I want you like you would not believe."

"But you once said you thought people shouldn't—"

"And you know I was talking with my intellectual mind. You ask too many questions, darlin'. My heart wants to have you in my arms loving you…" He was undressing her and fumbling with his own clothing, muttering to himself, "But I still ain't sure…"

He laid her down on the bed and kissed her mouth again and again, caressed her without hesitation, his touch hard-gentle and sure with intuitive knowledge, burning her up and melting her down. His body, a collection of stone-hard muscles, enveloped her with tenderness, and her senses took flight and soared, drenched and sated in the sweetness of his touch. And suddenly her physical arousal ceased.

Her mind came alive instead, at first attuned to the house—were her sons still sleeping? was Corey up?—then to worry about what she had done, dragging Hank into her confused misery. He had been pure in his friendship, had tried grandly to remain in control, but had become her victim instead. Her mind raced on. He was nothing like Denny or Paul. Everything about Hank fit everything about her so well, touching her so differently; if she could turn off her anxious mind and dive into the deep waters of sensation, she could easily remain here. With Hank. Forever.

When he stopped himself to pull free and ejaculate between them, her tears of regret began—regret for her actions, for some notion of infidelity which had thrown her into unfamiliar emotional territory, for the end of what might have been a sweet beginning. And tears of sorrow, because he would leave her now, alone. Of course he was aware that she had stopped responding to his quiet passion. Things were complicated now beyond her capacity to handle them, and she was afraid she had lost the one thing that had kept her going—his steady friendship.

His utter silence—only the bare betrayal of quickened breath—frightened her. Terrified that he would desert her without a word, she watched him through her tears. He got up and rummaged around in his clothing until he found a handkerchief with which he wiped her belly. Then he pulled on his pants and undershirt and lit a cigarette.

Finding her nightgown in her bag, he wandered back to the bed with a dejected air and stood there smoking. His hoarse voice broke the silence. "I ain't no good for you, Sarah," he said, dropping the gown beside her and turning away. "Go on and cover up your beautiful woman's body."

He stood across the room smoking, running his hand through his hair, shifting his weight from one foot to the other, then squashed out the butt. "I told you I ain't no good for you, that this ain't what you need," he said. Hurt was conspicuous in his quiet tone. She studied him through a blur of tears as he took hesitant steps toward her. "This kinda loving ain't gonna make things better." He paused. "Suppose we just say it was a mistake and we don't gotta do it no more." He shook his head vehemently as he sat down beside her. "I tell you, Sarah, I will *not* let this happen again. You hear?"

She only cried the harder, and he touched her arm. "Sarah, please don't cry no more. I cain't stand it. I cain't stand you hurting and me not being able to do nothing about it. Only thing I can think of to do when you start that is to tear him apart."

"I want things to be the way they were with you, Hank," she sobbed. "I... You're the only thing... the best thing in my life. I don't want to lose you. I don't want you to hate me and you have every right—"

"Stop that now. Didn't I tell you how much I care for you? That won't never change. Nothing's changed, except I ain't loving you like this again no matter how bad you think you need it." He pulled her close and held her until her tears stopped. "Sarah, look. I hope we got us a connection strong enough so's this here mistake we've made ain't gonna ruin it." Sighing loudly, he added in a passionate whisper, "Oh, God, please let's try to forget this happened."

PART FOUR

1

"DENNY, I'M TRYING to get supper." Instead of reaching for the whiskey bottle as he usually did when he had the coal dust washed off, Denny had pulled Sarah into his arms.

"So what? Cain't I kiss you?" She allowed it, fighting the repugnance she felt. "We gotta get things patched up. Hit ain't no good us living like this."

"I was going to suggest the same thing."

After supper when the boys went out to play, they sat down at the table for a talk. Because she was now as guilty as her husband, Sarah tried to ignore what she knew—that the mine guard's daughter was on her way to Europe.

"I guess you ain't perfect, but you come damn close, even if you's scrawny and..." Sarah closed her mind to the rest of his insults and remembered soft-spoken words: *your beautiful woman's body...* "And I been thinking maybe I's wrong about some things. I want us to start talking again, maybe start doing things together, maybe just me and the boys sometimes too. Think you could forgive me? A man ain't nothing without his woman," he continued. "You're my woman, Sarah. That girl, she wasn't much. And by heck, I miss you. I miss how you used to smile and talk about the garden and your pig. You'd get excited whenever Al learned something new. And remember how you used to put love notes in my dinner bucket? Boy, I miss that. I miss you. Let's try and get all that back, Sarah."

"How?" She asked. That afternoon she had seen Denny's blond girlfriend standing at the train station with an older woman, perhaps her mother. They were dressed in white linen and stood next to a mound of trunks and suitcases. Several official-looking men stood around as they waited for the train, and one of the men said, "...off on the grand tour..." to which the older woman nodded while adding something about California.

"Well, I told you I's sorry. You could say you forgive me."

"Assuming you're sorry, I could forgive you."

"I am sorry, Sarah."

"Then I forgive you, but I'm not sure if those things can be erased like they never happened."

"Why not?"

"Because they hurt me."

"Well, you ain't gonna hurt no more. I'm gonna try to treat you nice, and you're gonna forget all that."

That night in bed he pulled her to him. "I can't do it yet, Denny. I just can't."

"Why not?"

"Because I think about you and that girl."

"All right. I'll wait awhile."

In the coming days he asked her questions about the children and how her day went; he even carried water for her several times and praised her efforts in the kitchen. He looked at her more often and smiled when his eyes met hers. He pulled out his guitar and sang his old love songs to her, making her sit with him and listen, even though her chores were piling up. "Do 'em later," he said. Every night he held her close, suffocating her with wet kisses and pressing his erection against her thigh.

At a square dance one Saturday night he played half the time and danced with her the rest of the time. When it was over, she put the boys to bed while he helped himself to a few belts of whiskey. His expectancy had settled throughout the house, into every corner before they went upstairs. When they climbed into bed, he reached for her. "Denny..."

He pulled his hand away. "I been nice to you, Sarah."

"I know you have, but—"

"I been talking to you, doing things with you and the kids. I want you now, I wanna show you I love you, and you're gonna tell me it reminds you of when I wasn't treating you right. That ain't fair, Sarah. You ain't giving me a chance. Are you trying to punish me now for when things wasn't right?"

"No."

"It weren't all my fault like you try to make it out to be."

"I know," she agreed, although uncertain how she had wronged Denny before her tryst with Hank.

"We cain't make things all the way right if you're gonna decide to be some kinda virgin now. You ain't *never* pulled away from me the way you're pulling now, and it makes me think maybe you're letting some other man have what's mine."

"Denny!"

"You think I'm so stupid I don't know some of the boys stops by here in the mornings sometimes after I leave?"

"Where'd you hear that?"

"I just heard it. What're they stopping by for, Sarah?"

"If you heard they were coming by, then you know why."

"I heard you's buying scrip from 'em."

"And you should be glad. That way we have a little extra, and I can't believe you could accuse me of what you just accused me of."

"I didn't mean it, Sarah. I know you ain't that kind." He snuggled next to her. "You been tired and sad, but it don't have to be that way no more. C'mon, Sarah. Lemme make you feel real nice the way I used to."

Her skin shrank beneath his touch, and she tolerated his violation of her innermost privacy by disconnecting her mind until he was finished. But guilt was strong in her heart. Denny had become more pleasant; she even felt like laughing and talking with him more often, but her desire for the intimacy they had once shared was irrevocably dead.

2

Sᴀʀᴀʜ's ᴛʀɪᴘs ᴛᴏ Richfield continued, but Hank only saw her in the presence of Ben and Corey now. When she met his eyes, they held neither accusation nor desire, and he slipped guns and ammunition into her valise while her sons were distracted elsewhere in the house. She grew numb with a dull ache, increasingly aware of the chill as Hank systematically shut her out of his life, and she began to dread the trips.

But one night in late September he stayed after the rest of the household had gone to bed and sat with her in the kitchen. He asked her pointless questions and rambled about union politics. He made comments about her marriage, drumming his fingers on the table, and Sarah suddenly read him in the same way he often read her. He regarded his hands so he wouldn't have to look at her, and she knew he wanted to tell her something.

"I know you're trying to get things worked out with your husband. Sometimes marriages get off track with misunderstanding, but then they fix themselves. One of these days when your kids is grown, you'll be setting on the porch with your man and you'll count up all them years you had with him, and you'll forgive him. You just gotta get through these bad times, and I know you can 'cause you got a lot of courage, Sarah Sable."

"You sound like you're saying goodbye to me."

He glanced at her briefly. "I ain't exactly. Things is just changing. Lots of things. Just changing." He didn't speak for a full minute. Sarah felt distance growing between them.

He continued hesitantly. "A while back there you's thinking things was finished between you and your husband. Maybe you and me was both dreaming about things that wasn't real. Only way things'd ever be finished between you and him is for an accident or a bullet to get him. He knows that a lot clearer'n you do, Sarah, going in them tunnels every day, staring into pitch black and jumping every time a piece of the roof gives way, then looking at them guards with guns. That makes some men pure mad and reckless and game for a fight; others it eats at 'em, makes 'em scairt, maybe makes 'em wanna do a little too much drinking. You gotta allow that, Sarah. He's got a tough job and a tough fight. He's your man and you gotta stick by him."

"What's changing?"

"Well…" He stuffed a cigarette between his lips and frowned at the tabletop, still not looking at her. He lit up and smoked awhile. "Couple weeks ago coal miners in Kanawha County tried to march on the Guyan field. That's Logan County. The governor tried to stop 'em, district president tried to stop 'em. Only thing finally stopped 'em was a threat to bring out the national guard. Everyone's getting mad. Ain't nobody can get into Logan County on account of the sheriff, Don Chafin. He's got hundreds of deputies, and they's all on the coal companies' payrolls. Somebody leaves Logan County to testify in court about what goes on there, if they go back home they get beat up or kilt. Union sends organizers in and Chafin's deputies is all over 'em. Ain't nobody getting in there.

"And I don't know about no more guns, Sarah. The governor's scairt, thinks people's trying to assassinate him. He threatened the miners with the national guard. Now the national UMW is calling for a nationwide strike if we don't get a sixty-percent increase in wages. The federal government only wants to make it fourteen percent since coal production's down. They's plenty of spies crawling round, and they're getting wind of the arms we're accumulating. Mine guards is one thing to deal with, but the national guard's something else. I ain't sure what's gonna happen, but I get worried almost sick thinking about you and your boys on them trains…"

He talked on about politics, local happenings, his own and others' speculations. He didn't stop for anything besides lighting and drawing on cigarettes. He scarcely looked at her and he did not smile. By the time he ducked out the back door with a most impersonal leave-taking—"I gotta take a leak. Hit's getting late, so I'll just go on home"—she felt like some union contact with whom he had been obligated to meet.

The following morning as Sarah prepared to return to Dawson, Corey remarked, "I reckon Hank told you all about his girl last night. What d'you think of that?"

"His girl?"

"Yeah, he found him a girl. Didn't he tell you? I cain't tell which one of 'em's the craziest. Most of the time me and Ben cain't hardly keep 'em pried apart. Seems like nobody can. Her parents has about give up on her ever staying home. She's up there at the boarding house with him all the time. I cain't believe he didn't tell you."

"Maybe he did," Sarah mumbled. She knew he had tried. "Does she know about his involvement with organizing?"

"A little, I reckon. She don't help him or nothing. He didn't tell you?"

"What's her name?"

"Kay McGwinn."

"Well, you tell me about her, Corey."

"She's seventeen. Her daddy's got a union card, her mama's been married before. They's a lot of 'em in her family."

"Is she pretty?"

"A little. She's sweet, but I don't like her hair. It don't look good short, makes her cheeks look too chubby. Or maybe she just don't know how to fix it." Corey laughed and fluffed up her own beautiful hair that needed no fixing. "She don't have good teeth neither. She's smart though. She didn't go to high school, but she stuck around in school for a long time and helped out the teacher to earn a few dollars, so she's smart. But dumb enough to try to get herself hooked up with Hank. They's lots of gals trying all the time and I don't know why. I could see it if they knowed he's educated and don't have to be here, but ain't nobody knows that. All they know about him is that he's about the best worker Richfield Coal's got, always leading the weigh sheet and making good pay for someone his age, and he can hit a baseball. That's all them girls want."

Sarah forced a smile. "What else is there?"

"If I was one of 'em, I wouldn't want nothing to do with him, no matter how good he looks nor how much he makes or how good a house he could get."

"Why not?"

"'Cause he's gonna get hisself kilt one of these days just like Daddy done, that's why." Corey's voice caught, choking on her private terror. "He's itching for a fight with them company deputies. He'd love to get into it with 'em in some strike. I wouldn't wanna be married to him and have his young 'uns."

"Is he going to marry Kay?"

"If she has anything to do with it, he will. If he gets his say, well, you know he won't marry nobody. Nor have babies. Course they's accidents, and the way them two's a-going I'd say they's plenty of room for an accident."

"I'm surprised."

"Oh, why? Sometimes our men just gotta take chances. Sometimes there ain't no tomorrow. 'Specially with all this trouble in the air. You know that." Corey lowered her voice. "Listen, I expect he'd be madder'n blazes if he knowed I been telling it to you like this."

"Like what?"

"Like maybe they's some kinda funny business going on between 'em. She's all over him all the time, but I don't know if they're really *doing* it."

Sarah knew she should applaud this news of Hank's expanding world; instead she mourned privately as her own circumstances diminished. Denny continued to be attentive and pleasant, but she knew he'd had company while she was gone, for she found a black hair ribbon in the bed, half-tucked under her own pillow.

Lonnie stopped by with more gun money, but she had to refuse it, explaining to him Hank's warning.

3

It was October, and the weather had taken a cold turn. Everyone heard a muted rumble, followed shortly by the screech of the whistle, and Sarah joined the convergence of women at the mine's drift mouth.

The men were brought out in order to mobilize a force of diggers, and one by one each woman cried out in relief when her man emerged, black-faced, healthy, and whole. Sarah identified many of them—Lonnie Pierce, Med Givens, and Mace Elder among them. One after another, their dirty faces became recognizable: Owens, Hilling, McCartney, Caldwell, Morris, even Edward Billings, the Baldwin–Felts spy. In the end five women stood alone, their men unaccounted for, and Sarah was among them.

Digging was an all-day process, and Millie took Alan and Colin home. Mine guards, appropriately sympathetic, tried to talk Sarah and the other four women into going home, promising to notify them at once when they started bringing men out. Only one woman left, muttering, "My first one was kilt this a-way. Waiting here don't change nothing," but Sarah stayed. Fine particles of snow and rain began to fall, but she felt nothing except every separate moment she had ever lived and loved and hated with Denny. Each moment seemed precious now and she begrudged him nothing—not one drop of liquor drunk, nor one tedious chord played, not even the lies or the insults. She was thankful now for the falseness, that she had at least appeared to be good to him these last few months.

There was commotion at the portal when the car finally came up. Arthur Caldwell, Med Givens, and the foreman in charge of the rescue were shouting to a doctor and some nurses who had been standing by. Men hoisted a body from the car, and black and scorched as it seemed, Sarah recognized Denny at once. She rushed forward as they laid him on the ground. Med stopped her.

"You're lucky, Miz Sable. *He's* lucky. He's stunned but there ain't a scratch on him. Rest of 'em's goners. That's why we brung him up first." As Med spoke, Sarah saw the movement—the *life!*—in her husband's limbs as the doctor checked him over.

Denny lay in bed for two days, groaning over his bruises and complaining about the ringing in his ears, but there seemed to be nothing serious wrong with him. With a mixture of guilt, sorrow, and elation Sarah went to the funerals of the other men, wondering at God's whims. Denny, too, seemed touched by his luck. His eyes glistened with moisture when he looked at Sarah, and he insisted that his sons play in the bedroom with him.

"What happened?" she asked him.

"They had us opening Number 13. Gas musta come in. I don't know for certain. Course you cain't smell it. I seen dust and a big flash. Then it felt like something hit me and I figured I's dead."

"Why were you in that room?"

"Guys been working it for several days. They told us engineers'd fixed the problem. They was rotating us, I reckon, so nobody'd have nothing to complain about."

"I'm afraid there are four widowed women and a pack of fatherless children who have plenty to complain about."

"Not us though."

"Don't be so smug. We almost lost you. Waiting for them to bring you out was the worst time of my life."

"Waiting for 'em to dig me out was my worst. I didn't think Greskevitch was hurt none neither, but he just stopped breathing. I watched him, no, I didn't watch him, just felt him. We was holding onto each other in the dark. Once he was gone, I figured I's next."

An unexpected telegram was delivered. *Sarah, We heard. Praying you're all okay. Hank.*

When she showed it to Denny, he asked, "Who's Hank?"

"Corey's brother."

His questions continued. "She got a brother? He live over there? He got him a family?"

"Not yet, but Corey says he'll be getting married soon." She heard the finality, the imminence, in her own words.

Later Dry Creek Coal's owner, Orville Jones, knocked on the door. He removed his hat and stepped into the room. "Mind if I come in, Mrs. Sable?"

"You may come in anytime since this is your house."

"I'd like to talk to your husband if he's able. I hear he had him quite a scare."

No thanks to your shoddy practices, she wanted to answer but left the room saying, "Please wait here and I'll see if he feels like company."

In the bedroom Denny dozed with a children's story magazine across his thighs. Colin had fallen asleep next to him and Alan, at the foot of the bed, was trying to figure out a puzzle. Sarah wanted to lock her family away from Jones's unworthy presence, from his paternalistic, condescending curiosity, and she felt like telling him Denny was sleeping and couldn't see him. But Denny would be furious with her if she did so.

"Mommy, help me with this!" Alan exclaimed in frustration.

"Not now, sweetheart. We've got company."

"Who?" He scrambled off the bed and dashed toward the stairs, and Sarah let him go. She didn't care what the boy said to Jones.

She shook Denny and told him Jones was downstairs. His eyes flew open wide. "By Christ! I ain't even been outta bed yet." They heard Jones's tread on the stairs, and Denny grabbed the whiskey bottle from the nightstand and put it behind the bed. He glanced around the room, dismayed at the clutter.

"What do you care about impressing that bastard?" Sarah whispered.

Jones rapped on the open door and walked in. "Well," he beamed. "Looks like we've got one lucky fellow here." He approached the bed and shook Denny's hand. He turned to Sarah. "Suppose I could get a private word with your husband, Mrs. Sable?"

Sarah went to the bed and picked up Colin who whimpered and yawned and then laid his head on her shoulder. She closed the door and steered Alan, who had been standing on the landing, downstairs. In the kitchen she began chopping potatoes and onions for supper.

Jones left after about ten minutes. In the boys' room at the front of the house, Sarah sniffed at the scent he had left behind, an odor of soap and cologne, and it reminded her of a time long past when she had associated regularly with men who smelled similarly, who washed in the convenience of bathrooms with indoor plumbing.

While her children played with blocks on the floor, she gazed out at Orville Jones's lordly progress down the lane. With fury and tenderness she thought of the broken remains of the men who had come out with Denny, and she saw more clearly than ever before the difference between worker and operator, worker and mine guard, worker and politician.

For the first time Sarah felt completely Hank's fanatical concept of *class*. She had always known which side she was on, but she had never felt such pride so deeply before in the solidarity Hank spoke of, and she had no intention now of trying to talk Denny into getting out of the coal mines. Jones was joined by a couple of mine guards, part of his army of brave knights, and Sarah was seized by a renewed desire to feel her suitcase heavy with guns and ammunition. She'd bring in more firearms no matter the danger.

Upstairs in the bedroom Jones's scent lingered more prominently, and Sarah clenched her fists at the look of Denny lying there with a deflated air, staring at the floor. "What did that son of a bitch want?"

He looked at her sharply. "Since when do you talk like that?"

"Since whenever I feel like it. I asked him politely to wait downstairs and he didn't. He owns this house and he owns your life and I despise him. I wonder if he visited the widows."

Soon Denny was back at work, and Sarah couldn't help noticing the way he looked at her sometimes, slyly, as though he were sizing her up. Was he back to his old ways so soon? She put aside the foolish idea she was trying to make herself believe about fidelity in their marriage, wondering how it would fit into their old age together in rocking chairs on the porch.

A letter came with Corey's return address on it but not written in Corey's hand. Sarah checked it over carefully and saw that it had not been tampered with. Before opening it she stared at the handwriting, surprised that after five years she could remember the penmanship of a boy in her schoolroom.

Dear Sarah,

We were all shocked and angered when we learned of the explosion in Dawson. My heart goes out to you and your boys but especially to your husband who, although unhurt, must have suffered untold horrors while awaiting rescue.

Conditions are such right now that it's not a good idea for you to travel alone. We're not sure how the situation will shape up in November, but perhaps you could come over for Thanksgiving. I'll keep you posted and advise you later.

I miss you.

Love,
Corey

On November 1, as Hank had predicted, bituminous coal miners struck everywhere regardless of union affiliation, and Sarah took note of the fear evident in Denny's eyes, not sure what he was afraid of—the union, the operators, or the federal troops the governor actually called in.

On the eighth, UMWA District President Frank Keeney directed the miners to go back to work and accept a fourteen-percent increase, but it was another week before they did so. The military left at the same time and things returned to an appearance of normal. Sarah told Lonnie she was ready to go for more guns, but he seemed to think that things were not as calm in Mingo County as they were in McDowell and advised her to do nothing until she got word from Richfield.

Another letter came from "Corey" a few days before Thanksgiving.

Dear Sarah,

I'm writing again to tell you not to visit, even though I would rather see you than anyone else in the world. We've just had some bad news. Mommy's brother in Welch, our Uncle Slim, has passed away, so it looks like our Thanksgiving will be a family gathering there to pay our final respects and dispose of his few belongings. Mommy has already gone to see to the burial. Everyone else will join her there in a day or so.

Maybe things will settle down in the next few weeks and you can come over and stay for a few days. I look forward to such a time.

Love,
Corey

The next communication she received from Richfield was a letter from the real Corey with just a few short lines: *Things has finely clamed down. We would love seeing yall sometime soon? Christmas? Newyears? Any time?*

The invitation caught Sarah off guard. She had been counting on strikes, federal troops, and uncertainties to keep her in Dawson. Sometimes she dreamed vividly of Hank and awoke missing him with a profound ache and wondering if her connection with him had been permanently severed.

4

THEY WERE IN Richfield for a "family" Christmas gathering. Denny had agreed to come, and when he and Ben hit it off almost instantly, Sarah breathed easier. At supper Ben suggested to Denny that they go out to a saloon, mentioning that his brother-in-law would meet up with them there. But Hank came to the house instead, and Sarah wondered if she imagined the immediate dislike that seemed to spring up between him and Denny. After the men left, Corey observed, "Well! Suppose them two'll get a little friendlier once they get to drinking?"

Later Denny tumbled into bed smelling of whiskey and said to Sarah, "Where in hell did that sweet Corey get such a bastard for a brother!"

"You two didn't get along?"

"Damn him! He picked at everything I said."

"You imagined it."

"Nope. He's a hostile, unfriendly bastard, and I tell you, if he keeps it up, me and him's gonna get into it. I can only take so much lip from a wise guy like him."

"What did he say?"

"Just picking at me. Everything I said, he implied, not directly or nothing, just implied that I don't know shit. We talked about some places around McDowell County that's good fishing. Well, I don't know where I's talking about, according to him. Then he has to go dragging it out of me in front of everyone that I never even fish. Then he talks to me about my own kids. Seems there's things about 'em I don't know that he knows."

"Such as?"

"Like about how Al likes baseball so much. Hell, I never seen Al show much interest in baseball, but this son of a bitch claims he does. You ever noticed anything like that?"

"He and Hank have tossed a ball around a little."

"Then we get to arguing about ways to undercut a seam and the fastest way to get cars loaded. He's a damn expert. Ain't nothing I know that he don't know better. Ain't nothing I can do better'n him. He don't say any of that straight out, but it seemed like he was thinking it and suggesting it."

"I'm sure you can sing better than him," Sarah pointed out.

"He even had something to say about that. He said he knowed a fella that heard me play and said I weren't no good. He asked me if I was any good. Real arrogant like. Hateful."

"Try to forget it, Denny. We won't be here long."

"I tell you, Sarah, me and him's gonna get into it if he keeps picking at me. I know it ain't mannerly, but I'm gonna bust him if he don't leave me alone."

"You'd be better off to ignore him. I know you're a little taller than he is, but he might surprise you."

"And I already heard about him being such a great baseballer. He don't scare me, the goddamn punk."

"Please leave him alone, Denny. They say he's pretty good in a fight."

"Yeah and maybe we'll just see. I cain't stand guys like him."

"Now it sounds like you're picking at him. What's wrong with guys like him?"

"We walk in that there barroom, and everyone's got something to say to him. You can tell by the way he talks that he thinks he's smarter'n everyone else. The *way* he talks. And all them guys eating it up."

Ben and Denny were up early the next morning. "I'm gonna get me a doe, by golly," Ben said. "You gals better be ready to cook us up some venison steaks tonight."

While Ben cleaned his gun on the back porch, Denny sat on the couch next to Corey who nursed Gary. He strummed his guitar and made small talk with her, then he eased into song, crooning a worn-out ballad softly as though singing a lullaby to the drowsy baby. From the kitchen where Sarah was mixing up bread dough, she saw her husband's eyes moving slowly over Corey's face with such seductive tenderness it seemed he was caressing her. His gaze traveled to her partially exposed breast then back to her face, and all the while his voice stroked the air around mother and child.

Later that morning after Ben and Denny were gone, footsteps thudded on the front porch. Hank swung the front door open, exclaiming to Corey, "Look what we brung you, Sis!"

Corey came running and Sarah stood in the kitchen doorway. "Well, ain't you something!" Corey said. A small evergreen was tilted on its side on the porch. She clapped her hands with glee.

"Where d'you want it?" Hank entered the house followed by a girl dressed in miner's boots and jeans. Corey had already told Sarah that Hank was still with Kay. *How unfeminine she is! How unattractive!* Sarah thought. And how horrible of me to judge her, she concluded, noting Kay's loving eyes turned toward Hank.

Corey pointed. "How about there? If you moved the chair and the lamp." Hank and Kay set to work rearranging furniture, and Corey said, "Kay, this here's Ben's cousin, Sarah Sable. Her and her family's staying with us a couple days. Her husband's gone hunting with Ben."

Kay smiled pleasantly. "Pleased to meet you."

Sarah nodded and smiled, observing Kay with a constricting heart. She was short in stature with the look of a tomboy. Her hair was cropped short around plump, pink cheeks. She pitched in helping Hank situate furniture and bring in the Christmas tree, moving as though well aware of her own competence. Her laughter was warm, showing crooked yellow-brown teeth, and periodically she touched Hank or brushed against him. They accomplished the task of putting up the tree with the familiarity of a married couple.

Sarah was sure they could all see how it was for her—her husband's indifference, her petty envy of Kay at this giving and sharing time of the year, her isolation from anything joyous. She had not been prepared for such feelings of humiliation and exposure to overcome her and concentrated on her work in the kitchen.

Corey, Hank, Kay, Alan, and Colin bustled about the living room making plans to decorate the tree. When Corey, Kay, and the boys went upstairs to dig out decorations, Hank ambled into the kitchen. He rooted around on a shelf until he found a tin. Setting it on the table, he said, "You been elected to make the popcorn."

"Okay. When I'm finished with this."

"Making cookies?"

"Yes. Help yourself."

He poured coffee and lit a cigarette, watching her roll out dough. "I don't know if I can take anything back with me," she said. "Denny would notice the difference in the weight of the bags." She was aware of her hair, strands of it coming loose, and her smudged apron. He must see her raw emotional wounds clearly. "But I want to, Hank. I want to do something." She looked at him, surprised at the intensity of his gaze. "It'll be a while before I come back."

"Why's that?" His jaw was tight as his teeth clenched.

She looked away, wishing to disappear. "Winter's coming on and Colin sometimes gets sick with an earache. I can't have him out in bad weather."

"It's just as well. Transporting's risky now anyway." He smoked and continued to scrutinize her while she removed a tray of cookies from the oven. "It's been a long time, Sarah. How you been?"

"Hank, will you please leave Denny alone?"

"I ain't bothering him."

"He says you baited him last night."

"Is that what he said? He said it's *my* fault? Like he didn't do nothing first?"

"What did he do?"

His words were quiet, measured. "Last night? Nothing. He didn't do nothing. Last night."

"Well, leave him alone. You don't have a quarrel with him."

Corey and Kay and the boys were making noise at the top of the stairs. Hank leaned close to Sarah and said, "I reckon Denny Sable's gonna get what's coming to him." He put out his cigarette and left the kitchen.

Amidst the popcorn-making and tree-decorating, Ben and Denny returned, dragging the promised doe behind them. The event took Hank outdoors where he helped with the carcass. Corey and Sarah consulted about cooking chores, while Kay made excuses. "Me and the boys'll fix up the tree. I ain't much in the kitchen." *But you're probably really something in the bedroom*, Sarah thought. Throughout the morning she had endured the sight of too much of Kay and Hank's kissing, an activity that Kay continually initiated.

The midafternoon supper, with everyone crowded around the kitchen table, was a feast of fried slabs of floured and seasoned venison, potatoes, green beans, and fried apples. Sarah and Corey had also made biscuits and gravy and bread. For dessert there were cookies, a pumpkin pie, and coffee. Despite the shouting and confusion and laughter, an almost palpable friction sparked the air. At every opportunity Hank stalked Denny with his eyes and verbally assaulted him with subtle force, and with increasing regularity Denny challenged him.

After the meal everyone relaxed while Denny played his guitar. Sarah escaped the uncomfortable situation by insisting on washing the mound of dishes alone. Hank sat on the couch, his arm around

Kay and their fingers entwined, and every time Denny hit a wrong note, Hank muttered lazily, "Gosh darn!" Sarah could tell by the way Denny played and sang that his annoyance was increasing.

Corey asked if he knew "Henry Lee." When Denny began the tune, Corey sang along and encouraged Alan and Colin to join her. Soon Kay was singing too, and from the kitchen Sarah thought they sounded wonderful with Denny's smooth baritone carrying the higher voices.

When it was over, Ben rose and stretched and said, "I'm beat. I'm gonna lay down awhile." He picked up his sleeping son and climbed the stairs. Little by little everyone settled into separate activities. While Hank repaired a table that had come apart during the earlier moving, Kay sat in a corner and played card games with Alan and Colin. Corey insisted on relieving Sarah in the kitchen, so Sarah settled on the couch, taking her turn with stringing popcorn for the tree.

Soon Denny put his guitar down and went to the kitchen, and Sarah heard the clink of glass and bottle. The intermittent rap-rap of Hank's hammer and the occasional comments from the card game in the corner partially masked the voices in the kitchen. Sarah was unable to catch words, but the content of the conversation didn't matter, because she soon heard Denny's voluptuous laughter and knew he was openly flirting with Corey. Keeping her eyes on needle and thread, Sarah tried not to think or feel.

She looked up when Hank said, "That oughta do her, wouldn't you say?" But he was addressing Kay, showing her his finished product.

"Looks nice," Kay said. "I'll get that little mess for you after this game."

He rose. "That's all right. I was just going to get the broom."

Exactly what he encountered when he entered the kitchen Sarah couldn't be sure of, but she heard Hank's exclamation. "What the hell you think you're doing, Sable!"

"Minding my own business. Like you ain't."

"Looks like you're getting a little too friendly with my sister."

"I's just talking, so how about go to hell, will you?"

"Hey now, boys," Corey said warily.

"Anybody going anywhere it's you, Sable. Corey's got her a husband upstairs. And, you son of a bitch, you got yourself the finest wife a man could ask for in the next room." Kay and Sarah glanced apprehensively at one another.

"Get yourself settled down, Hank," Corey said.

"What's that supposed to mean?" Denny grumbled. "You been looking at her yourself?"

"You gonna get away from my sister, or do I gotta move you away?"

"I'd like to see you try, you little punk bastard."

A flurry of scuffling feet was followed by the unmistakable sound of fist slamming into flesh and bone. Corey shrieked. "Hank! God A'mighty! Don't be brawling in my kitchen! Get outside now!"

By the time Sarah and Kay and the boys reached the back porch, the adversaries were walking circles around each other in the yard. Denny, with a reddish bruise on his left cheek, was watching Hank guardedly, and Hank was muttering taunts under his breath. The remains of the now-mutilated deer hung from a makeshift scaffold several feet away. Denny began taking ineffective swings at Hank, who leaped quickly out of his way.

Then Hank planted both feet on the ground and said, "Let's quit fooling round. C'mon, asshole. Let's see if you can throw a punch any better'n you can play that guitar." He beckoned with an index finger, and Denny rushed toward him. His fist connected with a corner of Hank's chin, and then Hank was all over him, hammering him with both fists until Denny managed to make a break and back away from him.

A crowd gathered, with men coming out of houses or from the street to jeer and cheer or just watch with arms folded. "Anybody wanna put money on this'n?" somebody called out. Some men shook their heads, but most of them ignored him.

Anger seemed to spur Denny to throw a couple of solid punches, but it took Hank no time to recover and lunge forward again with such lightning agility that Denny could not avoid him. Hank caught him a right and a left in the gut and, when he hunched forward, slammed him so hard across his shoulders that Denny fell to his knees. As he slowly picked himself up, Hank took the moment to shrug out of his shirt. "I ain't even started with you yet, you dirty bastard." He spit out the words and Sarah saw murder in his eyes. "You wanna rest a minute?"

"Hell, no!" Denny snarled, curling his fists. "I just been playing with you."

He charged but Hank stopped him with a gut punch. Denny swayed forward and Hank drove a fist into his nose, knocking him backward. Denny crashed heavily into the dirt. Dazed, he barely struggled when Hank yanked him up by his shirt and slugged him again in the face. He promptly fell backward again. Blood covered his cheeks, dripped over his lip, and smeared Hank's knuckles. As Hank went after him again, Sarah blurted out, "Hank, that's enough. Stop it!"

He froze momentarily. Then he went to Denny, took his hand and pulled him up, speaking loudly enough for everyone to hear. "Get up. I ain't nigh finished with you, but looks like your wife wants you alive…" Then he growled something else the crowd could not distinguish and left Denny swaying on his feet. Hank went to the pump where he splashed water on his face and arms and picked up his shirt and dried off. Lighting a cigarette, he went to lean, sullen and brooding, against an adjacent porch.

The crowd broke up, and Sarah led Denny into the kitchen where she and Corey began the job of cleaning him up.

"What a way to get woke up from a nap!" Ben remarked. He sat at the kitchen table drinking coffee and rubbing his neck.

"Baby still asleep?" Corey wanted to know.

"Sure. Didn't bother him a bit." Ben turned to Denny. "What the hell you two fighting about?"

"Shut up, darling," Corey muttered in a silky voice. "They was just having theirselves a little Thanksgiving fun, wasn't you, Denny?"

"Sure was."

"Looks like your nose is busted," Corey crooned on. "That hurt?"

"Ow!" Denny exploded and jerked his head away. "Jesus Christ!"

"Denny, I don't care if you wanna fight with my brother or get drunk, but hit ain't right taking the Lord's name in vain. Now you stop that. It ain't gonna fix your nose."

"Then how about leaving my nose alone."

Sarah gingerly wiped up Denny's blood and cuts while their sons looked on. The back door opened and Hank entered cautiously, Kay behind him. Remembering Kay, Sarah felt a lump rise in her throat. The young woman had doubtless comforted him in the gathering dusk outside, while Sarah tended her husband.

"I suppose I ain't welcome," Hank said.

"You oughta leave," Corey agreed.

"I just come in to get my things, then we'll be going." Hank disappeared into the living room. When he returned, his gaze fell on Alan, who was watching him. "What're you looking at, son?" he asked. "Judging from the attention your daddy's getting, I expect it's a pretty clear lesson to you that it pays to get the tar knocked outta you."

He pulled on his coat, took Kay by the hand, and looked at Sarah, his eyes brimming with bitterness. "Night," he said and closed the door quietly as they left.

5

IT WAS WINTER and Sarah threw herself into the chores of motherhood and homemaking, trying to be watchful. Dawson was organizing, Lonnie told her, plotting in secret with the men of Tomahawk and Laura, Dry Creek Coal's nearby holdings, and once the weather broke in the spring, they would confront Jones with a demand for union recognition.

Sarah peered into her cache beneath the floorboard in the kitchen, dismayed at her dwindling funds. Money aside, she still had plenty: a healthy pig, egg-laying chickens, and canned garden produce. She brought in extra cash from teaching men to read in the evenings and also had the little bit of scrip she accumulated from the few who still sold it to her. She needed a boarder to feel truly prosperous but didn't dare ask for one as long as Edward Billings remained in town. She walked everywhere with eyes to the ground in search of pennies and dimes, trying not to think of her large savings account, into which she was no longer able to deposit much.

Now that her money and scrip were thinning out, Sarah had a glimpse clear to the bottom of the niche under the floorboard, and her eyes came to rest on Paul Lessing's pistol. She took it out and examined it. Suppose she needed to use it. Did it work? Had it ever worked? The gun had been in her possession for five years. Sometimes it had contributed to her feeling of safety, but now she wondered if she could rely on it.

Denny was so preoccupied anymore that Sarah could scarcely get his attention. News from Mingo County, only a few miles away, found its way into Dawson, and every few days Sarah heard talk out in the open of the discontent there. Lonnie predicted that the unrest in Mingo County would come to a head soon, and despite the personal resolve she had made, Sarah could not stop herself from traveling to Richfield. Even if it was February, and even though Lonnie hadn't compelled her, she had to know what was going on there.

"At last I got *family* I can talk to!" Corey exclaimed when Sarah arrived. "I wish Mommy were here." She spoke with a wide-eyed expression of childlike helplessness on her face.

"Corey, I'm not really family."

"God help me, Sarah, I'm gonna have another baby. What am I gonna do?" Tears brimmed in her eyes.

"The same thing you did before. You didn't have any problems before, did you?"

"No, but Sarah, these men are crazy. All they talk about is they ain't signing no yellow dog contracts and to hell with coal companies that say the union's against the law 'cause it violates the right to individual contracts. I'm sick of it, and I'm so scairt. If they strike, we're gonna be outta here. Company'll put us all out…" She threw herself sobbing into Sarah's arms.

"You won't be alone. Ben'll look out for you. Have you talked to him or Hank about it?"

Corey wailed. "Do you know how much bullying I'd get from my brother if I's to tell him I'm scairt? Sarah, he don't understand how it is for a girl. I don't wanna have a baby in a tent. And I gotta eat. I cain't starve while I'm carrying a baby."

"I'm sure he understands. But if things get tough, if they really strike and you need help, you can count on me. I've got a little extra money. But don't tell anybody." Her words brought immediate relief to Corey, and they spent the remainder of the day doing chores together and talking, catching up on things.

"That husband of yourn ever get his nose straightened out?"

"No. Looks like it's permanently bent."

Corey giggled. "You knowed he had it coming, didn't you? Hank was bound to go after him." Sarah did not want to rehash the events of their Christmas visit, but Corey felt a need to explain her part in it. "Might just as wella been one thing as another to set them two off. I hope you know that. I hope you know that's why I didn't get outta Denny's way while he was coming on. Sooner they got it over the better."

By the time Ben got home, Corey's spirits had much improved. At supper Ben told Sarah, "You gotta pretend to go to bed, that is, turn out all the lights, then set in the dark here in the kitchen and wait for Hank around twelve-thirty."

"What! Why?"

"Everybody's being watched. He wants to preserve this contact for as long as possible, but ain't no secrets gonna last much longer round here. I expect if you ever come back, you'll be visiting us in our new homes—tents."

"But Ben! It's winter!"

"And you're lucky they ain't no snow on the ground or little brother wouldn't be coming down here at all tonight."

In the dark after midnight Sarah peered out the kitchen window. A half moon gave ghoulish substance to the night. Rain barrels seemed to move and crooked fence posts rippled. Shadows swayed out of the corners of her eyes, then scurried behind outhouses, and moonlight seemed to glint off the gun barrels of cleverly hidden mine guards. The rumble of a train in the railroad yard reminded her of guns and explosions, and she nearly jumped out of her skin when she saw real shadowy movement coming into focus from the woods at the edge of the backyard. Hank entered soundlessly, and his nighttime vision found her instantly. He encircled her in his arms, and she shuddered against the icy cold of his jacket.

"This better be important, little darlin'," he said against her ear, "else I'm gonna kill that son of a bitch Lonnie. He oughta know better'n to send you here now. Things ain't safe."

"This isn't Logan County. I only saw two mine guards the entire trip."

"I ain't got no guns for you. What does Lonnie want?"

"I came on my own. I have a gun. The pistol Paul Lessing gave me in Clarkson. Will you look at it and tell me whether it works, whether I can use it?"

He moved away from her, and she heard him rummaging around a shelf. She saw his shadow at the window in the dimness for a moment before he covered it with something, and the room went blacker than before. Then he guided her to a corner and pulled her to the floor. A flash of light temporarily blinded her when he lit a kerosene lantern which he placed on the floor between them, turning the wick down low.

As her eyes adjusted to its light, she saw he was staring at her, a look of consternation on his features. "Where's the gun?"

"Here, in my pocket." She handed it to him.

He inspected the pistol cursorily, returned it, and said, "I cain't see nothing in this light. What do you need a gun for, Sarah?"

"To feel safe. I know something's going to happen."

"How do you know?"

"I just spent months taking guns to Dawson, and the men aren't organizing recreational hunting parties with them. I've had this gun for five years. I want to know if it works."

"Why didn't you ask Lonnie?"

"Because you know about guns." Was that the reason? She met his eyes in the muted glow of the lantern and stopped breathing. Her heart raced and she was suddenly swimming in longing for him. "And I… I trust you," she added weakly.

He sighed and swallowed. His hand closed over hers, sparking fire across every nerve in her body. She was, body and soul, saturated with need of him. "Sarah, I don't want you coming back here. This place, we're about to turn it upside down—"

"With guns?" Unwelcome fear intruded as she remembered Corey's words. And she knew there could easily be no tomorrow— nothing, nobody to come back here to.

"With a strike. We'll use guns on scabs and mine guards and—"

"When?"

"I don't know. Soon."

"Tell me what's happening."

He told her that Frank Keeney, district president, felt there was enough union strength in Mingo County that he could ask the coal operators to sign union contracts. The coal companies would refuse, lock them out, or try to make the miners sign yellow dog contracts, individual employment contracts stating that the signer was not a UMWA member and would withdraw his employment if he did join. "They do that and we're going after 'em. Scabs ain't taking our jobs."

"Maybe the company will give you union contracts."

He snorted. "Companies won't give up yellow dog contracts that easy. Ain't no union man's gonna sign one nor keep working under one. Not while we got so much momentum."

"I'm afraid, Hank."

"No, you ain't. You already proved you ain't afraid of nothing."

"What if something happens?"

He let go of her hand and lit a cigarette. "Then it happens. So be it." He blew out smoke. "You know things ain't staying the same."

"What about my gun?"

He glared at her with affectionate irritation. "Sarah, take that gun back to Dawson and ask Lonnie about it. I cain't look at no pistol in the light of a kerosene lamp."

"Did you know Corey's pregnant?"

"Ben mentioned it."

"She's worried, Hank. She doesn't want you to know it, but she is. I told her I'd help her out if she needs anything. I have a little extra cash, and there's an extra room at my house. I mean, if there's a strike."

He nodded. "All right. Thanks. I'll remember that." He shook his finger in sudden anger. "But I tell you, them two, they're having too much fun. They ain't got no business, I mean, Corey, she's only sixteen, they's a strike coming, and now ain't the time—"

"Look who's talking!" Sarah exclaimed softly, not caring if he saw her petty jealousy.

He stared at her as though she had slapped him. After a moment he said, "Look who's talking yourself, Sarah Sable!"

They were quiet for a long time, and he seemed boyish and vulnerable, sitting cross-legged in front of the lamp. "We're talking in circles," she said.

"I know."

"Well?"

"Well, what? You said it. Circles. Cain't be broken. Kinda like wedding rings, I reckon. It's how we talk."

"But what if something happens?" If he got behind a gun, or in the way of one, she might never see him again.

"What if?" He lit another cigarette, his mood utterly black.

"Hank—" She reached for his hand and he snatched it away.

"Look," he said. "You and me, we don't need to say things just 'cause something might happen. We already know everything without it being said. Ain't that right, Sarah Sable?"

His words brought a lump to her throat, and she allowed tears to begin in the hope that he would embrace her. "Stop calling me that," she whispered with a distinctive sniff.

"Why?" Hostility rang in his voice. "It's your name, ain't it? Sarah Sable. Mrs. Denny Sable." He dropped his cigarette in the ashtray, blew out the lamp, and rose. "I gotta get."

She leaped up after him. "Hank, please don't go!" she exclaimed. She threw her arms around his waist and he stood motionless and tense in the dark; his arms hung at his sides.

"I gotta get home. I gotta go to work tomorrow. I gotta two-and-a-half-mile walk tonight." She held onto him but said nothing.

Her head against his chest, she could hear his heart pounding, and she treasured it—his life, even if he was furious with her. His chest rose and fell, and she reveled in the feel of it, his breath. "Okay," he grumbled. "You want some words in case I get myself blowed away, is that it? Some kinda explanations or something?"

"Yes." Anything—an argument—anything to keep him with her a few more precious moments. The sound of his voice, regardless of cruel words, was a song—life's melody.

"Okay, well…" He hesitated, then exhaled. "You hurt me, Sarah. You hurt me about more'n I could stand, so what do you expect me to do besides what I done? But I ain't blaming you. I couldn't keep my fool hands outta the fire. So I probably hurt you too. Now there ain't nothing we can do about it, 'cept what we're doing. And there ain't nothing else to say about it. Talking about it ain't gonna change things." He tried to move toward the door. "Night, Sarah."

She held on with determination. "C'mon, Sarah. Let me go."

"Hank, please kiss me goodbye."

He put his arms around her and hugged her hard. "I ain't kissing you, Sarah Sable. I made that mistake before. You ain't mine, and I ain't gonna do it." He released her and eased away. "And I ain't yourn. You know I belong to another," he said, moving toward the door. He opened it and said as he left, "Be careful. Take care of yourself and your boys. Night."

6

THAT SPRING OF 1920, the secretly organized miners at Dawson planned to gather with those of Tomahawk and Laura to bring their recently formed union into the open. They would then demand recognition from Dry Creek Coal and strike if it was not granted. Three days before the planned meeting, Sarah had a bad night. She rarely had trouble sleeping and was surprised at her own restlessness. The next night when the same thing happened, she sat up in bed, certain now that something had awakened her. She tiptoed downstairs and grabbed her coat. It was close to two o'clock.

She sat down on the top step of the front porch, shivering, leaning her shoulders against the post. All was silent except for the power station hum, and yet she was sure something wasn't right. She thought of her hidden pistol. Lonnie had examined it and assured her that it was in perfect working order.

A sharp hiss startled her and she sat up straight, straining her ears to determine the sound's origin. Over by the rail yard she heard the rumble of a steam engine's slow start. It gradually gained speed as it rounded the bend. It might be pulling only one or two cars. From the porch Sarah should have been able to see the bright beam of the train's headlamp, but she saw nothing. Somewhere in the distance she heard a door slam.

Boots were softly chewing up slag in the street, coming from the direction of the tracks, and Sarah shrank against the post, expecting to see mine guards with guns. Instead three miners walked rapidly along the street. As they passed by unaware of her, Sarah strained to recognize them. Caldwell. Somebody else. Pierce. "Lonnie!" she called in a whisper.

The three of them froze. Lonnie waved the others on and came to her porch. "What're you doing out here?" he asked in a low tone.

"Something woke me. What's going on?"

"You hear that engine?"

"Yes."

"You see it?"

"No."

"Somewhere round fifteen men got off. All of 'em's carrying suitcases and weapons."

"Same thing last night?"

"Maybe."

"What does it mean, Lonnie?"

"Company's got wind of our plans and they's gonna try to stop us. We'll have to change our plans. We thought they had 'em a tight-mouthed bunch at Tomahawk and Laura. I thought they was sure of everybody. We got us a rat. Somebody's talking. Next time we ain't telling nobody, no wives, nobody." He turned to leave and stopped. "But I'll let you know. After all them rifles you brung us, you're like one of us. And hey. Suppose you could spy around town during the day? Maybe keep your eyes open if you head over to the Tomahawk store? See if you can find out where all them guards is and let me know if they leave."

Spring's full bloom was upon them, even if it was the beginning of what might prove to be war, and Sarah's heart was full. She hadn't been able to forget her meeting with Hank. *I ain't yours...* Those words had bounced around in her head through a sleepless night until she thought she would go mad with emptiness that hurt worse than a tangible wound. The following morning she had asked Corey about Hank's plans with Kay, only to find out that he had let her go right after Christmas. And Corey said there was no new girl. Sarah still didn't understand and Corey said, "He ain't got no girl 'cause he's all messed up in his head about some married woman lives over at Dawson. If you don't know that, then you're deaf and blind, but especially dumb as hell."

But—*You know I belong to another*, he had said. Yes, she realized, he belonged to the coming fight more thoroughly than he belonged to any woman. He had prepared himself for years, and now it was better for everyone if he went into it unfettered.

She threw herself into her own fight in Dawson. She took her sons to the playground when the weather was nice. There she had a view, even if it was a long view, of the train station. She often forgot to pick up things at the store, and had to make several trips daily, watching the company offices closely all the time. She scrutinized Silk Stocking Row and the boarding houses where mine guards lived. Were others there who weren't supposed to be, waiting, hiding—lulling the miners into a feeling of safety? She would find out. Heart pumping, she knocked on the first door. "I must be crazy," she whispered as footsteps approached and her throat went dry.

The woman had a pleasant face and hair pulled back in a severe bun. "Yes?"

Sarah forced a smile. "Hi, I'm—"

"You're the lady with the nice vegetables."

"That's right. I'm planning my garden right now, trying to make some extra money, and I was wondering, well, last year things got a little out of hand. So many people wanted to buy, and I had to make sure I had enough for my family."

They laughed together like friendly neighbors.

"I thought this year I'd line up my customers in advance and try to get an idea of how much you'd need, maybe the kinds of vegetables you might like."

"Well, ain't that an idea. You can sure include me."

"Okay. And you're Mrs.—?" Sarah pulled out pencil and paper.

"Brown. Randall Brown. And put us down for tomatoes. Mainly tomatoes. My husband loved your tomatoes last year."

"I'll do that, Mrs. Brown," Sarah said. "It's just you and your husband then? No kids?"

"My girls are off at school, but they'll be home this summer. And now that you mention it, Judy, she likes squash. I remember I got some from you last year. I'll take some of that too."

So Sarah went, canvassing the houses of the company employees. By the time she left the last house, she was exhausted and disgusted and had no information unless it was that everything appeared to be as normal as it ever was—no squads of company thugs hidden at these houses. Alan and Colin had probably worn out their welcome at Millie's, and she already had a late start on supper, but she forced herself to go to one boarding house before she walked down the hill.

Mrs. Harper glared at her as Sarah gave her pitch and afterwards said in low tones, "Miz Sable, you think I give a damn about what these creeps eat? Right now I got enough to do just keeping the extra laundry done. If you wanna make money, that's how you can help me out."

"Laundry?" Sarah regarded the woman with interest. She was large-boned and had the grim, homely look of hard times about her, yet her skin was soft and translucent with blue veins.

"Yeah. Didn't you used to do laundry?"

"Before I had kids I did. I don't have much room or time for that anymore. Do you need help? Can't you get it all done?"

"Not since they brung in these new men. All they do is set around and smoke and play cards and sweat and change clothes and eat. I cain't stand 'em and I don't have time for 'em. And yes, I need help."

"How much are you paying?"

The next morning Sarah told Lonnie what she had discovered. "There are four extra men staying at Mrs. Harper's house and four of them next door at Mrs. Mitchell's. I'm going to Harper's on Fridays and Mitchell's on Mondays to help with laundry. I said I couldn't take it home with me."

He said, "I imagine they's more of 'em stashed around at Tomahawk and Laura, at the boarding houses there."

Sweet breezes and longer hours of daylight, people spilling out of doors in the evenings, young boys bringing out bats and balls, made Sarah's heart yearn and worry. Filling the days and nights with her usual tasks along with her new spying duties gave her little time to think, but a nervous ache pressed close to her heart, a worry that wouldn't go away whenever she heard bits of conversation regarding unions and yellow dog contracts in Mingo County.

A routine trip to Welch to do some shopping, visit Aunt Sadie, and make a deposit at the bank took her momentarily away from the whispered tensions in the coal camp, until she glanced at Sadie's stack of newspapers. The headlines rocked her, made her forget the problems she faced in Dawson for the moment.

ANOTHER MINGO CAMP STRIKES
ONE KILLED AS STICKVILLE MINERS STRIKE
UNION LOCKED OUT AT WYATT HOLDINGS

So they really were going out in Mingo County! One town after another was shutting down. She scanned the articles with a pounding heart, but there was no mention of Richfield. It was time to catch the train home, and she hadn't had a chance to read the older papers. It might already have happened at Richfield, but she didn't have time to dwell on it because the return to Dawson was harrowing, and Sarah made Alan and Colin stay in the seat with her. Mine guards were everywhere, some of them wielding rifles and threatening passengers, and as the train arrived in Dawson, it did not escape Sarah's notice that none of them got off the train, and probably few, if any, would be stopping at the three or four remaining towns in McDowell County. This train, carrying so many mine guards, was heading west for Mingo County.

Sarah stopped at the company store to pick up items for supper, amazed that activity in Dawson could go on normally in the wake of what appeared to be a massive work stoppage just a few miles away in the next county. At the post office there was a letter, intact and untampered with, from Corey in Hank's handwriting.

Dear Sarah,

Richfield and Bear Hollow are out. Please don't get any crazy notions to come here. Armed company men are patrolling everywhere, including the railroad. They will try to bring in scabs—"transportation," as the companies call them—so there could be activity around the trains—unpredictable *violence that you <u>must</u> stay away from. There can be <u>nothing</u>, do you hear me—<u>nothing</u>—important enough to warrant a visit. So <u>stay</u> <u>home</u>.*

We had to spend a few nights sleeping on the ground, which wasn't bad since the weather is relatively warm. We've got tents now and many of our belongings. Ben and I and the baby have plenty of room compared to some with large families, so we let Hank stay with us. I don't know how long this is going to go on. My baby is due in September, and after I caused a big scene and acted like a spoiled little crybaby, Ben and Hank said maybe some other arrangements could be made for me. Hank mentioned you as a possibility. I'll let you know later on.

Sarah, I never expected to feel the way I do, but things look quite different out here. I'll tell you about it sometime, and I pray I'll have that opportunity. I was wrong not to say it all when you were here the last time, like you wanted. The way I feel now, I don't give a damn. The most important thing I could have told you, said straight out loud, is what you already know—I love you, Sarah. Every day I live, I love you, and I'll die loving you. I love you. <u>I love you</u>.

Corey

P.S. <u>Don't come here</u>. <u>Stay off the trains</u>. <u>No reason is important enough for you to come here</u>.

"Stop it, Hank," Sarah whispered. She brought the letter to her face and smelled faint cigarette smoke. Even if he had this need now, while he was out there derailing trains and facing gunfire, she knew he had been right to begin with. Nothing should have been said. Besides, what a chance he had taken writing those lines! If Denny had opened her mail…

Nevertheless the letter was so dear she didn't want to throw it into the fire where it belonged, and she kept it in her pocket, rereading it occasionally, sniffing its cherished scent, until she heard Denny at the door. Then she opened the stove and watched the fire consume it, remembering snatches of the stories she had read in Sadie's newspapers. *Two coal miners were killed... A gun battle with unknown casualties on either side... I love you, Sarah.* Perhaps there would be no further communication. Ever.

7

WITH THE STRIKE on in Mingo County, Sarah threw herself into surveillance with new fervor. One day Mrs. Harper said, "Ain't no way I'm getting all these here shirts pressed."

"Why don't I take some of them home and do them for you?" Sarah suggested and, to maintain her reputation, added, "For another dollar."

"Gotta have 'em sooner than next week."

After a brief bit of bargaining, Sarah said, "I'll have them for you tomorrow, and any you haven't finished I'll take home and have them back here by Sunday."

"You drive a hard bargain, Miz Sable, but you're fair. Anyway the company's paying me pretty good long as I keep them creeps happy."

Coming and going at the boarding house, Sarah established the practice of making herself at home. She did not knock and she took the longest way to get around to the kitchen where the laundry was done. If Mrs. Harper was occupied elsewhere, Sarah roamed the house to find her, often barging in on card games and half-dressed men and pretending utter disinterest.

One warm day in early May Sarah left the company store at Tomahawk. Walking slowly toward the train station, she felt prickly chills on her neck. She whirled around and saw nothing but the same two mine guards standing on the long porch of the store.

Glancing up at the second floor where lace curtains decorated an open window, she saw a hand, a man's left hand with a wedding band on the ring finger, letting go of the curtains. A glimpse of a figure in a dark suit coat was the only other thing she could distinguish.

Is someone watching me? She grabbed her sons' hands and led them toward the train station. *It's impossible. My cover is perfect.*

And yet she brooded on the train. If anyone had observed her scrupulously over the last year, if anyone thought to connect her to Lonnie and Hank in a more than casual way, she might be suspect. In a panicked instant she knew something wasn't connecting. She thought back to the union meeting she had attended at Mace Elder's a year before. Why was it she could have had a verbal confrontation with mine guards at what they knew was a union meeting and yet travel without harassment to and from Richfield and do laundry for the extra guards at the boarding house? Baldwin–Felts detectives knew what to look for, and her activities could not have been overlooked. But she had watched her back carefully with every trip to Richfield, always reaching the conclusion that she was not being followed or watched. Why not?

In Richfield Hank had remained undercover and unsuspected, thanks to his association with Beckworth, the operator. In Dawson people assumed Sarah did not associate with Denny's friends. If she were suspect, she would not be allowed to help with laundry at the boarding house. But for the first time she had a strong feeling that something did not add up. She dared to imagine that somewhere, not far away, she might be on somebody's list, on somebody's mind, her name on somebody's lips.

The next morning, seeing her crooked Welcome Friends sign, Lonnie stopped by, and she discussed it with him. His conclusion was similar to hers.

"You're just jumpy, Sarah, suspicious of everything. It's spring. People work in them offices over at Tomahawk. They're allowed to open their windows and look out."

"That explains yesterday. What about all this time, since last summer when I challenged those men at Elders' house, with my husband sitting right there? Think about it, Lonnie. Could Darlene Elder do what I've done with the immunity I seem to have? Could your wife, or Med's? It doesn't make sense. Something's not right."

"You might be right." Lonnie was thoughtful for several long moments. "But I don't see how. Didn't you write your cousin a letter after that meeting saying you wasn't involved with your husband's new activities?"

"Yes, of course. But still…"

Lonnie scratched his head, looking flustered. "And, well, it's a fact, Sarah. Everyone round here knows you and Denny's got differences. Including the folks in charge."

So that's it, Sarah thought. Her existence was defined by her marriage.

Lonnie surprised her at the back door one Friday night after Denny and the boys were asleep and gave Sarah the word she had been waiting to hear.

"Me and Med decided them guys ain't never gonna leave the boarding houses, and we cain't wait forever. We're gonna meet tomorrow afternoon. Most of our men was told today, and I think—I hope and pray—that we're all trusted brothers. Tomorrow's a good time. Company's shutting down the mine in the afternoon. We're spreading the word at Tomahawk and Laura tonight and tomorrow morning, and ain't no wives supposed to know. So you just go about your business as usual tomorrow and let your man go about his."

"I will."

"Well, I guess things is about to change, Sarah. You been a big help." He turned to go.

"Where are you meeting, Lonnie?"

"Over yonder, about halfway between here and Laura."

"At that old barn up in the woods?"

"Yeah. It ain't on company property. After we get things set, we're gonna march right up to Jones's door. We figure some to wind up in jail, but we gotta do it."

Sarah clenched both fists as he opened the door and wished him good luck.

The next morning Denny was as sullen and silent as always, and the tabletop seemed easier for him to look at than she or the boys were. When he was ready to leave, he picked up his dinner bucket, mussed Colin's hair and grinned, an old smile that Sarah had forgotten, one that made him handsome again. Then he turned to Alan and balled a fist for the pretend punches he and his oldest son exchanged from time to time. Alan, making a determined face, hit his arm hard, and Denny broke into spontaneous laughter that Sarah hadn't heard in a long time. Tears sprang to her eyes.

He turned toward the door and mumbled, "I ain't working all day. They're closing down early today. They're wiring a new section, have to keep shutting off the power. But don't count on me for nothing this afternoon. I got something to do."

"I love you, Denny," she called out as he closed the door.

She went about her business, as Lonnie had told her, transplanting tomato and pepper seedlings in a race against gathering rain clouds, and ironing shirts, also in an attempt to beat the storm. She longed to know, to be there, to be included in the men's plans, but union business, coal miners' business, was strictly for men.

Denny came home and changed clothes in a hurry and had as many words for her as he had that morning. Before he left, he stuck his trusty flask in his pocket, and Sarah tried not to feel the icy winter in the shoulder he turned away from her in that lilac time of spring.

She smelled the fullness of the blooms on her way up the hill, a part of her heart empty with Denny's rejection, another part full with her own planned bit of excitement during the men's hour of triumph—delivering freshly pressed shirts to a houseful of card-playing, half-dressed, unsuspecting Baldwin–Felts detectives who had failed in their mission. Lightning crackled when she was a hundred feet from the boarding house, and she ran the rest of the way, barely keeping the shirts out of the rain that was suddenly splattering everywhere as she shoved open the front door.

By the time Sarah reached the kitchen where Mrs. Harper sat reading a magazine and eating cookies, her footsteps were echoing in the emptiness, and her heart was beating louder than the thunder in the distance.

"Mrs. Harper! This place is empty. Where are they?"

The woman shrugged in unconcern. "How should I know? You know how them creeps is. Always attending to important secret business."

"But never all of them together."

"Nope."

"And next door?"

"Gone too. Don't worry about it. I'm having a vacation. Hang them shirts over there, will you. Sit down. Have some cookies. They just come out of the oven."

"I have to go." Outside rain was falling and thunder rolled, and halfway down the hill Sarah wondered where the lightning was that was supposed to come before the rumbling noise she was hearing. Was it thunder—or guns? In her backyard she stopped and steadied herself, catching her breath. Then lightning flashed across the sky, and she knew she had been imagining things. But the guards were gone, so they must be going after the miners. If there was a chance in a million that they could be warned, she had to take it. Inside she grabbed Paul Lessing's pistol from under the floorboard and pulled on a lightweight coat. Arriving at Millie's, aware of the precious time she was wasting, she spilled out her information in rapid whispers, watching Millie's eyes grow wide with fright and disbelief.

"You cain't go!" Millie cried, grasping her hands.

"I have to. Somebody has to." Sarah didn't want to admit that she was terrified.

"Don't go! Oh, Sarah, stay here! Let's wait and see."

"You want to wait and see somebody dragging Harry's body back here when there's a chance to keep him safe? Well, I don't want that for my husband. Look at our kids! It's their daddies. I'm going."

The barn was back in the woods, nearly two miles away and across a ravine that marked the boundary of Dry Creek Coal's holdings. Sarah knew of it because of her wanderings in the woods looking for new places to put her pig pen. The way was slippery and soggy. Rain fell steadily, pattering in the trees overhead and splattering against the coating of old leaves on the ground. Lightning flashed and Sarah ran, continuing to imagine gunfire in the thunder.

Near the barn the trees thinned out; fog and rain converged. The barn was surrounded by mist and the rapidly moving shadows of men, more confusion than Sarah could sort out. They were running and shouting; some were shooting, but most were scattering into the gray curtain that hung over everything. Taking a second look, it seemed to Sarah that the miners might be inside the barn while the company thugs were holding a position outside. From time to time men darted away from the barn in twos and threes. She wasn't sure what to do but hurried around to the back and slipped inside the barn, pulling the pistol from her pocket.

She heard a man cry out. Imagining it was Denny, she decided then and there that if there was one dead miner, she would make sure there was at least one dead company guard.

"Not *me*!" she heard the man cry out again in agony, and again it sounded like Denny's voice. "Jesus Christ! You know *me*!"

Entering the main section of the barn, Sarah took in the scene in a split second. To her right a man lay still in a pile of rotten hay, his arms and legs sprawling, a wide red circle on his chest, and on an almost subconscious level Sarah registered recognition: Med Givens. Other men were scuffling about and running just outside. A man cringed on the floor, while another in a coat and tie, a mine guard, stood over him with the butt of a shotgun menacing.

"Sure I know you, you stinking bastard," the Baldwin–Felts man was saying. He kicked his victim in the ribs, and in that split second, Sarah knew the man on the floor *was* Denny.

Her heart nearly exploded as she raised the pistol. "Get away from my husband!" she cried. She wanted to see this bully's face when she shot him. At the sound of her voice, the guard whirled around, and Sarah recognized Paul Lessing. Her jaw dropped and her finger went weak on the trigger.

"Good God!" he whispered. "Sarah? Jennings?" His eyes went to Denny who was doubled over in the dirt trying to get up. "*That's* your husband?" Paul's face twisted. "Bastard!" He spit in Denny's face, turned on his heel, and stalked out the door and into the fog.

8

PAUL LESSING DISAPPEARED into the mist. Sarah pocketed the pistol and rushed to Denny's side. He held his arms around his middle as he rose, groaning in pain and wobbling on his feet.

"What the hell you doing here?" he asked her.

Sarah blinked, staring into Denny's smudged face, but she kept seeing Paul's stricken, disbelieving face.

"Let's get outta here." Denny tried to shove her toward the door.

"We can't!" She shrugged away from him. Nothing made sense to her. Surely none of it was real—she was drenched to the bone, standing in a dilapidated barn with Denny.

"Why not? Come on, woman." Denny tried to take her arm. "I gotta get outta here."

Sarah ignored him and turned toward the body in the corner. Med Givens seemed unreal, as immobile as the wood-framed walls. She heard footsteps behind her but didn't turn around. Med was as motionless as a stone. She heard voices.

It wasn't Paul. I imagined it.

She watched two men, one with tears streaking his face, pick up the body and roll it into a dirty blanket. "Sarah, come on." Another man put a gentle arm on her shoulder and she looked up. It was Mace Elder.

"I was too late," she muttered to him as he led her out. "I tried to warn you, but I didn't find out till—"

"You done what you could," he said. They followed the men who carried Med Givens.

At Med's funeral Sarah separated herself from Denny, slipping in beside Millie. She sat through the service like the rest of the community—in disbelief. At Laura a similar event was taking place for two coal miners also killed by the Baldwin–Felts men who had ambushed the barn. Three Tomahawk men had suffered gunshot wounds, and one of them hovered near death. One Baldwin–Felts man had died during the fight.

"Me and Mace has done a lot of talking. There ain't nothing else we can do for now," Lonnie told Sarah as they left the cemetery. He looked old and confused, his way lost without his friend and partner. He wiped his red eyes and didn't try to hide his feelings of defeat. "This place is crawling with guards now, and to tell you the truth, I'm afraid to do anything till we find the rat. Mace feels the same. We're almost afraid to talk to each other. Everyone *seems* okay, but somebody ain't. You and Mace's about the only ones I ain't afraid of."

Dawson looked like an occupied military zone with mine guards everywhere. Sarah managed to get herself through the days by forcing herself not to feel. Or think. Or remember. That was difficult because Paul Lessing made himself prominent in the streets. He tried to catch Sarah's eye, even took several steps toward her on occasion, but she averted her eyes and moved hastily away from him. It's not him, she told herself. *Maybe* it's not him. He was heavier by some fifteen pounds. It had been five years. Maybe it was someone who looked like him.

But in the barn he had spoken her name.

In the streets his rifle hung loose at his side, the barrel pointed into the dirt; sometimes he didn't even carry it, while the others constantly had theirs at the ready, trained on the miners, even their wives, in a threatening manner, sometimes accompanied by abusive language. Paul tipped his hat when women passed, and Sarah noticed a gold band on his left ring finger.

She recalled things he'd once said. *If I have to put on a show of force, I pick on the snitch. They're scum, rats sneaking in the boss's back door, drinking his best whiskey, telling who did this and who said that.*

At home her heart was an unfeeling rock, and she was exhausted before her day began. She had to almost pick up her feet one step at a time to go to the woods and look after her pig. The animal's comfort, like that of her sons, was the only thing that stirred her to action. She isolated herself from everyone who seemed to be developing a new kind of community spirit, surrounded as they were and closed in by mine guards, bound together by grief— Med's death and the failed efforts of the men.

One evening, news—spreading like a wildfire out of Mingo County along the Tug Fork by way of the railroad and over the telephone and telegraph lines—reached Dawson: a strike on Red

Jackett Coal Company outside the town of Matewan, evictions of miners at gunpoint from company houses, and a gun battle in the streets of Matewan. Eleven mine guards had faced Chief of Police Sid Hatfield, other townspeople, and coal miners. Hatfield, once a coal miner and still a card-carrying member of the mineworkers' union, had become an overnight hero, having accomplished in the light of day what everyone secretly longed to do. The ten victims of the gunfight included seven Baldwin–Felts men. *Seven of them at once!* And two of them were brothers of Tom Felts!

The miners' cause, momentarily put down in Dawson, Laura, and Tomahawk, was alive and strong in Mingo County, growing into a war as increasing numbers of miners went out on strike. The shootout in Matewan escalated the mine guards' vigilance in Dawson. In the evenings Sarah watched the miners' slow walk home, their heads hung low, their spirits beaten down, and she felt unclean. *I'll bash the informer if I get the chance...*

She knew what she had to do, but the action it would require demanded more strength than she possessed. So she put it off for a day, and then another day. She let days go by. While everyone in Dawson went about his or her business with quiet admiration for Sid Hatfield, Sarah suffered a secret shame which grew with her continuing lack of action, but one night at bedtime when Denny reached for her, she leaped up, jumping clear out of bed, and switched on the light.

"C'mon now, woman," he said in a sensual, sleepy voice. "What the hell you think you're doing? It's been a long time for us."

Sarah stood away from the bed, her mind racing. "And it'll be a longer time," she croaked. Her time of indecision was over. *If I see you roughing some man around, I'll know right off he's an informer...* Stepping away from her blanket of denial, she enumerated in her mind all the things she had to do—the only choices available to her.

"What the hell you mean by that?"

"I'm leaving you, Denny."

"Leaving?" He sat up in bed and screwed up his face. "Where you going?"

"To Welch." She hadn't known where until that moment.

"Well, you ain't going tonight, so c'mon back to bed. I want you bad, woman. We ain't done it in quite a while."

"I'm leaving you, Denny, leaving our marriage, and I won't do it with you. I'd die first."

Anger flashed across his face as he sprang from the bed. "What the hell's come over you? Ain't no wife of mine talks to me like that. Now c'mon!"

He reached for her and she darted away, flying as fast as she could down the stairs. She wasn't sure how fast he might have come if he hadn't stopped to put on his pants first, but by the time he rounded the corner into the kitchen, she had the pistol out of its hiding place. His eyes and mouth popped open and he took a step backward, instinctively raising his hands.

"Now just a minute, woman. Where the hell did you get that thing? I thought I seen you with a gun in the barn but figured I'd imagined it."

"It's mine. And believe me I'll use it if you try to make me do anything I don't want to."

"Put the goddamn thing away. If you don't wanna do it, fine. I'll go get it somewhere else." He took the whiskey bottle down, sat at the table and drank. "C'mon, Sarah, put it away, and let's talk."

"There's nothing to talk about."

"You said you's leaving. You mean leaving? Like you ain't gonna live here no more?" Sarah nodded. "You cain't do that. You're my wife. I need you here. And I need my boys. I ain't letting you leave. I'll get the law after you if you try it." He looked at her hard. "Say, you got yourself another man?"

"You sold us out, Denny."

"What're you talking about?"

"You know what I'm talking about. You sold out your own sons and everybody in this town. Med Givens is dead because of you. And those men from Laura. Everything we've worked for is destroyed because of you. And why? So you could enjoy a little bit of good whiskey? So you could have some high-priced whore for free? So you could go in the mine without worrying about mine guards bothering you? You sold us all out for your own comfort."

"Don't say that!" he rose and stormed at her. "You saw that goddamn thug kicking me at the barn. I was with all them others, and I don't know what the hell you're talking about."

"Yes, I saw him kicking you, Denny." He took a tentative step toward her. "Get away from me."

He backed away. "You can ask any of them guys how good a union man I am."

"I know how good you are. I know when you joined, and now I know why you joined. And I know now why mine guards never questioned anything I did. I know where you've been sneaking off to all those nights. I know everything now, and I don't know why I didn't see it before."

"Sarah, you're a low-down bitch to accuse me of something like that. You ain't got no proof and you better keep your goddamn mouth shut about it." She looked him in the eye and said nothing. "You just made that up 'cause you're as cold as the North Pole and don't wanna give your man no loving. Well, you think I care? Who'd want you anyhow?" His eyes and his voice were full of contempt. "And I ain't afraid to say that to any man that'd listen to your ridiculous accusations. Now we'll finish this tomorrow, woman."

"I intend to finish this tomorrow," Sarah said to his back as he left the room.

In the front room she put her hand out the door and tipped her Welcome Friends sign, then scooted Colin over and snuggled into bed with him. She stared into the darkened room for a long time before falling asleep.

At breakfast Denny shook a finger at her. "Don't be getting no more ideas like you done last night, woman." As he left to go to work, she shoved away a tear and said a silent goodbye to the man she thought she had been living with for so many years, and when Lonnie came by, she told him, "I've found the rat."

9

SARAH SPOTTED PAUL Lessing on the street in front of the company store, lighting a cigarette and talking to two others who were leaning over the porch railing. Her heart began thumping so hard she felt sick, but she marched straight up to him. The moment their eyes met, she remembered all that had gone between them. "Can I ask you..." She swallowed, then glanced at the others.

He nodded and walked some distance away. She followed at his elbow, and when he turned to her, she said, "I need to get out of here. I didn't know. About Denny." He didn't answer, just narrowed his eyes and waited. "I've got to get to Mingo County."

He shook his head emphatically. "An eastbound'll be coming soon that'll take you to Bluefield where you belong."

"I have to go to Mingo County."

"Do you know what's going on over there?"

"Yes, but I have to go. I have a cousin who's expecting a baby. I promised I'd take care of her, but I'm leaving here, leaving my husband..."

He was shaking his head. "You could get hurt over there."

"Please, Paul. I've been hurt enough here."

"Where abouts?"

"Richfield. It's not far. Only about—"

He shook his head. "That's not a good situation. Those people are fighting with transportation. The N&W won't stop trains at places like that tent camp at Bear Hollow."

Sarah glared at Paul's unmoving face, feeling filthy for having asked him to help her. She had turned Denny over to Lonnie. There was nothing left for her in Dawson and apparently no one to help her. "Well, I'm going. Even if I have to walk."

Back at home she packed furiously. She sent her children out to play and refused to answer their questions. Everything of value belonging to her and the boys that she couldn't take along, she put in boxes and took to Millie's for safekeeping. When she told Millie her story, Millie cried and Sarah panicked.

"Millie, stop it. I can't let myself cry or think now. I have to get out of here before that train leaves." Her friend walked with her to the station where they waited together and made plans and promises to keep in touch.

The conductor studied Sarah for a long moment when she told him where she was bound. "I doubt we can stop there."

"Get me as close as you can then. Stop outside of town and I'll walk in." His gaze told her she had lost her mind. "I'll walk the whole way if I have to."

She made the boys sit beside her even though they thought they were on a fun holiday to Richfield and wanted to scamper around in the seats. Appalled at what she had just done in Dawson, terrified of the train's advance toward the tent camp, an unfamiliar and apparently dangerous place where she might not be welcome, she tried to reason with herself. *This train is approaching Richfield from the east. Don't scabs come from the opposite direction? What could the miners do to the train? To me? I'm a woman, with small children.*

As usual the train had plenty of mine guards aboard, and when one came and sat across from her and the boys, she didn't realize at first that it was Paul. She told herself she hated him, that she could do this by herself, just as she had walked out of Dawson, but she suddenly breathed easier. Not since his spectral appearance in the barn, pointing the finger that changed her life, had she felt so unburdened.

Holding his rifle as though it were an awkward package, he leaned across the aisle. He seemed uncomfortable with himself, with the extra weight that made him appear ten or fifteen years older. "I talked to the engineer. He says he'll try to stop, but he says he won't take responsibility for anything that happens. He hasn't tried to stop there before."

"Boys," she said to her sons, "I want you to trade seats with this nice man for a while."

As the switch was being made, Alan mumbled, "He don't look like a nice man to me."

Paul and Sarah exchanged a smile.

"If your redneck friends are controlling the area, they're gonna be suspicious when a passenger train tries to stop. There's some closed cars at the end. No telling what they'll think. You could have fifty loaded guns pointed at you."

"Do you think they'd shoot a woman with small children?"

"They're awful jumpy over there. They're looking for any kind of trick the coal companies can come up with. Charles Beckworth, that's the operator, refuses to talk to the union. All he wants is to get men in the mine who'll work—scabs—and get production going again."

"What if your side is in control?"

"More than likely we are, so I'll tell them to give you a safe passage through."

Sarah looked away from him, out the window and said, "I appreciate this."

"It's the least I can do. Anyway I hope it's that easy."

After a little while she asked, "You got married?"

"Uh huh."

"Are you happy?"

"I don't get home much. We live over close to Bluefield."

"Do you have children?"

"Girl and a boy." He lit a cigarette. "You're the same, Sarah. Still asking questions."

"I'm not the same at all."

"You're still uncommonly pretty and very smart, and I'll wager you've learned how to fight. You were working on it back then."

"I learned about fighting when you left Clarkson." She raised her chin.

"Savage make a try for you?"

She nodded. His question confirmed what she had always felt—that Paul had expected it. "I won."

"I knew you would. I hoped you would."

"You left me in the lion's den, Paul."

He stared straight ahead. "You don't know what I went through. Sometimes I think maybe I'm still going through it. Every time I pass through that town. Then something like this happens. They say that fellow Givens was a good man, like that fellow in Clarkson. Ferrell."

"It's never a fair fight. Our men are gunned down by cowards."

"You're telling me."

"Do you ever think about quitting?"

"All the time. I haven't killed anyone. If I got out now, I'd have no blood on my hands."

"I'd argue with that," Sarah said and he looked away.

They rode in silence for a while before he said, "Coal operators donate all kinds of money to charitable organizations and worthy causes. All anybody has to do is ask. They still have money left over to live it up and pay people like me to do things I ain't particularly proud of. They use every legal and illegal trick in the book to keep you people down, to keep you from organizing because they think it'll cost them. Well, what's all this costing them?"

"You've changed your views."

"I've just seen too much. Listen, it's too bad about your husband. Guys like him, well, they ain't much good. I knew about him, even heard him spill his guts, but how was I to know he was your husband?"

Sarah didn't answer. She wasn't ready to think about Denny. Something inside her wanted to defend him, to protect him from the Baldwin–Felts man who sat beside her.

"Did you ever go to college?" he asked. She wanted Paul to know nothing about her and remained silent. He looked across the aisle at Alan and Colin who were giggling and had their fingers tangled together in some kind of game. "Fine looking boys you've got there."

Glancing at her sons and then past them, Sarah recognized the landmarks just outside of Richfield station. "We're almost there."

Paul rose as the engine began to grind down, its whistle crying out in shrill notes. "I think we've got a mile or so up around here before we hit Bear. Come on." He took her bags and led her through the passenger cars to the one just behind the tender car. Another mine guard joined them, and Paul handed the man his rifle. "You stay put till I come for you," he told Sarah. "I'm going up to the engine."

When he opened the door, Sarah got a mouthful of hot wind and cinders. She turned to watch out the window. The engine was crawling, and she could see individual cross ties, bits of gravel, and dust-covered weeds along the edge of the track.

Alan cupped his hands around his eyes and pressed his nose against the window, and Colin tried to crowd in. "Mommy, why are we coming to Richfield like this? This ain't even Richfield!"

"Where are we, Mommy?" Colin asked.

"Bear Hollow, sweetheart." The train's whistle continued its sharp toots, announcing its intention to stop. The town, so like all the others, came rapidly into view, and Sarah suddenly thought of her pig. She had told Millie she could have it if Denny didn't want it, and she knew Denny wouldn't want it. She didn't think Millie would care for the pig as well as she had.

Bear Hollow town was empty and so was her heart. She missed her pig, the soft fur around its ears, and its awful grunts of happy greeting. The large sign on top of the company store announced *RICHFIELD COAL & COKE COMPANY, Bear Hollow, W. Va.*, and Sarah thought about her garden. She hadn't watered it before she left; it would be dry by this evening or tomorrow morning. There wasn't a station at Bear Hollow. The train came to a stop near the tipple, and Sarah noticed several men with guns raised standing back, under the cover of empty coal cars. The area was a hollow at the base of several steep hillsides shorn of timber and grown up in brushy vegetation.

Paul Lessing swung down off the engine, agile despite the extra weight, and Sarah realized she had left very little food in the icebox for Denny. She had not had time to make a stop at the store or to even think about what he would eat. Bear Hollow seemed desolate like a ghost town. She tried to imagine that Hank lived here. All these things, the tipple, the coal cars, the buildings in the distance, seemed like statues of things that didn't really work or exist. Paul took three steps, and gunfire from the hillside threw gravel and cinders around his feet. He dashed toward the empty coal cars, to the other mine guards. He would come back, braving bullets, to tell her to stay on the train. Relieved, she knew she could go back home now. She had tried...

Could she beat Denny home? she wondered, thinking of the note she had left him. *I meant what I said last night. I will be in touch with you about a divorce. I'm sorry.*

But not as sorry as he should be. If she went back now, he might ask her forgiveness. She could fry potatoes and mix in the leftover beans and salt pork and pick greens out of the garden. After supper he might put his feet up on the front porch and play the guitar while the boys played in the street and she carried water to the garden.

How long had he kept his awful secret from her? She recalled her surprise when Denny had unexpectedly joined the union and Med's prediction at that first meeting that the company would be sending in spies. They had, but they had also recruited Denny. Perhaps it explained his withdrawal from her, his preoccupation, which she had attributed to interest in other women.

Paul was returning to the train, strolling slowly, defying the snipers on the hillside to shoot him in the back. He entered the car and said, "Well, you saw it for yourself. Your redneck friends ain't close to the train, but they've got us covered. You step out there and they're likely to spray a few bullets your way."

"They weren't even close to you."

"They're letting us know they're up there. But accidents happen, Sarah. You've got two little boys there. I wouldn't risk sending them out there."

"They didn't shoot at you when you came back."

"If I open that door, they'll shoot. Watch." He opened the door and nothing happened. He stepped down, away from the train, and gunfire crackled and splattered rocks along the ties. An outcry came from some of the passengers as Paul returned to the car.

Sarah picked up her bags and said to her sons, "You boys stay here until I tell you to come. Stay away from that door, you here."

"Yes, Mommy."

She brushed past Paul.

"Sarah, I'm telling you—"

"They won't shoot a woman," she insisted, stepping to the ground. She stood in the open for half a minute and nothing happened. Paul, without his rifle, lumbered down the steps. He picked up her bags and walked beside her to where the mine guards were stationed at the empty coal cars. They returned to the car and she asked, "What did you tell those men over there?"

"I asked them if it was safe for you to get off, and they said if you wanted to commit suicide it was. I told them you were game for it and asked them if they could get you to the camp. They said they could get you within a few yards and still keep themselves safe."

"Thank you, Paul," Sarah stepped away from the train and called for her sons. As they emerged, Paul turned around and faced the hillside where the snipers were stationed. He pulled two new red handkerchiefs from his coat pocket and waved them in a wide arc. Then he tied one around each boy's neck. Paul's audacity astounded Sarah. Red bandanas were becoming the union's symbol of solidarity; wearing one was the same as flaunting a union card.

Alan, looking very much like his father in his gait and the tilt of his head, took his brother's hand, and the two of them stepped carefully away from the train.

"I won't forget you, Sarah," Paul said, grasping the rail. He raised his arm to wave at the guard who in turn signaled the engineer. The train whistle wailed. "Good luck to you," he called as the train groaned and lurched forward.

PART FIVE

Bear Hollow, West Virginia, May 1920

STRUGGLING WITH TWO suitcases, Sarah followed the man to whom Paul Lessing had spoken. He was a lawman of some kind who led her quickly along a partially wooded path. Stopping abruptly, he said, "This is as far as I go."

She looked up. Through the trees she saw the gleam of canvas tents in the afternoon sun and people—strangers, not her own Dawson community—milling about. The rifle barrels of sentries stood out among the trees. It was probably after four o'clock. She wondered if Denny had left the mine yet. He might be reading her note this very instant. *I'm sorry, Denny...*

"Mommy, what's everybody doing in tents?" Alan asked.

"I'll explain it to you later," Sarah said as she braced herself for a confrontation with a Bear Hollow sentry.

"Somebody said you's coming in," the man said. "What's your business here?"

"I'm Ben Stevens's cousin. I'm here on a family matter." The man stood aside. Sarah looked at the sea of tents, then back at the sentry. "Where's their tent?"

"Oh, sorry. C'mon, I'll take you." They began walking and he stopped. "Lemme get one of them bags for you."

When they arrived in front of the tent, Corey looked up from the fire she was tending and exclaimed with delight. She embraced both Sarah and the children and began talking, rambling about conditions at the camp, the progress of the strike.

But Sarah wasn't listening and neither were the boys. They were acquainted with several of the pack of children that was running around the camp and took up with them. Sarah didn't stop them. She stared into the fire and thought of how hungry Denny always was when he got home from work, how he liked hot water to wash off with regardless of the season. He always put his dinner bucket on the table, even though he knew she was trying to set it for supper.

Corey peered at Sarah. "What's wrong, girl?"

"I'm tired. I had a hard time getting in here. Mind if I just sit here and rest?" She sat down on a trunk, head in hands, staring into the dirt. So many things were left undone. The beds were unmade. The stove would have to be lit, and she couldn't remember if there was wood in the kindling box. He would come in, see the note she had left on the table. Or perhaps Mrs. Morris would tell him before he went in.

He would curse and throw things, reach for the whiskey bottle. Flop down on the couch and pick at his guitar, perhaps thinking about their marriage, determining to change, to make things right if they could only start over. To Denny, each day had always been a beginning. He could start fresh, not understanding that the past had accumulated.

Corey shoved a bowl of bean soup under her nose, and Sarah looked around for her children. "They already ate," Corey said and sat down next to Sarah. "You gotta tell me what's going on, Sarah. Is it your man again?"

"It's everything. I'll get around to telling you," she said, remembering the day, a long time ago now, that Orville Jones had visited Denny after his lucky escape from the explosion. No wonder he visited. They were friends. The thought nearly gagged her—*her husband*! She had stayed on with Denny after seeing Paul kicking him. She couldn't bear to think about any of it. "What's going on here?" she asked, trying to clear her head.

Corey embraced her gently. "Aw, Sarah, you poor girl. I already told it all to you."

"Oh." She had heard none of it. "Well, what about Hank? How's Hank?"

"I don't hardly see him. He goes off early in the morning, comes back late. He's fixing to leave. They's gonna send him somewhere else. He's awful quiet. Sometimes stead of working he'll hang around here and read half the day. He's been quiet ever since Harvey was kilt."

"Harvey?"

"One of the men. Got shot the first day everyone come out. He hung on a coupla days but never woke up, and you shoulda seen his wife. They'd had a fight or something and she went crazy when he died. They never got a chance to patch things up. He never woke up so she could tell him—whatever. Tore Hank apart. Tough ol' Hank. He sat in that there tent and cried."

Sarah thought of Med Givens and the Laura men. Now this man, Harvey. How many of them were to be taken from their loved ones in the midst of an argument, a conversation, a kiss? Hank's tears, his letter—*I was wrong not to say it all... I love you*— now made sense.

"You going back tomorrow?"

"I'm never going back, Corey. I've left Denny and my life in Dawson."

"God A'mighty, Sarah! What'd you do that for?"

"I don't know. I mean, I just can't tell you now."

Corey hugged her. "Sure, sure. You tell me later." But in a little while she asked, "Where you gonna go?"

"Welch, I suppose, if I want a divorce."

"A divorce!"

"Be quiet, Corey. I don't want everyone knowing my business. And I haven't told Alan and Colin yet."

"I'm sorry," Corey said and hugged her again. "Oh, Sarah, I'm so sorry."

Over Corey's shoulder Sarah saw Ben, Hank, and another man approaching, rifles slung across their shoulders, red bandanas around their necks. He was talking to her as he approached. "... and they told us a train stopped, and they don't never stop up here, to let off a woman and two boys, and she's got her an escort of company gunmen to get her in here, and I says to myself, there's only one woman with two boys who can get a train to stop up here and have company men bring her in." He stopped in front of her and Corey let her loose. "Damn it, Sarah," he said through his teeth, "didn't I tell you to stay away?" He took her hand and pulled her to her feet. "Didn't I tell you there ain't nothing important enough to risk yourself and your boys to come here for?"

After all the ugly noises, the confusion, the wreck of her day, and her ruined life, his voice was a melody, his rough hand the comfort she needed, his presence an oasis in the barrenness her existence had become. "Yes, but you were wrong," she said, her voice breaking.

2

LYING AWAKE ON the narrow cot Hank had given up, Sarah listened to the camp settling in for the night. Children whimpered; an argument between a man and a woman progressed, escalating for several moments before it died away; a fiddle cried. People strolled by on their way to and from makeshift outhouses and generally milled about.

It had been an impossibly long day, and her mind kept working as she tried to relax into sleep, her thoughts returning often to the long talk she'd had with Hank. The sun setting, they had sat on a rock ledge overlooking the tents, exchanging stories. He had complained about his circumstances. "It's a lot of setting round and waiting. I got so much time on my hands I'm about to go crazy. I do everything I can round here to keep myself occupied and I still got time."

"What do you do?"

"Cut wood, carry wood, carry water, build stuff, steal stuff—sneak into town at night for food. Lotta things. It takes manpower to live like this when you ain't used to it."

"This is what you wanted."

"Just 'cause you want something don't mean it's gonna be a picnic. I didn't know how much I liked working. This here's the most free time I ever had. Most men got families. Or a gal they're courting. I miss playing ball." He curled his fists and put one on top of the other, miming the swing of a man at bat. "This time of year I oughta be down on that field hitting balls!"

Discussing Denny's role in Dawson's failed attempt at unionizing, Sarah mused, "I should hate him. I can't bear to think about him or what he did or the fact that I lived with somebody who did those things. Or maybe… God, do I hate myself?"

"Don't start that, Sarah. It ain't your fault. Now that you know, you got out and that's all you could do."

"But I lived with him. Had his children. How could I have made such terrible choices? How could I have gone so long without seeing what he was doing? *You* questioned his joining the union. You saw he wasn't the type, and you didn't even know him. Why didn't we see it?"

"People don't wanna see something like that."

She mused about her options. "Go to Welch, get a job, get a divorce—what else is there?"

He picked tobacco from his tongue, thoughtful for a moment before he said, "There is something else. I wanna ask you something." But he remained quiet and the moment stretched out.

She touched his arm. "What is it?"

He dragged on his cigarette. "I suppose I ain't got a right to ask," he said, "but I'm asking anyway. I ain't got a job, and you're in the middle of all this. You ain't free. But when you are, and I got my job back… Well, I'm just gonna pass up the preliminaries, and say it. I want my chance with you, Sarah, and will you marry me?"

"Hank—"

"And I don't want an answer now. You cain't answer now. Just give me the chance later on. I meant what I said in that letter. I love you. And I wouldn't do none of those things to you, darlin'. I wouldn't cheat on you, nor lie, nor drink. And I'd treat your boys like they's mine. Anyhow, I wanna be first in line. I ain't gonna bother you other than to be a friend till you're ready." He paused and smiled at her. "Then I'm gonna bother you good."

Sarah finally lapsed into fitful sleep. Close to dawn when dew was heavy outside and a chill was creeping under the canvas, an owl trilled from a nearby tree, punctuating the stillness, waking her. Somebody coughed. Sarah pulled Colin close and groped beside the cot until her fingers rested on Alan's shoulder. He was bundled in a blanket and breathed evenly. Outside the tent she heard movement and then the soft snap and hiss of a match as Hank lit a cigarette. Evidently he also was wakeful in his bedroll by a dead fire.

Sarah rose early and helped Corey prepare breakfast. Through the mist she observed similar activity around neighboring tents. Ben and the children were still sleeping, and Hank was gone. "He ain't never here in the mornings," Corey told her. "He's out talking to the sentries."

"If you only knew how much food I left behind," Sarah murmured as she turned salt pork in a skillet. She wondered again what Denny was doing. Was he getting ready to go to work? Making his breakfast? Packing his lunch? Had *he* slept? In the quiet gray dawn, with white tents looming out of the chilly fog, the idea of Denny—befuddled, angered, or trying clumsily to fend for himself—didn't seem quite solid enough to be real.

Hank returned for breakfast. While the other adults engaged in small talk and fussed over children, he made another pot of coffee. Gritty and unshaved, he had little to say and less militant fire in his eyes than Sarah imagined should be there. She caught his eye once and was reminded of a cat stretched out in lazy contentment.

When she started to help Corey clean up, Hank said, "Stay here and talk to us." She stayed and listened to the plan he and Ben had worked out, and for the first time the permanence of her changed circumstances and the accompanying unknowns began to be real to her. With a job, she would need someone to watch her children, and Corey, her baby due in September, needed to get out of the tent camp. Hank and Ben proposed that Corey and little Gary go with her to Welch. "But you'll be back to work long before her time in September," Sarah protested.

"Don't bet on that," Ben said.

She turned to Hank for confirmation and saw the hard fire blazing. "It ain't gonna be over soon. Companies is bringing in more private deputies every day. We're prepared and committed to go against whatever they try. It's gonna be tough, but we gotta see things through while we got the strength. After Matewan the county's rallying together. We got the support of the district office, the national office. We ain't going back to work till we go on our terms. It's only end of May. Folks's hoping for a conclusion before the snow flies, but we can learn a lesson from the Kanawha County strike. They was out for over a year." He looked away. "Ben's gonna go with y'all to Welch. Help you get settled and make arrangements."

"Ben? Why not you?"

He gazed at her. "Ain't my place. And I don't wanna do nothing to compromise you while you're waiting on a divorce." He set his cup on a rock next to the fire and took off down the path.

He returned at noon to eat, and Sarah listened to his random observations as he shoveled in beans and bread. "Eat too many beans and you're about sicker'n you are when you're starving. Corey don't like cooking out like this. That's why we're eating beans. Once she's gone, I aim to carry firewood for some nice woman who'll take pity on me and Ben and hopefully feed us better'n this." Then he leaned toward her and spoke softly. "This move ain't gonna be easy on your boys. Ain't no easy way to explain things to 'em. It's hard on me too, and I ain't gonna tell you no lies. I hated him before when he hurt you. I hate him worse now for what he done to Dawson, for hurting his own sons. And you. But I'm so glad you ain't with him no more I can hardly stand it."

He set his empty plate aside. "I'd like it if me and Ben could take turns going to Welch, but I don't want no gossips knowing about my feelings for you. Till your divorce. I'm going to union headquarters in Williamson, and I don't know what they'll do with me, where they'll send me. I got me a little stash that I earned fair and square. I been figuring on holding onto it till kids here start needing food and medicine. Sometimes I think maybe I could keep a little of it for my own self. A divorce is gonna cost you. You gotta get a decent lawyer. Don't take no offense, Sarah, but if you need it, a loan, I'd be more'n glad to help out. If you need—"

"I don't need anything. I've got my own nest egg which will more than get me by."

Throughout the day and evening he continued to clarify the strike's possible consequences and the hardships ahead. "I'm committed to it," he reminded her, "for as long as it lasts. If it's two years, then I cain't be your man for that long. And I ain't holding back. We got guns, momentum, and solidarity. Scabs are coming off trains in Williamson every few days. I cain't hide, let somebody else risk taking my bullets even though I now got a chance with you."

"I don't expect you to do anything else," she assured him. It seemed that she and Hank were always on the verge of saying goodbye. Their parting this time was defined by the web of uncertainty in both their lives. Sarah was leaving the coal camps behind, but she felt strong, able to face an indefinite future because of the one thing she could count on—Hank would be there.

3

Huntington, West Virginia, October, 1921

SARAH JENNINGS GATHERED her books and left the lecture hall. She walked slowly across campus heading for home and her boys who were with a sitter. She shared the sitter and the rent on a house with the young widowed mother of a little girl Alan's age. Since her departure from Bear Hollow nearly a year and a half earlier, Sarah had overcome a mountain of obstacles, but most days now it seemed she had only painted herself into a corner full of options that went nowhere. Today was no exception, and she was steeped in sadness.

She was attending Marshall College courtesy of some coal operator she had never met. *Coal operators donate all kinds of money to charitable organizations and worthy causes. All anybody has to do is ask.* Taking Paul Lessing's advice, Sarah had asked, and Robert H. Styles, owner of Mason & McDowell Coal & Coke, had attached a condition to his open-ended loan, as well as a challenge. She must keep an 85% average, and if it remained above 95%, he would waive repayment and consider it a donation to, in his own words, "a very worthy cause."

Sarah had initially moved to Welch providing vague explanations to her children about her separation from Denny. She met with a lawyer, who had some trouble tracking Denny down, but little difficulty finalizing a divorce, an action which decreed that Denny was to pay five dollars a month, money she had never yet seen. And the return of her maiden name, something she had requested, at the time, for Hank Ferrell. She wondered now why she had counted on a future with him.

Corey and little Gary lived with her in Welch, Corey caring for the children, while Sarah worked a clerical job at a mining machine company that paid decent wages. When Ben visited, he and Corey sequestered themselves in Corey's bedroom for long visits, and after the birth of Corey's daughter, there had been a pleasant, somewhat prolonged visit from Belinda Ferrell.

The strike in Mingo County was officially declared on July 1, 1920, even though most of the miners were already out. With the support of District 17 and the national union, they were prepared to stop at nothing to prevent the coal companies from operating normally.

Although working in Williamson, Hank maintained sporadic communication with Ben, and Ben's many visits to Welch usually brought news of Hank, none of which Sarah liked. He had joined striking miners who shot up scab trains in Williamson and staged riots at the depot. Later he was involved in patrolling county borders for mine guards who tried to push union men out of the county. He accompanied organizers who tried to reason with scabs, tried to talk them into coming over to the side of the miners. Then he began dynamiting. Hank's messages all had similar content: Sarah was not to go to Bear Hollow, as he wasn't there. They were blowing up tipples and power stations and trying to derail trains; Sarah was to stay away.

Then the unthinkable happened. Ben brought news that Hank had been shot, and Sarah scarcely heard Ben's tedious explanation of the events leading up to the occurrence.

The governor had declared martial law, and federal troops were sent in an attempt to get control of the strike by protecting scabs and guarding mines so they could continue operations. Martial law was soon lifted, but the troops' brief presence allowed some previously idle mines to resume production. Hank and five other miners were attempting to take down the tipples and power plant at a mine when mine guards surprised them. Three of them, including Hank, were hit; one didn't make it. The other three took Hank and his wounded companion to the hospital in Williamson.

He had been hit in the chest, right lung, and somewhere around the gut.

"He shoulda been dead three days ago, doc says," Ben told Sarah. "But he ain't. He might be stubborn enough to keep hisself alive. He mighta got past the worst, but they gotta move him outta that hospital before he gets arrested."

Now strolling across Marshall's campus, Sarah let herself recall a few of the details of a dark, rain-swept weekend in mid-October, nearly a year ago now, in some nameless tent camp near Williamson, the last time she had seen Hank.

On the blustery night of her arrival, she stepped into the nurse's tent where he convalesced. A lantern on a crate beside an iron-framed bed emitted a soft glow. Hank dozed half-sitting, one arm on top of the covers, his hand on an open book. Several books were piled on a nearby table. There was a cot on the other side of the tent, along with a table arrayed with medical supplies, and an open trunk that held a jumble of women's clothing. Hank was clean and recently shaved, but appeared wasted. Sarah sat on a straight chair beside the bed, content to listen to his even, somewhat congested breathing. She was lost in reverie when the tent flap was raised and a woman stormed in, glaring indignant rage all over Sarah.

"Who are you?" she hissed. "Nobody's supposed to be in here." Sarah gazed into deep brown eyes framed in long lashes. Tessie, the nurse, wore a long-sleeved undershirt and miner's overalls, which fit her snugly, showing off a curvaceous figure. She had clear skin and long dark brown hair, thick and shiny. "Who *are* you?" Tessie demanded again. Her nose and lips were chiseled like the statue of a goddess.

"Who are *you*?" she asked the nurse, whose beauty caught Sarah off guard.

Hank stirred. "See what you've done," Tessie said. "Now get out and leave him be."

"I came a long way to see him and I'm staying right here," Sarah answered in a whisper. Tessie spun around and marched away, throwing an irate glance over her shoulder from time to time as she rummaged in her medical supplies.

"Sarah?" Hank's voice was weak. She turned toward him and took his hand. "That you, Sarah Sable?"

"I got my maiden name back, Hank."

"Didn't I tell—?"

"And don't tell me I shouldn't have come. I made Ben bring me. I've been trying to get here ever since I heard. Nothing could have kept me away."

He smiled feebly. "Well, I sure ain't much to look at."

Tessie was at his side, pushing Sarah's hand away and fussing over him. She glared at Sarah. "Please don't tire him out. I'll give you five minutes."

"Tessie," Hank mumbled, and the nurse turned to him solicitously. "Tess, darlin', this here's my sister. I ain't seen her in a long while, and I need—" He broke into a spasm of coughing, and Tessie put a glass of water to his lips. He gazed up at her, ashen-faced.

"You need to rest," she said sternly.

"Get out, Tess. I cain't rest now except with Sarah."

As Tessie retreated, Hank groped for Sarah's hand. She moved the chair closer and Tessie disappeared. Sarah was terrified of complications—pneumonia. Warm weather was long gone. He needed to be indoors, perhaps at her little house in Welch.

What had they talked about that weekend, Sarah wondered now, strolling tree-lined streets toward home. He talked about Tessie. "She keeps doping me up, putting it in my food. I cain't hardly get myself woke up."

His words had been affectionate. "I ain't never been so happy. I got so much to tell you…" There was evidence of a problem with Tessie. "She's taking too much care of me, taking too much for granted, and for sure taking too many liberties." And, another proposal. "I ain't much, Sarah. Half dead, out of work, most of the way starved, and pretty crazy a lot of the time. After I get myself put back together, let's get married."

"It's not a bad idea."

"Did you just say yes?"

Sarah sat with him off and on throughout the weekend, making herself scarce whenever Tessie gave the order. Talking to others in the camp, she learned that Tessie Connors and Hank had worked together earlier in the strike. Now she was nursing him back to health apparently with her own aims in mind, giving him better care than he'd received in the hospital, tending him like he was a baby—or like the husband she expected to make of him.

With little control over his circumstances, Hank nevertheless managed to engage his nurse in a contest of wills. "This is the best food in camp," Tessie announced, bringing in a tray of fried apples, oatmeal, and real bacon.

"Get that food away from me." His voice was thin, but there was no mistaking his anger. "I don't want no more dope. I cain't feel no pain, and I don't need it."

Tessie set the spoon down. She stroked his face, his hair, kissed his hand, and Sarah turned away. "You don't understand what's good for you, Hank." He glared at Tessie and she pushed the spoon toward his mouth again. "Just a little."

"You want me to eat?"

"Yes, honey," Tessie said with tenderness. "Come on."

"Let's see how bad you want it. You try it first. For every bite you take, I'll do the same." Hank and Tessie locked eyes, and Sarah saw in Tessie a powerful woman who wanted Hank for herself. Might he not easily become dependent on whatever liberties she was taking with him? The nurse nearly always found something to do in her tent; she had no qualms about changing her clothing or bringing in a pan of warm water and bathing in almost complete nudity.

On that one and only weekend visit a full year ago, Hank and Sarah often sat together in silence. Sarah did not want to share her cares or her life with the nurse, and Hank did not press. He wanted to talk but Sarah didn't want him to wear himself out. Although far more alert than he had been the first evening, he was still far from well, and they sometimes settled for the pleasant diversion of Sarah reading to him.

Hank rambled gloomily about the strike, saying, "We ain't gonna win this."

Sarah drew in her breath. "How can you know that?"

"Coal companies is the same as the government. We're fighting the companies, the governor of West Virginia, the legislative branch as well as the judicial system. All of 'em's in the operators' pockets. The only weapons we got is our wits and our guns and the jury system. For now we at least got the jury system, but I wouldn't be surprised if the politicians found a way to get juries in their pockets too. Then we got our last constitutional right taken away."

"But the union's backing you."

"This here's an expensive strike, Sarah. Do you know how many thousand people the union's feeding? Their funds can only go so far. Then we're on our own."

"You sound hopeless, Hank. You've done so much yourself, and all this time you've seen things this way?"

"I seen it before I was shot, the resources the companies got. The scabs they can get. And the federal troops. Think of what that means. Federal troops. They're supposed to be for protecting American citizens. But they was protecting operators' property, fighting against us. Don't you see how powerful they are—they take away our rights and get the support of the government. Yes, the troops was withdrawn, but it showed me what we're up against. We're gonna fight 'em though, do whatever it takes."

"You say it's hopeless, and yet you risk your life. Why are you doing this?"

"You think the only time I ever played good ball was when I knowed we was gonna win the game? I messed up last time, but I ain't gonna get in the way of no more bullets."

"You mean you're going back into it?"

"Course I am." At the end of her visit, he asked, "Sarah, do I still got that yes you give me the other night?" And went on to say, "If this thing lasts a couple years and I wind up blacklisted and crippled and cain't get a job nowhere, I reckon you'll change your mind. You got your boys, so I can understand if you cain't wait on me. I'm keeping your promise with me to warm up my lonesome heart, but I expect you to tell me if you change your mind."

"I love you, Hank, and it's a promise I'd never go back on."

He closed his eyes and grinned. "I ain't never heard you say that before. Tell me again."

"You know I love you, Hank, and I'd want you to do the same for me—tell me if you change your mind."

"I ain't changing my mind. We probably ain't gonna be seeing much of each other for a while, but I ain't changing my mind, Sarah. No matter what."

Sarah had returned to Welch to face a long fall and a longer winter. Waiting. And waiting turned into worry. About Hank's health and safety, and about him and Tessie Connors. Ben said she was from a family of miners and railroad men, she had left home and gotten a nursing degree, but once the trouble started, she quit a steady job in Beckley and volunteered her time for the miners' cause. She didn't have to be there, but she was anyway. Just like Hank.

Sarah didn't hear from Hank over the winter. She knew he was gaining new perspectives, meeting people, working with others whose intellect and selflessness might equal his own. He was moving, changing, living, nearly dying, all with Tessie, a beautiful woman who Sarah knew was courageous and dedicated, a woman worthy of him.

As days and weeks passed, Sarah looked with growing distaste at her reflection in the mirror and with increasing hopelessness into her mailbox, where the only letters she received were from Millie Owens and her parents, and her expectations shrank. Around Christmas she received a rambling letter from Belinda Harmon, in which she mentioned Hank: *The strikes hard on everybody I pray its over soon. I worry about Hank all the time. As you must to. He's way more stubborn than his daddy was. Refusing his own happiness til its over. He ain't never looked out for his own self and I pray for the day when youll be able to and when youll give him his own children to look out for stead of everyone elses.*

"Me too," Sarah muttered as she folded the letter and returned it to the envelope, uplifted for the moment by Belinda's confidence in her inclusion in Hank's future. But she was fairly certain that she and Belinda would be the last ones to know about any changes in Hank's plans.

When Ben visited, Sarah would ask, "How's Hank? What's he doing?"

Ben confirmed her growing fear when he looked away, then at Corey, and replied, "Don't see him much. He's working outta the office in Williamson. In and outta lot of camps."

In February a letter finally came, and Sarah shut herself in her bedroom to read it. It had been four months since she'd seen Hank.

Dear Sarah, he wrote, *Something has happened. I can't explain it on paper because it would take too long and you might not understand. But I know you will when I tell you. It's important to me that you understand. It has changed everything. Everything. My life, my future. For the time being, though, I'm bound to this place until the end of the strike. I'm afraid that if I go to Welch I'll never come back here to the daily misery and suffering, that I won't have the strength. That's why you don't see me. It's easier for me to keep my shoulder to the grind here than to stop for a breather. Just like writing. If I go on much longer, I'll never be able to stop. But I may yet break down and write you long letters. I compose them in my head all the time.*

Sarah reread the letter, memorized it, but understood none of it. Something had happened. What? There could only be one happening to change his future so drastically. Only one thing he had to tell her in person. He would try to smooth it over with pretty words. As for his closing—*Love*—of course in some way he still loved her, still had a sentimental place in his heart for the woman who had once been his teacher, who had smuggled arms for the coal miners.

When Ben visited again, he and Corey were in and out of the bedroom all evening, using the bathroom, seeing to children, eating. Sometimes they shut the door, sometimes they didn't. Sarah had never paid much attention to them, and tonight she didn't either, until she heard Corey speak Hank's name.

"What's Hank up to?" Standing stock still in the kitchen, Sarah tried to hear Ben's response, but his voice was an inaudible rumble. She had no trouble distinguishing Corey's higher voice. "Still with Tessie?" And Ben's one-syllable reply was easy to understand. "Yeah."

The last words she and Hank had exchanged—*I ain't changin' my mind. No matter what*—meant nothing now. She had heard it straight from Ben's mouth. He must have been with Tessie for some time, otherwise Corey would not have asked if he was *still* with her. They were deliberately keeping it from her.

At night her tears fell silently. He had been the one person she had unfailingly trusted, even when he was thirteen years old and kept the schoolhouse warm. For months she had waited for him, counted on him, defined her life in terms of him, while he had moved on. And so she made up her mind—she would not remain in a place where Hank Ferrell might find her someday in order to explain how "something had happened" to him that had sealed his future, changed his life—and ruined hers.

In March with warm weather on the way, Corey returned to Richfield's tent camp with her children, and Sarah set about disappearing, her heart empty of all but an ache. She left no forwarding address with the post office, her landlord, or her employer. She had taken the original precaution of having Denny send any correspondence through her parents. She visited Aunt Sadie, giving the elderly woman her parents' address but asking her not to give it out.

With Welch behind her Sarah paid a short visit to her parents, instructing them to tell no one who might come looking for her where she was. Hank didn't know either Sadie's or her parents' whereabouts, and he might not attempt to find out, with all the trouble it would take. He did possess honor though, and she thought that eventually he might try to contact her to inform her of his change of plans.

4

AT FIRST HUNTINGTON was refreshing, as no memories abided there. Sarah met new people and was distracted with making living and child care arrangements. She was worlds away from her former life in the coal fields, and if she had not continued to read newspapers, she might have left it all behind. But the strike continued in Mingo County, and trouble escalated as winter gave way to spring, a new governor clearly on the side of the coal companies took the reins in Charleston, and strikebreakers continued to be imported from the north.

In May Sarah read of a violent standoff in the town of Merrimac, in which miners blew up the power station, cut telegraph and telephone wires, and gathered in the hills, firing at will into the town at anything that moved, including scabs and coal company officials. When mine guards, state police, and sheriff's deputies came to the town's defense, the battle spread to points up the

Tug Fork River and into Kentucky, and the shooting continued for three days. The result was hysteria among the business population in Williamson and elsewhere in the county, and the governor implored Washington for a resumption of martial law and the support of federal troops.

Sarah tried not to care, but she bought and read every available newspaper. Sometimes she felt that the miners had lost their collective mind, were drunk on violence, or plain crazy with uncertainty and starvation. Many mines were operating at almost normal capacity with scab labor; thus the continuance of a strike seemed almost without purpose.

President Harding was not forthcoming with federal troops, but that did not stop Governor Morgan from taking his own measures. After declaring martial law in Mingo County for the second time, he oversaw the establishment of a special police force, a militia consisting of almost three hundred townspeople from Williamson. The governor also restructured the West Virginia National Guard, encouraging able-bodied men to join, but refusing union men in the ranks. The guard commander made it a crime for two or more union men to meet together and began arresting men by handfuls without warrants, raiding the UMWA office in Williamson as well. Such events quietly haunted Sarah. In the middle of the night she awoke with fearful dreams of violence still thundering through her head, as if in warning.

Why should I care? she asked herself. But Hank could easily be killed, and now that she had erased a trail that he might follow only with difficulty, Sarah realized that neither Belinda Harmon, Corey, nor Ben would have a clue to finding her if he should die. She read all the papers with renewed diligence, carefully searching for names of the deceased.

She also worried about Corey with pangs of guilt, knowing that under conditions of martial law, the girl would be overwrought. State police, state militia, and the national guard had effectively replaced mine guards, and now they were the ones who forced their way into tent camps, smashed furniture, verbally and physically abused women and children, and provoked confrontations with striking men.

In early June, just as she was about to begin school, Sarah received a short letter from her father with a clipping from the Bluefield newspaper. *I thought you might be interested in this. I know he was a good man, and I pray for him.* Paul Lessing's obituary was an unexpected blow, hurting her with tears that stung and left her gasping for breath. He had drowned in the Tug Fork in Mingo County, shoved in accidentally by a fellow mine guard who mistook him for a striking miner they had been chasing in the dark.

"Oh, Paul!" Sarah moaned aloud. She had thought of everyone dying but him. She hadn't even been thinking of him. Now she couldn't stop. "Look what you've done to your family! You should never have stayed in that filthy business." She wrote to his widow to let her know of Paul's kindness, how he had helped her and her children get out of Dawson. She remembered everything about him, for the first time with no shame, and wondered why he hadn't quit a job in which he had admittedly found no pride.

Sarah started school, gingerly carrying Paul's memory with her. Her thoughts about the Mingo County strike were jumbled and out of focus, and she had the feeling that if she could somehow lay Paul Lessing to rest in her mind, things would become clear to her.

In her classes she listened hungrily to ideas that were fresh and exhilarating to her. What she had been missing in her years of physical drudgery in Dawson! She was determined to meet her benefactor's challenge. She would not merely keep her average at 90%, she would keep it at 100%. Studying long hours, caring for her sons, sharing chores and cooking with her housemate, Sarah did not have much free time. She attended an occasional party, and let men flirt with her, even if she wasn't willing to take it any farther.

Amid the changes, however, she led a secret life, quietly grieving for Paul Lessing and rehashing each new development in the strike. Repeatedly she read Paul's obituary, pondering it, trying to keep a living image of him in her mind. Remembering how he had defied rifle fire during their last meeting, she muttered to the wrinkled lines of newsprint, "You didn't deserve to die, Paul." With those words, her vision cleared somewhat. He had been a mine guard. But Paul hadn't deserved death.

Later she read of an incident at a tent camp at Lick Creek. State police raided the place, rounded everyone up, insulted and threatened the women, and destroyed tents and furniture. Before marching the striking miners to the Williamson jail, they pulled one of the men out of the crowd and gunned him down in front of everyone—for no reason. *He* hadn't deserved death. To the miners in the rest of the county, the killing was an outrage, the last straw. The men at the Charleston UMWA office were indignant, ready to escalate the fight, ready to try new tactics. Frank Keeney announced his intentions of sending scores of organizers into Mingo County, forcing the police to arrest them, thus filling up all the jails in that and surrounding counties.

Sarah understood the issues, the flagrant violations of constitutional rights by state law enforcement officials. Men were arrested without warrants, jailed without bond, charged falsely. But the violence was suddenly beyond her comprehension. Paul Lessing had not deserved to die, nor had the man at the Lick Creek camp. She thought of the others she had known over the years. Dominick Cinelli, Drew Ferrell, Doug Burnside, Med Givens, Albert Felts. There were untold others—men in explosions, children in sickness, women in childbirth. And others who had missed death by some miracle—Denny Sable, Hank Ferrell.

In southern West Virginia the U.S. Constitution had also been ruthlessly murdered. With the power of absentee money, legislators met and judges sat to carve out and interpret laws that suited a privileged class that had no interest in the state or its people beyond the exploitation of natural resources. There was plenty of money to outfit a fighting force; there was no consideration for a working man's housing or his safety on the job. There was little for his widow or for the education of his children.

Violence and oppression pervaded the coal fields. Searching anew for the perpetrators, Sarah saw for the first time that they were not even people like Doug Burnside or Tom Felts. The responsible parties were the coal operators, and they never got killed. Tom Felts's goons, the deputy sheriffs, the state police—might all of them be just so many more pawns in a rich man's game? The governor himself held office courtesy of the buying power of coal barons.

At the end of July when she read that Sid Hatfield and Ed Chambers were being taken to Welch to stand trial for charges of a highly suspicious nature, Sarah saw the power behind the coal operators' money in a new light. With fresh indignation she understood laws like the "jury bill," which allowed juries to be imported from other counties, the presence in the governor's mansion of a man who championed the coal companies, and the blatant detention of hundreds of poor people in the jails of Mingo, McDowell, and Logan counties.

Coal was king. The operators ruled with a quiet, powerful hand that clutched millions of dollars. There was only one thing more powerful than money, and that was the law of the land, but in West Virginia those who made and controlled the law had a price. Coal was king in a state of corruption, all made possible by the ignorance of so many. Strikes ultimately made no difference. Power stations blown to bits, mine guards gunned down, and a thousand similar incidents were just annoying flea bites on a bear.

And so Sarah came to see that there was yet another side of the line that she had never considered before—the side of reason, enlightenment, justice, and ethics. Silently she crossed alone to that new side and vowed to spend the rest of her life educating, teaching people to think and make the most of their own resources. From her new perspective, she recognized that she had grown beyond Hank Ferrell and all the guns in southern West Virginia.

Then on August 1, brutality erupted on the steps of the Welch courthouse, a supposed haven of law and order. Sid Hatfield and Ed Chambers, on their way in to stand trial in the courtroom there, were gunned down in broad daylight by a pack of Baldwin–Felts agents. When the smoke cleared, Hatfield and Chambers were dead of multiple bullet wounds; their wives, who had been by their sides, were unhurt, and both dead men, after being momentarily surrounded by Baldwin–Felts men, suddenly had smoking pistols clenched in their lifeless hands.

All too familiar with that trick, Sarah knew that the killers would never be tried for their actions in what appeared to be self-defense. The assassinations, along with all that had happened since spring, would doubtless precipitate more violence; and on August 7, Frank Keeney, the UMWA District 17 president, called miners together in Kanawha County to present demands to the governor. The newspapers said five thousand men met for ten hours at the grounds of the State House, where Keeney reported to them he had failed to persuade the governor to lift martial law from Mingo County.

You have no further choice, Keeney in effect said to the miners. The only way left to get your rights is with rifles, and if you don't arm yourselves, you are not good union men. He told the men to await a call to mobilize. It was a challenge, it was tacit permission, and miners from many of the southern counties prepared themselves to answer Keeney's call.

Two weeks later they met ten miles south of Charleston, and Sarah could scarcely keep her mind on her studies as she read accounts of the formation of this "citizens army," with numbers estimated between seven and fifteen thousand men. They came from the southern coal fields—Kanawha, Fayette, Raleigh, Boone, and McDowell Counties. Several papers also reported the presence of large numbers of participants from Mingo County, and Sarah's interest heightened regardless of how often she told herself that it was none of her personal concern.

It was clear that they'd had enough, and no matter where Sarah then stood, her heart swelled as she read of the miners' intentions: to march on Mingo County and overthrow martial law. To get there, they would cut a path through Logan County, where they would find Sheriff Don Chafin, who ruled the county like a despot at the behest of the coal companies, hang him, and then blow up his courthouse. But they wouldn't stop there. They would also see to wiping out the mine guard system and unionizing the entire area.

Sarah felt certain, though, that no matter how great their numbers or how thorough their preparations, the miners still amounted to nothing more than a swarm of gnats armed against a mighty grizzly bear, and any inroads made would only enrage the powerful animal.

As the men moved southward, their numbers swelling as they went, reporters from all over the East arrived, and Sarah was able to find out what was going on from the *New York Times* and the *Washington Evening Star*, as well as the *Charleston Gazette*. She learned that Don Chafin was prepared to meet the miners with his own army of two thousand men made up of state police, state militia, Baldwin–Felts men, and deputies from both Logan and Mingo Counties. They were entrenched along the twenty-five-mile ridge of Blair Mountain, which guarded the entrance into Logan County.

Reporters were unable to break the miners' secret codes and passwords, but they managed to paint a picture of the march's progress. The miners were grimly sober, to the point of confiscating stills and searching newcomers for liquor. They looted selectively along the way, taking, usually from company stores, only guns, ammunition, and food. They were respectful to the residents of the towns they passed through. It was a march of surprising preparedness with the miners' inclusion of doctors, nurses, large foodstuffs, and medical supplies.

Veterans of the Great War had charge of units of fighting men, and they drilled the men in shooting, marching, and facing machine-gun fire. Advance troops went forward to prepare trenches, cut telephone and telegraph wires, and drive out any mine guards or company officials in the area.

The stories continued for days, coming from reporters who followed the ranks of armed marchers and those who waited with Chafin's forces on top of Blair Mountain. As the event grew in reality, it grew in Sarah's mind, and she didn't know how she managed to complete her courses earning 100% in each, as she was more concerned about the coal miners' commandeering of trains and pilfering of company stores.

Dialogue among the men in charge entered the accounts—a proclamation from President Harding demanding that the miners end their unlawful march, a meeting between Keeney and Governor Morgan in which Keeney refused to back down, a declaration from U. S. Brigadier General Bandholtz insisting that the miners put down their weapons and go home.

Sarah stopped cheering and cringed in horror at the things she imagined. Reality was ghastly enough—an orderly, purposeful mob on its way to claim the rights it had so long been denied. But she envisioned something far more personal—a wild march of men, once her own neighbors, whose frustrations she knew well, had felt herself, many of the determined faces recognizable. Competent veterans led these men and deployed Hank Ferrell on dangerous missions of intelligence-gathering and sharpshooting. Included in their ranks were able nurses like Tessie Connors. And at night at the campsites when they bedded down, Hank and Tessie came together... They were already together and had been for some time, fighting together for a cause they staunchly believed in.

More clearly than she ever had, Sarah *felt* Hank and Tessie together, which underscored her isolation. Was it possible that she herself had once had secret conversations with illegal union leaders? Transported rifles in her suitcase past unsuspecting armed detectives?

She tried to make sense of the march and concentrated on causes: the governor's lying statement at the beginning of the Mingo strike that the coal companies did not hire mine guards; the companies' privilege to use state police and state militia as their private armies; the hiring of a Mingo County circuit judge to assist in prosecuting Sid Hatfield; the coal companies' output of $750,000 to help elect the present governor who now did everything in his power to break the strike; the enactment of the jury bill; coal company control of local elections; illegal detention of miners and organizers in jails; but mainly—the assassination of Hatfield.

Sarah thought of a book by Zola that Hank had once lent her. In it, nineteenth-century French coal miners had been driven by company exploitation to the same frenzy of mob action, and no matter how many there were, they were crushed lower than they had been to begin with. In West Virginia in the twentieth century, Chafin had an army of two thousand. By the time they reached Blair Mountain, the miners numbered between ten and fifteen thousand. Both sides were armed, both prepared.

And Hank and Tessie were together.

Once the actual fighting began, Sarah read no encouraging news. Sharpshooters, machine guns, airplanes with explosion bombs, gas, gunfire with no letup—it went on for a week. The entire state was put under martial law by order of President Harding, and suddenly the action was taking place right in Sarah's backyard as General Bandholtz marched federal troops into the state by way of Huntington. Ten miles down the road at Barboursville he divided his forces. Half he sent down Coal River to come upon the rear of the miners; the other half took the Guyandotte River to flank the rear of Chafin's army.

On September 3, Bandholtz's split forces arrived at the battle zone at the same time, and after an order to end firing, the various factions broke up and made their slow way home.

Both sides claimed that victory would have been theirs if not for the intervention of federal troops. During the battle both sides had taken prisoners, and both sides had suffered casualties. But there were no lists, and Sarah sometimes imagined a dying Hank cradled in Tessie's loving arms. She also saw the broken back of the union momentum the miners had struggled so diligently for, and regardless of her new conviction that violence was not the answer, she felt the bitterness of defeat the men were taking with them as they returned to work, as much under the heel of the coal barons as they had ever been.

5

THE FALL SCHOOL term began. Sarah resumed her studies as the miners were returning to work, and she tried to close the door to additional heartache by not dwelling on the subject. Life in the coal fields was simply not her concern anymore. Her life must go forward.

But at the most unexpected times, she saw Hank. Cooking a meal, she imagined him asking Beckworth to give him back his job. Discussing literature in an English class, she envisioned him scratching his head after an unsuccessful search in Welch as he boarded a train back to Williamson, back to Tessie. Lying down at night, she saw a plain ceremony, Hank and Tessie exchanging vows.

When Sarah's housemate decided it was time to start seeing men again, she urged Sarah to do the same. "It's been a year since you divorced, longer than that since you lived with him," she reminded Sarah. They discussed the assets of the various men who expressed interest in them. The men who admired and pursued Sarah telephoned; they showed up on her doorstep, and a couple of them sent her flowers.

But it was hard to ignore the feelings that haunted her and reminded her far too often that she was inadequate in some basic way, a failure, regardless of her shining academic potential, despite the interested men. And she tried not to hear the other, louder voice. *I won't change my mind no matter what.* But more importantly—*Everything has changed.* She shoved it to the periphery of her thoughts, unable to understand why such words, now so far in her past, from a man she had moved beyond, could possibly make any difference to her.

She settled on a graduate student. He often walked with her after class either to the library or to her house. Sometimes they stopped at a cafe, and she began to halfheartedly anticipate his company. Her smile was her armor, every day making her stronger, and the fall season helped, the changing leaves splashing color and spicing the autumn air, a few insects still humming in the grass, a eulogy to a past that was surely dying, all but dead.

On this day of brilliant October sun Sarah was going straight home to tend to her sons. Alan and Colin were the only real comfort in her life. At the house she dismissed the sitter and sat down with the mail, waiting for her sons to wake up from their naps. There was a fat letter from her father, an envelope within an envelope. On the inside envelope he had written: *This young man nearly convinced me to tell him where he could find you. In the end I allowed that I would send you this letter that he composed surprisingly quickly. He sat at the kitchen table and wrote furiously for over an hour, not even drinking the coffee your mother set in front of him. Of course you will draw your own conclusions and do what you will, but my advice to you (which you have ignored in the past) is to accept this kind, thoughtful, and intelligent man. He has been a coal miner, but he has an uncommon lot to offer by way of a future.*

There was no time to prepare now for what was coming. Sarah laid the letter down and paced around the room. She didn't have to read it now, did she? She could wait until evening. Or she could throw it out unopened. She snatched it up and sank onto the sofa where she carefully pried open the envelope and pulled out several pages scripted in Hank's neat, but hurried, hand.

Dear Sarah, I've been trying to find you, but have discovered instead your deliberate attempts to prevent that. I don't care about your changed plans or your protective parents, I intend to find you. You made a promise, that you would be my wife, and then you gave me another one, that you'd tell me if you changed your mind. You owe me an explanation and I'm holding you to it. In case you have doubts about seeing me, I'm putting it all down here.

I wrote to you several times after Corey came back home. I got a post office box where I could hear back from you, and I got damn tired of staring into that empty box and making excuses. Then all my letters were returned unopened, so I telephoned. I thought there was something wrong with the line because I couldn't get through. I called again after Hatfield was shot because I was worried. It seems I worried for nothing because you weren't even in town. The operator said your telephone was disconnected, so I went to Welch looking for you.

There was no forwarding address, your landlord didn't know where you'd gone and neither did that machine company where you worked. I figured you must have found yourself a new man and a new life and didn't want me to find you. I decided to show you how successful you could be running out on me, but first I had to go back to Mingo County.

I had to wait till the strike was over. The way things heated up and fell apart at the end, I couldn't leave. But afterward I found Aunt Sadie. She claimed she didn't know where you were, so I said I

346 | *Catherine Cometti Samargo*

worked for Dry Creek Coal and there'd been a mistake in the accounts and you were owed money for some work you done in Dawson for a boarding house. She gave me your folks' address all right, but, Sarah, do you suppose I would have given up if she hadn't told me? I would have gone to Bluefield and started with the telephone book. I could have found your father's store without Sadie's help. I could have looked up Ray Alan Jennings.

For a moment Sarah hated the resourcefulness she must have known he possessed. So much trouble he had taken to maintain his honor, to keep *his* promise. Still, he could have written it straight out in the original letter. She read on.

Here's what I want you to know about me. Most important, there is still nothing I want more than to share my life with you, and if I'm lucky enough to find you, depending on your circumstances, I may stick around and try to bust up whatever you've got going with somebody else, as I'm not ready to accept your rejection. I like to remember a time when you were a little bit crazy about me, and I want to try to rekindle it if there's any kind of spark left in you.

Sarah stopped reading. What was this? What about Tessie? But most of all, what about her own new direction? Hadn't she outgrown Hank? What if he asked her to go back to Bear Hollow and keep his house using rusty water she had to carry from a spring? She closed her eyes and breathed, trying to conjure his face, trying to hold onto her resolve. And knew there was no question—she would abandon her studies and go with him. She read on.

I am fully aware now of the mistake I made not seeing you in Welch. Ben took the time to visit Corey, and you are no less precious to me than Corey is to him, so why didn't I make the effort? I had good reasons not to, but I should have come.

My reasons. First off, before you left your marriage, I'd gotten used to thinking I'd have to live out my life without you. After you said yes to me, it seemed easy waiting for you only until the end of the strike. The only time it was hard was all that time I was with

Tessie, whom you met. As I'm sure Ben told you, while I was recovering from the bullet wounds, she convinced me I might catch something and drop dead if I was running around in the cold wet woods fighting scabs and mine guards. So she and I became a team—I was her medical assistant...

No, Sarah thought, Ben did not tell me.

Meanwhile, she and some organizer had become very close. She has since married him, but there were plenty of nights I had to sleep, or try to, in her tent with them two getting mighty friendly on her little cot, and I missed you terribly on those cold and lonely nights.

Second, I knew that if I went to see you in Welch I wouldn't have gone back to the strike. I know that sounds weak, but it was true, and still is. Sarah, if I've lost you because of it, I will understand what a terrible mistake I made, but if there is any doubt in your mind, please hear my explanation. I wanted to tell you in person, but I had no idea how long the strike would drag out, and I didn't expect you to move on in my absence or because of it.

In January I was pretty near all patched up from the bullet wounds, so I went back out and started raiding places with the other miners. I was still crazy then—I loved blowing things up, loved having my strength and ability back. And the challenge, figuring how much explosive was needed and where to put it.

We were staying at some tent camp planning a job—to hit a nearby power station. A woman from the camp got into an argument with a mine guard. That was before the state police took over. Then some guards shot up the camp, not really shooting to kill. Later they took to exchanging insults with some of the camp residents. The camp was on somebody's farm, not company property. The guards started cutting holes in tents and real shooting started. The miners were angry and defending themselves, and I did my share of shooting. The guards took off through the trees still shooting at us, and we fired back. Finally they left, but one of them was hit. He'd fallen, landed face down, and we went out to see about him. We turned him over and, Sarah, it was the strangest thing. I thought he was your friend Paul Lessing. I hadn't seen him since he threw us out of our house in Clarkson—6 or 7 years ago? I learned later on it wasn't him, but at the time that's who I thought it was.

He was hurt bad and I panicked. It was the first time a mine guard ever seemed like a human being to me and here he was dying and maybe I'd shot him. He was fighting for his life. I fell to my knees and prayed out loud for his life, that it hadn't been my gun that'd shot the guy, because I thought it was Lessing. I watched him suffering, and it turned into me feeling his pain and his life slipping away— that same thing had already happened to me. Life draining out your guts. Besides praying, I talked to him, telling him—hold on, you can make it. While I knelt there with him, one of our men finished him at close range. Blew his head into a hundred pieces.

It was horrible of course, but no worse than many things that went on, that I took part in or knew about or advocated. I just saw it up close happening to somebody I thought I knew, to somebody I knew was a good man. Watching him die was bad enough, but that gun blast, up close roaring in my ears, unexpected, and that poor guy's brains blown all over. About as quick as his head disappeared, I saw everything different. Paul Lessing wasn't a bad guy for a mine guard. He helped my family out, and in many ways he was a friend to you. I saw all of us fighting each other, mine guard and deputy against coal miner and nobody winning but the companies and politicians. The one buys the other, but none of them are dying. They're taking advantage of a population of ignorant people who will never get a chance, strike or no strike, unless the laws are changed and enforced.

After that I never picked up another gun, never destroyed no more company property. I was committed to the strike, so I stayed and helped out with things like transporting food and taking care of kids and sick folks. That's when I should have come for you. I stayed and helped, but I'd lost my fire and I couldn't be an inspiration to no *one. I was finished with the violence—but not with the cause, you understand. Something different about my father's memory made me stay, something about commitment and loyalty, standing by my brothers.*

If you followed it, you know it got worse. Martial law, gun battles, Hatfield and Chambers gunned down like my daddy. And all the time I was saying to myself, this ain't the way, it'll never work. I used to think you were either for us or against us, on one side of the line or the other, that there weren't no other choices, but I saw there was another side, another way that I'd never thought of. I used to remember my daddy lying dead in a pool of blood, thinking there was only one thing I could do to right that wrong. I hated mine guards, I suppose because they were so visible, but now I realized the operators and the bought politicians are the real evil, and they won't be stopped except by changed laws.

If you're wondering if I went to Blair Mountain—no, I didn't. It was pointless. Many went because they were angry about the Hatfield murder. They felt powerless and wanted revenge. I'd already felt that way for years as a result of my father's murder. I saw it was a lost cause. If every coal miner in the state had been there, we still would have lost. The government was not going to let that go on. Federal troops was bound to show up.

Sarah, I am not the man you once knew. I saw my daddy get killed and I went crazy. I watched that mine guard I thought was Lessing get it, and I saw reason—the answer, at least for me. The others who don't have no other way out will keep shooting and striking. I'll not fault them for that as long as they have to watch their women carrying impure water, and as long as they don't have resources to get schooling for their children, and they are looking death in the face every day. But it's not for me. In the long run, battles against coal companies and Logan County sheriffs will not be won in the woods or in the coal fields with guns. They'll be won in the courtroom and in the ballot box and in the legislature.

Coal miners and the UMWA need representation by smart men who aren't controlled by anyone. They need sharp, dedicated lawyers who have the miners' interests at heart, who've seen how they have to live and work, who aren't afraid to go head to head with slick-talking politicians and judges and operators. I'm talking about the law. For me.

I've started with Beckworth. He knows I talked scabs out of his mine, sabotaged his tunnels, and destroyed his equipment, but he tried to persuade me to go to the School of Mines in Morgantown, wanted to pay to train me to be an engineer. I said I'd prefer to do it my own way, and he still said he'd pay. I didn't tell him I intend to go through undergraduate and law school, and I don't know how much I'll take from him, but I <u>am</u> going to school. If I use his money, I'll repay it. Once I'm finished, I'll come back and fight for the miners and the union in the courtroom. Against the likes of Beckworth.

And I so much want you with me. If I haven't heard from you in a week, I'll start looking. Beginning in Huntington. If that fails, I'll bully your parents until they tell me where you are. I love you, Sarah. Please save me the trouble of a search. Write to me.

Sarah reread the letter and sat immobile for perhaps five minutes before she went to her small writing table and got out paper, pen, and ink. Looking down at the blank page, she realized she had never before written a letter to Hank.

☞❧

ACKNOWLEDGMENTS

Unlike many Appalachian-born people steeped from an early age in their coal-mining heritage, I grew up unaware of any such family roots. But in my early forties I sat with my father's three sisters one Sunday afternoon as they reminisced about a quaint town in McDowell County. They recalled traveling there periodically by train from their home in Bluefield to visit their beloved grandmother, my great-grandmother, who died in 1931.

I had grown up with family stories, but this was the first I had heard of what turned out to be a company-owned mining town. My aunts' nostalgic descriptions brought to my mind a sleepy, picturesque village nestled against verdant mountains, and I yearned to write about such a charming, old-fashioned place.

Subsequently I began reading about southern West Virginia in the early 1900s. I also spent many hours talking to one of those dear aunts, Elizabeth Cometti, learning large portions of family history I'd never known. I wondered, did these proud people try to minimize or hide their humble beginnings as Belgian and Italian immigrants in the coal fields? The answer must be yes, because during those sessions with my aunt I would sometimes have to ask her a question several times and in different ways before she would give a reluctant, and sometimes vague, answer. She did not, however, mind describing her experiences as a seventeen-year-old teacher in a one-room school in rural Mercer County.

Nor did an aunt on my mother's side of the family, Opal Johnson, who is at the time of this writing one hundred years old. Her early teaching days were in Roane County. (Both of these aunts went on to earn advanced degrees and won numerous accolades in their chosen field of education.)

My aunts Josephine Ritter, Elizabeth Cometti, and Anita Hutcherson have all passed away, but I credit them as the inspirations for *Another Side of the Line*, a story I had no idea would become one about the struggle for unionization. It's what was happening in those days, even though my ancestors, who apparently remained old-world and unsavvy, were not much involved.

I labored through a first draft of this novel with the tireless, critical help of my daughter Mary Samargo Herring, and I was supported in numerous other ways by my daughter Emily Samargo Stolarski.

This work, in an earlier, much longer form, won first place in the annual West Virginia Writers novel competition. After many rejections from agents and publishers, the novel slept untended in a drawer for years before I pulled it out and dusted it off. Trimming it to its present form was not an easy job, and I greatly appreciate the many readers who provided me with helpful criticism and advice, all of which I considered and much of which I took to heart.

And special thanks go to Rae Jean Sielen, without whose assistance this project would never have been completed.

About the Author

Catherine Cometti Samargo's covert writing career was launched with the receipt of a lock-and-key, one-year diary at the age of twelve. Since opening that little book, she has rarely been inclined to put down her pen or, in later years, remove her fingers from the keyboard. Throughout her child rearing and breadwinning years her yen to shape words into narrative boiled on a back burner and has resulted in an unruly body of work. *Another Side of the Line* is the first piece to reach completion.

The author, a recently retired teacher and education supervisor, works as an editor and writes fiction, memoir, and non-fiction. She lives in Morgantown, West Virginia, where she enjoys family and friends and pursues an interest in photography.